2116

DISCARDED

To the
Edge of
Shadows

JOANNE GRAHAM

Legend Press Ltd, The Old Fire Station,
140 Tabernacle Street, London, EC2A 4SD
info@legend-paperbooks.co.uk | www.legendtimesgroup.com

Print ISBN 978-1-9101628-4-2
Ebook ISBN 978-1-9101628-5-9
Set in Times. Printed by Clays Ltd.
Cover design by Gudrun Jobst www.yotedesign.com

Joanne Graham lives in rural Devon, UK, with her two children and too many cats. Being the youngest of five children, her love of the written word began when she would escape the busyness of her childhood home by diving into a good book. She has been writing since the tender age of eleven when her mother bought her a typewriter for her birthday.

Joanne was the winner of the 2012 Luke Bitmead Bursary and her first novel, *Lacey's House,* was published by Legend Press in 2013.

Visit Joanne at
joannegrahamblog.wordpress.com
Follow her @YarrowH

For my Mother
With love always

Chapter One

This is what I was. I was nothing; I was lost in the darkness. For a long time I was only the sharp bloom of agony, the rush of adrenalin, the light tingling of someone else's movement against my skin. There was silence where I drifted and the quiet became vast in the shadows, it was bigger than me, bigger than everything. I was invisible against it, a fragment of black on black. And time passed. I felt it flowing past me like oil and had no way to measure its depth, its length. Until suddenly there was something more and I didn't know where this other began or where the silence ended. I recognised its absence, yet did not see it leaving.

Into that moment moved a shadowed hand in vague focus, a staccato beep, a sharp sigh of murmured platitude that shrunk the silence to something softer, more tangible. What I heard and what I saw, they were noise and shape, yet still unknown with their blurred edges. And abruptly it seemed that there were monsters of a kind in the darkness, roaring monsters with gaping mouths at the edges of a vision that seemed new and tenuous. I felt fingers grasp at my wrists and sharp teeth sink into my skin, I felt them pull at me, dragging me with them deeper and deeper into the billowing darkness. I was lost.

There was pain and confusion where I drifted in the

emptiness. Words were familiar inside my head; they made sense to me there where no-one could see them but they lost their way in my mouth, drifted against the edges of my teeth and stuck there, sour and worthless. My lips would not open and in my head I was screaming and screaming, willing my teeth apart, my tongue to move, my voice to sound a klaxon into the stagnant uncertainty.

"Should I talk to her?"

My mouth didn't move, these were not my words, I could not claim them. They were soft and small and there were tears in them, they swam in the air around my head and I tried to follow them, recognise them but they were chased away by a reply, a deeper voice.

"Of course, if you would like to. She may be able to hear you."

And the words in my mouth drifted deeper, higher as I tried to say that I could hear them; that I was in there and they could not see me in the dark.

There was warmth in the palm of my hand, soft and small. It clenched lightly, curving around fingers that felt weak and could not squeeze back. Somebody's hand in mine, a small fingertip tracing the bones in my wrist. The hand touched only the places where I did not ache, the tiny spaces where there was no pain and in its gentleness there was a kind of loss, an urging to respond, a resignation.

Into that moment the music fell. Quiet at first, shy almost, I felt my ears strain to catch the sounds as they gathered momentum, becoming firmer, less shaky. "Baby love, my baby love, I need you oh how I need you." I did not recognise the tune, the words were unfamiliar. It was sung with a sorrow that worked against the tempo and the voice hitched, faltered, started again. The softness in that voice was like texture on my skin, I felt it caress my cheek, touch at the corner of my mouth.

"She smiled!" the music left instantly as her voice called out with breathless urgency. There were squeaky footsteps, the sound of breathing. "I'm sure she did, only a little, but I saw it."

In that instant, light flooded into my eye, chasing agony beneath the hard curve of my skull. I tried to blink against the finger holding my eyelid open but I was frozen until the hand moved away and the darkness brought relief. I faded away into the nothing behind my eyes and I swam there for a time that had no measure.

The next time there was sound something had changed, it was less muted, more real, it could be grasped, held in my mind, examined. I opened my eyes to greet it and across the void I saw neat blonde hair. I looked into blue eyes that held tears and exhaustion. I did not recognise them and the person they belonged to stared back at me for long moments, a frown spreading across her forehead as she looked at me. Her eyes flicked to somewhere beyond my shoulder then back again. The clarity hurt my head and I winced against it as she gestured to someone I could not see and then footsteps approached.

Another woman bent over me, shone light in my aching eyes, watched for a reaction. She must have seen what she wanted to see because she nodded to herself and scattered words over her shoulder like salt at the waiting woman with the worried eyes.

"I'll get the doctor," she said and I heard the other woman's breath catch.

"Can you hear me, Sarah?"

I wanted to reply but I was thinking, 'is that my name? Is she talking to me? Of course she must be, it's only the two of us here now'. But the name was unfamiliar and I did not recognise the voice that spoke it.

I felt tiredness sweep over me and struggled against it, wanting to hold back that moment of return into the nothing. I fought to be free of it and it was a birth of sorts, a squeezing into life, a labouring. This was the moment I began, the moment of my first cohesive memory. I would feed it over

9

the years until it grew with me, became more adult, more solid. This was the time of my becoming and I floundered helpless and weak as a newborn. But I was not new, I was older, grown, and later I would find out that my life began there, in the month of my fourteenth birthday.

Chapter Two

Where do words come from? Were they born in me, absorbed somehow from a mother I couldn't recall? Did they wait latent and calm for the starter's whistle when they would rush into my mouth and announce themselves? And if not, if they were painstakingly learned, patiently taught, then why were they there in my vacant mind, why did I still know them when everything else had gone?

The words filled the silent spaces; they were grasped from the air around me when the nurses thought I slept. I heard them talk about my emptiness, about being broken and all the things I could not do and, in their conversation, I saw that words were all that was left of the person I once was. Apart from the woman who watched me, who seemed to fit there in that space as much as I did, who became as familiar as the ever-closed blinds and the routines of checks, refreshments, lights out.

She had small features, large eyes, an air of sadness. I took in the gentle, youthful femininity of her and there was no-one in her face that I recognised, she belonged only in that room, a patch of bright, floral fabric against clinical white and beige. I did not know her at all and when I told her this, light, whispered words carried on weak breath, the pain of the knowledge rippled across her face.

"You will," she said and her hand touched mine as if she sought to assure me of her reality, her presence, "I'm your Aunt Leah."

It seemed that she was ever-present. I did not know what the chair beneath her looked like, I had never seen it empty. I had not yet woken from sleep to find her gone. There was comfort in her presence, in her increasing familiarity; the room would not be complete without her. In the vague moments of waking, when I was not quite there, not quite anywhere, she was the anchor that drew my eyes and held me still.

The doctor came in as I drifted, talked to her in hushed tones. There were signs of improvement, of growing stronger. He referred to me as 'she' as if he too had forgotten who I was and I wanted to tell him, shout out loud that I am me, I am here. But I didn't know where here was and even in my own mind I was Sarah, and that was all.

The chair creaked as she sat down and I realised that I didn't want to open my eyes while it was vacant. I did not want to question the solidity of the things I knew for certain: my name was Sarah, Leah always sat in the chair, the doctors always spoke in whispers.

There was a magazine open in her lap, her eyes skimmed across the surface, never stopping on any one thing long enough to take it in. She turned the page, the sound soft and appealing in the silent room, I felt the gentle breeze of its turning on the back of my hand.

I wanted to talk into her reverie, to ask her questions, but I was afraid then of what she would tell me and what she might keep hidden. I wanted to ask how I came to be there but then I wondered 'where else is there?' It seemed that all I had ever known was right there in that moment.

There came a subtle shift in the balance of sleeping and waking. Moments of clarity become less haphazard, stretched into measurable time. I marked them against the ticking clock on the bedside table. No longer fragmented and sporadic, time formed patterns in front of my open eyes. I woke and watched the gentle play of morning light against the edge of the window, I felt sleepy when it grew dark.

The nurse came to change the dressings on my head. Small movements chased dizziness through me, and flooded limbs with weakness. I wanted to stand, to walk, to see if I remembered how but I was fed water from the too-heavy glass by my bed, other people's hands held it to my lips; it seemed I could not be trusted to get even that right. Leah moved the straw slowly to my mouth, wiped at my chin with a tissue when I pulled away too quickly and all the while I looked over her head at the blinds covering the window and wondered what was beyond them.

Eventually I asked the question.

"What happened?"

She sighed theatrically. I was the prompt that fed her the beginning of the line she had practiced over and over in her head. She turned her blonde head away from me, breathed deeply before she answered.

"There was an accident, a car accident. Your sister and your dad, they didn't make it." Her voice caught against the simplicity of the words and she began to cry, quietly so as not to intrude on the grief I too should be feeling.

My emotions were strange, twisted things. I did not know how to react, what to say or do. I felt a sense of sadness coil through my chest, hitching at my breath. Somehow it was not complete, not whole. I felt sorrow at the idea of these people, the fact that they were there and gone, my eyes grew wet at the sight of someone else's tears, someone else's grief. But the depth of that grief was not my own, and tears were shed for no more than the emptiness, the nothing that they were. I had no memory of them, I cried only over their absence from me, from my thoughts.

"What about my mother?" I asked. "Where is she?" and it felt strange to ask because I only knew the word, not the person it belonged to. There was something in Leah's face, a tightening, a closing. As if she recognised that the moment was not then, that I had heard too much in too short a time. Even before she opened her mouth I knew that there was no answer in it.

"You look tired. We'll talk about this another time, when you are rested."

And of course she was right. The exhaustion was there in the pale sheen of sweat against my top lip, in the trembling in my chest as though I had run for too long. I looked at the room that was my world and felt as if I had always been there. I wondered, if I were to open the door and see beyond it, would the smells out there be different, would the light be the same as here?

I pointed to the dressing on my temple, careful when I moved the hand with the needle in so that there was no pull against tender, bruised skin. The bandage was smaller than it had been when I first became aware, when I first ran my fingertips gingerly over its rough surface, its thick wadding.

"What's wrong with me?"

She dried her tears before turning to look at the white beneath my fingers, her eyes were rimmed red and she sniffed twice.

"You hit your head, really hard. Your skull was fractured and your brain swelled up. They had to remove a little piece of the bone there. You were in an induced coma for two weeks to give your brain a chance to rest, to recover. It took three more weeks after that for you to wake up. Then when the swelling had gone down they gave you an operation to put a small plate in."

I ran my fingers up my left cheek, feeling the tenderness beneath soft skin. I felt where the edges of the dressing began, to the left of my eye, just above the swollen curve of my cheekbone. There was bruising there, I felt the difference in sensitivity as I explored. I followed the path of the fabric across my temple, behind my ear, stretching upwards almost to the top of my head. Around the edges where the dressing

14

ended there was the soft spiking of newly growing hair. I pressed against it and moved my hand across my crown where the growth was longer, less brutal. I knew that its colour was dark and dull, I saw the longer threads curl across my right shoulder. But I did not know what it looked like; I did not know the colour of my eyes, the shape of my face. I wouldn't recognise my own reflection.

"I want to see it," I said.

Leah drew her bottom lip between her teeth and bit down gently for a long moment.

"I'll bring a mirror in with me when I come back in the morning."

I realised then that she was not always there after all, that she did not sleep in the chair waiting for me to wake up. I realised that I did not want her to go, that I didn't want to open my eyes and find her absent, I wanted things to stay exactly as they were so that I knew where I was.

"What's the matter?"

Her hand reached up and brushed tears from my cheeks before she moved to the edge of the bed and perched awkwardly on the mattress. I felt the tension in her muscles as she ignored her discomfort in order to hold me carefully while I cried.

"I don't want you to leave," I said as I breathed in deeply and found her scent soft and unfamiliar. She held on as tightly as she could as if she, too, were afraid to go. I winced against her and it was a full stop falling into the moment.

"I'll stay until you're fast asleep, I promise."

I wanted to protest but I knew that it would not be long before she was given that freedom. Everything, however small, exhausted me. And crying took its toll all too quickly. I drifted and did not hear the door close as she left.

Chapter Three

The doctors and nurses all walked like it was the easiest thing in the world, a dance almost, as they placed one leg in front of the other, adjusting their weight easily. Aunt Leah moved with a kind of grace that the others didn't quite have, she swayed gently, her full skirt skimming around her knees, the kind of walk that people must surely envy.

How did I walk? With stumbling lack of grace, with hands that blistered against the frame I leant on, with pain in every part of my body. Leah walked alongside me, pushing my intravenous drip stand so I didn't drag it with me like a reluctant dog. A large, round nurse with a voice softer than it should be encouraged me forwards, and I felt the trembling begin in earnest, the weakness take over, the collapsing.

There were arms behind me that did not let me fall, arms that held me as the wheelchair slid beneath my bottom. Those arms, which belonged to a healthcare assistant, pushed the chair, with me in it, back to the side of the bed. I knew that when my heart rate was normal, when I was breathing more calmly and slowly, when the sweat on my forehead had dried, they would encourage me to get into bed by myself. They would go over the techniques they had already shown me, ways in which I could compensate for my weakened muscles.

They waited for me to grow still and calm but inside I

was raging at myself, for being useless and pathetic, for being stuck there and yearning desperately to be elsewhere, anywhere. The anger grew, blossomed inside me. It tingled in my sore hands, my aching arms and felt powerful and alive. Without thinking I reached for the mirror that Leah had brought with her, the mirror that showed me wide brown eyes in a pale face that perhaps once was pretty but had grown too thin, framed by bandages and spiked hair. I threw it as far as I could, which was only feet away but felt like it should have been further. In my head I saw it smash against the far wall, but instead it limply fell down on the tiled floor and shattered in its wooden frame.

There was a pause, long and deep as the sound of breaking faded away. The three of them stopped like statues when the music fades. No-one knew what to say into that moment, it was a pause, a nothing. I held my breath. And then as if a switch was flicked they began to move as one. The healthcare assistant, whose name badge said Becky, moved to the destroyed mirror and began collecting the larger pieces, the nurse left the room and returned with a broom. Leah came close to where I was sitting and sat on the edge of the bed, reaching for my hand.

Nobody spoke, not then. Leah's hand was warm in my own and anger dissipated into her palm leaving a feeling of embarrassment and shame. Becky left, came back with a wet cloth and wiped it across the floor, gathering any tiny shards that the nurse's broom had missed. The two of them left the room together and I watched as the damp smear caught the light and shrunk on itself, becoming dry and dull before disappearing altogether. The room was as it had always been, nothing had changed.

"Do you want to talk about it?" Leah asked into the stillness.

I looked down at our hands, her nails were polished a pretty shell pink and she wore a ring shaped like a flower. My hand was covered in the yellow-green tinge of an old bruise and the pinky roughness of sticking plaster that held the needle still beneath my skin.

"I feel weak and stupid. I'm sick of these walls, sick of this room. I just want to get better and go home." And then I paused, hitched in a shaky breath because I did not know what home was anymore, where it was, who would be there. Beneath the urge to get well, to be strong, there was fear to keep my frustration company and perversely I realised that there was safety here, in these boring walls. Beyond them there was an unknown world that I would have to find my way through.

"It won't be long now, I'm sure. Your drip is coming out today and your wounds are healing nicely. As soon as we can get you a bit more mobile you will be able to come home."

"Wherever that is." I tasted my own bitterness and spat it out with greater force than intended.

Leah blinked her eyes against it but nothing more. "Your home is with me, Sarah. It always will be. We still have each other."

Her sentences were clipped, her voice low and she was close to tears, so little time had passed since she lost her brother and the grief never seemed far from her thoughts. It was not just for my sake that she was there with me.

"Where's home?"

"In a little terraced house in Exeter. It has two bedrooms so you will have your own room."

I nodded a little but her words did not paint a picture for me, I was no less blind. "I don't know Exeter," I said and it was meaningless, unnecessary because we both knew that I didn't know anywhere, that everything was forgotten.

"You grew up in Exeter, you were born at the old maternity hospital there. You lived in the city until you were almost ten but then your parents separated and you went to live near Glastonbury with your dad and sister. Maybe coming back to Exeter will help nudge your memories a bit, help to bring them back."

I wondered if it were possible, if the familiarity of a place I used to know would fill in the blank spaces of my mind, give me a past, something to mourn. There were things that I could still do: I could talk, I could move, albeit slowly, I could think and write. But I was void and empty of the many images that surely existed inside me before. I looked again at our joined hands and tried to absorb my childhood from the only person I knew who had known me then.

"What was I like?"

She smiled and lightly touched my face. "You were smart, funny sometimes, often serious. You were enormously protective over your little sister and acted more like a mother to her at times. You took your role as the eldest child very seriously and you were incredibly close to your dad. He adored both of you girls so much and sometimes, in the school holidays, he brought you to stay with me and we would do fun girl stuff like shopping and going to the park or the swimming pool."

"I wish I could remember," I said and she smiled again softly, consolingly, before leaning over and pressing her soft lips to my hollow cheek.

"You will," she whispered against the shell curve of my ear. "We just need to give it a little while longer."

And in that moment I believed her, I thought it could only be a matter of time until I was whole again. But she was wrong. Mine was a dandelion clock memory and the wind blew too strongly and scattered it.

Chapter Four

When I walked out of the hospital next to Leah it was no longer on the shaking legs of a newborn foal. My back was straight, my stride small, careful. I felt the tension of determination lock into the sinew and muscle, holding me more upright than I should have been under the circumstances. Leah pushed the wheelchair ahead of her; it held my suitcase and nothing more. It did not hold me, I held me and there was a strength in that, a sense of relief.

Tucked somewhere amongst the folds of the few clothes I was taking with me was the sheet of exercises that the physiotherapist had told me I must continue with. And I knew I would even though I hated them with a passion. It was the exercises, painful and arduous as they were, that gave me back my legs, my ability to walk properly.

The tall, gruff physiotherapist had guided me gently through the steps, never changing his tone, even when I cried or shouted at him, which was often. He rewarded my ill temper with the freedom to return to the home that had never been mine. I said thank you to him before I left, he smiled and told me I was welcome. As I walked towards the huge doors and smelled the morning in the air I realised that I was not effusive enough in my thanks and that it was too late to change that.

The ambulance that would take us home waited for us near the doors, the driver smiling our way as we emerged into the cool morning and I thought, 'is it nicer for him that he gets to drive someone who is well, who is getting better? Do the journeys bring more joy when they happen this way around?' And then I wondered if this was the same man who brought me here three months ago, if he recognised in me the wreckage of the child I was then.

Leah helped me tackle the too-large steps into the back and once there I laid down quickly. The lengths of the corridors were mapped out in trembling muscles and deep aches, I felt every step shudder through my body. She covered me with a blanket and I was grateful for it. During the last few weeks of my hospital stay, I spent more time in the gardens, watching as the flowers began to bloom and spring began to head towards summer. I was less pale because of it, health had returned to a face once hollow and shadowed. But I still felt the chill of outside too easily, the over-warm hospital preventing me from acclimatising quickly enough.

The drip had been gone from my hand long enough for the skin to show no sign of it being there other than a tiny mark, easily overlooked. The dressings had been removed from my head. I cried when I saw beneath them for the first time, the scar that I would always carry, this permanent reminder, a deep 'v' leading from in front of my temple, behind my ear and then up towards the top of my head. One line from the accident, one from the operation that saved my life; they met in the middle, pathways on a map that lead me somewhere new, somewhere alien.

The doctor said that in time the scar would fade, become paler, smaller; the opposite of my own transition back to health. Eventually my hair would grow to cover it, I would have a strange parting and the line that travelled from my eye to my ear, would be hidden by sunglasses on hot days, or by a strategically grown fringe. I reached up and pulled at an awkward tuft of hair, willing it to grow.

"How long will it take to get there?" I asked and Leah looked thoughtful for a moment.

"Well it normally takes around an hour and a half from Bristol to Exeter, but that's in a car rather than an ambulance, so maybe a little longer." I looked around me at the metal walls, the boxes holding medical equipment, the seatbelts, and there was something there that found its way into my lungs, I breathed it in and suddenly I was gasping for breath, I was drowning. I reached for the blanket and threw it to the floor as if the weight was crushing me, my heart hammered, bursting in my chest. My terrified screams echoed in my own ears and all other sound evaporated. I felt hands grab at me, saw mouths moving soundlessly in front of wide-open eyes. I fell headlong into darkness and there was no-one there to catch me.

When I woke up I was lying on a soft, squashy sofa in a front room with small windows and rose-patterned curtains. The metal walls were gone and they had taken with them my rapidly beating heart and the terror in my lungs. Leah sat on the floor next to me with eyes full of sorrow.

"They sedated you," she said and there was guilt in her voice as though it were her fault. "You slept for the entire journey. They are gone now. I'm so sorry, Sarah. It never occurred to me that you would react like that to being in a vehicle. I should have thought and I didn't."

"It wasn't your fault," I replied and she nodded in response. I could see the disbelief in her eyes but she let it go and I watched it bounce away from her.

"When you're feeling up to it, I'll show you around. There's not much to see though, the house is tiny."

"Okay," I said quietly and wondered how long it would take to find the patterns here, would the scents become familiar, or would day and night look the same as in the hospital?

"As soon as you are well enough, we'll go shopping to get

22

some clothes for you. You can decorate your room how you like, obviously I'll help you with that."

She talked in sharp disjointed sentences, her voice over-loud in the small room. She looked bleak, nervous and I asked her what was wrong.

"I'm scared that I will let your father down. Tom and me, we were so close, and I want to get things right, to do the best I can for you. That's all." In the light from the window, Leah's skin was painted with youth. I reached out my hand to her and tried to smile, the kind of smile that was at once sympathetic and consoling, the smile I had seen often on her face as she watched over me.

"How old are you?" I asked and she smiled a little, as if the question were out of place in this moment.

"I'm twenty-eight. Tom was ten years older than me."

There was discomfort in the slope of her shoulders. They seemed too small to hold the burden of me, the weight that I was. I wanted to tell her that it would be okay, that we would walk these days together but I could not bring myself to tell her something that could have been a lie. I didn't know how either of us would cope with the newness of our changed lives. There were shadows in her eyes, the grief that she hid so well from me and I realised that I could not bear to see it, when her shoulders were already bowing under the weight she carried. I couldn't hold her heartache in my hands; they were too weak, too fragile in that moment when she needed them to be strong.

I pushed myself to sitting, feeling vague and shaky.

"Can you show me the house now?" I asked and opened my eyes wider, feigning enthusiasm, hoping to pull her away from the edge.

She smiled and got to her feet. "Of course," she said and stood up to lead the way. I felt the tremble in my legs grow stronger as I tried to stand, the remnants of whatever sedative it was that had coursed through my veins and pulled me into oblivion. I could do this, I could do this but my legs were lead-heavy and stiff. Perhaps if I broke it down, took it one piece at a time. I watched her feet trace the path for me, counted the steps that she took, forced my own legs to follow close behind as I counted slowly in my head. There were five steps from the sofa to the lounge door.

Chapter Five

So this is what I learned that first day. There were five steps from the sofa to the lounge door and only three steps in an L shape between the lounge and the kitchen that was decorated in lemon shades and pastel checks. My legs trembled through eight steps to the foot of the thirteen stairs. The hallway was dark through lack of light, the small window in the wooden stable-style front door making little difference.

I paused halfway up the stairs to catch my breath and Leah was there instantly, concern on her face. The curving lines of worry between her brows, the slightly down-turned mouth, spoke of her care of me and, in that fraction of time when I saw my tiny reflection in her eyes, I knew that I would grow to love her, the delicate woman who would become my constant, my stay. She waited patiently beside me for my strength to return, offered her arm for me to lean on as we moved side by side up the remaining steps.

My bedroom was opposite hers, only two steps between the doors. Her room was sweet and feminine with vintage-style bed linen and white painted walls; there were frills around the bed base and above the window that looked out onto the quiet street. My own room was a little smaller and plain by comparison, a single bed, wardrobe and chest of drawers, all neutral tones and lacking in character.

"We'll decorate as soon as we can."

She squeezed my hand as we took the six steps to the bathroom next to my room. It was small and warm, the same shell pink as Leah's fingernails.

"Would you like a drink?"

I nodded my response before we turned to head back down the stairs. In my head I still counted the steps away as we returned to the kitchen and found them to be one less. Where did it go? I looked around as if it would appear before me, leaping out from its hiding place. I sat at the little round pine table and watched Leah bustling to make me feel at home.

"It's a nice house," I told her and she smiled over her shoulder.

"I know it's small but I like it." She carried a tray to the table and placed it between us, there was milk, sugar and a teapot covered in a woollen tea cosy.

"Do you live here alone?" I realised I hadn't asked before. It never occurred to me until I sat within that moment that there could be someone else, a partner for Leah, another stranger I had to learn about, one who hadn't sat with me for hours praying that I pulled through. I felt the concern of my intrusion into her life blossom inside before she shook her head.

"I was seeing someone for a little while but it wasn't anything serious. We drifted apart when I was spending so much time in Bristol." She spoke quickly to reassure me. "We were on the verge of going our separate ways anyway, it was never going to become serious between us."

I wanted to feel reassured but I didn't, I stood on the edges of her life and changed things without even trying.

"Would you like sugar?"

The silence grew as I stared at the china sugar pot and wondered if I would, if I was the sort of person that took sugar in my tea before, or whether I had milk. I didn't even know if I liked tea at all, I didn't have any at the hospital where they patched me together with plates and staples, they had brought me juice and I hadn't thought to ask for anything else. She reached over to lift the teapot and carefully poured the hot liquid into small china cups. I was frozen by indecision over something so ridiculously small and she saw it in my face.

"Why not taste it without first? It's easier to add it than it is to take it away."

And so I did and discovered that I did like tea and that it tasted just fine without sugar. Leah added one spoon to hers and let me taste that too, it was not as nice and I felt better knowing that I had a preference. There was something of me that remained here after all. I was not just brand new and lost, likes and dislikes were hidden somewhere beneath my skin.

"I have something for you."

She got to her feet and left the room. I stared at the space she vacated and tried not to feel out of place in this strange house that I was told was home. I heard her rustling somewhere beyond the door and when she returned she was carrying a book and a brightly coloured pen set. She placed them in front of me and returned to her own seat. The book was light blue, fabric-covered. It had a dragonfly on the front made of coloured thread and sequins and the pens were bright and glittery, all the colours of a rainbow I couldn't remember ever seeing, though I knew the word and what it meant.

"The doctor suggested that I get you a journal, something to write your thoughts and feelings in. It may help in your recovery. Recording your thoughts will help you to see patterns in them, perhaps clues to your memories. Apparently they have helped other people in similar situations."

I wondered at that, at the thought that somewhere there could be another girl or boy, someone just like me, walking away from a point in the past that held their memories. I wondered if they ever found their way back, if they ever managed to open that box. Perhaps mine were there too and they took them by mistake.

"Thank you," I said. "I'm not sure I'll be able to think of anything to write."

27

"That's fine too. There are no dates in that journal, you write your own so if you have nothing to say then it doesn't matter. It's just there if you need it." She smiled at me but there was tiredness there too and I saw a need in her that everything should go okay, in that moment where it became just the two of us, together.

I asked her if I could have a lie down when I finished my tea and she was instantly on her feet as though my words were strings that pulled her taut, upright. I placed my cup gently on the table and Leah led me up the stairs. I counted as I went, holding tightly to the book and the pens as though they could bring me comfort while I slept. She helped me into bed, pulled the plain curtains over the day and leant in to kiss me lightly on the cheek.

"You smell of jasmine," I told her.

"I do, it's my perfume." And I thought that here was another of those things, a dandelion seed. It floated past my mind as I breathed in the scent that I remembered from another time, from somewhere lost. It had a tiny thread that hooked into my skin from the dark memory places, the vacancy inside. I fell asleep before the smell dissipated and this was the sleep into which the dream stepped, taking root and refusing to let go.

I woke to a pounding heartbeat and the frantic soothing of my aunt's voice, her hands were on my shoulders, the night heavy outside and I drowned beneath the weight of it. Leah didn't ask me what was wrong, she didn't encourage me to speak; she simply held me against her chest and rocked me like a baby until I felt calm.

"What happened?"

She asked when I was still and I became mute before her. I shook my head and could not bring myself to vocalise the trauma of it, the horror. My breath returned to normal beneath her hands as she kissed my scrappy hair.

"Do you want to talk about it?"

I shook my head again, knowing that there were no words, that even in the immediate aftermath of the nightmare the visions were already leaving, breaking down into dust behind my eyes. She motioned me to lie back before reaching down and flipping the duvet over so that it was fresher, more pleasant against my cooling skin.

"I'm here if you need me."

She looked smaller without her make-up on, with her long blonde hair falling in waves over her shoulders. I sought to reassure her that I was okay. I smiled a little, though my heartbeat still throbbed in my veins.

"Do you want me to wait while you fall asleep?"

I wanted to say yes, to feel her beside me, dipping the mattress slightly, holding my hand. But in her eyes there was a deep sadness, she looked pale and tired and I did not want her to regret that day, to lament the time before it when there was just her inside those walls. I told her that I was all right, that she could go back to bed.

When she stepped from the room after saying goodnight she left the door open and turned on the landing light; there was reassurance there in the soft glow. I reached down beside my bed and picked the journal up from the floor, and as I opened it to the first page, snapping the lid off the pen, I heard the soft sound of crying coming through the open door, a hidden, secret sound that was not meant for my ears.

Chapter Six

This became my truth. It was a simple, painful thing, a recurrence that my mind would go back to over and over until it was a constant, a thing that I could rely on, ultimately perhaps the only thing. Why did it begin there, in the house I needed to learn to call home? Perhaps because somewhere inside me I remembered those walls, I had been there before, they had once been a part of me, part of the life that was absent, gone. Maybe it was enough to pull other memories forwards if only in my sleeping, subconscious mind.

From that first night of waking it grew, it became an element of my blood and sinew. It was a truth that I could not walk from, that I could not change. It was the same dream that, even now, appears over and over, taunting me with a fragment of the memory I thought gone. Until I could no longer remember what it was to wake feeling refreshed. There was another me in that dream, the me that came before, the me I wish had survived. We are not the same, she and I. She is light, full of laughter and comfort; she is surrounded by the sweet familiarity of things being just as they should be. I envy her! I envy her innocence, her ignorance.

We sit in the car, the three of us, my dad in the driver's seat. From where I sit I can see his arm curving to the steering wheel, his knuckles shiny against taut skin. He is wearing his

'Dad' jumper, the one we got him for Christmas. I know it embarrasses him slightly – I see it in his face when his hands find it in the washing pile – but he wears it anyway because it was from us and because he loves us more than he hates its gaudy pattern and lumpy texture.

My sister and I sit in the back, with me behind the vacant passenger seat that neither of us ever asks to sit in, as if there are ghosts there or spikes or itching powder. We know that it is our mother's seat, or it would have been had she not told our dad one day that we stifled her, that we stole her air. She walked away to find somewhere better, a place elsewhere that would help her breath come easier. So her seat is forever empty and we call ourselves the three musketeers.

We are playing the supermarket game the way we always do when we go shopping. It is a memory game and there is a bleak irony there because that day was the one that changed it all, that made my mind a scrambled, tentative thing and my past an echo that I only recall properly when I sleep.

"I went to the supermarket and I bought a packet of beetroot." Dad's voice rumbles, gruff and familiar from the front seat and spills over the two of us. We stick our tongues out and make sicky noises as Dad laughs and says to me, "Your turn, Sarah." As it always is after him, it's an age thing he says and I fall in the middle between him and my sister, the sandwich filling. Sometimes soft and sweet, sometimes sour and sharp.

"I went to the supermarket and I bought a packet of beetroot and a bar of chocolate." I know that chocolate isn't on the list, it rarely is when we count every penny and find them too few, but I think it is worth a try, I think that if I say it quickly it will sneak into his subconscious and lodge there among the other boring everyday items and Dad won't realise, that he will buy it before seeing its superficiality, its luxury.

"I went to the supermarket and I bought a packet of beetroot and a bar of chocolate and a box of eggs." My sister's voice is smaller than mine, softer and nicer. She has the sort of voice that makes people want to listen closely, as though they might miss something and it will be a great loss. In the dream her voice is hard to hear above the car engine and I have to repeat what she says so Dad knows what came next. I think it is a bit of a cheat really, for me at least. Repeating her words helps me to remember more when it is my turn, it gives me an advantage.

The game stumbles on as we get closer to the supermarket, down the narrow, tree-lined road that turns the sun into a strobe and makes me blink against it. There is a clarity to the light that brings everything into sharp focus, all crisp lines and edges that flash against the backdrop of trees. We add milk, bread, cheese, orange juice, dog food, washing up liquid, fruit pastilles and what seems to be hundreds of other items that make me concentrate so hard that it hurts.

Dad's final item is tobacco and it is the last thing I hear him say in the dream, the last time I hear his voice. The sound pushes into my subconscious memory and lodges there among the dark and debris, the shattered glass. Tobacco, his famous last word. How dare it be something so insignificant? I screw my eyes shut and try to think of the sequence, of what comes next and in that fraction of darkness everything changes. The world becomes a different place.

How can sound be so loud in a dream? It isn't here anymore, it doesn't exist in this moment, fading as it did years ago into silence and yet I still cringe away from it, the tearing, wrenching, crunching sound of my life being cut away from me. I open my dream eyes to chaos, the world spinning away as I see daylight where the roof should be. I open my mouth to scream and feel something hard slam into my head before everything becomes still and so silent that I think I have lost my hearing.

With dazed eyes I look to the side of me and my sister is there, curled up and still. Her soft, dark hair curls slightly across her cheek, catching a little in the breeze that comes through where the roof used to be, her eyes are closed, her head resting against the back of her hand. She looks so calm, so comfortable and I wonder how she can sleep now, how can she not be awake and terrified like me?

I try to move as I feel the pain begin to grow behind my eyes and down through my neck but my body feels heavy and bloated, like there is a weight on me that holds me still, pinned like a butterfly. I look down and my hands are pale and faint, soft-focussed as everything grows indistinct and vague. I look up and see the curve of my dad's chin, his short, feathery eyelashes brushing against his skin. I can see his hands on the steering wheel, still gripping tightly, the knuckles still white. I see the sleeve of his Dad jumper pushed up to his elbow but there is blood on it now and I think that he will be cross if that doesn't come out, like he was with me when I got grass stains on my school shirt.

From where I sit I cannot see his face, there is no wry smile curving his cheeks out, a smile I can usually see from this vantage point. He is still and silent and I want to hear his voice, to hear him say what has happened, to make sense of a world gone awry. I open my mouth to ask him what is happening but my own voice is a silent void, a nothing. I feel my mouth move, dry tongue rasping against tender lips, but nothing emerges, as though my voice decided to get up and leave when I wasn't looking. I turn my face to the roof, see its torn edges and finally my mind seems to make sense of what has happened, like puzzle pieces falling into place.

I reach round and unbuckle the seat belt that may or may not have saved my life and I try to lift my unusually heavy weight as I move forwards, squeezing myself between the gap and into the empty seat that was never mine. I try to lift my hands to my father's face to pat him awake, to seek out his reassurance but I falter and stall as I see that his skin is slack; that half of his face, the part that is furthest from me, is red and misshapen. The white of his eye gleams through it, open and fixed.

I reach up and begin to shake him, my too-small hands grow slick with blood and I falter as his head drops towards his chest, his hands still gripping tightly onto the steering wheel. I try again and again but there is no response. I find my voice in a scream that propels from my throat, tearing out of me and sweeping over my dead father as if it could wake him, as if it could take the death from his one open eye and give me his smile back. I don't give up, I shake him and shake him, my arms aching. Fear and disbelief explodes inside my chest and it is my own horrified scream that penetrates my sleeping mind and propels me into a world where my heart still hammers but my hands are clean.

In those moments after waking I remembered everything in fine detail, every moment of the dream that appeared to hold my one and only memory, but as I became more awake – as the more rational day gripped me with determination – the images faded and became lost. I remembered the noise, the fear and the pain, but no matter how hard I tried I could no longer remember what colour my sister's eyes were. In those moments after waking I couldn't remember her name. It slipped away from me and scattered like sand and there was only a patch of silence where it used to be.

I tried to write things down in that time of shocking wakefulness, I reached for my journal and attempted to put into words what she looked like, how she smiled, but the memories faded into the morning quicker than I could write them.

Later, Leah fetched a bag of photos from the loft and I pored over them, trying to absorb the detail through my fingers, but the dream was long gone by then and I was looking at a stranger; someone who was never part of me, someone who never mattered. My memory could not hold on to the face in the pictures. All I seemed able to hold on to was the envy I felt as I looked on her apparently sleeping form, wishing desperately in that moment that I was her, that I was calm and still, that I wasn't the one who had to try and piece my father back together.

Chapter Seven

She asked me how I was and I pulled my eyes from watching the interplay of light across the window, the flashes from the passing cars that I heard less and less as the days passed. The pain in my head was absent in that space. There were days when it was crippling in its intensity, days when I could do little more than turn on my side in bed and drink water from a straw. But not that day, that day was light and soft.

There was relief in her smile when I told her and I knew that it was for me, that she was happier when I was well, that she worried she would lose me too. I asked her, on another morning when the headaches were absent, how she had learned of the accident. I talked away the initial reluctance to tell me. Perhaps she realised that my experiences were limited already, that I needed to learn more, to feel more, even by proxy.

The events that haunted my nights, that I saw over and over projected into a subconscious sleeping mind, had never been seen by Leah. The horror of it, the blood, all that I witnessed seemed nothing more than rumour to her, heard third hand from the family liaison officer who knocked on the door as she was getting ready for a night out.

By the time of that interruption, a hammer blow into calm stillness, the words had gone through so many people that she

35

wondered if they may have twisted and changed, if they might be wrong. She held tightly to the possibility that they could be nothing more than some awful, cruel game of Chinese whispers. She even wondered, she told me with a smile that hurt to look at, if it were some kind of terrible, humourless joke. *Knock, knock. Who's there? The police.* These were the thoughts that had gone through her mind as she tried to make sense of the awful events of that day.

She sat on the flowery sofa, half-dressed in her bra and skirt, stockings in hand – she had opened her door without embarrassment thinking it was her lover turning up a little early – as the policewoman's words stole her family away. Now you see them, now you don't. The officer told her as gently as she could that there was only one survivor and it didn't look good, as if it would have looked better if I was merely the walking wounded instead of the shell that I became.

I'm terribly sorry that your brother and your youngest niece have been killed outright but look on the bright side!

Right then in that surreal life-changing moment had I seemed like a bright side? As Leah tried to make sense of her cherished older brother's death, as she tried to take in the words that couldn't possibly exist in the planned version of her life, I lay in the hospital surrounded by people trying to keep my heart beating, trying to hold me in the here and now. She still felt guilty that there was a delay before she got to my side, that I was alone in the dark for the first few hours.

By the time I woke up, the season had begun to change, becoming summer-warm and hazy and my aunt had begun to accept that her life had altered forever. Ten years younger than the brother she buried while I was sleeping, Leah worried that she was too young to become surrogate mother to a pale thin fourteen-year-old whose mind was a damaged shell with little left inside.

She had plans of belated further education, of chasing her newly found dreams to become the next big thing in fashion design, in her mind she had seen herself carving an international path. She put them on hold, willingly she said, because in that moment I was the most important thing, the only important thing. Her plans for the future were placed carefully in the coffin that held my father and sister and she didn't mourn the loss of them, there was no wistfulness in her eyes when she spoke of them in the past tense, as though they too were gone forever.

Life changes, she had said, and sometimes those changes bring a different perspective, a different journey. But I couldn't help think that her future, the one she had planned was just one more thing that had been destroyed in the car that day. When I passed the open door of her bedroom it was too easy to imagine a smell of decay lingering around the tailor's mannequin that stood naked and ignored in the corner.

I watched her then as she curled into the arm of the sofa, her legs coiled beneath her, hair caught in a loose bun that fought to be free. She was pretty, delicate in the soft light, as familiar to me as the skin that I wore because I met her at the same time I met myself; those relationships equal and new. I watched her peace and felt a sense of guilt, a subtle undertone of it threading through my stomach, bringing wishes of a changed past, a different future.

What would life be like if I were only one of a pair of nieces that visited sometimes? If we had nothing more than a few days within these walls interspersed with trips to the park and too much ice cream? How much more could Leah have been without me?

"What was my father like?" I had asked before but the answers slipped away in the time between the questions. I did not like to ask, to interrupt her stillness, to remind her. But I was compelled by the empty places, the slow drift of my thoughts. She put her book aside and stretched her legs, still pale despite the warmth of that summer because she had spent her time inside with me, teaching me about the world all over again. Her hand patted the seat beside her and I moved to it, leaning against her as she placed her arm around my shoulders.

There was no reluctance in her movements, no regret that I asked this question. I think that she liked to talk about him, to remind herself too, of the place he occupied in her life, of where he stood. She looked down at me and rested her hand softly against my cheek; it had a gentle curve by then, filling out as I returned to health.

"Well, Tom was more sensible than me, more inclined to responsibility. I used to tease him about it, say that he was all slippers and hot chocolate where I was more mini-skirts and vodka."

She smiled down at me and I didn't move, afraid to interrupt as I tried to pull the words into my pores, make them always a part of me.

"He used to watch out for me, even after he had moved out. I wasn't much older than you at the time but I was the flighty one who stayed out 'til all hours worrying our parents. So many times it was Tom that got between us when I argued with my mum after coming home at four in the morning. He was dependable like that, my protector."

"What about my mother, what is she like?" I knew I shouldn't ask, that in all the lost memories I had been told up until then, my mother didn't exist and there was something in Leah's face when we talked about my hidden past that made me hesitate, fall silent. It seemed that my mother was gone, was absent from me. I wondered if she even knew that I was broken. I asked because it seemed a good time, but Leah's face turned away, telling me that it wasn't, that it may never be.

She sighed and drew breath in slowly as if to fill the time before she must use it to propel hesitant words forwards. And when she spoke I understood more of her reluctance in those moments, she had wanted to avoid telling me of another death, another forgotten shadow I must grieve for.

"Your mother and father separated when you were eight years old. I wish I could paint a better picture than this one but, the truth is, I didn't know her very well, I was off travelling for some of the time they were together."

Her eyes could not meet mine, she looked away and there was unwillingness in the set of her shoulders, hesitation in the words she said. She breathed in deeply and held the air still in her lungs. "She died when she was too young. Cancer took her."

As if the disease had come along in a car and hastened her to get in before driving off into the distance. I felt smaller, vague, as if every death learned diminished me, stole my life too. I thought that in future I wouldn't ask; every question led to something less, something gone.

"I didn't go to the funeral and I don't know where she is buried. There's nobody... "

And I heard the words she didn't say, that she could not extract the answers she needed from the cold pile of earth that blanketed my father and sister, the earth that told me that I was an orphan. I thought that perhaps one day I would try to find her, take her flowers maybe. I wondered where I would even begin to look, to be able to fill that empty memory with one more carved name on a headstone.

"But we know where my dad is," I said and my words were thieves that tried to steal her sadness, while ignoring my own.

Her eyes met mine, still troubled and dark. "We do. Would you like to go?"

I nodded in response, thinking that it was past the time I should have gone to see for myself the place where they were.

"I'll get my bag," she said.

Chapter Eight

I had not set foot outside the house in the three weeks since my arrival. I did not know what the house looked like from the pavement. I didn't know what colour the front door was. I had sat with Leah in her small courtyard garden, I had felt the light evening breeze that carried the smell of the distant sea against my skin. But outside was unknown, outside was alien and fear lived there.

I had heard the cars go past, seen the rippling silhouette of the postman through the small frosted glass window before letters fell onto the doormat and sat in the lounge while Leah brought in the delivery from the local supermarket. I had not yet stepped over that threshold to see the street beyond and Leah kept vigil with me inside, she had not left me alone in the house for a moment. I didn't know what I would do if she did.

I didn't realise how strange I would find that first journey until I stepped down over the front step, until I saw the glossy white painted wood and the number forty-eight in black ironwork above the letterbox. The road was quiet, the path two paving slabs wide and curving slowly downhill towards a green space surrounded by trees. It was not a through road; the traffic I heard from safe within the walls was only the people from this one street, or those visiting whatever hid beyond the trees.

I felt a pull on my hand and realised that Leah had walked on and failed to see that I was not keeping time beside her. My face must surely have told her a story of fear and anxiety, and she bent slightly to be level with me.

"What is it?" she asked.

I could think of nothing to say, of no way of explaining that I was too small to be beneath the huge open sky, that I couldn't remember how to do this.

"I'm scared," I told her and she didn't ask of what, she didn't tell me not to be silly. She looked at me with kindness and pulled me against her so that I could see nothing but her pale blue sundress.

"Okay, this is what we can do. We can turn around and go back inside, we can think about this, and try again another time. Or, we can take one step at a time. We can walk down the hill, across the park to the little churchyard. I will hold your hand every step of the way, we can stop anytime you want to, you can keep your head down and I will pull you along. It is up to you Sarah, you don't have to do anything you don't want to."

I thought about it, the weight of the sky above me, the absent weight of grief I should have felt. I was not sure if I could do this, if I could walk into a distance I could not yet see.

"How far is it?"

"Not far," she replied and she lifted my chin from its position against my chest, and gently turned my face towards the hill, the trees. "If you look where those trees are there is a little green park. In the park you turn right and walk on the path for a little way and up another hill, the church is up there. At the bottom of the hill, you'll be able to see the church tower. From here it's probably three hundred metres at the most."

The thoughts rushed through my head: 'three hundred metres, that's about six hundred steps, which is one hundred

41

and twenty times from the sofa to the living room door'. Perhaps I could do this if I counted in bands of five, if I imagined I was inside, if I pretended I was surrounded by familiar cottage walls with the lounge door ahead of me. It may be all right if I keep track of the steps. I nodded at Leah and told her I would try, she smiled and once more held my hand as I stepped forwards and began to count silently down the hill, keeping my face turned to the ground so that the sky could not tell me how small I was.

By the time we stepped through the gate and onto the winding gravel path lined with overlong grass, the count had become so familiar I could think of other things; of our destination, of surnames that were the same as mine yet belonged to people my mind told me did not exist. An ache in the front of my thighs created the map in my head as we turned up the hill, and soon the grass was long enough to paint my ankles with dew. I did not raise my head to see the church tower, finding the sensory journey enough without my sight; the warmth of Leah's bigger hand in mine, the turned soil of new graves, the earthy damp scent of it.

There was only one mound of earth where there should have been two. I risked a glance around me and all that was nearby was a smaller mound, already sinking to be almost level with the edges of the grave.

"Why is there only one?" I asked, wondering if we would have to walk further, if I would have to begin the count again.

"They are in the same coffin. It's what Tom would have wanted."

What about me, where would I go when the time came, when the sky fell down? Would I be alone, nearby but never close enough to touch, would I feel cold? Do they? I wondered if they were even there; if they had tunnelled out, found somewhere better to be.

"Do you believe in Heaven?"

She closed her eyes against the question and her hand grew tighter against mine.

"I do now."

I let go of her fingers and turned to look at her, finding her eyes fixed in the distance, somewhere other than this graveyard, somewhere beyond a severed family tie.

"Why now?"

She turned to look at me, her eyelashes bound together by dampening grief.

"I can't imagine them being gone. They had so much life in them, so much to give. And I think they must surely be watching out for you, making sure you are safe and well. And they couldn't do that if this," she let go of my hand suddenly and gestured towards the mound of earth, "is all there is. There has to be more, it makes no sense otherwise. All that energy, it had to go somewhere. It couldn't have just blinked away into nothingness. They couldn't have just evaporated." Her voice came faster until it hitched rough and unsteady against the last words.

I reached for her hand again and she skimmed over my grasp, pulling me tightly into her arms. I felt the tears bubble up through her chest and into her throat, felt her sorrow drip softly onto my hair and when her grip loosened a little I turned in her arms and looked at the wilting daisies someone had left here; a faceless stranger that grieved in my place. The fading white petals rested where the headstone would one day be and I blinked against the fading of them where they rested above the dead.

Leah reached into her bag and pulled out a packet of seeds, she sniffed a little and wiped her nose against the skin of her wrist.

"I hate those horrible vases." She pointed to the nearby graves, at the little containers with the metal slots in the top. "Your father would have hated them too, he wasn't a vase of flowers kind of man, he was beautiful and vibrant and natural."

She showed me the front of the packet, the mix of wildflowers, colourful and eclectic and I found myself agreeing with her, I looked at the vases and found that I hated them too. I absorbed her emotions like a sponge because I could not remember what it was to feel my own, to make up my own mind. The taste of my loathing was bittersweet in my mouth because it didn't rightfully belong to me, because I simply borrowed it as I desperately tried to learn the world again, to make sense of the unfamiliar.

Leah opened the packet and began to scatter the seeds haphazardly across the soil before bending to rake them in with her soft hands. She didn't appear to notice the reddish brown streaks the earth left against her skin.

"I think when the headstone arrives we'll plant some jasmine against it, it'll look beautiful when it grows."

I thought about the roots, of where they would grow and how they might pull life from the dead and the cycle would continue on and on. I wondered how long it would take for this space to look different, how long before it absorbed the muted colours of the surrounding graves and became less new, less raw.

Eventually the grass would grow a little too long, a little too wild and the green mound would become intertwined with poppies and cornflowers. There would come days when I would sit there for hours among the wild blooms, resting my head against the names carved into the polished stone and the scattered flowers would speak of remembrance in a soft tone. I would no longer be afraid that the sky could fall in on me, that I was too small beneath it.

But in that moment all I could hope was that the day would come when I stood before their grave and remembered the smiles and the love from when they had lived, that there would be memories within me of the people that lay beneath my feet. I prayed for their restoration, that I would know them enough to grieve equally alongside Leah, who should not have to carry the burden of being the only one to cry for them. I would be able to see them in the jasmine flowers that curved over the future gravestone. I wondered how far beneath my feet they were. I looked at where my shoes left indents in the soft earth and thought it seemed there were only three small steps from their feet to the top of their heads.

"Are you ready to go?" she asked and I nodded, turning when she turned, stepping when she stepped.

We did not speak at first and the counting in my head filled the silence until we stepped through the gate that led to the street where Leah's house was.

"Are you okay?" she asked me and I was, I had coped with the outside world. Breaking it down into smaller pieces that my mind could make sense of, made it less threatening somehow, small, like me.

"What will the headstone look like?" I tried to imagine it, above that ground, the marker so that others could see who we grieved for, so that even when we were gone they wouldn't be forgotten, they could still be found.

"It's just a plain one really, pale marble, simple words. I don't like all those intricate ones with the carvings and the clichés. It is unnecessary, grief is a basic, raw thing, it doesn't need a disguise."

And I stored away another dislike, another borrowed opinion. I filed it with the slotted vases where it became a pet hate of mine too, another layer to a fragmented identity.

I looked at the floor as we walked and thought of the two that we had left behind, of how they were part of my life now, but only in their absence. I looked at our hands clasped together and wondered what it would have been like to hold a smaller hand in mine, to not have lost them both.

Chapter Nine

Her name was Annie. I wrote it in the front of my journal when Leah told me and I hated that I didn't already know, that I hadn't even held onto something so small, so significant. It would become a fixed point, an anchor; I will write it in the front of every journal I have, copying it carefully when the pages are crisp and static. Then, I wrote it in my special new pens – the ones with the glitter in them – the ones that came in every colour apart from boring ordinary black and blue. I bubbled around the letters in gold, to make it precious and bright. Those five letters became all I had to make her feel part of me. Somehow they mattered more than the glossy still photographs that were years distant and did not stand in the place where I was.

I did not remember her apart from in those snatched fragments of dreams, our last moments together. Why did it have to be that the accident not only took my family from me, it took my memories of them too? As if it weren't enough that they were gone, that it had to be as if they had never been real, that I had always been without them.

Was it any kind of consolation to know that they still lived somewhere in my subconscious? If only enough that they appeared in my dreams, repeating forever the final moments they shared with me? It wasn't enough, I felt cheated, alone.

I wanted to remember the way they laughed, the way they smelled or how their hair looked first thing in the morning. I wanted to remember birthdays and Christmas mornings with presents and excitement, when Father Christmas still existed and so did they.

And so in place of her, I wrote her name where I would see it every day, it was the tentative thing that bound us together; the bridge that allowed me to think of her. I touched the letters gently with the tips of my fingers every morning. Sometimes tiny fragments of glitter stuck in the dips and whorls of my fingerprints and I carried her with me, shining, and pretended that it was enough to fill the empty space in my memory.

What life would she be living if the outcome had been different, if the back seat had been a haven for both of us and not just me? She would be there too, in those cosy walls, in the house that was becoming more familiar and easier against my skin. I thought of her as a dancer or an artist, something bright and colourful, someone vibrant and alive. I imagined her as everything I had lost, as everything I was not. I wondered how it would feel to only visit one name in the graveyard and have someone who grieved equally at my side. I tried to think of the things she would enjoy doing, of the way she would laugh or the expression on her face when she was lost in thought, but it was hard to imagine someone that my memory told me never existed. No matter how hard I looked there were no clues there.

Sometimes in the night before the nightmare found me, I felt sure she was watching me; when the moon was tentative and vague behind the clouds, when sound became muted and echoed dully from dim walls. I felt suddenly as if I were no longer alone, felt the chill of eyes across my skin, goose bumps following in their wake; a feeling so strong that my head jerked round to try and catch sight of an echo, of someone long gone.

Was she angry? At a life cut short? At the utter waste of all her possibilities, of what she could have become? I was

47

the older sister, having had two years more in that moment of her ending than she would ever have. I should have known enough to cover her, should have wrapped my arms tightly about her as the world changed around us. I should have held her safe.

Did I imagine, then, the bitterness or blame in the shade she sent to keep company with my guilt? Was she raging at the unfairness of it all, stamping a little foot that would never grow into my old shoes? Was she the reason I felt trapped, unsafe beneath a wide sky, because my life wasn't deserved, because it shouldn't have been me that lived? I felt the anger in the presence that surrounded me and I understood it.

But in daylight hours where sense returned and ghost stories became nothing more than fiction, it wasn't Annie that hovered at the edges of my plain room and mourned her own loss. It was the guilt of the survivor that had held on tightly enough to live, and it was anger, the isolation of being left behind. I thought about a life that could have been, three lives that should have been and I began to grieve for them all.

I pulled the diary from under my pillow to record the events of the day and her name leapt into my mouth, pushing forward over a malleable tongue until it burst forth and blossomed, calling her to my side. I wanted the world to hear me thinking of her. I wondered if she could hear the sound of her name on my mouth, or if she was gone entirely and all that was left were these five letters that spilled over my lips into an empty room.

Chapter Ten

Days passed and the evenings brought tiredness and aching muscles. Every morning at the same time, half past eight, we left the house. We turned right when we went out of the front door, not left; left was the past, left were graves and loss and sorrow. We turned right and right was the city, the future, but it was more distant than the graveyard, there were more steps to count, more blocks of five. I did not know then that she was teaching me to make my way through the streets for a reason, that she could already see the changes that I was blind to.

The first time she said the same things she had said before: we will go only as far as you want to, I will hold your hand, we can turn back any time. We made it to the second street, not quite as distant as the graveyard but more frightening, less green. The cars were louder there, the road busier. I was knocked by a lady with a pushchair coming towards me and I flinched away from her and stepped quickly behind Leah. She placed her arms tightly around my shoulders.

"It's all right," she said. "The lady just didn't see you."

But the damage was already done. My voice was small when I told her we had to leave and before I turned I looked in the direction we would have gone, had I not been afraid, and in the distance there was the awning of a shop. I could not make out the name of it and I wondered if next time I would get close enough to see what it was called.

By the time we stood outside the white door with the black numbers my heart was calmer, my breathing slower and I could feel the frown that furrowed my brow. I tried to work out how it could be that there were six hundred and ninety-two steps to the point where we stopped but six hundred and ninety back to the door. There was no balance there, no normality. I knew I could have lost count, I could have slipped somewhere along the way, my steps could have been slightly bigger.

No matter the explanation I felt uncomfortable, off balance, and I didn't like the feeling of insecurity that raced through my arms, my legs and made them feel weak and pointless. I thought that the next time I stepped out the front door, I would walk up on one side of the road and back on the other and that would be enough. I would understand then if the steps were different, there would be a reason, it would make sense.

And then it was the next day, the next time and we got further. That time I anticipated the cars, the people walking closer than I would like. I focussed on my steps and tried to imagine the noises and the bustle as distant from me, less conspicuous. I discovered that the shop I saw was a small craft shop; there was patchwork in the window, sequins and knitting needles. I felt the pause in Leah's steps, the slowing down, the interest before she smiled briefly at me and walked on.

The unevenness in my steps was no longer important, I did not pause and wonder, I did not feel my heart race. Leah did not question when I crossed the road to return on the opposite side, the side that may have more or less steps. She looked a little pleased that I was taking the initiative and I wanted her to believe that it was okay, that I was stronger and so I smiled back and she pretended not to notice the worry in my eyes.

Later, when the sky had darkened and I was feeling weightless, almost beyond tired, she brought hot chocolate and placed it next to me with words that were heavy. I watched as bubbles of frothy cream spilled over the edge of the cup and raced each other to the saucer.

"We have an appointment at the hospital next week," and she pointed at her head to indicate which doctor so there was no confusion in me, so that I knew it was the specialist, the one who would handle my recovery, who would try to find my absent mind.

"Which hospital?" I remembered the blue signs with the 'H' on as we walked and somewhere inside me, in the hidden places, I knew what it meant and wondered if it would be there, down a road I hadn't yet walked.

"In the children's hospital in Bristol." She reached for my hand, lightly held the fingertips in hers. "I have a mild sedative I can give you for the journey, we can go on the train, over the next few days we will practice the walk to the station. It will be okay. I know you can do this."

Was it right that I felt a sense of betrayal? That suddenly the morning walks seemed cynical and cold, a training of sorts to make it easier for her to get me on the train, to get me to the doctor's office miles away? I hid behind my cup and did not speak. After a few moments she got to her feet and moved towards the kitchen. I heard the whisper of the door as she pushed it open, the creak of the cupboard, the bang of one pan against another.

I put my empty cup onto the sticky saucer and counted my way slowly to my bedroom, hearing the pause in the sounds from the kitchen and knowing that she was standing there, head to one side, wondering about me. Even when I walked slowly with my head bowed, when I felt heavy and afraid that life was running away from me, too fast for me to keep up, even then the number of steps was the same and I found comfort there.

Chapter Eleven

The room was still and airless. I was pinned by the weight of it, pressed into the soft floral throw on the sofa as the clock ticked the room's pulse. Slow, sluggish days of routine and sameness, a sigh fell from parted lips into the lazy room as my toes curled under and released, curled under again. I closed my eyes and watched the slow shifting of the light outside the window, red against my eyelids. If I sat like this for long enough would I forget how to move? How to breathe? Would the rest of my memories – the ones that reminded my insides how to live – decide to leave, to find somewhere else more interesting to be? How long would it take for me to become a statue? I was vague, distant and I swam through thoughts that sought to pull me beneath the surface, hold me until my breath could no longer be held.

When I opened my eyes again and blinked them into focus, Leah was watching me with a half-smile on her face; she stretched her bare feet out, arching her back slowly as if she too were becoming statue-like and had only just remembered how to become fluid, graceful.

"Do you think you would be up to a visit to the hairdressers today?" My fingers reached up to my head, following the same route they always took when I pressed at the scar there, when I checked its tenderness. The hair around it was wild, eccentric. I saw it in the small bathroom mirror when I brushed my teeth, it was the reason I wore a hat or a head scarf even when the weather was hot and itchy. It had grown longer in the weeks since leaving the hospital but it was uneven, strange, like unkempt woodland where wild things ran and brambles grew.

"Which hairdressers?" I asked, because I had to know before I agreed, but thought I already knew the answer, it was there in the previous day's walk into the city centre, past the window showing sleek banks of sinks and young stylists dressed in black. She had paused, looked in and I could read the thoughts as they crossed behind her eyes. I tried to think how it would be to stop outside with the intention of going in, how the door would feel beneath my hand, how it would be to step into a moment that was unknown.

What was it like for Leah to be there in that space with me, to feel trapped by the ghost in the room? I still heard her crying sometimes beyond the door to her room, it was always night-time when I heard her, always when she thought I was sleeping. Her tears were hushed and I thought of her grief as a quiet thing, dignified, but it was also a secret that she kept from me, a weight that she carried alone with no-one to balance the load.

I had lain in bed and wondered how she would feel if I made the two steps over the hallway, knocked lightly at the door and offered her my company, my sympathy. I watched the light spill over the threshold of my half-open door and held my breath, torn by the indecision, afraid that if I were to appear next to her, to place a soft hand gently on her shoulder, she would know that I had always heard, that there were no secrets. Perhaps she would have stopped crying, held her grief inside until it became twisted and cold. I thought of her life as an altered place, somewhere altogether different now that I was in it, now that home was here.

"Can we leave if I don't feel up to it?" I asked and her reply was preceded by a light touch against my upper arm;

her fingers were warm, barely there.

"Of course, as always, you only need do what you think you are up to and nothing more."

"What if the hairdresser is halfway through when I feel I have to go?" Her eyes moved to my hair, starting on the side with the scar as if it were a magnet for them as it was for my fingers. I wondered if it would always be this way, if those pinkish lines would always be my most obvious feature, the thing that I was remembered for when I stepped out of a room and left people talking.

"Well," she said and one corner of her mouth turned up a little, "even if that were the case, I really don't think it could look any worse."

I began to laugh before she did and I think it surprised us both. It was a small thing, a barely-there sound, as if my body had forgotten how to do it but it built in volume until it equalled hers and when the laughter faded away she pulled me into her arms and squeezed me tightly. The room became yellow-tinted, edged with life stolen from forgotten laughter and she held me in the air of jasmine that surrounded her. I felt light and happy as she kissed me on the end of my nose with a smile and placed her palm against my cheek.

Afterwards I found that it was a small thing after all, the change in my appearance. I still feel the shying away from too-harsh fingers as they pressed, rubbed at my damaged places, my broken skin. I heard the gentle reproach in Leah's voice as she warned them to take care, to soften their touch and when they did I relaxed into their hands and eventually opened my eyes to a changed reflection that needed no covering, an elfin face that began to lose the ghosts of an operation that haunted it.

We walked back along the cobblestones of the side streets. The wind blew softly through my evenly cropped hair and it was new, different. The scarf was folded into the corner of Leah's bag and I could not help but reach up and touch the changed landscape, the taming that had occurred.

When Leah stopped I held the number of steps I had reached in my head and turned to follow her eyes. Nestled between a tiny fabric shop and gift shop with leaded windows was an empty unit, the windows a little dusty, the interior painted white. She was contemplative, her eyes narrowed as she looked far deeper inside than I was able to see, to a future place where the dust was wiped away and the shop open for business.

"When I stayed in Thailand, I used to earn a little bit of money crafting bouquets of local blooms for the tourists and selling them on the streets. Perhaps that's what I should do, floristry, what do you think?"

It occurred to me that things were changing, that she was planning the next step she should take. I watched as she stepped tentatively forward to meet her future self and I wanted to ask 'what about me, what can I be?' but I didn't, knowing that it would be selfish in that moment when there was light in her eyes. I couldn't reply to her question, I couldn't tell her what I was thinking.

"You used to live in Thailand?" I asked instead, and she nodded with a smile.

"I travelled to many places." I counted our way home and her story accompanied the metronome in my head. I heard her vibrancy as she stepped into an altogether different life of travel and spontaneity. I smiled as she looked at me and spoke of exotic memories that I envied simply for the fact that they were there behind her lovely blue eyes when my own were empty of secrets and tales to share.

Chapter Twelve

There were forty-eight floor tiles in the short corridor outside the doctor's office. Off-white with grey and blue swirls, a poor man's marble that pressed softly against my feet instead of being hard and unyielding but they shone as though someone cared for them a great deal and the soles of my shoes slipped as I walked. Counting them over and over I sat in the tubular, chrome, puffy-seated chairs and pretended not to hear the muted voices that spilled across the threshold of the open door, marring the carefully polished surface.

Would this space ever become familiar, comfortable, somewhere that held no mystery? Would it become like the walls in Aunt Leah's house, safe and known? I felt too small, too exposed to sit in that place alone, surrounded by pictures of landscapes I had never seen and smells that were alien to my slight, flaring nostrils.

That day was a good head day, a no-pain day. I woke from the usual nightmares with my neck feeling surprisingly free and light, my head a balloon bobbing freely on the end of a short string. I brushed my short hair carefully, moving gently over the still-tender scar that wasn't quite hidden yet despite the hair stylist's attention. Careful consideration was paid to the edges where the separation in my skin had been reunited, the shiny thick line that looked frayed and untidy. The scar looked like little more than a separation of fabric and loose threads that I tried to press inwards with the tips of fingers that marvelled at the lack of sensation in the skin there.

"Good days and bad days... " Leah's muted voice tip-toed into the corridor, chased by a deep rumble of the doctor's reply. Good days, bad days, good days, bad days. It repeated over and over in my mind, finding a natural rhythm. It became the sound of the train on the tracks, the train that brought us there because I was too afraid to climb into the seat of the car and relive the feeling of my family being gone.

I surprised us both by enjoying the journey, watching the countryside pass in a blur beyond the oval window. I found a kind of freedom in the movement without the constant litany of counting that seemed to move deeper and deeper into my subconscious. I even managed the subsequent bus journey, though I held tightly to Leah's hands and kept my face pressed into her shoulder until it was time to disembark.

Good days and bad days. I thought that Leah was being kind making the scales seem balanced, calm. She didn't say that there were days when I seemed to fracture a thousand times, days that she followed closely behind me with a broom to sweep up the pieces. I did not hear her speak of the darkness of my past, the shadows that became a vacuum that I suffocated in as she struggled to pull me to the surface. I floundered through the unfamiliar, confused by everything around me and she was always there, normal and serene, her arms outstretched.

I nibbled at the ragged skin around the edges of my nails and stared at a painting of a wild mountainous landscape that looked dull and rainy. What had the artist been thinking? Why had he enjoyed the day so much that he wanted to share it even though it looked bleak and harsh and cold? I wondered if I had ever stood where the artist stood, in my other life, in my before.

Leah's voice, no longer vague, became a blunted arrow directed at me.

"You can come in now, Sarah," she called and I heard concern there, though it wore a disguise of nonchalance. I moved across nine floor tiles in an L shape and stepped onto thick carpet that made me feel off-centre. The room was bright and clean. Huge windows allowed the sunlight to bleach away colour and texture from the walls and furnishings, making the room appear colossal and vague at the edges.

I stopped in that spotlight, frozen. Leah's pink-tipped nails waved in front of my face as she held her hand out to me across the void. I reached out and allowed her to pull me forwards and the room shrank to normal size. Her arm felt warm as it curled around my shoulders and pulled me closer.

Doctor Marsden looked like a bear, his hair too long, his face and hands too big, his chin gruff and bearded. He didn't look like a doctor at all and I pulled my gaze from his as he stared at me. I looked intently at the silver balls hanging on string at the edge of his desk.

"Hello Sarah."

I found it strange hearing my name cross a stranger's lips and so I ignored him and carried on staring at the balls. I heard Leah begin to tell me to reply and his hand lifted in my peripheral vision, stalling her words before a single one was formed.

On the surface of the balls, the office windows curved around the edges, fading to points that weren't real, that weren't there. The blonde of Leah's hair, the red of her jacket, the soft carpet, all reflected around the gleaming surface of the five silver orbs. I moved closer, fascinated, saw myself moving in perfect synchronicity, distorted and weird. The reflection of my face filled the orbs entirely as I stepped nearer, bending curiously. I lifted my hand to touch my cheek and the reflection twisted and curved with the movement. My face came closer, filling the space more and more until there was only my eye, huge and warped, slowly blinking five times over.

"Look," said the doctor and he reached out. I took a tiny

step backwards as his fingers stopped level with one of the balls, lifting it before letting it go to careen into the others. The ball on the other end lifted and dropped back again, the balls in the middle staying still. I watched, fascinated, before glancing up to see Doctor Marsden smiling at me. He was smaller, folded in on himself, and the barrier between us was no longer there.

"What is it?" I asked.

"It's called a Newton's cradle. It's named after Sir Isaac Newton who was a physicist."

"A Newton's cradle?"

"Yes. He was a clever man, Newton. He also discovered that white light carries all the colours of the rainbow. Come and see."

He stood then and walked towards the big window, gesturing for me to follow. I counted across the carpet until I stood near him, not close enough for him to put his outstretched hand on my shoulder but near enough to see what he was looking at. A many-faceted crystal hung on a string in such a way as to catch the light pouring in through the glass. He reached up and spun it between thumb and forefinger and small bursts of colour danced in unison across the windowsill and the hairy contours of his face.

He smiled at me. "Who knew science could be so lovely?" he said.

I thought then that I would like this man, with his shaggy hair and his warm smile. He was different from the doctors at the hospital with their sterile clothes and their hushed tones. They belonged to the past, to the hospital room where I began. Doctor Marsden was in the now, present in my new life, my new beginning, and I accepted him in with little trepidation.

We sat back down and the room seemed much smaller now than it had when I stepped through the door into brightness.

"Has there been any change in your memory, Sarah?"

I knew this question was a repeat, that he asked Leah the same thing. Perhaps he hoped that the answer would be different, that we would be two sides of the same coin, where Leah spoke of heads but I had tales to share. I shook my head and thought that perhaps I disappointed him.

"Sometimes I remember little things, flavours of sweets before I try them or I know how certain types of material will feel in my hand. Just little things, I don't have any memories of me or my life."

"Hopefully, the little things are just the beginning. In cases of neurological amnesia we would expect to see an improvement of memory fairly quickly during recovery. Do you have trouble remembering new information?"

I thought of the dream that escaped me quickly after waking, of Annie written in glitter on my fingertips and how I couldn't seem to remember the colour of her eyes, even when I had just looked at them in a photograph. I thought of journeys with counted steps and how every count was known.

"Sometimes. I remember certain things and not others."

"That, too, can be an issue with severe head trauma. We would expect to see an improvement in that area as your convalescence continues."

He smiled again, a reassuring smile that told me I am not so unusual after all, that this had happened before to other people and their experience was a signpost to my own recovery.

"What I would recommend is to keep a note of any memories that appear to be from before the accident, no matter how small, such as flavours and textures. You may find a pattern emerging which may prompt further awareness."

I nodded in response and he turned to Leah, telling her to call if she had any concerns and in the meantime to book an appointment for the following month. We all stood at the same time and he shook both of our hands in turn, my own small hand disappearing into his vast, warm paw. I smiled at him as we turned to leave and he said goodbye as if we were friends.

Chapter Thirteen

Everything began to slide from beneath me. The more I coped with and the more change I absorbed through skin that became thicker, less sensitive, the more it seemed I was given to hold in hands that seemed too small, too weak. There were no backward steps, there was no way to reverse the changes that gathered their own momentum and pulled me with them.

Doctor Marsden had told Leah that I was okay to return to school. But he was wrong because it would not be a return, it was a new thing, a source of fear and confusion. How could I return to something that never existed in the mind I had then? It was essential, he said, for my social awareness, my recovery. And in those words there were hooks that attached onto Leah's conscience, prodding her sharply into feelings of guilt at her own ignorance. She apologised to me for not having thought of this, as though it were something I missed and desperately needed back.

September approached far too rapidly and we filled the days with uniform shopping and walks to and from the school that was past the church, up the hill and down a narrow street. I counted the steps until they were familiar and did not feel any better because the change still came and only the path to the large glass doors was known; there were secrets beyond them, unknown places.

Eventually the doors opened and a man was there, middle aged, non-descript, forgettable, but he smiled warmly and introduced himself to me first for which I was grateful, I was not yet invisible there.

"I'll show you around the classrooms you will need to be familiar with and give you a map to study at home. Eventually you won't even have to think about it, it will become second nature."

And he smiled at me as I thought that he was wrong, I would have to think, I would always have to count my steps down these corridors. I would look at my feet as they stepped onto the grey floor and close my eyes and ears to the people, the sounds around me and then maybe I would survive it all, maybe I would make it through.

By the time we were finished, Leah's face was a theatrical mask of worry and pleasure. Her smile a tentative thing that begged me to tell her that everything was okay.

"I'm scared," I told her and even those small words struggled to the surface as if speaking them made my fear real, and once loosened I could never contain it again.

"I know," she replied.

And her arms were around me, shielding the building from my line of sight, making it disappear. I breathed her in and wondered how it would be, walking these places without her to protect me, to keep me safe.

"Shall we walk back a different way today?"

I looked at the delicate curve of her jaw line and shook my head. I was beginning to forget how many steps there should be for some of the paths I had mapped out. It seemed, perhaps, that there were too many to remember, too many journeys stored in the weakened spaces. I realised that I must limit my choices, my directions until the cold solid statistics of them became so memorable they could not be crowded out by new paths.

I could walk into town or visit the shops on the main streets, my feet knew the way to the school and my eyes would lift to acknowledge the sleeping place of my family as I passed. I could find my way to the train station, to the doctor's and back home again. For all of these journeys I held the count in my head. But I daren't add anything new unless it was essential because what if, one day, I forgot the numbers and couldn't find my way back home?

Chapter Fourteen

I was not like the other children. That was the fact that lived dark and still in those first few weeks, in the silence I pulled around me. It was there as I walked into the school on the first day of the new term, as I trod the bustling corridors and danced softly through the crowds, head down, eyes on the floor. Would it have been different if we were all new together? If I hadn't started in Year Ten, when everyone else had walked this space together for three years? Perhaps if I could have gone back to Year Seven, reversed time somehow, then I could have filtered through quietly, become invisible among the crowd.

In my new tutor room I bounced off the tight-knit groups that had formed in the spaces where I did not exist. I was sidelined, afraid, and the other students looked at my short hair, my pale skin, the still-visible scar, before turning back to their own conversations. I wanted to turn and leave but the teacher, Mrs Perrot, materialised behind me and ushered me deeper into the well of conversation and familiarity. She introduced me to the class and there was heat in my skin that I knew must be obvious to anyone. I slid into a seat at the edge of the classroom halfway down the row and tried not to exist in that moment until someone whispered behind me:

"Are you the girl whose family got wiped out in the car?"

I lowered my head further, my chin grazing lightly against my chest and saw for the first time the label that I would always carry around my neck: 'the girl who... '. What was I? The girl who lost her memory, her family, who didn't fit in, who counted her steps? I was all of those things and for the first time I saw it clearly in one complete image. Without turning around I nodded my head slightly and I heard his intrigue, his strange admiration and tried not to shed tears against it.

I became defined by all the things I was and all the things I was not. I wasn't there at the beginning, I was not smart, I was not pretty enough. I was not the same as everyone else. I didn't know how people found out about the accident, perhaps they overheard a conversation between teachers, a note accidentally left on a desk for prying, uninvited eyes, but it was one more thing that set me apart. After the initial curiosity, the sidelong glances, they turned from me and I floated like a ghost at the edge of their vision.

I saw the concern on Leah's face as I walked in at the end of each day. She stopped asking me how things went, replacing her words with back-rubbing hugs that made me feel even more like an object of pity and sympathy.

"Things will get better."

There was hope in her voice, bordering on prayer and I wanted to believe her. The weeks passed and my school days were a test of endurance, one more mark on the calendar. I kept my head down and worked as hard as I could, wishing away the hours, days, weeks.

Towards the end of the first term, Alex found me. In the canteen eating lunch I watched the table of popular girls holding court. Everyone knew their names apart from me; for some reason they would not stay in my head, slipping out whenever I turned away. What was it that set them apart from the rest of us, that made them what they were? I did not realise at first that someone had sat in the empty seat beside me. "You're Sarah." A voice stated.

Startled, I looked up. "Yes."

"My name is Alex."

She was shorter than me, pretty with green eyes and freckles. I had noticed her before simply because the other girls stayed away from her too. She was an invisible, like me, though she seemed indifferent to it. I looked again towards the other girls and she followed my line of sight and smiled towards them.

"You know, they'll end up waxing some old lady's hairy legs when they leave school!"

I laughed into the virgin space around me, the sound making the air seem lighter.

When I arrived home, Leah looked less concerned when I smiled a little as I stepped through the door.

"I met a girl called Alex today, she seems nice."

I didn't realise then how common that name would become within these walls, how inseparable we would become. Leah turned from me and walked to the kitchen, getting two bowls, the tub of ice cream. We sat at the table eating quietly and it felt like a celebration.

Our lunchtimes together became everyday, routine and eventually they spilled out into the corridors and beyond the school walls. We walked home in the same direction and it was good to have company, to have someone else to talk to other than the muted greeting to the grave as I passed by.

"Why do some of the others call you dykey?" I asked her, knowing that it couldn't be true, that she wrote 'I love Harry' on the inside of her pencil case.

"It's because my mum is a lesbian and her girlfriend lives with us," she said simply.

I shook my head as I watched the other girls heading home, laughing together, sharing lipstick and secrets. I realised then that I was glad I was not like them, that I didn't fit in.

"Would you like to come in for a bit?" I asked and there was a surge of relief as she agreed. I did not have to feel embarrassed that I had read more into this tender beginning than I should have. I found Leah in the front room and asked if it was okay for Alex to come in.

"Of course," she said, getting to her feet, "she can share the cake with us."

I waved Alex forwards and introduced them as I wondered what cake Leah was talking about.

"We've met before, a while ago now so I doubt you remember. I know your mum, she owns the fabric shop in Gandy Street."

"Yeah she does," Alex replied and we were all smiling as Leah told Alex she was welcome anytime, that she could come for a sleep over whenever she liked.

I heard in the rapid fire of her words the desperation to keep that door open for me, to smooth the path of friendship as much as she could so that I no longer stood alone. She waved us into the kitchen where a huge chocolate cake spilled over the edges of the table; it was covered in coloured sprinkles, sugar crystals, marshmallows.

"Well, we'll be neighbours of sorts soon then. Working neighbours at least," Leah said and we both looked at her curiously. "I signed the lease today on the empty shop unit. I'm going to open a florist there."

I threw my arms around her and told her I was happy for her but underneath it all I owned that happiness too; here there was another reason to make the new friendship work, another reason to be able to hold onto it. And it was only then that I realised how afraid I was that it would fade away.

Leah added another glass to two already sitting on the table and poured us all a small amount of sparkling wine before looking at Alex's slightly bemused face.

"Your mum won't mind, will she?"

"Probably not."

"Well, that's good enough for me," Leah smiled and raised her glass theatrically above us, "Here's to Rose Tinted, may it be a great success!"

"Hear, hear," I replied and met Alex's eyes across the

table. Her smile was wide and genuine and she winked at me as we simultaneously sipped at the wine.

It was in that moment, as we sat together looking to the future, the bubbles tingling a pathway down my throat and sinking into unexpected warmth in my stomach, that I realised what I was feeling was real happiness. It was the first time I could remember feeling that way. I didn't ever want to let it go.

Chapter Fifteen ~ Six Years Later

So this is how it begins. With a simple truth, with three small words, a tiny statement and it is this: I saw her. Long before she ever noticed me, long before change had blown through both our lives and brought us together in a scream of confusion. I saw her emptiness, the void, and found her intriguing, compelling.

I found her in the impersonal corridors at the school she had joined late, where she drifted from class to class; on the playing fields where she sat hunched beneath the weight of her life, shoulders round and spine curved. I closed my eyes against the way she carried her grief like a companion, a long lost friend, a security blanket that hid her from prying eyes. It set her apart and nobody bothered to look beyond it.

Except me, of course, I saw who she was beneath it all. Saw her shadows, the ghosts that hovered over her head. I saw her self-pity, her fear, the bitter taste of it that pulled her cheeks in tight and puckered her lips. It was all too easy to think of her as a fragmented image in the hospital bed where she faded in and out as the doctors tried to stabilise the ebb and flow of her heartbeat. I imagined her struggle, her fight to survive.

I don't think she ever noticed me there, too wrapped up

as she was in the life that had handed her trials that other people would never understand. She was brittle and sharp-edged, fragile, the best china kept locked away for a day that would never come. In some ways she reminded me of my mother even though we are close in age, Sarah and I. She had that same look in her eyes, the one that had once made me so afraid. I felt that if I touched her even slightly she would break beneath my fingertips, crumble into dust, and so I kept my distance and remained no more than an observer, keen, unobtrusive.

And afterwards, when school was done and we had all been frozen into the former student photographs that lined the school reception, I still saw her, waiting for her along the same paths she always walked; catching an occasional glimpse of her reflection behind me in shop windows as I waited for her to notice me there watching her, with her arms full of flowers brighter and more colourful than she was. She was a moth, drab and colourless. I felt like a butterfly against her, my colours bright yet short-lived. The bleak slant of her shoulders drew me in.

How would she feel if I forced her to see me, if I said hello? Would she recognise me as the girl who sat with her in the final year photograph? Would she remember seeing me in the shadows, silent and watchful? Would she know my name was Ellie, that my favourite colour was red, that I loved the taste of garlic? Or would I remain invisible to her as I always had?

Sometimes I wondered what it would be like if she were to feel the delicate touch of my hand brush lightly against the soft skin of her cheek. Would she recoil? Or lean into my touch, pushing against my hand, the palm moulding to her cheek? I could easily imagine the tenderness, the affection in that touch, just as I could too easily see that same hand grow sharp and cruel, leaving marks that would glow against pale, taut skin.

Sometimes beneath the tenderness, the yearning for

attention, for her to notice me, I hated her. I envied her lack of memories, the ignorance of her forgotten childhood when my own burned in twisted, agonising paths inside me. I don't know why I had never stepped forward before. There was some thrill, some dramatic irony in watching someone who didn't see me, as though I were privy to all her secrets while sharing none of my own. I knew all about her, all about the accident, her struggle to survive, her grief at the loss of her family. And she knew nothing of me, she had never looked into my eyes and guessed at the person behind them, she had never heard me speak or paid any attention when I laughed. I was little more than a ghost for her and I loved the secrecy of me even while hating her for her lack of awareness.

She never knew that I observed her like a scientist stares at a specimen beneath a microscope, fascinated yet aloof. She was unaware of the constancy with which I watched, with which I learned her routines, the patterns of her days. I wanted to see the expression on her face when she saw me, noticed me for the first time; when she realised who I was, who I have always been.

Chapter Sixteen

The morning dawns fresh and clear as I jolt awake to the sound of my own heart beating loud in my ears. My skin is hot, clammy and laying here with the sheet damp beneath me I know that today will be warm and humid. Hidden beneath the easing breath, the slow descent to calm, there is something new nudging my still half-asleep mind to pay attention. I try to grasp back into the fading moments, feeling my way into the fear already alleviated by daylight. I think over the vanishing tiny detail of the dream before it evaporates into the morning.

I find what I am looking for in amongst the shopping game we played in the moments before my world altered and I wonder why I never noticed it before. I quickly write it down before it can leak onto the pillow, tearing the sheet of paper free from my journal and knowing that I will place it in my pocket, carry it with me as I go to work so that I do not forget to ask about it later; this tiny thing that is new and suddenly important because I have never considered it before. I prod at it gently, scraping at the surface, waiting to see the glitter of gold beneath the dust but there is nothing more, only this question.

By the time I head up the street, I am late. My watch tells me that it is ten to ten but it is not as simple as looking at the crystal hands and walking faster. Leah's concern threads its way down the road towards me and hastens me onwards, pulling at my feet with a lack of subtlety.

Time is a strange thing, it bends and twists on itself, patterns that are not linear, that circle and alter as I lose myself in them. I should have been at the shop an hour ago. Often we go in together but this morning Leah needed to leave early, to head to the flower market and collect fresh stock. I hadn't been woken by my nightmare until long after she walked quietly out into the still-dark morning.

I set my alarm, knowing that I often return to sleep after the bad dreams, fumbling for it when it startled me awake, breathing out a yawn as I sat up, pushing the covers back as I moved. I made myself a mug of tea and curled into the sofa as I drank it and somewhere between then and now time has played tricks on me as it often does.

I have heard others ask the question in simple conversation, rhetorical, exasperated, 'where does the time go?' and I imagine it hiding from me, perhaps keeping company with the memories that never returned, my 'then' life that I hear tales of and wonder if they are true. Tales of my father and sister, descriptions of our little house, stories from Leah's past. The anecdotes have long been exhausted, mined for every nugget of information but I find that I do not mind the repeats. Surely if I could remember myself I would often revisit these moments, finding company in them, or solace. Leah doesn't mind, I think she likes to talk of them too. And now, in the curve of my pocket, held tightly in my fingers there is a new memory to be told about, something I have not heard before, something overlooked. I am impatient to hear this new thing, to discover where it sits in the life I do not know.

Thinking of Leah prompts me to walk faster still. It is all too easy to imagine her sitting behind the counter, fingers busy, mind churning. In the years since I left school there have been many times to be grateful for her understanding on days such as these, when time runs ahead of me and though I sense her impatience I know that it is not for herself and her lack of a colleague, a helping hand, but out of the concern for me that never faded even as I grew into adulthood.

I walk in the company of a subtle undertone of guilt, sensing it in the background like the quiet hum of electricity, barely noticeable after a time but always there. The guilt of being a survivor, guilt about Leah and all she has sacrificed for me, about the life she could have had. I compare her possible life with her real one and despite the success of the shop, the throngs of customers headed her way through personal recommendation without need for advertising, I find that the present day comes up lacking somehow. She could have been so much more without the weight of me.

She knows I sometimes feel the drag of these feelings, reading it in the familiar shadows behind my eyes.

"I don't want you to feel guilty," she has said more than once. "I want you to understand that it was a selfish thing that I did. I was terrified they would take you from me and I would lose you too. I had no-one else, you are my family. I couldn't have got through it without you to care for."

And so we dance in symbiosis, equally reliant, equally needed though I still feel guilty and she still despairs of it. And beneath it all, beneath her assurance and her emphatic words, threads another reason equally valid and bright. She would have seen giving me up as a betrayal of my father; in some vast unacceptable way she would have been letting him down had she admitted defeat and been unable to cope. Not just for me then, the sacrifices she made, not just for herself. They were for the ghost of the brother she adored. The father I had lost.

Chapter Seventeen

My mother sang when she was happy. I heard her from my bedroom as I put my school uniform on and brushed my teeth. I watched the me in the mirror, blurred by a smear of toothpaste on the glass and a trail of dusty cobwebs, smile as I heard her voice bathe the kitchen yellow and warm. Her feet slid and rasped across the floor to a beat only she could hear and from the doorway I saw clearly, outlined against her wistfulness, the man she imagined she was dancing with. Her shoulders flexed beneath his invisible hands and there was a sigh in her voice as the song grew soft. Something in the way she moved, in the way she sang, made me sad and uneasy; that invisible man was never my father and somehow I knew it.

Her voice grew lost and desperate, too small for the room she had expanded with her joy only moments before. The change fluttered in the air, pushing against me until I backed away, to the very edges of the room where her eyes found mine.

"I see you there you know, little girl of mine. I spy with my little eye something beginning with Y."

"Yacht?"

The shake of her head fanned dark curly hair. A wisp of it twisted into the corner of her mouth and I fought the urge to reach up a finger and pull it free.

"Yak?"

Laughing, she looked around the kitchen and raised her shoulders, her palms upwards as if to say where, where could I hide a yak in this tiny kitchen? I caught sight of the tile near the kettle plug, the one she varnished over, the one she let me paint with a big, blotchy sunshine in happier days, so long ago that I could hardly remember it. I thought the answer was right there.

"Yellow," I said. There was certainty, strength in my voice, but she shook her head again.

"Oh no! The Y that I see is Y O U and you know what that means?" I shook my head. "That means it is tickle time!" And I ran.

She chased me through the door, down the hall, into the front room where we leapt onto the sagging, worn sofa and buried ourselves beneath prodding fingers and laughter. Inside I filled up with bubbles of contentment that made my footsteps lighter as I carried them with me to school.

Later, when they had all burst and the day was passing, the front door opened to reveal a sadder face, an air of despondency. There was no singing, no games. The house smelled different, of someone else's clothes, someone else's feelings and she seemed to flounder against them. I tried to imagine where the strangeness came from as I sat quietly and felt out of place, vague, like a stranger in my own home. I tried to feel the echo of laughter in the fibres of the sofa, but it was gone as though it had never been.

She walked up the stairs and I heard the change of mood in her feet, the way they landed on the stairs with a slight echo, the way she made them heavier somehow. I slid sideways along the hallway, the bones in my slight frame catching against the lip of the kitchen door as I followed the shape of it. I remember thinking to myself that perhaps she had a headache, perhaps that was what painted the frown lines between her eyes. There was a tiny leap in my chest as I grasped for a better option, one that wasn't me, my father, this house.

I dragged a chair to the sink, careful not to make any noise with it. I gave no thought to how I would get down again without spilling anything from the full glass until the water was in my hand and it was too late to think of another plan. No matter how slowly I stepped there would be a jolt at the end. Water cascaded over the back of my hand and I lapped at it like a cat as I stepped around the tiny puddle I had created on the floor.

My own footprints made no sound against the worn stair carpet. She was in the bathroom when I reached the top. Her spine pushed against the curve of her back as she bent over the sink, her face submerged in the water that lapped against the porcelain brim. I stood holding the glass, holding my breath, wondering if she was dying in there, in the tiny sink with its brownish water stain and mismatched taps. Time stretched out and I stood mute until I reached my empty hand towards her just as her head pulled free of the surface and the oxygen in the tiny room disappeared noisily into her lungs.

"What does it feel like to drown?" I asked her as water dripped from her chin and she rubbed at her eyes with the sleeve of her dress. She pulled out the plug and twisted quickly to face me, her eyes were bright and narrow.

"What does it feel like? I'll show you." She gently took the glass from my hand and placed it on the edge of the bath, launching my toy wind-up boat down the curve of the tub as she did so. Her hands ran softly up my arms until they tangled into my hair and pulled my head sharply back with a sudden wrench. My throat was constricted and all I could manage was a squeak as her mouth came down on mine and she exhaled. I desperately tried to push myself back as her breath forced its way into my lungs and pulled the control, the free will, away from me. I grew taut, huge against the onslaught and thought that perhaps she meant

77

to kill me, that this was where I would end. When she abruptly let go of me my legs crumpled beneath me and I collapsed onto the floor. I sat crying in front of her as she looked down at me, her eyes bored and dull.

"You want to know what it feels like to drown? Look into my eyes and you'll see it. I drown every day."

I heard her footsteps as she walked down the hallway, as I struggled to my feet and felt my own breath chase the invasion of hers out of my body. I heard the swish of her curtains being drawn, the creak of her bed as she laid down. I knew she would be lying there in the half-dark with her hands pressed dramatically across her eyes. I hoped that she would be there until the day was ending, when Dad and I could tiptoe around the house in case she shattered like a crystal vase, when he would be with me and keep me safe from her unpredictability.

The day that started off so well, so sunshine-bright and happy, had become distorted and bleak. A dark thing that bound my mouth shut and silent, spilled oil in the mouth of a seabird. That morning and that afternoon did not belong together; they were two distinct things, separate and opposite. That day was not this one. This was a black day, a cold day for her and she carried it like a storm in her eyes, in her soul. It was there when she spoke, her voice a sharp thing that cut through the air and dug into my skin.

I walked quietly back down the stairs, moving slowly, feeling hunted. I sat so still, so very still in the living room that smelt masculine but unfamiliar as the bed creaked again from her bedroom. I heard the beginning of her rage wash down the stairs and fill every room. The sounds of something smashing spilled from the bedroom, surrounding me like a whirlwind, trying to pull me into it where I would be injured, carried away, lost forever.

I flinched and wondered when my father would be home from work. The light pouring in through the half-drawn curtains was too bright for it to be any time soon. The afternoon would chase the sun beneath the horizon before I heard his key and, in that moment, his arrival seemed too far away from me to take the fear that grew in the pit of my stomach.

Upstairs the calamitous noise began to fade to a more ominous silence. I slid beneath the kitchen table and thought that if I were really still it would be okay. If I didn't move, didn't speak, didn't even breathe, then no-one would see me, I would be invisible. She would walk right by. She would forget that she was not alone. I tried to imagine that I was a flower, to picture the roots stretching, leaving my feet, pushing through brown cracked lino; deep, deeper into soft moist earth. Leaves pushed through hair follicles, growing, unfurling. They pressed along the underside of the table, pushing softly against the wad of gum stuck there by my guilty little fingers some time ago.

Flowers don't feel afraid. I tried to be a flower and get everything that I needed through invisible roots. I heard her step into the room and I sharply drew in the smell of her cigarette, her perfume, her rage. A hand grabbed tightly onto my ankle and I was pulled backwards. My stubby, bitten fingernails clawed for purchase on the rough, worn floor. She turned me with harsh hands and I looked up into a face that was emotionless and cold. My mother looked beautiful, pale and faint like a ghost. I thought that perhaps I should look away. If I looked away she would fade like the smoke that curled from her parted lips and become nothing against the ceiling above me.

"What the hell is this?"

Her voice climbed in pitch as she thrust me towards the puddle I had left on the floor. Like a puppy who had peed where they shouldn't, she rubbed my face into it, pressing down until I felt the inside of my cheek grind against my teeth. I tasted blood and tried to pull away, bracing against the iron grip of her palm. She hauled me to my feet and the slap rocked my head backwards. I saw stars against the nicotine stains on the ceiling.

By the time I heard my father's key in the door, the shouted greeting that emerged in blissful ignorance from between his lips, I was in my room with the light off, my hot cheek pressed against the damp patch on my too-thin pillow. Muffled voices rumbled through the floor against a backdrop of plates and cutlery. No doubt she told him that I was unwell, that I mustn't be disturbed, I was obviously sleeping.

I knew that at some point in the night she would sneak into my room and beg forgiveness, and that I would struggle to hear her words against the sound of my hunger. I knew that by the time we all sat in the kitchen to eat our breakfast the following morning she would be all smiles. My father would ask me if I was feeling better and I would nod and smile as she looked on with worried eyes. I knew that there would be extra chocolate in my lunch box at school and that dinner that night would be my favourite. Dad would smile and say I was lucky and my mum would nod as if she agreed, as if the treats made up for the cut on the inside of my mouth, for the poison she had breathed into my lungs.

Chapter Eighteen

The cobbled street where Rose Tinted sits is a step out of time, untouched by car tyres and surrounded by whitewashed walls and leaded windows; the sense of peace that hangs over the wide alley provides a slower pace beneath people's soles. It is the feng shui of the place, Leah says, transporting people to another time where the pace of life was slower and worries were less significant somehow.

Whatever the ambience is, it leads to a steady stream of customers, a more than adequate income to offset the inheritance we both received, Leah from her own parents and me from my father, a legacy which remains relatively untouched, waiting for the day I grow older, become independent; something I, as yet, have no desire for.

Thanks to Leah I know how to make bridal bouquets, funeral wreaths and bunches of roses held together with birthday wishes or guilt. My hands don't have her dexterity; my eyes lack her sparkle and flair for the dramatic. Her creativity, particularly with modern arrangements, outshines mine a million times over but I do the best I can and Leah seems pleased regardless.

It is a blessing to work with someone who knows me so well. I wonder if I would be able to work at all without the shop to offer me understanding. Anywhere else I would surely be fired for taking too much time off, for the headaches that have never stopped plaguing me.

Leah understands if my head hurts too much to come in, or if time moves away from me too quickly to keep up. If it is one of her busier times she simply works longer hours and I try to make it up to her on the days when my head is together, rather than being torn apart from the inside. Sometimes we stand, working side by side until the clock turns night into morning, one day to another.

She never complains at the way things are, all she asks is that I call to let her know on the days when I wake after she has left for the market and find it impossible to raise my throbbing skull. She worries otherwise. This morning I have let down my side of the agreement, I haven't called and I walk as fast as I can as if every step will steal away her apprehension.

A pigeon suddenly flies towards my face, jolting me from my reverie and into the here and now and I wonder as my heart clamours and I collect my handbag from the floor, 'was it that?' Could it have been something as simple as a startled pigeon? This is a game that I often play with myself as I puzzle the why of it all, the pointlessness of it.

The crash that killed my family wasn't caused by anything as dramatic as a drunk driver or a speeding car. Nobody stepped into the road, my dad didn't have to swerve to avoid a small child or someone's pet. It wasn't a hero's death and there was no-one to blame. I think it would be easier if that were the case, if I could point my anger in one particular direction and sweep those responsible away with it or see a reason for it in some way. But I can't. It simply was what it was: a pointless, stupid accident that may have been avoided if Dad had started the engine a second earlier or a second later. If one of us had needed the toilet before we left, or if we hadn't. If the wind hadn't blown the way it had or if the birds had flown in an altogether different pattern, if the moon hadn't been full or the signs hadn't appeared as black clouds in the shape of a dragon. Or perhaps if a pigeon hadn't flown up and startled a father distracted by a shopping game he always played with his children.

I had picked through and tried to sort out the lack of answers, the imaginings or dreams from the truth. I looked for my story in the fragments I could find. Reaching into my pocket I drew out the piece of paper I had hastily scribbled on as I woke with the dream fresh in my mind. Another question for which an answer must be found or it would eat away at me, in the same way that the lack of other answers did almost every second of every day.

I pushed open the shop door.

"What happened to the dog?" My voice keeps time with the bell over the shop door, my sentence finishing before the ringing does. I hold out the piece of paper as if it is proof that it existed, a paw print in black ink. Leah, wearing her favourite overalls with the ditsy daisy print all over, her blonde hair tied back with a head scarf, replaces the old-fashioned phone receiver into the cradle. The air is thick with the heady scent of lilies.

"Well, good morning to you too," she says, a wry smile dancing across her lips.

"Sorry. Good morning, Leah," I reply and go to her side to place a conciliatory kiss on her cheek. She smells of jasmine and hair spray.

"All these years and you have never asked me that question."

Her voice is lacking in inflection, as if it has been ironed flat by my query and lost anything that gives it shape or substance.

"I've never thought of it before. But I wrote it down when I woke up this morning, it was in the dream, it was… it was." I feel the frown knit my brows together, feel the confusion that pursues the paper in my hand and tries to snatch it back into the world it belonged to, the dream world I escaped from. I can no longer remember where the question fits in, cannot, in this moment, place it among a shopping list shouted by playful voices. It blurs around the edges and becomes indistinct, slowly erased by the distance between then and now.

She discards the gardening glove that protects her delicate skin from rose thorns and reaches out to take the paper from my hand, reading the question written there in blue glittery ink. 'What happened to the dog' followed by three exclamation marks and one question mark, as though it were obvious and I should have asked a long time ago. There is sadness in the tiny smile that tries to grow upon her lips and fails.

"His name was Patch, he was a Springer Spaniel."

Her voice is small as she plays with the fingers of her discarded gloves, pulling flecks of dirt from them, dropping them to the floor. In an absent-minded gesture she reaches up and tucks a loose tendril of hair that has escaped her head scarf behind her tiny ear before reaching over and flicking the switch on the kettle.

"Your father got him for you girls some time after he and your mother split up. I don't know how old he was, but he was still young enough to be a little too boisterous and bouncy. He was lovely though, liver and white with these huge floppy ears."

She smiles at me over the insignificant detail, knowing that I crave it, that she is putting an image in my mind that fills a space, one that will remain after I wake in the morning, because she has painted it in the present and it cannot be washed away by the sound of grinding metal and screaming.

As she speaks, Patch begins to walk through my thoughts leaving footprints on the virgin surface. He greeted everyone who came to the door with a gift of some kind in his mouth: a stone he had found, a cuddly toy or an old sock. He was exuberant and wet-tongued. His appetite vast, his loyalty unquestionable.

"I couldn't take him. I was at the hospital all the time, it would have been impossible to care for him; and besides that postage stamp of a garden wouldn't have been right for a dog like him, he needed space to run around. I felt so guilty though, taking him down to the Blue Cross. I couldn't let go of his lead at first and then when I did I cried into his fur."

She smiles though her eyes look wet and shiny as I reach over and rub the back of her hand.

"I phoned them every week to see how he was doing and then one day I called them and he was gone. He had been taken in by a young family that had a farm out Tiverton way. I was happy for him and for me too if I'm honest. I felt less guilty thinking about him running around fields with his new owners." She frowns a little, "I hope the animal shelter told them not to give him sweet things, they made him drool."

"I wonder if he's still alive," I say and her eyes find mine; her mouth curves into a gentle smile.

"Let's just think yes and be happy for him," she replies.

And so we do and it is easier.

Chapter Nineteen

I am watching today, as I often do, with curiosity, and a little contempt as yet again she keeps her face firmly pointed towards the pavement in front of her feet; as if she is afraid to look anywhere else, as if she is afraid of what she might see if she looks at the world and all its life and vitality. Would she be infested with it, with its pulse? Her, the little ghost girl who lived when she shouldn't have, who only seems to embrace a half-life as if she deserves no more than that.

The frustration builds inside me as I watch. I want to tear apart the shell around her and scream until she looks up, sees what is in front of her. Why won't she look, why is she so pathetic? Today is a bad day, today is a hating day. I wonder what I can do to change things, to shake her up, shake away the blindness of her fear. How can I force her eyes to be more open?

The pigeon flaps upwards into her face, startled by her heavy footfalls, her haste. Her fear is palpable as she scrambles for her dropped bag. I imagine it threading through her heartbeat, in the flush that floods across her rigid jaw. My rage is a physical thing. I bear witness to her timidity and it angers me. How is it possible that she is so weak, so bound by her past when she was set free by her forgetting, by her lack of any childhood? And I am the one that is drowning in mine.

I think about my mother and become powerless in my anger. That this weak creature in front of me should have the pleasure of forgetting, that she should mourn her lost memories, her family. Not for the first time I wish I could be like her, that I could cast my memories into the darkness, that my own mind could be fractured and broken. How much easier would it be to not know where I had come from? How much easier would it be to step into a future unfettered by the past? I have watched as she squanders this gift of freedom she has been given and I loathe her for it.

She was a fool to look for answers, a fool to hope for any kind of returning. It can do no good at all to remember, she doesn't realise how lucky she is to have only now, only this. If only there were a way I could jolt her into the present, into the life she should be living, if only there were a way to show her all she misses out on by locking herself away in her ivory tower. Perhaps I can find a way to drag her into a life worth living.

Later, I leave her behind and walk lightly through the market in the city centre, running my fingers through multicoloured scarves and pashminas, too unseasonal to sell. Placed as they are on the pavements of the busy city streets, the stalls – with their bright awnings and eclectic wares – look awkward and out of place, as if they don't quite fit. A little like me.

I bounce between the stalls like a ball bearing in a pinball machine, smiling at the goods on display, trying titbits of food proffered on the end of a stall holder's disposable fork.

"How about it then, are you up for it?"

I turn towards the deep voice and look first at the leaflet waving in front of my face and second into the deep-set eyes of the man that holds it. His face is weathered, attractive.

"Up for what?" I say, flirtation in my voice as I smile up at him.

He raises one eyebrow and smiles back. "Anything." He answers and laughs, holding the leaflet a little higher to catch my eye.

I reach over and take the leaflet from his fingers, glancing briefly over the glossy images of a light aircraft, parachutes, people smiling as they plummet through the air. I wonder if they ever doubt that the chute will open, if there is a moment before the cord is pulled that pushes ice through their veins. I wonder what it would feel like to question, even for a second, one's own survival.

Reaching forward, I lightly tap the leaflet against his chest, noticing as I do the curve of the defined muscle beneath.

"I'll think about it," I say.

"Do," he replies, his eye winking so slightly it could have been nothing more than a twitch.

I hope that maybe it is more, there is promise behind his light smile.

"Will you be here next week?"

He looks down at the paper in my hand and nods. "You could sign up for our mailing list too if you want, we'll send you invitations and information about the events that are organised, see about getting you involved."

He turns and lifts a clipboard, the pen hovering in his hand somewhere in the air between him and me, as though he isn't quite sure if I would take it or not, as if I might leave him hanging and he will feel slighted, embarrassed. Something occurs to me then that I haven't thought of before. I feel the thrill of it as I reach my hand out.

"Why not?" I ask and take the pen from his hand. I smile to myself as I write down Sarah's name, her address, her mobile phone number. He takes the board from me when I am finished and glances at it.

"Nice to meet you, Sarah Phillips, I'm Matt."

I shake the warm, rough hand he offers and feel a little bite of regret. "Goodbye Matt," I say and turn to walk away.

I feel pleased with myself, knowing how shocking the idea of jumping out of a plane will be for Sarah, knowing that the idea will cause her thoughts to go into overdrive. I can only imagine the fear that would come to the surface, the horror she would feel. The stirring it would bring to her pathetically stagnant days.

I head towards home, a journey that takes me past banks and estate agents and that is when I see the advert. Later I will think all sorts of things about karma and synchronicity, about how apt it was that I saw the advert just after the idea had occurred to me to write Sarah's name instead of my own.

The advert is reasonably small but bold enough to be noticed. It is perfect for a day when I wondered about jumping alone into a blue sky and questioned the security in that. Perfect too for a day when I planned to shake someone else's life awake.

I am amazed at how quickly my mind reaches the decision; at the speed with which I know what it is I have to do. The perfectly groomed, middle-aged woman behind the desk looks up as I walk in, her face set in an automatic smile of welcome.

"I'm interested in the new apartments that are reaching completion in the city centre," I gesture vaguely towards the advert in the window. "Do you have any literature I could take a look at?"

"Of course, in actual fact we also have a show apartment available for prospective buyers if you wish to take a look yourself."

I think about it for a moment. "Would I need to make an appointment?" I ask and the woman, identified as Jill by the black name tag with curving gold script, shakes her head.

"Not at all, we have representatives in an office at the complex, simply turn up during normal office hours and they'll be happy to show you around."

Her smile is brief but warm, used like punctuation to

finish off her sentence.

"Perhaps I could take a brochure away with me?" I say and watch as Jill moves towards a filing cabinet and withdraws a glossy folder that she promptly hands over. With a smile of thanks I turn and leave, glancing at the glossy card and wondering at a whole new set of possibilities.

Chapter Twenty

It is a ritual of sorts, this kind of evening spent in the courtyard. Would it be possible to even begin to count how many times we have sat in these seats, drunk from these cups, sighed in unison? She is in her place and I am in mine. Have we ever changed, swapped places, seen each other from a different perspective? I think that no, it has always been like this, a dance between the two of us where we both know the steps to perfection, where we move simultaneously without stumbling, without fault.

Our conversation is always innocuous. We discuss the weather, the shop, films we like, articles we have read, it is the symphony in the background; one that we have both heard many times over and yet never tire of. And this is what I love, this sameness, this routine. It is ours in the same way that we have our own seats at the kitchen table, or the way that the sofa curves into the perfect shape for me when I curl into the right hand side of it.

These are the things that I love because they never change. Like the number of footsteps to my front door, the marks on the pavement that I memorise as I walk. They are always the same and I embrace this sense of constant rhythm, this harmony. If nothing changes, if nothing alters, then everything will remain just as it is right now; there will be no loss, no grief, no fading into black.

Leah sighs into the air around us. It is a sound of discord; a negative tone and I wonder how I know this when it is nothing more than an exhalation. Her cup moves against its saucer as she leans forward and meets my eyes with a direct stare.

"Sarah, you know how much I love you, don't you?" I look down at where my hands are curled around my own drink. We are drinking jasmine tea poured into little china cups from a squat, painted teapot. It tastes of somewhere far more exotic than this tiny courtyard garden, where we sit bundled up in coats and scarves against the growing chill of the evening. I hold tightly to my tea trying to warm my numb fingers as they are caressed by the cooling twilight.

"Yes?" I reply and I hear the question in that tiny word. I wonder if any good could follow what she has asked, the way she has asked it. I know that the question mark that punctuates her words is really a 'but' and that I may not like what follows. I wait nervously, a child called to the headmaster's office.

"Okay," she says, "please hear me out on this and understand that what I am saying comes only out of concern for you."

I raise one eyebrow against this moment that does not sit right with us, in this place, where things have always followed the same design, the same pattern. She leans in towards me and lightly presses the smooth skin of her forehead to the pale white line of scarring at my temple. Even now, so many years later, it still feels raw and tender to the touch; it still feels obvious.

"Sarah, you are twenty-one years old."

She pulls gently away from me and squares her shoulders as though preparing for a fight. Her voice has altered, her words marching towards me in crisp clean lines, I have never heard this voice before. She even holds her head differently, angled towards me and taut as though looking over imaginary glasses and were I not so worried about what comes next I would giggle her posturing away, make light of it somehow.

Instead I hide my concern in the steam that rises from my tea.

"All right, I want you to tell me honestly, have you had a boyfriend since Robert Jay?"

I automatically shake my head a little, as if I have anticipated this question, predetermined my answer. Leah watches me carefully, reading the movement of my face as I wonder at the origins of her question, at why it is here in the first place. Why now when I have long since stopped thinking of that name with any kind of emotion?

To say he had been the love of my life, when I sit here at twenty-one and see time stretching far into the future, would be meaningless; though I had once believed it to be true and that he could never be replaced. Perhaps it is more apt to say that he had been a love in my life, thus far the only one.

We had met in our final year of school and I think it fair to say I had mourned the loss of our relationship for longer than it had lasted. What do I remember about him now? That I steadfastly refused to call him Bobby as he wished me to, choosing Rob instead, because Bobby sounded ridiculous on a teenager that stood at six feet and at fifteen already needed to shave.

I remember that before the time in art club when we bonded over a dramatic piece of pop art by Lichtenstein, there had been only myself and Alex and we still existed on the periphery of everyone else's school days. Our friendship had grown closer, stronger as the terms had passed and by the time we were in Year Eleven, with GCSEs looming and study taking the place of fun, she and I knew each other's every secret. She knew about the car accident, the blank void in my memory, the headaches and the counted journeys. I knew about the bitterness of her parents' break-up and the older brother who had gone off the rails when her mum came out. He was in a young offenders institution serving time for robbery and Alex didn't talk about him much, though I knew she missed him.

When Rob joined art club to get help with his coursework

I couldn't take my eyes from his. He was gorgeous, tall and broad-shouldered with dark scruffy hair and dimples when he smiled. Like us he was not part of the popular crowd. He was severely dyslexic and struggled with written tasks so was duly labelled as a failure by the more able children who said he must be retarded. He was intelligent, kind and artistic but none of that mattered, the labels given in school stick like super glue and can never be altered or removed, can never be completely erased.

In true teenage fashion I loved Rob with all my soul after spending less than half a day alone together. We caught the train to Exmouth and walked along the beach, our hands tightly clasped together, I told him about the accident that I couldn't really remember and the memory I had left in the wreck of the car. He said he understood and kissed me right there on the sand, our bare toes sinking in and making me feel unsteady.

After that day I doodled 'Mrs Sarah Jay' on a million pieces of paper and tried to imagine what our wedding would be like. We talked about what college we would go to, where he would study art and I would study journalism or business or media or any one of the hundreds of subjects I hadn't identified yet as fitting perfectly around me. It was intense, incredible, perfect. Until suddenly it wasn't anymore.

There were no dimples on his cheeks when he told me that his father had been transferred to Edinburgh with work and that they would be leaving shortly after the exams were over, there was no perfection in that moment. How could it be that pain could be so sharp, so pure, without physical cause? My exams suffered and I grieved for him in a way I had never grieved for my father and sister, even while he was still there in front of me, even as I tried to memorise every line on the youthful face that would soon be kissing me goodbye. I was sixteen and thought my life was over.

At first we wrote to each other and spoke on the phone whenever we could. He told me that Edinburgh was cold, that he felt isolated, that he missed me. I told him that nothing was the same without him and fought back the tears so he didn't get embarrassed, so that he didn't have a reason not to call. And slowly the stories of his days became more rich and full. He began to mention names, new friends that had been made. His voice took on a tone of life, of excitement and I felt the shift away from Devon, from me.

The phone calls grew further apart, becoming shorter and stilted until eventually receiving them became more awkward, more painful than the silence in between. The last time we spoke I told him not to call again, that I needed to move forwards and away from him. I pretended not to hear the relief in his voice.

Five years later, nobody could get close to me, the torch I once carried still hot and uncomfortable. I had gone on dates, often double-dating with Alex and her latest man. Some of them had potential and once or twice the date had become a second and then a third but there was always something lacking: their sense of humour, the way they smiled, the wrong aftershave.

"You know your problem?" Alex had said as I turned down another potential suitor. "You're too damn fussy! You're going to end up a crusty, lonely old maid at this rate."

I agreed with her and found that I didn't mind so much. I was happier following the bland, familiar middle line, as I tended to in everything.

My thoughts fade and I am back in the courtyard garden, which has grown still and prickly, the pause in conversation heavy and obvious. My cup of tea is stalled halfway to my mouth and Leah watches me closely, gazing into the zoetrope eyes that have played out the story for her, given her an answer. I look down and see the reflection of my eyelashes in the amber liquid.

"I don't really want a boyfriend," I say and she sighs with discontent.

"Darling, it isn't just that. You seem to look at life as if it's something to try and get through, something to tolerate. It's like watching someone going through the motions. You go to work, to the library, you read and watch TV, you hang out with Alex, but I get the feeling you are just filling in the hours. You're breaking my heart, angel, breaking my heart."

The passion in her voice stirs inadequacy and failing through me, the words seeming like criticism coming from the mouth of one who has always held my hand, told me I'm strong, held me up when I thought I would fall. She has changed the floor beneath my feet and I stumble against it. I do not know how to respond against the unfamiliar and I speak with petulance.

"I don't see why, I'm happy with my life just the way it is."

"No you're not, don't you dare tell me that you are happy."

Her voice grows sharp, pointed and I wince from it.

"I can see the shadows you carry. You are not living your life, you are enduring it and I am so afraid that one day you will wake up and realise that all the good things have passed you by. Jesus Christ, Sarah. By the time I was your age I'd had at least ten boyfriends, I'd travelled abroad, got pissed far too often. Hell, I'd even been arrested twice for being drunk and disorderly and while I am not condoning that kind of behaviour, and certainly not suggesting it, I can look back at my life and say wow, I really lived! Will you be able to do the same?"

Her voice grows higher and louder and I shrink before her, this stranger in my safe haven. Leah rarely talks without moving her arms and, as the words pour out of her, her arms flutter and shimmer like the wings of a wounded bird.

"I'm not like you though, I'm not the sort of person who takes risks and lets loose, you know that."

"I do know that, yes, in the same way that I know you don't take risks because you are terrified of leaving your comfort zone. You say you can't remember the accident and I believe you, God knows, I have no doubt about that. But believe me when I say that you are controlled by that day as surely as you would be if you relived it every second. You don't live your life because you are scared of what might happen if you do and I know damn well that Tom would have wanted more for you than this."

She conjures my father, moulds him into a stern, disapproving effigy, tells me that I am no longer good enough for his memory, that I am letting him down.

"Don't speak for my father, you don't know what he would have wanted." My voice, too, is louder now, taking on a tone of defensiveness, of discomfort. I want to get up, to walk away, to change this day to a new one where the balance is restored, where I am surrounded by familiarity and a gentle voice.

"Oh yes I do missy, because he would have wanted the same thing as I do, your happiness. It's all he ever wanted. I bet you're still a virgin too!"

I startle at her change of direction, even as I withdraw inside myself, and feel my cheeks going red which she takes, rightly, as assent.

"I thought so. My heart is breaking for you right now. Can you not see that? This world of ours is a wonderful, magnificent place and you are blind to it."

She gets on her knees in front of me and I look away embarrassed as she takes my hands in her smaller ones and looks at me with pleading eyes.

"I know it has been hard for you, with everything you have been through, with losing your family, your memory. But you survived, don't ever forget that, you survived. Please don't forget to live too."

My head is beginning to throb and I squeeze my eyes shut against the pain. I pull my hands away from hers and look towards the door, thinking that now would be a good time to leave, to go for a walk, to put some space between myself and Leah's words. As she moves back to her seat I stand up and take a step away from her without turning my back.

"I'm going for a walk," I say and my voice shakes a little as I step towards the door.

"But we haven't finished talking."
I look away from the worry she wears as clearly as a mask.
"Yes we have," I say and I leave.

Chapter Twenty-One

She leaves the house and I trace the anger in her steps, it rings into the night like sparks striking from the pavement. Her hands thrust into the pockets of her coat, her shoulders hunched, the tension in them tangible. As usual she is looking down at her feet, keeping the rest of the world away. I am not concerned. Even if she looks up she will not notice me.

This is not what I planned when I got the brochure, I had not really thought beyond that event, had only possessed the threads of possibility that I could collect and weave into something of substance later. But this works well, this is a perfect moment and the parts come together rapidly, unbidden; a story that tells itself. I think that I will leave it a few moments before attempting to find my way into her house, into her room. I will give her time to get further away before I take this chance.

I wonder for a second if Leah will follow her, try to talk her around, try to ease the anger. It would be easier for me if she did. I wait a little longer but the minutes pass and there is no sound of a door opening and closing rapidly behind her, no tell-tale footsteps hurrying to match Sarah's pace, hurrying to make amends. By the time she has faded into the darkness I have already turned to make my way towards the front door.

The little terraced house where Sarah lives with her aunt looks smaller than those it is attached to, as though it is being squeezed out of shape from the pressure on each side. Its windows are small, boxy, the rooms inside seem dark no matter how bright the day, how clear the sky. This won't be the first time I have crept softly inside its walls or walked as soundlessly as I can up the hallway. It won't be the first time I have found my way into Sarah's bedroom, though my visits were shrouded, secret. I don't think she ever sensed I had been there, standing in the place where she had stood.

There is a light on in the upstairs bedroom. It shines yellow against the window frame and I can see the vague silhouette of someone moving inside. The shadow moves from left to right, right to left. Her anger palpable in the staccato steps, in the rapid turns and I find myself smiling. The circumstances couldn't be more perfect than they are in this moment, I couldn't have planned it better than this, to have them both choking in the vapour trail of harshly spoken words. Their anger will work with me, adding impetus, adding reason. I can only imagine the bitter taste left in both their mouths.

With one final glance at the moving shadow I reach for the door, pulling my hood low over my head as I step inside. Downstairs all of the rooms except the hallway are in darkness, a message perhaps, a rebellion from the woman who has always cared for her, since her vacant life began anew: *I didn't wait up for you.*

I move silently towards the foot of the stairs, knowing which creaking steps to avoid. I pause at the top, my heart hammering in my chest as I listen to the sounds from beyond the bedroom door. Leah's voice is loud and irate through the wood as she talks to someone on the phone, no doubt trying to strip herself of her anger before Sarah returns.

I step quickly to the opposite door and open it just enough to squeeze through. The room smells familiar and warm. A trace of her deodorant spray hanging over everything and I inhale deeply as it blends with the smell of clean linen and polish. I look at her bed, still rumpled from the morning, and feel my eyes grow heavy and weak with the length of the day. Knowing that there isn't much time, that I have to be out of here as soon as possible, I reach down and place my little gift for her on the pillow where she cannot fail to see it. I pull the duvet straight and tuck it in at the edges, using the flat of my palm to smooth out the creases and wrinkles of her unmade bed.

Straightening up I glance towards the wardrobe, to the junk that litters the top of it. Old teddies, books, dolls, toys, even paintings from a childhood she can't remember. Pathetic sentimentality that was pointless, wasteful, under the circumstances. What did it matter if she kept them when her mind was empty of any knowledge of their existence, when the objects she held onto had no place in the abyss of her mind? As far as she was concerned anyone could have painted them, they could have come from a car boot sale, someone else's bin. Yet my face grows soft as I look closer, as I see that tucked amongst the debris lies something familiar, something that pulls my heart roughly against unyielding ribs. By the time I reach up and lift it down my eyes have blurred.

I stare at the fashion doll and try not to sniff, not to make a sound. Her vet outfit is familiar, though one of her sensible shoes is missing and her coat is dirty. My mother bought a vet doll just like this for me once. It had been a day when she was full of smiles and sunshine, when the house didn't smell of strange men, when she still loved me enough to want to make me happy. A proud smile had played across her lips as she handed over the box wrapped in purple tissue paper and tied with tattered, frayed string.

"It's not my birthday," I said and she smiled wider.

"I know," she said, "its Mummy Loves You Day."

It was the best present in the world because there was no reason for it, a 'just because' present to push away the dark things. I look at the doll in my hand and feel the weight of a million memories sink onto my shoulders, the tiredness, the sadness. I head back towards the stairs, suddenly aware that the voice from the bedroom has fallen silent.

"Sarah?" she calls out as I reach the top of the stairs.

My voice is a small still shadow held tightly behind pursed lips as I move as quickly as I can.

The door opens above me as I reach the hallway. Her footsteps echo on the stairs as I hurry towards the door. By the time she reaches the bottom she is greeted by nothing more than the rapid closing of the front door and I run quickly down the hill, not stopping to hear whether the door opens again.

Chapter Twenty-Two

I let myself into the house quietly, hours after I angrily walked out on the conversation I didn't want to have. My breath forms clouds in the early-hour chill, my hands shaking slightly as I fumble the key from my pocket and slide it into the lock; metal on metal echoes, the sound trickling into the hallway as I pull it free. The darkness is complete, the silence claustrophobic. I can't remember the last time we argued like that, can't remember if we ever did. Perhaps, perhaps not, maybe we had but it had fallen between the cracks in my mind and disappeared from view.

I hold my breath as I step inside. I know every floorboard that creaks if stood on, every pitfall, every alarm even in the darkness. Moving in a staggered, disjointed dance I head towards the kitchen and the kettle, desperate to feel that warmth between my palms. Sliding my hand around the door frame I slowly press the switch down, knowing that this light is safe, that it cannot push its way under Leah's bedroom door and alert her to my late homecoming.

I move between the old shaker-style cupboards, the vintage rose fabrics, the out of place modern appliances and think, not for the first time, that my aunt should have lived in a different era. The fifties with their full petticoats, tea dresses and beautiful, feminine style hold her in their grasp. It is written in the seams that sometimes run up the backs of her legs and disappear beneath the hemline of her pencil skirts.

The kettle is still warm despite being switched off. Warm enough to think that she is lying upstairs with her eyes and ears open for any sounds. I pause and listen, until the silence plays tricks with my ears, swelling and churning and it seems there is sound everywhere. I move in slow motion, listen carefully after any noise made that is louder than I intend it.

I don't want my aunt to come downstairs. I don't want to face her questions, her recriminations, my own guilt. I know that her words, her actions, were created out of her love for me. I know she thinks I do not live enough, love enough or simply feel enough. That I treat our home like an Anderson shelter that will protect me from the debris that falls around me.

I tread the unfamiliar landscapes of my life as if I walk on nails or broken glass. The steps between the familiar things are light, easy, bearable. I shy away from other journeys, other detours, lacking trust in them. There is security within the normality and confines of my every day. I know myself that I have become a creature of such immense habit that it will be hard to break free. I read the same authors over again, shop in the same stores, even wear the same style underwear, without change or variation. My hair looks the same as it has for years, grown out from the original neat crop to become fuller, heavier. I tell myself it is easier, better, to keep it long and wear it down to cover the now white, faded scar.

Everything is static, stagnant and I need it that way. If everything stays the same, if there are no peaks or troughs, no deviation, nothing different, then my life will be the same. There will be no peaks or troughs, no deviation, nothing different and I won't have to be afraid of waking up one morning and finding that it has all been swept away. That Leah and her chintzy, eclectic house have been torn away by a tornado and I am left alone in Kansas with no memory of anything; with nothing more than another name to write in glittery pens.

I stand in the doorway of the kitchen with the full cup in my hand, the light folding around me from behind leaving my shortened shadow in the illuminated pool at my feet. Preparing for the possibility that my aunt waits on the other side of her bedroom door and will appear the instant I lay my hand on my own door handle. What would I say if she asked me where I have been?

Would she believe me if I told her I have been in a pub, a nightclub, a man's bed? I doubt it. She would see through any lie I came up with, no matter how much she wants one of those things to be true. I could tell her the truth – that the hours passed vague and uncertain, that I can't quite remember them – but how could I bear the questions, the fear, the insistence that I tell her where I have been? Stood in the doorway, feeling self-conscious, I try to plan for a question I won't be able to answer.

I take slow steps towards the staircase and puzzle through my options. Leah calls me Dilly Daydream sometimes. I get lost in thoughts she isn't party to. She doesn't know what my daydreams are about but she tells me they must be immensely appealing to pull me so totally from the here and now. I wonder what she would say if I told her that sometimes I am thinking about a family that is gone, of where I would be in that moment if the accident had never happened. Would it hurt her that she wasn't enough? Would she understand?

This is what I will tell her if she comes out of her room and catches me carrying my coffee, my remorse, up to bed. That I was lost in thought and didn't know where I was, that I was being a Dilly Daydream and I lost track of time. I know that she would accept those answers and that even as she did concern would thread through her acceptance. It would be harder for her to pick up on a partial lie than a total one. But I don't want to tell her that I am not sure where I have been. I don't want her to know that the stress of the argument has pushed away any certain memories of the last few hours, that this is what stress often does to me; it breaks the tenuous, fragile bridge in my damaged brain allowing my new memories to run and hide, keeping company with that which is lost and gone.

I pause at the top of the stairs. There is no movement from beyond the doorway, no rustling of bed clothes or deep drawn-in breathing that indicates sleep. The house is so quiet that I wonder if she is in there at all. But even as I think it I feel sure that she must be. Leah rarely goes out without me and therefore she rarely goes out at all. I gently open my door and sidestep in.

She has made the bed while I was out and I see the brochure on the pillow immediately, out of place as it is on my plain cream cover. It has been opened and folded back on itself so that the full-page advert looks out towards the ceiling. It would have been hard to miss: a big circle in red pen marks one of the apartments being sold. Putting my mug down next to the bed, feeling the soft fabric against the back of my legs, I sit down and reach for the booklet. Sniffing at the air as I do so, trying to detect a trace of Leah's perfume, I wonder how long ago she came in and placed it here, waiting for me to stumble across it.

The pictures are bright, attractive, the people in it smiling and looking vaguely smug, as though they have something I've always wanted. The beginnings of hurt spread up through my belly and I wonder why it is that Leah felt unable to wait for me to come home to talk to me about this. Why didn't she leave it to the next day when things were calmer, more normal? Or was she eager to drop this massive hint, to rid herself of the tarnished chain around her neck? My heart is hard and weighted in my chest, sinking into the pit of my stomach.

I skim over the pictures of the show apartment for the new complex in the city centre, the bright modern furniture, the neutral palette, the cathedral visible through the French window that opens onto a sunny sky. It looks beautiful, the sort of place that would be perfect for a young person like me. But it makes me feel sad to look at it, marginalised, unwanted. The walls around me are my haven, my security and I can't imagine leaving the normality of them, the routine of them.

The more I think about it, the more afraid I feel. How could I cope with the walk to work, the different streets, the unfamiliar paths? I look around me at the familiar colours and patterns, the familiar smells and comfort of my only home. How could I change this? How would I ever feel secure in a place I didn't know?

I look again at the advert, at the tariff. I could afford it. The insurance pay-out after the accident and the proceeds from the sale of our house have barely been touched. The funds sit in a bank account waiting for me to grow up and start living, waiting to pay for a brand new life of my own. They have waited a long time.

I lay the paper to one side and try to swallow the lump in my throat. Surely Leah doesn't want me to leave just because of one argument. There has to be more to it than that. I look for clues in the subject matter of our row, search for the thought processes that could have led her to believe that this is the right thing to do, but reason comes up scarce and slight. Is it simply there in her desire for me to live, is that enough to push me away from her in the hope that my own two feet find solid ground on which to stand? Or is it more personal for her? Perhaps it is simply that she is tired of looking after me, that she wants her own life back.

I shed tears along with my clothes, trying to cry silently so as not to wake her. I decide that I will say nothing about the brochure. I will wait to see if she mentions it. I will not make it easy for her to push me away, choosing instead to say nothing at all to bring the conversation to the foreground. Spoken words can never be unsaid, can never be unheard and I am too afraid that I will open my lips and wash her away with a tide of reproach and angst that she in no way deserves.

Not for the first time, I curl up in the darkness and wish

that I could reverse time, go back to yesterday so that this moment has never been and everything is just the way it should be, so that nothing has changed. Yesterday was Tuesday, a day which sits happily in my memory. But this day is Wednesday, a cold ash kind of day, bitter and overcast. I close my eyes against it and futilely wish it to fall into the black hole of past memory.

Chapter Twenty-Three

My father didn't believe me when I first hinted at my mother's cruelty. I saw it in his eyes, in the slight turning away from my quietly spoken, nervous words. She would stand in front of him looking pale and beautiful and his eyes would cloud over, become blind to anything but her perfection, her smile. He grew misty, becoming transparent enough for me to see his thoughts, to read them clearly through his skin and perhaps he was right, how could anyone so delicate, so perfect, lift their hand in anger, particularly towards a child? When he looked at me his eyes were full of questions, a trace of guilt perhaps that I should feel the need to tell such awful lies.

One day when he walked in he was carrying a box and a smile. He held a finger up to his lips as he looked at the freshly painted happiness on my mother's face and then carefully placed the box on the floor in front of me.

"Don't shake it!"

I moved my hands towards the cardboard and it moved slightly. I jumped backwards and Dad laughed.

"It's nothing to be afraid of."

With weak fingers I prised open the two flaps and peered in as two chocolate brown eyes peered back. We blinked at the same time and I smiled. As he emerged further, a wet black nose surrounded by brown fluff, I couldn't help but squeal my delight, it was love at first sight.

The puppy was a no kind puppy, a mixture of a hundred different breeds, all thrown into a pot together and mixed up until he looked like no-kind of dog I had seen before. His legs were too short, his head a little too big. He had a swirling pattern in his brindle coat that reminded me of a snail and I called him Brian. He had razor sharp needle teeth that nibbled at my bare toes whenever I sat down. I cleaned up all his mess, took care of him, fed him and cuddled up to him at night where he wriggled and whimpered in my arms as he had little puppy dreams. I loved him more than I had ever loved anything. I loved him for the whole of his life, which turned out to be only six weeks and four days after I had first locked eyes with him.

She said it was an accident and unkind though she was, cruel though she had become, I believed her. The back door was open where I had been playing in the garden and the postman came and knocked on the door with terrible, fatal timing. She opened the front door just as Brian bounded after me into the living room. The interior door slammed with sickening force onto his neck. He didn't make a sound. He just broke and fell and didn't move again. My mother came running when I screamed.

She told me that she would bury him in the woods behind our house the next day when I was at school, that I couldn't go because it would make me too sad. The house was so empty without him, my bed so lonely. Even now, so many years later, I still curl my toes up when I sit on the sofa, waiting for those needle sharp teeth to take hold. I remember the days after his death as being empty and silent. It seems that there was no speaking at all in the cold, still house.

For months after I would walk in the woods and think of him, would still look around for his ghost, for a little mound of earth, a focus for my grief. Even after my mother had grown further into her cruelty and told me that she hadn't buried him at all, that she had taped his little broken body with plastic bags and thrown him in the rubbish bin, I still imagined him out there, his tongue lolling happily as he chased rabbits and falling leaves.

When my father asked me if I wanted to get another dog I turned away from him and went to my room without replying, closing the door quietly behind me, without anger so there could be no reprisals later. There would never be another Brian, he had been my friend, my ally, and when he died he took with him all the secrets that I had whispered into his tiny, quivering ears when I should have been sleeping. He was the only one that didn't turn away when I spoke, the only one who believed me, who never questioned the truth of what I said. He was the only one who had witnessed the anger and the casual cruelty of my mother.

Chapter Twenty-Four

I walk to the town centre taking the same route I always take, past the museum, up through Gandy Street, out into the rushing crowds. I walk on the same side of the road I always walk on. My steps are slow and measured so that the count is just right. I am not tempted to veer off, to take a different path, to go somewhere new. I never feel the pull towards brightly lit shops in the distance, the urge to climb on a passing bus. Nothing changes.

If I keep on walking the same way, avoiding the cracks where I can; if I look straight ahead and not to the side where I will see unfamiliar turns, unfamiliar faces; if I always salute when I see a magpie, or cross myself when a hearse passes; if I turn and spit when a black cat crosses my path; if I don't walk under ladders; if I always throw a pinch of spilled salt over my shoulder; if I follow these rules and a million others, carving routines and repetitions into every day then everything will be okay. Everything will stay the same, no-one will die, my life will follow the same old path, staying exactly as it has always been since I woke up in a strange new world. Nothing will alter, nothing will fade. What did I do on the day of the crash that altered things? It is a question that has played on my mind from the moment I became aware. Something must have changed that day, something large enough to roll through my life and scatter everything, destroy everyone. Had I tied my shoes wrongly, put them on the wrong feet? Had I not brushed my teeth or combed my hair? Had I argued with my sister and made Dad pause in his routine so that we didn't leave on time?

Perhaps it was none of those things or maybe all of them. Perhaps it was something I have never even thought of, a great mystery that follows behind me, hiding in my shadow. Surrendering to these compulsions, embracing this lack of difference means there is no room for change and the routines close around me like a steel trap. There is security within them, I need them beside me, holding my hand, telling me everything will be okay, that nothing can change if I don't change.

And now I walk the familiar route to an unfamiliar destination and the weight of this moment settles on my shoulders. If I count the new steps I will need, will I forget another pathway, perhaps the path home? Will the familiar fade away to make way for this new, this other? What sacrifice will be made to make room for this day?

The apartment block is ninety steps from the main shopping precinct with its pavement cafes and high street shops. The façade is gleaming glass and wood advertising its newness to all who pass beneath the jutting balconies. I have looked on a map, plotted it out, measured as precisely as I can. It is not too far from my known rhythms, my regular steps. Perhaps I can make it without losing something else. Perhaps not.

Undulating clouds reflect in the angled windows as I look up. I am tiny, afraid. I can feel the tension in my skin as I imagine the butterfly effect of my actions spreading out through my life, a whirlwind to sweep everyone away. Muscles clench and tighten in my legs as I prepare to turn and walk away. I was stupid to come here, to think that I could do this.

I tighten my grip on the brochure – that has still not been discussed – in my hand and think about Leah and how she wants me to do this, how she wants me to leave the safe, dark space beneath her wing. I think of the shiny brochure on the pillow of a freshly made bed and walk quickly towards the small office beneath the apartments, forcing one counted step after another until I am too close to back out.

I will take a quick look, nothing more, and then I can go home and pretend I haven't done it. If Leah mentions the apartments I will tell her that I went to see them and found them cold and lacking. I imagine she would be pleased with me for even making it that far, that just looking might be enough for now.

The woman who greets my stumbled entry is nondescript, forgettable, perhaps purposefully so. A person so easy to overlook will not detract from the apartment she guides me to, which is anything but nondescript and forgettable. Neutral tones and sleek clean lines surround me as I step into the living room. I recognise the window that frames the image of the cathedral from the pictures I have seen. At any other time, and for anybody else, this beautiful space would have been perfect.

"There has been tremendous interest in the available apartments so far. In fact, there are only three left."

Her tone, her words tell me to hurry, don't miss out. I turn away from her enthusiasm to look at the view.

"This show apartment is for sale too, once the others have gone, which will no doubt be very soon judging by how quickly the others have been snapped up. All of the furniture and soft furnishings are available by separate negotiation."

I walk away from her through to the bedroom and try to imagine myself here, in this space with its sleek mirrors, its king-size bed. How different it is from the shabby vintage glamour of Leah's house. Would I ever belong somewhere like this? I had never explored my own sense of style before, fitting neatly, instead, into the old-fashioned world that surrounds Leah.

At the window I look down at the shoppers hurrying back

and forth. There is no sound from them at all, just a strange kind of silent haste as they walk purposefully, striding with their heads up and their goals clear. I watch their lack of hesitance, their freedom and know that I am not like them, doubt that I ever could be. I hear footsteps on the wooden flooring behind me and turn away from the soundless rush beyond the window.

"I'll leave you to look around for a little while," the agent says, sounding disinterested now, in the face of my lack of enthusiasm.

"That's okay, I've finished now," I reply softly and turn to lead the way out of the door, past the agent's disappointment and onto the street where I put my head down and walk quickly back home, the buildings around me blurring in my peripheral vision as I stare at familiar paving slabs that tell me where I am by their maps of scratches and chewing gum.

Back in my room I try to imagine my belongings sitting amongst the flawless lines of the apartment, I look at bags and boxes of solid memories and struggle to see them anywhere but here, where the wallpaper I chose years before looks jaded and furniture jostles for space. I try to imagine what it would be like to sleep in such a huge bed when Leah comes in through the front door, high heels clipping in the silent hallway.

Her voice climbs the stairs towards me and I am already opening my bedroom door to reply when I realise it isn't directed at me, that she is talking on her phone and making no move towards the rest of the house as she speaks in the tone of one who has no desire to be overheard.

"Look, you know I would love to, it just isn't possible right now."

She pauses to catch the reply as I step through my doorway and move slowly towards the banister.

"Well no," she says, "perhaps it never will be, I have no idea. I just know that it isn't at the moment."

There is another silence before she laughs, a husky throaty

sound that bubbles towards the space where I listen from.

"That's not fair, I love the food there. You're just trying to put temptation in my way."

She pauses for quite a while then and perhaps I only imagine the vague rumble of a deep voice coming from the other end of the phone.

"I'll just have to see. Sarah's been having quite a difficult time of it lately. I don't want to rock the boat, you know how things are. Please try to understand, she is all the family I have left. I can't just up and leave her for a couple of days, not at the moment."

I turn to head back to my room, not wanting to hear any more. Her last words chase after me.

"Well if you can't be patient then there can't be any 'us'!"

She disconnects the call. I close my door behind me as quietly as I can. My head hurts and I reach for the painkillers that are never too far from my side before the headache can deepen into a cloud of agony that will obscure my vision and render me motionless. It reminds me that I am overdue for my yearly appointment with Doctor Marsden, that I can't keep putting it off even though nothing changes, and he has become little more than a familiarity, another habitual thing to maintain.

The bed is soft against my side as I curl into it, as I allow my mind to touch lightly upon the argument of the night before. She told me – amongst her pleading, her longing to help – that she had really lived and I didn't realise until this moment that she used the past tense, as if her life is over, as if my being in it has prematurely ended the exuberance with which she once moved. I am her cage as surely as the accident is mine.

The man on the phone is a first as far as I am aware. I can't remember her having a relationship of any kind before. If she had it would have had to fit in the tiny spaces where I wasn't with her. Why have we never talked about it? Why have I never noticed her solitude? For the first time I see the true extent of the sacrifices she has made. I feel selfish, thoughtless. I look around the room again, take in my clothes, my belongings and in this moment it all seems different, out of place among the stagnant waters of Leah's stalled life. I float among them and finally fall asleep as I try to remember if she has ever mentioned any man's name.

Chapter Twenty-Five

Sometimes I wonder if we are delivered screaming and protesting into a life we have already chosen. If it is the case for all of us that we know what to expect before we are even born. Do we make a conscious decision to step into a particular body and know that we will have experiences that set us apart from others? I wonder sometimes if I once walked somewhere beyond here, through a kind of pre-life, a mystery. I imagine that there is a library there with walls stretching far beyond my field of vision. Shelf upon shelf of brand new lives, where dust motes float in the light from the windows set high into the walls and people talk in hushed tones as they peruse the shelves looking for their perfect life story.

Did I walk through this vast library and lay my hands on this particular tome? Did it look good to me, appealing somehow? And Sarah, what about her? Is it possible that she chose her life story herself, that she read the words, the scenes contained in her life and pictured them perfectly, happily? Were our paths entwined even then? Had we met among the shelves and decided that yes, our paths lay together, our books next to each other, forever linked by their proximity?

I wonder if she read, too, the life stories of her father,

her sister. If she got to the end page and thought theirs a story complete, a tale well told despite the brutality of such a shocking ending, despite the lack of happy ever after.

I wonder these things because there seems to be a beautiful kind of synchronicity in the way that our paths cross, in the way that I am everything she is not. I am her mirror and she is mine. If there is such a thing as fate I have to ask what it was thinking when it brought the two of us together; when I looked at her and thought that hers was a wasted life, a pitiful shadow of existence. Perhaps I was fascinated by her, am still fascinated by her, simply because of these opposing experiences.

She holds her life with fear, trepidation; too scared to make waves, to fly into the face of her fears. There are days when I find her loathsome and wretched, nothing more than an object of scorn and ridicule. I envy her very existence because if I had her life, her empty past, how different it would be, how worthwhile. I seethe in the wreck of my childhood and think that she should be glad, ecstatic that hers is gone forever. One day I will make her see it. One day.

But that day isn't now, that day isn't this moment. In this moment I know that she has gone to look at the apartment and I prepare myself to step into the shadow of her footsteps, to see what she saw, to sense how she felt. How thrilled I was when I watched her and realised that was where she was heading, that my plan might just work. I saw her hesitation, her slight pause before she dipped into her limited courage and entered the building. She stayed only a short while and then left and headed towards home, her head forever angled towards the ground.

I do not hesitate or begin to turn away, I bluster in, surprising the bland agent and insist before she can say anything, before she can start her hard sell, her practiced pitch, that I be alone. I walk the floor of the show apartment planning what I would do if it, or one like it, were mine. I study the brochures of the other apartments, their floor plans and angles, their balconies that overlook the youthful vibrancy of the city below. What would I buy, where would I place the furniture? I look at the muted tones, the wooden floors, the beautiful carved wooden balcony and excitement crawls sensuously up my spine. I am overwhelmed by the possibilities.

The agent seems taken aback when I join her at the door almost immediately and say that it is exactly my kind of place. I tell her that I will be in touch, that the show apartment is exactly what I am looking for. She must be pleased because she hands me her card with a mobile number, telling me to ring her any time before ten at night.

"Are you on commission?" I ask and she laughs a little and nods self-consciously.

"In that case, I wouldn't dream of calling anyone else if I decide to sign on the dotted line." I give her a big smile as I leave and she seems a little dazzled by it.

Rather than taking the lift, I walk slowly down the wide stairs, planning everything out in my head as I descend. How perfect it would be if Sarah went ahead and bought an apartment here. I allow myself to dream, just for a moment that she will go ahead with it, that she will embrace her life, that she will become solitary like me. The two of us under the same roof, with no Leah to watch out for her. There would be less need to hide, to sneak around. It would be just us, just as it should be, just as it was always meant to be. I can't wait.

Chapter Twenty-Six

"You will never guess what happened to me last night!"

Alex's voice rushes loudly ahead of her, drawing eyes other than mine to her smiling mouth, the froth of curls that tumble across her shoulders. Her words are an introduction as the door begins to swing shut behind her, before she has taken a step towards our usual table in the window of the cafe, before she has begun to remove her coat. Her words spew out on a bubble of excitement.

"You're right, I'll never guess so you might as well tell me."

Her smile fades and she rolls her eyes theatrically. "Where's the fun in that? You have to at least try and work it out. Go on, please try and guess, just for me." She bats her long eyelashes across the table and I laugh.

"Okay, okay, put the puppy dog eyes away. Now let me think." I stir sugar into my coffee, watch her try to sit still as I take my time, pondering.

"You won the lottery?"

"Nope." A big beaming smile forms around the straw from her milkshake showing perfect teeth, a trace of her pink gums.

"Steven Spielberg spotted you walking down the street and wants you as the star of his next movie?"

"Uh uh. Though that would be pretty cool wouldn't it?"

"An elephant broke free from the zoo and trundled you off to the circus?"

She raises one eyebrow. "Now you're being silly."

"Well I don't know, do I? It could have been anything."

"Could have been, but it wasn't. It was, just wait until you hear this… Sean Jamieson." She bends her arms up and forms jazz hands that frame the joy on her face.

"Who?"

"Oh my. Why am I even friends with you? Sean Jamieson. Plays football for England, six feet and four inches of perfectly honed blond sex god. That Sean Jamieson!"

"Oh right, the six feet, four inches blond married god, that Sean Jamieson?"

She bats my words away.

"He was in the pub last night. Honestly, it was pathetic, girls were hovering around him like flies around shit."

"You were one of them right?" I smile as she nods sheepishly.

"Well, yeah but I pretended I was getting a drink so I was being cool about it. But then he actually spoke to me. I almost fainted."

"What did he say? Did he offer to whisk you away from it all?

"Not exactly," the flush spreads up from her neck.

"So what exactly then? Come on, you can't keep me in suspense now, you've built it all up and everything."

Her eyes slide from mine and she looks around the room before sighing.

"He said 'excuse me love, you're standing on my foot'," she blurts, "I was wearing those huge boots of mine, how was I to know? Anyway it was better than nothing."

I sip at my coffee and smile into the warm liquid. "Of course it was. It's an exciting story to tell your children one day."

Her thrown napkin hits me in the face, the corner of it landing in my coffee and soaking up the brown liquid. I consider throwing it back but she is wearing a white top.

"I ordered for us both when you texted to say you'd be a bit late."

I am not working today but Alex is and her lateness cuts into the time that we have, the conversations. She nods her thanks to me as the waiter appears over her left shoulder and sets our lunch out on the table. We are quiet for a while as we tuck in.

"Your mums are good friends with Leah right?" I ask her and she nods, even though she knows that I know the answer myself and that this is no more than an introduction to the conversation I need to have.

"Yeah, of course. They don't see her as often as they used to since giving up the shop but they talk on the phone quite a bit. Why?"

"I was just wondering if she had mentioned a man at all. I heard her on the phone, she was definitely talking to a man. She had a flirty voice on."

Alex lays her fork down beside her plate. "Not as far as I know but it wouldn't surprise me, she's lovely your aunt."

"I know, she's gorgeous. It's just that I've never known her to have a boyfriend before."

"Look, Sarah, you know I love you to death. Always have, always will. But I can't imagine it would ever be easy for Leah to bring someone home. You know what you're like with change."

"I wouldn't stand in the way of her happiness though," I reply and there is a thread of hurt caught on my words, I leave it hanging there and do not try to pull it free.

"Not deliberately no, of course you wouldn't. But the reality is that every day for you is pretty much the same. You stay at home, you work if you're well. Sometimes we talk on the phone, sometimes we go for lunch, always to the same place, always here."

Her arms sweep expansively outwards taking in the walls, the corners, the familiar faces of the waiting staff that know us well enough to call us by our first names.

"I can't imagine that Leah would find it easy to introduce someone into your environment. She's probably too worried about the impact it would have on you and she loves you far too much to risk upsetting you after everything you've been through."

"Has she said anything to that effect?"

"Not as far as I know. It's just common sense isn't it? You know how seriously she has taken her guardianship of you, you mean everything to her. You're the only family she has left now."

I look away, out through the window at the same scene I always look at, from the same seat I always sit in.

"I'm really boring aren't I?" I say despondently, feeling the weight of my familiar patterns pressing down on me.

"No, not boring. But you are damaged and you have limitations. We all understand that. Look, you're my quiet time friend, my chilling friend. The person I hang out with when I need a bit of peace. It's a good thing to me. You're a good friend to me. Though, hey, I'd love to see you let loose and party more often."

"Why?"

"'Cos I think it would be hilarious, I've seen you dance around your room, remember, no way should that be done in public."

I laugh and hear the relief in my voice as colour sweeps back into the dulled room.

"Cow."

"Yeah, yeah, you know it!"

The silence grows more comfortable as we continue eating, just as it always does. I watch her as she eats and think how lucky I was to have found her. She is my moment of lightness in a difficult week, a role she has always taken on willingly, always with a smile.

"I'm thinking about moving out," I say and realise as I taste the unfamiliar words in my mouth that the notion has gained momentum in my subconscious, has become more viable, more real. As though in the quiet moments when my mind wanders and becomes vague I have visited it, watered it, allowed the thought to grow and produce an altogether different future in my subconscious. My eyes lift to meet hers and I'm made silent by the frozen surprise that stalls Alex's face. It seems that forever and a day pass as I wait with growing impatience for her to reply, to share her thoughts with me.

"How did that come about?" she asks and I find that I can't tell her, that I haven't prepared myself for her to ask this particular question.

I don't want to vocalise how I felt in that moment when I discovered the brochure on my bed, or what had led up to Leah taking that action in the first place. I don't want to say that Leah thinks that I am nothing more than a shell, that I left my life in the wreckage of the car and it is about time I found it again and tried it on for size now that I have grown.

I tell her instead about the overheard phone call, the barrier that I represent to my aunt's happiness and the guilt that I feel because of it. She nods as I speak, confirming the truth of what I say, making me feel selfish for never thinking of it before. Have I ever seen Leah as anything more than an extension of myself? Did I believe that all her feelings were the same as my own and that she needed nothing more than our home and her work?

"I went to look at one of those new apartments in the city centre, I think… " I pause and glance around, looking anywhere except at Alex. Not wanting to see the slight frown, the poignancy of her understanding. I swallow hard to clear the pathway for the incongruity of my words. "… I might go for one of them." There is silence in response and I watch as she flounders for something to say.

She clears her throat and forces a smile."Really, Sarah, I would be so jealous if you did! They look fabulous. Just think that would be the absolutely perfect place for us to stagger back to after one of our rare nights out."

At my wry look she smiles and shrugs her shoulders. "Well, who knows, this could be the start of a whole new you. You could become a total party animal like me. Before you know it you'll be down at Jewels on the Quay surrounded by pink fur walls, getting your tits out and having fivers tucked into your sparkly G string."

"Hmmm, sounds like you know it well." I laugh and she blushes a deep crimson.

"The mums, you know. I overheard them talking about it once."

"Well, before you've sold my body into sexual purgatory can we maybe just take things one step at a time, Alex. I'm really scared at the thought of moving out you know." I look down at the table, my eyes growing suddenly wet, spilling over. I feel the palm of her hand against the top of my clenched fist.

"It will be fine, Sarah. I'll be there with you. I'll help you through it. I promise." With her free hand she holds out a napkin and presses it to my damp cheek. "One more thing," she says as I feel my skin against her palm, "what do you think me and Sean Jamieson would look like together?"

I smile into her hand and shake my head resignedly, letting her distract me.

Chapter Twenty-Seven

She watches me furtively from behind bunches of roses, cellophane. I pretend not to see her, instead keeping my head down, keeping busy, humming lightly under my breath. If I act as though everything is fine and normal then surely she will see nothing other than the perfect mask I pull down to hide my eyes. But it is a ruse, a pretence and surely we both know it, surely we sense the change in the air as easily as a snake tastes its prey on the tip of its forked tongue. I cannot pretend in front of Leah when she has spent years watching me closely for signs of healing, signs of change and so I hide among the flowers and feel her eyes graze my skin.

The bell over the door sounds and from behind the counter I watch as a tall, good-looking man comes in. He is smiling at my aunt and I cannot stop myself from wondering if this is him, the strange man on the end of her phone, the one I stand surreptitiously in front of and refuse to let through. He moves towards her, his eyes glancing in my direction first and it is the child that still lives somewhere in me that speaks as he passes me by, confrontational and slightly too loud.

"Can I help you?"

My voice is a blade that cuts through the space between us. He pauses briefly and then changes direction where he flounders against my severity.

"I'd like a dozen roses please."

His voice seems too small for him now; he has become unsure, hesitant.

"Well now, would you like red for love, yellow for friendship or perhaps white for innocence?"

Leah's smiling voice washes over us both and I look up to see a frown in her eyes as she meets mine, disguised by her friendly customer smile. I look at her and think 'not him then, not him,' as he once more steps in her direction with a slow growing smile. I feel shame at the uncertainty, the insecurity I served him and walk carefully across paper-thin eggshells towards the back room.

"Not yellow then, definitely not, perhaps a mixture of red and white. Would that look nice?"

I hear the smile in Leah's reply but not the words as I think of the houses of Lancaster and York, of a battleground and bad omens. I wonder if she thought of this too, if her unheard reply advised against that particular symbolism. I sit at the small table where we often drink tea together during quieter moments and press my cheek against the cold surface, closing my eyes against the unfamiliarity of feeling awkward around her.

The sound of the bell heralds the smiling man's exit and sends tension up my spine, pulling me upright. Seconds later I feel her standing in the doorway watching me.

"Are you going to tell me what this is about? You've been edgy all morning, please tell me what it is. Is it your head? Is it hurting more than normal? Have you arranged to see Doctor Marsden?"

These are the things that define me: my head, the doctor. It seems sometimes that this is all I have, there is no experience beyond the walls they create. I shake my head to erase the concern I see in her eyes.

"I'm leaving." Shock flashes across her face and she eases herself stiffly into the seat opposite me.

"What do you mean you're leaving, you mean for the day?"

She reaches for my hand but I move it, afraid that physical contact would dam the words I am finding so difficult to say. I know that she takes my withdrawal as a slight; her hand flutters back to the table like a wounded bird. I feel the panic rising as the moment comes closer, knowing that once I tell her, then it becomes real and I can never take it back. I shake my head and gesture expansively with the hand that denied her, at the tiny room that holds us still within this moment.

"Well, to begin with, I'm handing in my notice here. It isn't fair on you for me to work here when you could have someone much more reliable in my place. You only gave me this job as a favour and because of it there are times you have to do the work of two people. So I quit and now you can hire a better assistant." I try to smile, to show her that this is a gift, a good thing, but my lips are stiff and cold. I look at my hands instead, seeing a tiny trail of red from a jagged rose thorn, wondering how I hadn't noticed the moment it tore at my skin. Her voice is barely more than a whisper as it crosses the table towards me.

"To begin with? What else is there, what else are you leaving?"

I glance at her face and wish that I hadn't. She looks stricken, anxious. I cannot hear her breath as she waits for a response.

"I'm going to put an offer in on the new show apartment in the city centre. I spoke to the agent yesterday. I think it's time I moved out, spread my wings a little." I try to make light of it, attempt a little laugh but even to my own ears it sounds as though I am trying not to cry, as if I sit in this increasingly claustrophobic space choking on my words.

"I don't understand," she says, her voice smaller, almost whispered. "Why now, why all of a sudden?"

I don't mention the brochure, choosing not to bring up her part in starting the tower of cards tumbling so that she can tell herself it was my choice, so that there is no guilt for her over this decision. She looks genuinely taken aback and I want to wind the minute hand backwards, start over and stay silent, tell her that I am simply tired. But I can't do that. It is too late.

"You gave me a life, Leah, and I owe you so much for that. Now I want you to have yours back."

Her cheeks are wet and I turn away from them.

"You are my life."

Her voice is smaller still as she rises to her feet and leaves the room.

Chapter Twenty-Eight

The room hardly changes. There is the same number of tiles, the same art on the walls, the same chips in the paintwork, though perhaps there are more of them now and I simply haven't noticed their increases over time. The chairs look older and worn around the edges, their colours muted as though the years have sought to erase them and haven't quite succeeded. The tiles no longer shine. Strange that everything seems on a smaller scale than it once did, as if it has shrunk around me, grown closer, less threatening.

The previous decade has whitewashed Doctor Marsden's hair and thinned it; his beard grows grey around the edges, darker in the middle. He still looks like a bear only now I imagine his hibernation lasting longer, his bones more tired when springtime wakes him. He looks pleased to see me, surprised, as if I am not the next name that is written on his appointment list.

"Sarah, how lovely. Please come in, have a seat."

Nothing more than a guest who has come for tea, different from all the other patients that must walk through his door, more welcome perhaps. He presses the intercom button.

"Julie, some tea please if you wouldn't mind, and pop some of those nice biscuits on a plate, you know, the chocolate ones."

She replies and quickly appears with the tray. She looks doughy, round and colourless in her beige trouser suit. She speaks softly, almost whispering, as though she were in a church and when she leaves she closes the door gently behind her, with quiet discretion.

The years have altered our meetings, changed their patterns. Because we both know that nothing is changing, that there is nothing he can do for me when my memories stayed ever absent. Seeing him has become routine and nothing more yet still I come because I do not wish to lose this familiarity.

"Now," says Doctor Marsden, "how have you been?"

I don't know where to begin, because it seems that so much has changed, and yet so much more has remained the same.

"Where should I begin?" I say, my words a pause that my thoughts try to fill.

"How about with the Post-Traumatic Stress symptoms, how are they?"

I turn to look out of the window, wishing I could tell him something other, something better. While he busies himself pouring tea for us both I brace myself for the suggestion that always comes, the help that I always turn down.

"I still have the nightmares most nights, problems concentrating sometimes. I still have the panic attacks when I feel things are out of my control. I still struggle with my memory. Not my childhood ones, I know they're probably gone for good, I just have blank spots now and again where I can't quite remember what I was doing."

"Do you mean like those moments where one goes into a room and forgets why they went there?"

"Yes that kind of thing, I struggle to hold onto new memories still. And I'm still getting headaches." I look down at my fingernails. They are a little ragged and need cutting. I try to pretend I do not find it embarrassing to talk of my many weaknesses.

"Still on the left hand side where the scar is?"

I nod and lean forwards to take my tea, staring into the rich brown liquid and wondering when it will be polite to say I have to leave, wishing I had not made this annual pilgrimage to have the same conversation, the same lack of answers.

"How about cars, do you still avoid travelling in them?"

I thought of the train journey to Bristol, of the walk to the station, the bus ride to the hospital. I thought of a life of walking everywhere and missing out on trips to the beach, to the moors, so many other places that are not found along a bus route. I nod.

"Okay then. The most likely cause of the headaches, as we've discussed before, is stress. The tests we've given you have shown up no further anomalies. The injuries to your brain tissue, while serious, have been predominantly overcome. Of course there's some scarring of the tissue, but my opinion would be that your symptoms are almost wholly psychological." He glances my way and I see the concern in his eyes. "I think it has been discussed before, either with your aunt or with yourself, that the amnesia, forgetting your childhood completely, is unlikely to have been caused by your head injuries. In the short term such amnesia would be possible, even expected, with such a physical trauma, but there is almost always at least partial recovery of the memories over time, whereas you have had no recovery whatsoever."

He looks at me with a smile that avoids his eyes, it is sympathetic, heavy and sad.

"So the implication is that it is all in my mind, a psychological concern rather than a physical one."

He nods and his eyes are above my head, beyond the space where I sit and fight the urge to turn and see what he is looking at.

"Dissociative Amnesia most often occurs when someone is trying to block something out, a horrific and traumatic experience for example, such as the one you have suffered in the crash. It isn't connected to physical trauma in any way other than by the fact that the normal function of the mind has broken down and seals those memories away in a little box where they can no longer be seen. The good news is – if you look at it as good news – those memories still exist inside you somewhere, hence the nightmares. They are buried deeply inside of you, they are not gone, which means there is the possibility of recovering them."

"How though? Surely if they were still there, I would have had some sort of sign by now, some kind of breakthrough, even a tiny one!"

"Hmmm, now that I cannot tell you, the mind can be an incredibly strange thing and it's a total bugger when it goes wrong. What I can say is that your compulsive behaviour, keeping everything the same, your avoidance of situations you find threatening, your limited social interactions, and yes, even your current amnesiac episodes, all of that 'stuff' is most likely caused by the Post-Traumatic Stress. I can't give you back your past but I can refer you to someone who may be able to help with discovering where it went and why and he can help you with your other symptoms too. Now, I know I have asked this before, but would you like me to refer you to a psychiatric colleague of mine? Psychiatrists can really have good results with PTSD, awareness of the condition has grown and so have the therapies on offer."

His tone is resigned, he has asked many times before.

"It worries me that people will think less of me if I'm seeing a psychiatrist. I'm not mad."

"I didn't say that you were. Psychiatrists aren't only for the truly insane and you know it. In fact I think this is just another example of avoidance; your excuse to not get better, so you don't have to face these things."

"Maybe."

"Maybe what? Maybe it's avoidance or maybe I can refer you to a psychiatrist?"

I take a deep breath and my answer is a sigh, nothing more. "Both," I say.

He looks surprised.

"Well, that's certainly a step in the right direction from the resounding no that you've always given me."

I look away from his smile into my lap and his tone grows gentle, I know him well enough to imagine the softening of his face, the kindness.

"You know, this is the first time you've come to see me without your aunt. Is everything all right?"

"I made her wait downstairs. I thought that I needed to start doing things on my own."

"Then you should be feeling more than a little proud of yourself Sarah, that is a huge step in your recovery and you've achieved it all by yourself."

I feel like a child at the dentist, as though any moment he might hand me a sticker and pat me on the head. And I think that no it isn't really something I have achieved by myself, that it is because I feel I have little choice in the matter, that it is what Leah wants.

"Can I let you know, about the psychiatrist I mean?"

His eyes are kinder still as he nods across the vast expanse of the desk that still holds the Newton's cradle I coveted as a child.

"Of course you can, whenever you're ready. Though please try not to leave it for many more years, I may well have retired by then."

I stand up and shake his hand, thanking him for the tea as I think with a strong sense of loss that nothing is forever, even Doctor Marsden, who knows more about my brain than I know myself, even he will be gone one day and where will I be then? Who will talk to me with respect about the things I fail to understand? Who will be kind and sweet and gentle when I refuse help time and again?

Leah waits for me with an air of calm that is false, weighty. I feel her hesitance, her awkwardness, the way she seems to shrink in size beside me as she fights the questions back into her throat. She has never stood on the outside looking in, not in something such as this, in matters of my health and recovery. She treads the virgin territory delicately and I speak before she can ask me how things have gone, before I hear the unfamiliar tremor in her voice.

"I told him I would think about seeing a psychiatrist, for the PTSD." My gaze fixes firmly on the rooftops ahead as I find it strangely uncomfortable to invite her into the solitary appointment.

"Oh, well that's good isn't it? I mean Doctor Marsden has recommended that for you quite often."

I hear in her voice that she wants to ask why now, what has changed? Was the difference only that she wasn't sat beside me, ready to step in when I couldn't think of anything to say?

"We'll see," I say, and turn towards the bus stop, painfully aware of the wall of thorns that is slowly growing in the space between us.

Chapter Twenty-Nine

I sit in the window of the cafe wearing a jumper with a fraying sleeve that I don't remember buying and shoes that have worn a matching pair of blisters into the delicate skin of my heels. With a pounding head I clutch at the too-hot cup hoping that the double espresso will send energy through my veins, lift my spirits above the many cracks that edge their slow way across the floor. My stomach rumbles loud enough to hear over the coffee machines and I try to recall what I ate for breakfast; probably nothing knowing me but there isn't much I can do about it now. I have left my purse somewhere and only have enough change in my pocket for the medicinal cup that has come all too quickly to an end.

Light pours liquid and smooth through the windows, reflecting from cutlery and tables, hitting my eyes like a laser. Pushing sunglasses gently into place I study my chipped nail varnish and think what a mess I must look to other people. How little I care.

Since Sarah's offer has been accepted on the show apartment, the days are dragging. I expected there to be some urgency, some haste, but instead she walks through this change like a condemned prisoner, dragging her feet, hanging her head as usual.

I see for myself the differences, the damage in their

relationship. The concern Leah feels when she looks at her niece, the hurt on Sarah's face. How funny that such a simple action so perfectly executed, so perfectly timed, has brought them tumbling down, blossom in a sharp wind.

I saw the advert go up in the shop window for a new assistant, recognising Sarah's writing, so much neater than my own scrawl. For a few moments, as I read the card, I entertained the thought of applying for it myself. I wondered what would happen if I did, if I stepped forwards and asked for the position, if I said who I was. I fantasised about what Leah's reaction would be if I told her my name. Would she recognise me? I felt it a shame that it was impossible under the circumstances to do such a thing. I thought about it on and off for the rest of the day though, smiling to myself each time I did.

Paying for my coffee I step out into the sunshine, the roads still glistening from a downpour I barely even noticed; it must have been brief and sharp. I meander through the closely built streets giving little thought to where I am going, paying scant attention until I see the spire of the church ahead of me.

I pick my way carefully across the gravel path, knowing I could find the way with my eyes closed if I wanted to. I wince at the rawness that flashes across my heels with every step and kick my shoes off with sighing relief, choosing to carry them instead.

Jasmine grows up from the headstone now, twisting a meandering path over the curve of the letters, adding a rich beauty to the sorrow of the epitaph. Leaning forward I move the delicate leaves aside and trace my fingers across the carved lettering, feeling the coolness of the polished stone. The meadow flowers and grass, damp from the prior deluge, brush against my sore bare feet, cool and pleasant. The green tendrils curl against my skin and a slight movement of my foot brings a spiky, sudden pain. A laminated card rests in the grass, its corners unrounded and sharp; tucked into the wilderness around the headstone it would have been easy to miss had I not pressed delicate skin against it. It is written in the same hand as the advert in the window of Rose Tinted, in sparkling purple ink.

I wish I could remember you. Even though I can't, I miss you both every minute of every day. Love from Sarah.

She has drawn a love heart beneath her name with two kisses inside it, one for each part of the decaying waste beneath my bare, damp feet. I skim the card as far away as I can, watching it cut sharp through the air before curving to the side and into the hedge at the edge of the graveyard. I look at the father's name on the stone, *Thomas Edward Phillips*, who was a beloved father, beloved brother. And beneath it, *Annie May Phillips* who is apparently forever in his arms. *Do not stand at my grave and weep.* As if I would, as if I would stand here and shed tears for them, as if I would waste my sorrow on those who do not deserve it.

A large, rough-edged stone lies on the ground not far from my curled reddening toes and I grasp it, holding it like a dagger in my hand. I scratch it across his name, his good wholesome name, his beloved father name. A trail of white chases the point of the stone across the surface, neither deep enough or damaging enough to remain if another downpour appears to wash the blemish away. I scratch harder and the stone resists, as if mocking me. I can almost hear laughter from beneath my scrabbling fingers but carry on anyway. Will my anger seep into the soil, wet and red hot? Will it leak into the space where they lie, rank and mouldering, together?

I cast the stone aside and begin to grab handfuls of blooms, tearing them from the ground and throwing them aside. I don't stop until the earth is ragged and bare and my hands are stained green with the pulped juice from the stalks. I look at the waste around me and feel no guilt, no shame at this desecration. I feel tired and sad, full of hatred and bitterness.

As I sit amongst the wreckage breathing hard, I hear the tell tale squeak of the gate that has needed oiling for as long as I can remember. Turning, I see a blonde head moving above the line of headstones. Maybe it is Leah, maybe not. It isn't worth waiting to find out. I have no desire to see her, to be seen by her. What would she do if she found me sitting here? I stand and hurry away in the opposite direction, weaving through the graves, bending low so as not to be seen. It is only as I reach the path – with the intention of doubling back to the gate and to freedom – as my foot touches the bare gravel, that I realise I have left my shoes beneath the destruction behind me. I think of where I got them and find that I don't mind losing them after all.

Chapter Thirty

With every little thing that I place carefully wrapped, in a box, the room feels less and less like my own. The delicate pink walls have not changed since those first months when I made it my own; the patchwork throw is the same, the curtains an image of home that I always needed to remain as they were. Yet everything changes as I remove from sight those things that say this room is mine.

I have taken my time over the packing, holding that moment of departure at arm's length, even though the fog of an outstayed welcome hangs heavily over me. I gently wrap fragile things, ornaments made of glass and china, place books in size order and stare for hours at old toys I am told were once mine, wishing for some kind of response from the cold abyss behind my eyes.

I am sitting on the floor surrounded by half-full boxes when Leah knocks lightly on the door.

"Come in."

She is slow to respond, the handle moving slightly then going back up as if she has changed her mind, as if she has to pause to gather her thoughts. This is how it is with us now, hesitant. She smells of fresh grass and flowers as she comes in, and she sits on the unmade bed. Shadows play across her face and she looks old suddenly.

"What's the matter?" I ask.

"I've just come back from visiting Tom and Annie."

Her eyes meet mine as though looking for something and I feel pinned beneath them. It makes no sense to me that she should be so sad after a visit to the graveyard, not now. Grief is a strange, twisting thing. Raw and tormenting in the early days, where all she could think about was how different she could have done things, how much better she could have been. It changed with time, becoming smoother, more gentle. The grief, the sense of loss, is still there, but its path has altered and now she looks less at what could have been done differently and more at the people they had been, the joy they carried, her love for them.

Leah has told me all of this before, how time is indeed a great healer, not because it takes the grief away, not because the loss is ever easier to bear but simply because the wound changes, scabs over and becomes less raw and intense, less painful to the touch.

I look at her for a few moments before realising she is avoiding my eyes.

"What is it?" I grow tired of waiting for her to speak, of the way she fills the room with trepidation.

"Somebody has vandalised the grave."

I am stunned into silence as her eyes move over my face, scrutinising my response. I put my hand over my mouth as though holding my words in to check them thoroughly before setting them free, so shocked that I can't be sure of what the correct reaction should be in this moment.

"I don't understand."

"I went to tidy it up," she says, "to have a chat with them. When I got there, all the flowers had been pulled up, every single one of them." She starts to cry. "And there were these scratches all across the headstone, like someone has tried to wipe their names out."

She puts her head in her hands and starts sobbing. I move beside her, put my arm around her and feel her flinch beneath my hand.

"What about the other graves?" I ask. "Were any of them damaged?"

She shakes her head, sniffing.

"I don't understand," I say again. "Why would anyone do that?" I pass her a tissue from the half-empty box on the floor and wait as she composes herself, delicately wiping beneath her eyes to neaten the black smear of her eyeliner. "Have you called the police?"

She shakes her head and seems uncomfortable when I ask why. She turns from me then, reaching into the carrier bag she brought in with her, slowly pulling out a pair of worn black shoes. I recognise them instantly, noticing in a split second the space on the front where some of the decorative sequins came off and I stuck multicoloured beads in their place. I take them from her hands and stare at them, trying to find answers in the worn, patchy silver of the insoles. There are tiny stalks of grass stuck to the leather.

"They were by the side of the grave."

And that is all she says but I feel the weight of those words settle hard around me, feel the enormity of them. She looks directly at me then, meeting my eyes with the challenge in hers.

"I got rid of those shoes ages ago! I put them in one of those charity bags that we left outside the door."

I hear the defensive tone in my voice, like that of a child desperate to be believed, who only results in convincing others of their guilt by their extreme, unguarded reaction.

"Please tell me it wasn't you, Sarah. Please tell me you didn't do this because you're angry with me for some reason."

I grow cold inside, frozen beyond words, beyond comprehension. How could she suspect this of me? How could she believe for one minute that I have done such a thing?

"I gave them away," I whisper, getting to my feet, moving away from her as though her presence is a contaminant that I can no longer tolerate. My voice is quiet, so very quiet and though she tilts her head towards me she doesn't catch all of the words.

"Pardon?"

I step forward rapidly and bend down, screaming them again into her face, driven by my shock at the accusation. My voice so loud that it hurts my throat, a voice propelled by the unbelievable pain that she thinks I might be capable of something like this. For the second time she flinches away from me, her face stunned as she gets rapidly to her feet and backs towards the door, opening her own mouth and easily matching my volume of moments before. I stand fast against the wave of it, the sheer rage of it.

"So I'm expected to believe that you gave these shoes away to charity and that they were taken to a central depot, sorted, taken to a store, sold to someone and then somehow, by some incredible coincidence, they end up on the newly vandalised grave of your family. That's what you want me to believe is it?"

"Well that's more believable than me doing it! Surely you can see that. How could you even think this of me?"

She sighs then and the volume leaves as quickly as it rose, the power diminished. When she speaks again her voice is soft, resigned, as if letting me know that she understands, that there could be good reasons for my actions and that she will understand them, whatever they are.

"I know you Sarah. These last few weeks... I know you've been having a hard time. If you would just let me in maybe I can help you, maybe together we can get to the bottom of it."

I look at her sincerity, her struggle to understand and see the belief that it was indeed me who left the shoes by the grave, that in some way, perhaps, it is a cry for help, for attention as I sense her slipping away from me and into the arms of her lover. I feel cold, empty.

"You're wrong," I say and my voice is a small, faded thing.

She looks up at me.

"You obviously don't know me at all." I push past her and leave.

Chapter Thirty-One

The water moved softly, stirred by the oars in my mother's hands, her fingernails bright red and shiny against the worn rough wood, the flakes of old varnish beneath her fingertips coloured yellow by time. The day was fine and hazy, the ripples golden in the sunshine. I held my fingers under the surface of the lake and felt the pushing resistance against the palm of my hand, the occasional slimy thread of weed as the insects buzzed softly. I looked to the shore a little way away, distracted by the upside down world of trees and sky that shimmered in the surface of the water.

It was a soft focus kind of day, a lazy day. My mother sighed and rested the oars for a moment as she pressed a tissue to her face and blotted the damp sheen away. Her sundress clung to her slender frame beneath the wide brim of her straw hat. More than once I saw the eyes of men in the few boats that passed us, noticing their intensity as they moved over her briefly and with subtlety. Those glances were long enough to stir possessiveness in my stomach, to make me want to tell them to stop it, she wasn't theirs. My mother seemed unaware of the magnet she was. She looked peaceful, content and after a little while I allowed myself to relax into the calm haze of the day.

My father waved to us as we drifted by, his palm flashing

white before he turned back and continued laying food out on the striped picnic rug. His mouth was moving as though he were talking to himself and he kept looking up as if reassuring himself that there was nobody there listening. If I made my eyes go soft and lazy I was sure I could see the air bending around his imaginary friend, like he was talking to ghosts that only he could see. I turned away and leaned back against the wood with a sigh.

"Happy Birthday, little sweet-pea. And how old are you today?"

As if she didn't know, as if this were a secret I had kept somehow. I heard the smile in her voice and was glad of it, that it was here today of all days, that she seemed light and relaxed. The boat tilted slightly, beginning the slow turn around the central island. I watched the ducks that made their home among the rushes, smiled as they put their bottoms in the air and reminded me of tiny, feathery dolphins.

"I'm eight," I said

"Eight years old!" she exclaimed, mock amazement dripping from her words. "How did my little girl ever get to be so big?"

I smiled at her. "In two years time I will be ten years old. That's double numbers, almost grown up." My words were a rapidly thrown shroud over her face, her smile suddenly hiding in its folds.

"Don't be in such a rush for that. There's nothing great about being a grown-up. Far better to be a little girl and not have to worry about grown-up things."

"Like shopping and cooking and cake and television and work and make-up and parties?" I meant it to sound light and funny, I wanted her smile to come back. But half way through my list I looked towards the ducks and they no longer looked funny to me, now they looked like they were flailing at the water, drowning. I realised that we had drifted completely around to the other side of the island where the

146

trees hung in the water, where there were dark shadows I couldn't see into. The branches were closer to the boat, the plants grew taller and all of a sudden I couldn't see anyone but her, the other boats hadn't come this far round yet. It was just the two of us and her smile was still gone because somehow I had chased it away. I could no longer see my father talking to himself as he prepared our lunch. I felt cold and scared.

"Well now," she said, "that isn't at all what being a grown-up is like. Being a grown-up is very different. Being a grown-up feels a little like this."

Her hand moved so fast I had no time to react. Her slim, red-tipped fingers gripped the front of my dress, twisting the thin material until I felt it grow close and tight across my back, digging in. I saw the muscle in her arm tense and become corded, I saw it shake as it took the strain of my weight. Her other hand gripped tightly onto the edge of the boat. She pulled me sharply to my feet as I stared horrified into her empty face.

"Please Mummy, I'm sorry, please don't."

"But darling, you wanted to know about being a grown-up. I just want to show you how it feels, that's all."

Her voice was calm and pleasant; it held a sing song quality that was perverse, out of place amongst the threat, the dread that swelled the back of my throat. I heard the smile in her words and thought that it had been hiding there in her mouth all along, that it wasn't my fault that it had gone away. And then there were no thoughts left in me. She leaned forwards abruptly and I jolted backwards, the boat rocked sharply and I thought we would tip over and further shatter the glassy surface of the water before it settled back into its slow drift, ripples fanning out away from us across the surface as though they were running, trying to escape. I watched them with envy as they began to fade at the edges of the lake.

If I turned my head I would have been almost parallel

to the water, its golden ripples painting the side of my face with reflected light. I saw the tension in her jaw, the tremor in her arm again as she took all of my weight in her frail, weak hand. I grasped her wrist with both of my hands as I felt her grip on my dress grow slack and light.

"Please Mummy, pull me up!"

"This is how it feels darling, just like this. This is what it is to be a grown-up. Like I am going to fall all the time, like the thing that is holding me could let go at any moment. I am always moments away from the worst kind of danger, from the worst kind of fall. I look down and there is no bottom, there is no end."

Her voice was almost a whisper and I was chilled by it, terrified, because there was no strain there at all, even though she held me dangling above the chill water with one hand, even though her jaw was clenched, her teeth clamped together, she sounded peaceful, content almost.

I turned and looked down at the lake, seeing my fractured self reflected there. And beyond my broken image – deeper beneath the surface – were the dark flowing shapes of the weeds that clung to the lake bed, drifting gently with the movement of the water. They looked further away here, deep and secret. How easily they would curl around an ankle or a wrist or a neck and hold on forever; they would cover over my head and hold me still and no-one would see me down there among the shadows, cold and white and dead.

I turned back to look at her and she was smiling at me, her lovely Mummy smile. I felt the loosening of her hand, the letting go, the sudden terrifying sense of release. I gripped even tighter to her, feeling the bones in her wrist grind a little beneath my desperate fingers. I didn't feel the damp spreading across the lower half of my dress as my bladder let go.

"Please Mummy, I can't swim, I can't swim."

I heard the reedy whine of my voice, tightened by terror.

She sighed and shook her head at me.

"Neither can I sweet-pea. Neither can I."

She sighed and pulled me back into the boat. Her hand moved from my dress to my face, gently touching the flushed skin. Her thumb brushed gently against the wetness on my cheeks and for a moment she looked concerned for me. She seemed not to notice how I flinched away from this lightest of touches. Looking me up and down she turned and gripped the oars with a sigh and rowed us purposefully back into the sunshine, back to the shore and to safety. As soon as her feet were back on dry land she marched off quickly and I rushed to keep up, scared that she planned on going without me, that she would leave me here among the trees and the strangers.

"Darling, it's no good, we're going to have to leave."

My father looked up in surprise from the feast he had just laid out on the mat.

"Why on earth would we have to leave, we haven't been here long?"

She gestured towards me without even looking to see if I was there, if I had caught up with her.

"She's wet herself!"

His eyes took in my discomfort, the wet clothes and tear-stained face. He must have read the guilt there, and the shame. He didn't see the fear, he never could.

"Do we not have any spares in the car?"

"She's eight years old, for goodness sake, I thought she was past this." Derision tainted her voice, shone in her eyes as she stepped firmly away from what she had done and saw only me to blame, found belief and justification in her lie. My father's shoulders slumped as he reached forwards with a deep sigh to start returning the untouched food to the plastic tubs. I tried not to see his disappointment.

"I'm sorry Daddy."

I felt the injustice of it all coil through me, icy cold and sharp. He reached up and smoothed my tangled, sweaty hair.

"That's okay kiddo, it can't be helped. We'll just eat this at home eh?"

I nodded and started crying, wanting to stay here in the sunshine, to feed the ducks with my leftover sandwich crusts and run around the trees. I wanted to stay here and not think about home, about the way things were when my father's eyes weren't looking too closely at us. He saw his own disappointment reflected more keenly in my eyes.

"Don't be sad, we'll come back another time, bring another picnic."

He stood up with a groan and we walked slowly back towards the car, my wet clothes flapping coldly around my legs.

We never went back. I never saw the pond again, with its ducks and the dark side of an island that held people's secrets in its hidden places.

Later that night I curled up in bed and listened to their raised voices curling through the gap around the door, fragments of anger that held me firm in my bed, too afraid to move. We had arrived home and I had splashed around in the bath while the food was laid out again on the kitchen table. I sat in my clean clothes and ate food that had sat too long in the warm and didn't taste quite fresh enough.

After we had eaten I sat curled up on the sofa with Dad as my mother carried in the cake she had made while playing at being a good parent. She looked proud of herself, pleased at her achievement and I smiled, blowing out all the candles as they sang happy birthday.

"Make a wish," my mother said and I looked at her and wished that she would disappear, that it could just be me and my dad and that she would take with her the fear and bleakness of her dark moments, her twisted world that she forced me to live in. Afterwards I would think that my wish had floated into the sky and become warped like her, the words becoming mixed up and wrong and opposite. Afterwards I would always be careful of what I wished for when I pulled on a wishbone or sneezed only once.

As she left the room to cut the cake my father reached for the television remote. It had fallen where it usually did, down the side cushion of a sofa that had seen better days. When he withdrew his hand it held only a small golden cube which he looked at with a frown, turning it over and over in his palm. I watched his face closely and it looked sad, unsurprised. When she bustled in with three plates containing too-large pieces of cake, mine with the special pink icing and silver balls, she didn't immediately notice the change in the air.

I took a plate from her hand as she offered it but Dad didn't move, he stayed looking at his palm as if he hadn't noticed her there. Her hand hovered in front of him, the cake held out level with his eye line and he didn't move at all. She laughed, her affected laugh, the one designed to draw attention to her and only her.

"What have you got there that could possibly be more important than my yummy cake?"

"It's a cufflink."

His voice was hollow, void, and at the words which seemed like nothing at all to me, her face began to slowly fall apart. Hurrying to the coffee table she put the two plates down and reached quickly for the gold in his hand as if she could make it disappear, a magician with a coin. He closed his fingers over it and she took a faltering step backwards.

"I don't wear cufflinks."

She tried to tell him she had no idea where it had come from, whose it could be. He held up a finger towards her.

"Don't."

He turned to me and smiled lightly with his mouth, his eyes staying sad and empty. He leaned over and touched my arm lightly, as if afraid that pressing too hard would make me break beneath his fingerprints.

"Hey kiddo, could you take your cake upstairs and eat

151

it? Mummy and me need to talk."

She visibly wilted as he spoke and as I left the room, her face looked stricken.

I sat on the edge of my bed and ate, spilling crumbs onto the floor and licking the icing from my fingers. Through the floor I could make out the higher pitch of her voice pleading against the harsh depth of his. I put my pyjamas on and climbed into bed, knowing they wouldn't ask me if I had brushed my teeth, not tonight, and after a while their voices blurred and became insignificant.

When I woke up the house was dark. The bare bulb in the hallway bled beneath the closed door and I used it to navigate my way across the room. No-one had turned on my nightlight for me, though whoever it was that had come in and looked down on my sleeping form had thought to turn off the main light on their way out. I shivered at the thought of my blank-eyed mother watching me as I slept. I shuffled down the hall to the bathroom and opened the door.

She was in the bath with her eyes closed. There were traces of pink-tinged foam still on the surface, the water beneath them red and viscous. I touched her cold arm and she groaned a little, but her eyes stayed closed and the water still looked like blood. I don't know how long I stood there staring at my naked, bleeding mother. Suddenly her arm slid from the edge of the bath, I stared at the drip, drip, drip of red, watched as it trickled slowly across her palm, down her fingers, swelling into fat, round globs at the tips of her nails before falling and splashing into a vile circle on the floor. She groaned again and the spell broke. I ran to get my father.

Everything grew blurry after that. My father was running around frantic and breathless, an ambulance arrived. Mrs Cambridge from next door came round to sit with me and she let me eat cookies with milk even though, she told me, it was two o'clock in the morning and children should be sleeping. Eventually she took me up to bed and didn't seem to notice the crumbs around my mouth, in the spaces between my teeth, the chocolate smears on my fingers.

When I went to use the toilet, the bath had been drained of its water but there were thick red smears leading towards the plughole as if they'd raced each other. The drops on the floor had become hard. I turned away from them, the milk and cookies churning in my stomach. I stepped over damp, discarded towels, more red against pristine white. Hurrying back to bed I curled up into a tight ball and failed to sleep until morning.

Three days later my pale, insignificant mother came home with bottles of pills, a bandage on both wrists and my father left us both. My wish had gone completely, horribly wrong.

Chapter Thirty-Two

"I say we pop into the Duke for a couple of warm-ups then go onto Geisha's until we're too tired to move and too pissed to care. What do you think?"

"If we're too tired to move how will we get back to the apartment?"

Alex shakes her head at me disapprovingly.

"Sarah, Sarah, Sarah, ever the sensible one. We stagger of course, whilst singing out of tune, via the kebab shop for fuel to sustain us on the way back."

"Sounds delightful." I smile and wish I meant it, that my enthusiasm matched hers.

I know that I am grieving; beneath the smile and false enthusiasm I am mourning the loss of the only home I can remember living in. I want to curl up among the generic furniture of the new apartment and spend my first weekend there in the company of my sadness. But I can't because Alex wants to take me out to celebrate and I owe her too much not to go.

She turned up at Leah's with her tiny car. I looked at it dubiously but it turned out to be big enough to carry my boxes and bags after all. We put down the rear seats and crammed until the car seemed lumpy and misshapen, as though the seams were going to pop. There was no furniture to take. Nothing urgent needed that I hadn't already packed and surprisingly little that mattered: a handful of photographs of smiling lost memories, my diary.

I deliberately chose a day when my aunt was working and couldn't get away, I hadn't told her until the last minute. I didn't want her to offer help. I didn't want her to pretend she didn't want me to go. She still hadn't mentioned the brochure on my pillow and it hung between us like a ghost, vague yet cold, empty. I felt the hesitation when she tried to speak to me, as though she were nervous and afraid that her words might carry dual meanings, sharp stings within them. I found I didn't know what to say in return as we became like strangers, our former easy familiarity seeping through the cracks in the floorboards, leaking out from the tiny spaces around windows and doors.

I tried not to overhear her words when she talked on the phone, afraid of what she might say when she thought I couldn't hear her, afraid of what secrets she may be keeping from me. I no longer asked about her day, or the shop and how the new assistant was working out. I was afraid she would think my interest disingenuous. We ate our meals in silence, and on the rare occasions we did speak, it was in monosyllables, all attempts at conversation falling flat. Eventually, I stayed in my room as much as I could and Leah spent more time out of the house, leaving me to only guess at where she was going or who she was with.

Although I was nervous about the move, afraid to be alone for the first time in my life, I realised that in many ways I already was, that I had become solitary, singular, that I was already the thing I feared. I began to count down the days, wishing them away, wanting the move to come closer, if only to avoid the stilted awkwardness of what had once been my home.

I only told Leah the night before that I was leaving the next day. I tried not to see the flicker of pain that crossed her face as she turned away. Later, as she came upstairs to bed, she peered around the door into my impersonal, box-filled bedroom. With her face scrubbed of make-up she looked young and lost.

"I'm sorry, for what I said about the grave and for whatever it is I have done to hurt you. I'm sorry if I have pushed you away. I wish I could make it better."

She turned away, pulling the door closed behind her, not waiting for a reply, perhaps afraid of what it might contain. She was gone when I got up the next day. I stayed in bed as the sun came up, listening to her calm morning routine; the sound of cupboards being closed with extra care, of light footsteps. I heard the gentle click of the front door.

I left a note on the kitchen table saying thank you for everything and telling her she was welcome to visit. I didn't know if I meant it, if I could ever forgive her for the accusation she had thrown at me. That single act had undermined years of gratitude and trust, making me believe that she had never really known me, that beneath it all I was little more than a stranger she had come to care for.

While Alex drove the car around to the glossy new apartment, I walked as I always did. I followed the route I had counted almost every day since the papers had been signed, trying to make the paths familiar enough that I would no longer be afraid to leave my footprints on them. Counting back and forth, back and forth, until I had worn an imagined groove into the paths and made them my own. Made them safe.

We met at the entrance that was tucked slightly away from the bustle of the main street and loaded everything into the lift before the doors opened and she saw my new home for the first time.

"I don't know whether to hate you or pretend I love you in that way so you'll marry me and I can live here too. Sarah, it's amazing!" She stood in the centre of the room with her mouth open as she took everything in.

I put her eyes in front of mine; saw the clean lines, the sophistication as I counted the steps to the sofa and sat down.

"That's it, I have to get a place of my own. It is so not cool living with the mums at my age."

By the time she reluctantly left – 'dinner on the table, so not cool' – she had made me agree to go out with her that Friday to celebrate my new home, the shiny new phase in my life. I had tried to say no but Alex reminded me of how long it had been since we had spent any real time together, and what a crap friend I was in general. In the end I agreed just to get her to be quiet and stop making me feel bad. I was not strong enough to carry another load of guilt.

When Friday comes and she arrives at my neatly unpacked new home an hour early it is to find me still not showered or dressed. We finish discussing the night's plans and she pushes me towards the bathroom impatiently. When I emerge, she has a determined look on her face with her make-up out, ready to paint a party girl over my indifference. I sit still as she dries and styles my hair, wincing a little as I feel the brush pulling a little too hard, punishing my reluctance.

I look brighter when she is finished, more colourful and animated and I fight the urge to scrape my heavy, long hair back into a pony tail as she flicks through my wardrobe and selects something that she finds suitably shimmering. I change quickly and don't tell her as we head out the door that I feel as if I am wearing someone else's personality.

The High Street is bright and bustling with people heading out ready to party, the familiarity of the buildings settle around the exposed skin of my arms, my chest. Alex holds my hand as she steps forward to cross the road and rolls her eyes good-naturedly as I shake my head and walk a bit further, stepping into the ghosts of my former footprints, before crossing onto North Street.

The Duke is standing room only, the gaps between people filled with a noise so dense it seems malleable. We fight our way to the bar, battle to be heard. I breathe in the tang of perfume and sweat.

"Busy tonight!" Alex states redundantly and I look around in mock-surprise.

"Really! I hadn't noticed."

She smiles and digs me in the ribs. "Shall we just have the one here then and go on to the club? If it's this busy in town the queues will be hideous."

It is a struggle to catch her words and she repeats them for good measure. I nod my agreement and take a big sip of my drink, eager to finish and step away from my increasing claustrophobia.

There are one hundred and twenty-three steps from the door of the pub to the door of the club. I have counted them before on the other occasions we have gone out. Our routine never varies that much and I know that Alex finds it a little frustrating.

"You don't know what you're missing out on you know!" she said one time. "There's this great new club opened down the Quay, great music, rather attractive young men. It's brilliant, I'd love to show you it."

I heard the hope in her voice and told her I would try to gear myself up for it and she sighed, knowing how long that may take. She put up with it out of loyalty to me and stuck to the same routines, trying new places with her other friends, friends who weren't bound by the chains of repetition and counting their steps.

I count automatically as we walk, the digits clocking up in the part of my brain that doesn't interfere with my ability to listen or speak. So subconscious is it that half the time I don't realise I am doing it, though I notice if it is not there. One hundred and two steps to the back of the queue heading into Geisha's.

"So how are you finding it, living on your own, being independent?"

It has only been a few days but within them the hours are longer, the clock moves in slow motion.

"A little strange really," I say with a shrug. "I don't quite know what to do with myself, especially now that I'm not working too. It's like there's a huge blank space in front of me. I'm trying to work out how to fill it."

We shuffle forwards: one, two.

"There's no rush though is there? I mean, you can take your time deciding what you want to do next, where to go from here."

"True. I could maybe open up my own shop or something like that."

I taste the words for the first time, giving voice to something I have only considered as a vague possibility.

"What would you sell?"

"I don't know, the sort of stuff I like I guess, wind chimes, fairies, that kind of thing maybe."

"Weird hippy shit you mean."

I smile at the expression on her face.

"Not just weird hippy shit, nice stuff, like presents for people. There isn't anything like that around here."

"How would you know? When do you ever walk up the little side streets that might just be hiding something like that?"

We reach the front of the line and any retort stays in my throat as we bustle into the noise and flashing lights. The next two hours pass in a blur of dancing and alcohol. No matter how hard I try afterwards, I will never be able to pull the flashing images into any kind of linear cohesion. I clearly remember going into the club, the vague feeling of distaste as I am reminded it is the kind of place where feet stick to the carpet and everything smells of spilled alcohol and underlying sweat. I remember laughing at something someone, probably Alex, says before I turn my back and head for the dance floor. The music is too loud and the space too small and crowded to feel comfortable but I dance anyway, no doubt closing my eyes and pretending I am alone as I always do.

After that comes the stumbling vague feeling of having too many drinks, the lack of awareness or concern in my surroundings, the feeling of vertigo, the lightness about my shoulders as I forget to care about familiarity.

But I remember Cam.

159

I stand at the bar, in the crush of people waiting to be served.

"Excuse me," he says and has to repeat it twice before I realise he is talking to me.

I look at him, at his blue eyes, his gentle smile, and wait, hoping that he isn't going to come out with some cheesy chat-up line that will have the reverse effect to the one hoped for. Instead he says nothing more, just stands there looking at me, his eyes expectant. I get tired of waiting for his next words.

"Well?" I say.

He indicates with his hand. "I'm trying to get past."

I look around and see the crush of people blocking the way to the toilets. He had meant 'excuse me' in the literal sense, not as a way of initiating conversation. I feel like an idiot as heat travels up from my neck, tingeing my cheeks red.

"I'm sorry, I thought… "

"You thought I was going to come out with some hideous comment that would make your insides crawl. Well maybe I should, I'd hate to disappoint you." He smiles and looks me up and down. "That's a lovely outfit you're wearing, it would look really good on my bedroom floor."

I laugh, I can't help myself and he laughs with me before his face grows serious.

"You have a beautiful smile and I am very sad to leave it but I really have to go." He inclines his head towards the gent's toilets and I step carefully out of his way.

I think that it will be the last I see of him but I am still waiting to order my drink when he comes back and joins me in the crowd.

"Would you allow me to buy you a drink, to make up for the terrible chat-up line?"

I nod, pleased that he has come back. I hear him ask for a coke as well as my wine. He sees me looking at it as we walk towards the seating area that looks down on the crowded, pulsating dance floor.

"I'm tonight's designated driver, lucky me!"

"Well, look on the bright side, you won't have a hangover tomorrow."

"True, true." He smiles and gestures for me to go on ahead of him.

I wonder where Alex is and scan the dance floor, eventually catching sight of her as she dances wildly opposite a round man with a nice smile. She will no doubt come and find me when she has exhausted herself, which could be some time yet.

"I'm Cam, by the way."

We sit down in two outdated vinyl bucket seats.

"Sarah," I say with a smile.

He hands my drink over and as he does so I see a small tattoo on the inside of his wrist. Tiny angel wings with a date beneath them written in a fine curling script. He follows the line of my eyes, looks at the wings with a slight frown, an air of sadness that tells me that not enough time has passed for this to become easier.

"My father," he tells me and I think how beautiful his voice is, how deep and gentle.

I look at my own bare wrist, at the pale skin and tiny threads of blue before meeting his eyes with the familiarity born of empathy.

"Mine too," I say and he nods.

I sip at my drink, glancing towards Alex and the dance floor and from that moment he slowly begins to disappear with the rest of the night into vague, vacant memories.

Chapter Thirty-Three

I lean against the tacky wall of the club and feel eyes on my skin, feel them trace a pattern across my arms, over my breasts before going lower and deeper. The club is heavy with perfume and people, an underlying scent of desperation oozes from the pores of the painted ladies and their consorts. I watch them all – the keen and the indifferent, the lonely and the strange – as they move languidly through tiny spaces in the crowd, pulsing like bees on a honeycomb. I watch them and feel his eyes upon me.

Reaching up a hand to push the thick hair away from my face my eyes sweep across the human wall before me. I see him as his gaze moves over the swell of my hips and down to the hem of the tiny skirt I wear. He is tall, gruff and dark, shadows and coloured light moving, alternating across his throat, across his face, his eyes vague and half-hidden. His hand lifts to his head, my mirror image, and I smile to myself as I begin to move.

The path I follow meanders and weaves in his direction, I sense him leap and come alive as I move nearer. Closer I see how much taller than me he is. I see the underside of his chin rough with five o'clock shadow, the swell of his Adam's apple. At the last moment, when we should come face to face, I turn away but as I do, I take a deep breath, smelling him as an animal would, discovering whether I can bear to be close to him, close enough to feel the burn of his stubble against my lips. He smells of spice and oranges and leather. I think that his skin would taste of salt and musk. But I don't stop to find out, to get even vaguely close to that kind of invitation.

I take the two steps down onto the dance floor, threading between the other dancers, knowing that he watches. Past the poles that grow like stalagmites on a raised platform to my left, paying no attention to the drunken girl that wraps her bare legs around the cold steel and prays for attention from anyone who notices her. I begin to dance even before I find enough space to move in, even as I move sideways through the frantic, bouncing crowd, the trance beat crawling through my feet, into my bones. Faces curve into grimaces, sweat-soaked brows and upper lips, dark stains beneath arms, a flash of soft abdomen when arms are raised. I love all of it; this nightmarish quality, the depths of longing reflected in drunken eyes. There is so much life here, so much energy, both good and bad.

I find a space where my arms can fan out from my sides like wings and begin to move more slowly, more sinuously than the beat of the music. It is too loud and the beat is an altogether different one than I would normally choose but I dance anyway. Pretending to be alone, yet knowing all the time that he watches me, that I move more seductively for no other reason than because I can feel his eyes on me.

I sense his movement, his presence behind me, before I open my eyes to see him, before I feel fingertips brush lightly against my upper arms, hesitant and easy to ignore. There is a vague glimpse behind my eyes of a day by the river, of my father and fishing rods, of being told to move gently, softly lest the fish is scared away. Firm hands grip my upper arms and spin me around to face him, chasing the vision back into darkness, the fish back beneath the reeds.

His eyes are dark enough to hide his pupils and I marvel at the lack of depth, at the emptiness there. His gaze lacks intellect, and even in the immediacy of this moment I feel a little cheated. He meets my disappointment half way with an arrogant look and my skin contracts, as though moving from him by minuscule degrees. He leans forwards until his mouth breathes damp onto the tender skin beneath my ear.

"Can I buy you a drink?" His voice is deep, vaguely accented and I nod against the warm breath of it.

"Of course," I say with a small shrug of one shoulder and his fingers slide down my arm to grasp my hand and pull me through the throbbing crowds of dancers, my consent seemingly giving him the right of ownership.

As we move towards the bar I catch the looks of a group of young men, open and unguarded. They have the muscled physiques of residents at the nearby army training camp and I smile towards them as they nudge each other and gesture with their heads. I feel the bristling of my companion as he moves between them and me, forming a barricade they will not attempt to clamber over.

"I'm not yours," I say and he shrugs in response.

"Whatever." He replies lightly but does not let go of my hand.

I look at the side of his face, at the set of his jaw and think that he is not nice, this stranger. But I go along with him anyway, wanting to see more of what he is, of his desire for possession despite his lack of knowledge, his ignorance of me.

I say nothing as I wait beside him at the bar and merely nod my head in thanks as he hands me a white wine and takes a long drink of his lager, chasing it with a pantomime sigh.

"I'm going outside for a cigarette."

I hear the vague question in there, the wondering if I will follow, if I smoke, if I am his after all. I meet his eyes and it is enough of an answer for him as he turns from me and edges his way towards the dingy smoking area at the rear of the equally dingy club. I do not like him but I follow anyway, the drink he bought still cold and full in my hand.

In the grey stone space carved into an alleyway he stops and offers me a cigarette from a half-crushed packet. I decline but watch as he lights his own and breathes in, releasing the deep and satisfied sigh of an addict. There are two girls in the corner, one smoking, the other crying as she slides down the wall, the rough brickwork pushing her dress above her waist as she slowly folds into a heap on the dusty concrete floor. She is wearing unattractive underwear that sags in places and looks grimy and off-colour, it has clearly seen better days. Had she been able to glimpse the future and seen into this moment, would she have chosen better, chosen something prettier to show a world that lacked care towards her and made her cry? I turn away as her friend tells her that all men are bastards, it is in their genes and in their jeans ha ha.

She is still laughing at her own feeble joke as her friend stands again, adjusting her clothing as they turn and leave the alleyway leaving the two of us alone. I meet his eyes, his cocksure smile and feel like a spider under a glass. His hand reaches up and brushes against my cheek and there is the catch of a broken nail sharp against my skin. He holds his cigarette between his lips as he physically turns me, placing me with the wall to my back and him to my front. I hold his gaze and see in his eyes the soul of a bully. Alone with him I feel caged, trapped and the twist of his smile seems predatory and self-satisfied.

"I'm Ian." His words carry to my ears on a cloud of smoke and alcohol fumes.

"I don't care," I say and mean it, he is nothing to me, I don't want to know his name.

He frowns for a second, puzzling over what is obviously an alien response before he turns it to his advantage and pushes his expression upwards with a smirk.

"Oh, like that is it, no need for names? A woman of action, huh?"

His hand strokes, uninvited, along the underside of my breast and I stare at him, my face motionless. I look down at his fingers and there is coldness in his touch that moves upwards.

"Not with you. I don't think I like you," I tell him.

He looks surprised. "You don't like me but you let me buy you a drink?"

I can see that I'm not upholding my end of the bargain by not liking him, by not wanting his hand grabbing at my breasts.

"It was worth finding out, I liked the look of you from a distance. Close up though," I let my gaze sweep from his face to his crotch and back again, "I think you are a bully."

He looks away and laughs but I see a mask come down, or maybe come off; his face becomes harder, tighter.

"A bully?" He smiles at me as his hand reaches up and grips my throat, pushing me hard back into the wall.

My head hits the stone, though not hard enough to leave a bruise. I stare back into narrowed eyes and see that he waits for my submission, my fear, not doubting at all that it will be there. He presses his body forwards until he meets mine from chest to thigh. I feel the soft slight swell of his stomach, the hardness of his erection and think how pathetic he is.

His fingers grip harder, almost but not quite hard enough to restrict my breathing and I shift slightly beneath the weight of him, the force and anger of him as he grinds his lips against mine and forces his tongue between my teeth. I think of another mouth on mine, of another unwanted invasion, of my mother filling my lungs with her madness and I think he can do no worse than that, that this is nothing compared to her breath where mine should have been. I taste his cigarette, stale and rank, before he lifts his face and stares down at me. He looks pleased with himself as his thumb presses harder and my blood thumps in my head.

I am not afraid of him, I am not even afraid to die, what is my life anyway? Sarah appears unbidden in my thoughts, I wonder what she would do here, in this moment, with this threat surrounding her. How would she act? Would she be afraid? And I know the answer immediately, of course she would, of course she would be afraid; so afraid in fact that I doubt she has ever set foot in this tiny space where the lights are dim and the shadows in the corners are too dark.

My heartbeat escalates at the adrenalin of a new experience, of something different and I begin to smile at him as though he were a lover, an altogether more gentle man. I reach up my hand to gently stroke away the clench of his jaw, the baring of his teeth and I feel him soften slightly against my palm. I see his confusion and in that moment a trace of trepidation creeps into his gaze as he looks into my eyes and sees acceptance, something akin to affection and a lack of the fear he expects to see.

I raise my chin above his clasping fingers as if to kiss him and my confidence meets his uncertainty above the place where our chests still touch. I watch the march of perplexity across his face, see clearly the child inside him. He slowly lowers his mouth to mine. A trace of skin peels against the softness of his lower lip. And in the second before I feel it, before his skin presses against mine, I open my mouth and scream into his face with all the energy I can muster.

His hand releases its grip on my neck and shock blossoms in his eyes like ink in water as he flounders against the wall of sound. I scream as loudly as I can as he stands mute and baffled in front of me. He grips the front of my top and raises his other hand as if to hit me and I do not flinch from him. He stands, statue still, his hand raised above his head as two bouncers barrel into the space where we are and grab hold of him, forcing his arms behind his back, tearing my clothing as his hand pulls roughly from me.

I reach a hand up and rub at my throat and three pairs of eyes follow the movement, my two defenders seeing the fading red handprint against the pale column of my neck. I follow the wave of disgust that washes across their expressions as they turn and manhandle Ian, the now vociferously protesting bully, out of the smoking area.

The calm, the stillness that settles after their departure is all-consuming. The throbbing in my ears subsides and my heart rate slows. What would I have done if he had taken it further, if he had squeezed a little bit harder for a little bit too long? Who would be there to regret, to grieve? And Sarah, she would never learn the truth of me, the reason for me and sooner or later I want her to. I want her to know who I am. I want her to flounder as she tries to deny me. The tremor begins in my thighs, moving slowly upwards through my belly, down my arms. I try to breathe slowly and calmly, to push away the shock of my belated reaction as the tension seeps out of me and into the cold grey bricks.

I lean against the wall that looks like part of a cave and take a deep breath just as the door opens and laughter cuts through the stillness. I move, meaning to leave, to take with me the low feeling in the pit of my stomach. A hand reaches out to me, gently, as its owner takes in my expression, my torn clothing.

"Are you all right?" A deep voice, husky, belonging to a man with kind eyes who looks puzzled but genuinely concerned. He has the look of someone who is sober, aware. His friends look over at him curiously. They nudge each other and laugh and he pays them no attention.

"I don't suppose you have a safety pin?" I ask gesturing at the torn material of my top and he smiles softly in return, reaching both hands out slowly as if I am a fragile thing, a bird about to take flight. I see angel wings tattooed on the inside of his wrist as he reaches out and think how apt they are, how right for this moment. He takes the torn material in his hands and ties it together, not perfect but better.

"Good enough?" He asks and I nod and smile and think why not you? Why could it not have been you that I saw first with your lovely smile and your consideration?

I look into his blue eyes and mourn the loss of him, curse the poor timing, the lack of synchronicity.

"I have to go," I say and he nods again and looks a little disheartened.

"Is there anything I can do for you before you go?"

"Yes," I say. "Build a time machine so I can start the night over again."

With a smile he tells me that he will see what he can do and as I turn to leave he calls after me.

"Maybe we'll bump into each other again."

"I hope so." I close the door on his smile and instantly regret leaving.

With my head down I almost don't see Alex until it is too late. Her head is swivelling around, seeking someone and as I watch her eyes begin to move towards me, I step quickly behind the fleshy wall of a bouncer, imagining her eyes to be lasers scanning the space between us. I do not want to see her, I don't need the inevitable questions, the social niceties.

A group of young women, dressed scantily and wearing smiles bigger than their skirts, head towards the bar, a route that will take them past Alex. I tuck in amongst them all and keep my head down, curling into myself, until the group reaches the edge of the crowded bar. I break away and slip out of the main door, unseen by anyone. I slide a hand into my handbag looking for change and feel the smooth hard line of a key, the key to a brand new, shiny apartment. Looking back towards the door of the club, I have an idea of how I can stir things up, and make the ground seem a little less stable beneath Sarah's feet.

Chapter Thirty-Four

This is what I am. I am nothing. I am lost in the darkness and even as I drift I remember this feeling well, though here there is little pain; the waters are surely different. I swim beneath a surface I cannot see and I flounder as I reach for an invisible edge to pull myself free, knowing it must be here somewhere.

How strange that senses come to my awareness one at a time. There is that vague yet distinct perception as things fall into place, like the turning of a dial on a safe, and before the fear comes there are fragments of confused realisation, scrambled and indistinct. The first sense that begins to pull me out of the abyss is sight, even though my eyes are shut tight against the headache that pushes sharply at the inner curve of my forehead.

Light flashes, rhythmic and soft, sweeping past my closed lids in equal measure. The light is the first thing I know. I am not yet aware enough to question it, to even think what it might be or give it any consideration at all. It simply is the first thing there in the darkness of my consciousness. For a little while, maybe only seconds, though it could be hours, I drift with it; light and dark, ebb and flow, there and gone. In this space I am not yet thinking, I am not yet afraid.

And then there is touch: against my skin, beneath my legs, under the palms of my hands and my feet. There is softness where I sit, a foam seat, a bean bag perhaps. Hands curl against a curved edge, material soft. My face presses against something smooth and hard and cold that jolts in brief snatches. I cannot make sense of these things, their confused fragments, and only later, with the benefit of hindsight will my brain organise them; place them into a whole terrifying image.

I smell leather and aftershave, faint traces of both that are unfamiliar and vaguely disguised by a stronger scent, artificial and fruity. There is dust too, irritating and harsh in my nostrils, and the underlying smell of wet shoes, of something shabby and uncared for. And then there is the music, gentle easy listening sounds that drift into my ears.

Is this the moment I step back in to the present? Enough to realise where I am? Is it in this moment that conscious thoughts begin seeping in? Slowly I make these separate senses into linear patterns that create an awful, terrifying image. I recognise the song, the beautiful tone of Norah Jones, her name moving into my drowsy mind and beneath the voice, the music, beneath everything else, is a constant deep thrum, at once recognisable and alien.

I know what it is even though it lives nowhere except in the void of my childhood. I feel it in the jolting of my head against the hard, smooth, unseen surface. And I feel it in my heart as it takes flight, as it moves faster and harder, as its beating becomes a single tone, a humming sound at one with the horrific resonance I merge into. I feel the tension in my muscles, the moment of hesitation as I wait for the tearing, grinding sound of metal being torn apart.

I sense all of these things while still blind and helpless. Before I even open my eyes and see for myself, before I have given solidity to the fear pushing at high speed through my veins. I know where I am, I know what this is even though I have no memory of the last time I was in a car. I fight the terror that courses through me, to force my unwilling eyes to open. My head tilts sideways and backwards against the window as I look up at the rhythmic flash of the streetlights

171

passing, the residual glare against the glass, the smear of other people's fingerprints that make the bright yellow glow seem altogether more gentle.

I move only my eyes as everything else remains frozen. I see the dark stretch of the dashboard, the curve of the glove box and air inlet grills, the strange perspective of sitting in the front passenger seat. I feel a weight in my lap, soft and yielding and my heart is against my tongue, blocking my throat. I am too afraid to look around, to confirm where I am, to see the road flashing past beneath the wheels. I cannot bring myself to turn around and see the unknown driver steering me into oblivion.

I squeeze my eyes shut again as I open my mouth and scream my fear, the sound becoming solid, bending and twisting into words as I shout 'let me out, let me out' over and over and over again. My senses mingle everything together, sweeping it into a puzzle form that I will never be able to untangle, that will remain forever scrambled and fragmented.

The car screeches to a halt and there are hands on my arm, uncertain at first then more urgent as though trying to wake me from a nightmare that I am already conscious for. There are words said urgently and with guttural haste that make no sense to me. They are spoken in a deep voice, a voice that worries and grows into panicky desperation. They penetrate into my terrified mind and become louder, harsher as they seek to be heard above the scream after scream that rides the crest of my terror.

There is a hasty click, followed by the seatbelt sliding across my chest, the weight of him leaning into me, the smell of garlicky breath, the unlatching of the door. Cold still night air drifts in as his hand pushes me gently at first then with increasing urgency.

"Get out, get out, crazy lady."

I realise that he has an accent, strong and Mediterranean as I slide across the seat, scrabbling to get my feet out before I am pushed to the edge and have to face the added danger of falling. The hard road rises up to meet the soles of my shoes and as it does so the weight in my lap shifts and falls to the ground. He drives away without bothering to shut the door, I watch as the wind pushes it back gently, not hard enough to latch completely. There is a taxi light on top of the car, a license glued next to the number plate.

Stumbling forwards on legs that are too weak and thin brings a crunching sound and I look down at the spilled contents of my handbag, a broken pen, a perfume bottle, my purse and mobile phone. The rough surface of the road cuts into my knees as I bend to gather my belongings.

The street is in semi-darkness. There are a handful of streetlights, the murky expanse between them too large to feel safe. The buildings – a small thatched cottage, a tiny post office in the distance – appear far more rural and distant than the city would contain within its old Roman walls. I am shaking and crying, with no idea where I am or how I came to be in this situation. This night has become strange and twisted, a hidden thing and I am lost somewhere in its folds.

I try to find the markers laid down in my head by a memory that has failed before. There is Alex, the Duke, the flashing lights of the nightclub and that is where the fading begins. Would you allow me to buy you a drink? The question is still there in my mind. Did I say yes? And I'm sure I did, because there is the feeling of a cold, condensation-covered glass in my hand, of sitting down, of feeling sad. I push a little further and remember the angel wing tattoo, a flash of grief in blue eyes. Later, when my heart is no longer wild and disturbed, when events are calmer and less traumatic, I may remember more, but just now I don't know how I came to be standing at the side of an unfamiliar road in an unknown village and it matters. It matters a lot because there is nothing within me that speaks of what happened. I don't know what fills the dark spaces in between the before and after, in between there and here. I know for certain that I would never have got into a car through choice, that there must have been force, coercion.

The narrow road leads away from me and I follow in the direction that seems most promising, away from ever-increasing pools of black, hoping that this path leads out of the maze. I force my legs to move step after step – feet aching from the pressure of high heels worn for too long – until with relief I find there is a wider, better-lit pathway. I have only walked a hundred yards but it is enough to lift the scarf of unfamiliarity from my eyes, to place the scene in the brighter parts of my memory.

I stand at a junction near a bus stop. Yards away across the street is the local inn from which there are no sounds and the windows are in darkness, telling me that midnight has passed, that the day has changed. If I follow the road around I know there will be a long, narrow stone bridge that is too thin for two cars to pass safely. If I keep on going and going and going, past the railway line I have previously travelled, beyond the bridge, if I walk along the twisting dark road, past avenues of trees, if I do that then after a few miles I will come to the outskirts of Exeter, not quite secure outside the walls I often feel held and safe within, but still nearly home, still better than here.

The timetable in the bus stop shows the last bus as leaving at half past ten. I glance at my phone to check the time and there is a sense of loss, of abandonment. I am three and a half hour's too late and four hours too early for the next one. I unlock the screen and start to press numbers into the phone. Leah's number still comes easily, automatically, despite recent lack of use, but before I press to connect us my thumb hovers over the button to erase the call. What would she be able to do? She can't come and collect me, I can't get into a car to get home. I'm not entirely sure that under the present circumstances she would care enough anyway and I am uncertain enough of her feelings to be reluctant to find out.

Feeling defeated and scared I turn towards the bridge and begin to follow the road home. By the time I reach the edge of the village, where the streetlights end along with the

174

houses, my high heels have been pulled away from the tacky, raw blisters that flush pink against my skin and now dangle from chilled fingers. I try not to notice the stones biting into the curve of my insteps.

The last póol of light blends into a landscape of vague shapes and shadows; each step is soft and flat as I try to place the whole of my foot down at once, a carnival act balancing on a bed of nails. By the time I reach the crest of a small hill, the village lights are no more than a pale glow emanating from behind silhouetted trees. The air is colder somehow, more insidious. Rubbing at the goose bumps on my arms, I tread carefully and slowly upon the ground and pray repeatedly for the night to be over, the litany in my head joining with the numbers as I pointlessly count and set the pace I walk to.

Chapter Thirty-Five

I curl beneath the sheets and find pain in every part of my body, in each tiny movement, every little turn of my head against the soft pillows. I can barely breathe when I think of the trees looming above me, the rustling in the leaves. And yet I cannot turn from it, cannot prevent my memory from reliving the endless night in all its stark terror.

I had walked and felt invisible eyes on me from all directions, certain that someone was watching. The fear that crawled slowly up my spine, needle points along my scalp, it almost rendered me immobile, petrified. Almost.

I sang songs in my head, counted to a hundred over and over to make me forget that I was alone. I tried not to think of the moments that led me here, of what I may have done, of what may have been done to me.

The horizon was still invisible by the time I stepped onto familiar pathways. The journey had seemed so long, so slow that I was surprised the sun wasn't high in the sky. I looked for the barely perceptible lightening that would herald the dawn, that would wash away the night and make the ground seem softer, more forgiving against my naked tender skin. The sun stayed hidden, out of sight and I began to hate the dark that rested like a heavy cloak upon my shoulders.

I walked towards the city centre, dirty and tear-stained,

becoming one with the ragged drunks that staggered home as the dawn of a new day approached for them to sleep away. A man in a delivery van, whose eyes I could not meet, stopped and asked me gently if I was okay, if I needed any help. I looked at his mouth, downturned with concern and I forced my lips into a semblance of a smile and said I was fine, pretended not to have eyes swollen from crying, that it wasn't me leaving blood stains in the shape of toes on the concrete.

He nodded and put the engine in gear, slowly pulling away, reluctantly it seemed, as if he meant to stop again, as if he were having second thoughts and should have insisted on helping me despite my remark that there was no need. I forced my painful feet to speed up, kept my face parallel to the floor and moved out of the frame of his wing mirror until he rounded a corner and was gone.

There were others, people who woke before the sun. Shopkeepers just like Aunt Leah who had put in a full day's work by the time most people were sipping at their morning coffee or brushing their teeth. Even without looking I could feel their hesitation, their turning away. I saw a reluctance to get involved, to even ask if I needed help just in case the answer was yes.

The van driver had been an exception and I belatedly realised his kindness. I felt people's fear of me, the flaky drunk on her way home from partying too hard for too long. The shoes in my hand and the limping gait indicative of over-indulgence, of a life lived to excess; there was no reason, therefore, to pity me. It was the height of irony that anyone might be thinking that of me but I was glad of their unwillingness to get involved. Their concern, any offer of help, would stand between me and the security of the apartment.

By the time I slotted my key into the door I felt I had been away for days. My heels stuck to the laminate flooring as I stepped into the hall, the soles of my feet covered with bloody patches that mingled with dirt from the road and looked solid, crusty. Small stones stuck to the bottom of each foot and dug in a little more with each gingerly taken step on the warm, smooth surface.

The mirror displayed a face I could hardly bear to look at: dark make-up smeared across red cheeks, hollow, wide eyes that hadn't let go of the depth of my fear. Even when I sat startled every night in the shadow of my nightmares, the fear dissipated quickly, leaving a vague trace in my slowing heartbeat. I had never felt this level of terror before, this gripping, solid crush that held me in its grasp.

I dropped my shoes, my bag, onto the floor and walked tentatively into the bathroom, the pain in my feet escalating at the acceptance that for now I was finished walking, I could stop and try to catch my memories in a fragile gossamer net. Leaning over the bath I slid the plug into place and turned the water on, emptying half a bottle of bath oil into the flow. Every movement slowed by the ache in my muscles, the tiredness that hung over me.

Removing clothes that felt greasy and damp I threw them into a corner before going into the bedroom and standing in front of the full-length wardrobe mirror, looking for signs on my skin that someone had been there, someone uninvited. The skin on my breasts, across my stomach and thighs, looked mottled and purple. I ran the palms of both hands across the soft yielding flesh, testing for tenderness, for bruises that shouldn't be. I felt the raised sandpaper roughness of goose bumps, felt the coolness of skin exposed to the morning chill for too long.

There were no scratches, no inexplicable injuries, nothing untoward. With a rising sense of fear at what I might discover, I slid my hand between my thighs, bracing myself against the possibility of unexpected discomfort, against the trepidation of what it could mean. In that split second a million possibilities and fears rushed through me and I braced against them. But there was nothing there, no injuries, no wounding, no sore areas. The tips of my fingers felt cold against the inner warmth of my sensitive skin as I sighed my relief into the noiseless air.

The gleaming white and chrome of the bathroom became dreamlike as it filled with steam and I stepped carefully into the too-hot water, feeling the stinging in my feet increase as I did so. With slow deliberation I scrubbed at my skin with the rough edge of a loofah, washing away the grime of the night while trying to disperse my confusion about the taxi journey and the long walk home. Forcing myself to remember was futile. No matter how hard I concentrated, how firmly I tried to push my mind back and grasp what had happened, it was not there. The memories were gone, evaporated into the air and I knew from experience that however hard I looked, they were almost certainly gone forever.

Stepping from the brown, gritty water I wrapped myself in a towel and walked slowly towards the bedroom, praying that, even if just for one night, for what was left of this night, the nightmares would stay away.

Chapter Thirty-Six

The apartment is in semi-darkness, lit only by the lights of the modern shopping centre far below; orange sodium dancing with multi-coloured neon, reflecting from the chrome and glass façades of well-known shops and restaurants. She is restless and awkward beneath the sheets and after a moment or two, a checking of the depth of her slumbering, I step slowly and quietly through the strangely coloured twilight space.

I hadn't planned things the way they happened. In my head I had imagined the scene differently, the ending one of dramatic irony, of secrets. I didn't think it would end with her walking out of the night, bleeding and afraid. I hadn't planned it that way at all. I knew she was at the club with Alex celebrating her recent move, her enforced steps into independence. I knew she, too, spoke to the man with the angel wings and the gentle smile. I watched as they sat with their drinks in their hands trying to pretend they were somewhere altogether quieter, that they were somewhere more alone, more inviting.

Was it my fault then? Her distress, the tears and disturbances that plagued her as she slept? I pulled all the pieces into play, put an extra shot or two unobserved into her drinks when I could, picked up the phone and called the taxi when I noticed how drunk she was, how vacant. It was me who slid her pliant body next to the driver, me who told him where to drive, where to return to. I just wanted to see...

I hadn't expected her to wake up. It would be my little secret, this journey, something I would know about and she wouldn't, something that would make me smile when I thought of it, a power that I could have over her. The taxi driver could have returned and I would have taken her, semi-conscious, back to her apartment, let her in with the key that nestles in my pocket. I would have tucked her up into bed where she could sleep off her unknown adventure and wake up forgetful and confused, blaming tiredness, too much alcohol. But no, she had woken up too soon, and it had ceased to be my secret, my private joke.

Would I have done it if I had known her reaction? If somehow I could have foretold the future, seen the bloody footprint in her hallway from the wounds on her feet? Would I do the same again?

I like to think that I wouldn't be so cruel, that with hindsight I would be altogether more gentle, kinder somehow. I like to think that I am not cold-hearted enough to deliberately hurt her the way that I have. Yet I think that perhaps in some ways I am that callous, I am that cruel. There Is part of me, the part that stayed silent and smiling, that thinks I have done well, that I have succeeded in changing things somehow. The part of me that believes, during the moments of terror that surely coursed through her, that finally she may be alive inside, that she could at last be feeling something other than the pathetic safety net beneath her.

Even through my vague sense of guilt, my discomfort, I am congratulating myself for achieving something I always believed to be impossible. Weak, vulnerable, pitiable Sarah Phillips was finally jolted free of her constricting armour. She finally stepped, screaming and shaken, into the reality we all have to face sooner or later. There was no-one around to keep her hidden away. No Aunt Leah to turn on the nightlight and scare away the monsters under the bed. No boringly familiar path to tread in security and peace, always the same, never digressing, never changing.

I catch sight of myself in the mirror. The same mirror that captured Sarah's image as she ran her hands over her body while I watched, unseen. I reach for the lipstick on her dressing table. Is it the one she wore as she walked through the night trying to keep her terror at bay? I think that perhaps it is. I throw the lid back onto the surface and carry the tube across to the mirror and apply it to my own lips, exaggerating my smile in the semi-darkness, going around and around until my lips become huge, clown-like. My teeth flash white in my reflection. What would she do if she were to wake up now, see me standing here? I press too hard and the lipstick snaps at the base, rolling across the floor. I walk towards it and bend to pick it up before thinking otherwise. Reaching out with a bare foot I tread the red stick into the carpet, twisting until the lump beneath my sole is flat and smeared and then I step, leaving partial footprints, the edges of my toes, part of the pad.

I paint my presence in garish red against her carpet before turning and stepping softly out of her bedroom as I realise that, even with hindsight, I would do things exactly the same way. I would stand and watch as it all played out. Perhaps if I get the chance to do it all again I will enjoy it more, I will watch in delight as the precious princess in the tower flounders and realises she is utterly, completely alone. Just like me.

Chapter Thirty-Seven

With hesitant fingers I pick up the phone and dial Leah's number. For the first time since we argued, since our lives unravelled, I desperately need to hear her voice, to have her comfort me and tell me everything will be okay, the way she always has when the world becomes dark and painful. I am a child again.

I curl up on the huge sofa, my feet beneath me, wrapped snuggly in a voluminous, sugar pink dressing gown as the ringing goes on and on. Will Leah ever get round to buying an answer phone? I have mentioned it to her before, she always said there was no need, no-one called her at home. I glance at the clock and feel stupid at my mistake: at ten o'clock on a Saturday morning she will be at work. I am not thinking clearly. I disconnect and redial, imagining the old-fashioned phone ringing amongst the flowers. It is answered with a breathless hello.

"Leah, it's me, Sarah," I say quickly before closing my lips on the tidal wave of words waiting to sweep us both away, feeling the rush threaten.

There is a tinkling laugh from the other end, girlish and light.

"Oh hello Sarah, it's Jane, I'm sorry Leah's not here at the moment. Can I help you at all?"

It is the new assistant. I have only met her a handful of times, she is young, pretty, quietly efficient and far more reliable than I ever was. She offers her assistance down the phone as if all I am calling for is to order flowers, that this is nothing more than a business call, as if she can help. I grit my teeth against the sinking disappointment.

"Can you get her to call me as soon as she's back please? It's important."

"Well I would, but I'm afraid she isn't back until late Sunday night," her voice drops in tone, to the level of conspirators, salacious and secretive, "she's gone away for the weekend with Matt."

Just for a moment the world spins, the voice on the phone becomes distant and wet, bubbles in oil. Matt. Is that his name then? The man Leah had been talking to on the phone? The man I stood in the way of. How long had I been out of the house before she called him to tell him I was gone, that the coast was clear, that a weekend away sounded perfect? And how is it that this assistant who has been in Leah's life for moments as a mere employee knows his name before I do? If I needed confirmation of the distance between us, this is it. She has kept it all from me and now she is gone and I can't reach her. I hang up without saying anything else, without saying goodbye.

I know that Leah has a mobile phone that she rarely uses but keeps with her, I can always call her on that. Maybe she would come home, call around, help me. But even as I search for her number in my address book I find myself hesitating. I remember the disagreement she had on the phone while I listened, her insistence that the man on the other end be patient. What if I do call during their first weekend together and it is the last straw for him, what if he can't cope with finally having the chance to spend time with Leah only for me to prise her away?

My emotions are all over the place. Is it selfish that I feel annoyed that she isn't there when I need her so desperately? I fight the urge to dial the number, torn between my own needs and not wanting to disturb the first chance she has of a life for herself that isn't inclusive only of me.

I stare at the phone for long minutes without dialling the number and as I move to put it down on the coffee table it rings in my hand, startling me. I bring it sharply to my ear.

"Leah?"

"No, it's Alex. Where the hell did you get to last night?" Her anger seethes through the holes in the receiver, pushing Leah out of my head for the time being.

"I can't believe you left me there by myself. I felt like a total twat when I realised you'd gone!"

Words of explanation swell and lodge in my mouth, there is no good place to begin, no easy way to explain my lack of cognition, the absence of any explanation.

"Look, I know you're mad at me and, God knows, I would be too if the situation were reversed, but please believe me when I say there is no way I would have done that on purpose."

Her answering laugh is sharp, brittle, the antithesis of Jane's tinkling giggle of moments before.

"Not on purpose! Go on then tell me, Oh Great Wise One, how do you accidentally ditch someone in the middle of a club? One minute you were sitting with some cute guy, all smiley and sweet, flirting like there's no tomorrow, and the next you're gone. I looked everywhere for you. Got some pretty strange looks knocking on toilet doors I can tell you, and I got told to fuck off by a huge intimidating blonde, before realising you had actually deserted me. I even got the taxi to detour to your place in case you'd been taken ill or something, I wanted to make sure you were okay, but nope, no sign of you. Thanks a bunch Sarah, I really appreciate it."

"Alex, I'm so sorry, I really am but I am so confused." I know she hears the tears in my voice, even though I am trying to hide them. I know it from her silence, the conscious biting back of her anger.

"I don't remember what happened last night. I remember

seeing you on the dance floor when I was having a drink with Cam, the cute guy, but after that it's all blurred. I can't remember leaving the club." The sob leaps from my throat and pushes against her ears before I can stop it. "The next thing I remember is coming round alone in a taxi, miles away from Exeter."

I hear her sharp intake of breath and feel a surge of gratitude that I do not have to explain this, that she understands the terror in me.

"I think I might have been drugged or something. I was so scared, Alex, so, so scared. I didn't know what to do."

Tears make the telephone slippery against my cheek and I close my eyes tightly to hold them in, listening to the silence from the other end.

"Alex, please say something."

"I'm coming over," she replies, all traces of anger gone from her voice, and it is my turn to stare at the receiver as someone hangs up without saying goodbye.

The coffee is brewing in the cafetiere and my face is scrubbed pink and shiny by the time Alex knocks on the door. I am still not dressed, she has been too quick for that but I have done the best that I can to make myself look comfortable, rested. The lines around her eyes tell me I haven't succeeded, my own eyes are still too wide and my smile too false. She throws her arms around me and squeezes tight. I cry again into her shoulder as she makes soothing sounds and rubs at my back as if I am a child.

When I finish she makes me sit down while she pours the coffee. I tell her everything I know, all that I can remember about the taxi ride and the painful walk home. She gets on her knees and examines the cuts on the bottom of my feet.

"They're not too bad really," she tells me. "They aren't deep but they will be a bit sore for a couple of days. Where are your plasters? I'll put a couple on the worst ones just to cushion them and make it a bit less painful to walk."

I direct her to a drawer in the kitchen and sip at my coffee while she plays nurse. When she has finished she sits next to me and takes my hand in both of hers.

"Have you got any other injuries?" she asks, her voice so gentle I can barely hear it. "I mean, like, you know… "

A blush warms my face as I shake my head. "Nothing, I checked when I got home. I don't think anything happened like that, an assault or anything."

"Well that's a relief anyway."

She rubs a hand across her forehead as I take a deep breath.

"I'm worried that maybe this is something to do with my head injuries. You know Doctor Marsden thinks I should see a psychiatrist? What if it's because he thinks I'm going mad? Because that's how I feel Alex, right now I feel like I'm going mad. I feel so confused, so all over the place. The forgetting is the worst thing; my memory doesn't seem to be getting any better. Like not remembering last night."

"Have you mentioned that to Doctor Marsden?"

"Yeah, last time I went to see him. He thinks it's probably connected to this Post-Traumatic Stress thing as it's quite a common symptom, he said the psychiatrist will probably be able to help with it."

"And do you think you'll go, to the psychiatrist?" I look away from her and nod, feeling a little ashamed, feeling that admitting it means that I have a problem, that I am going mad after all.

"Well it's about time you did something a bit more proactive about your issues. Who knows, maybe he'll be able to help you break out of your little bubble and start living a bit." She reaches over again to pat the back of my hand. "I think the first thing we need to do is go to the walk-in centre and see if they can find out if you've been given anything nasty. It's only round the corner so it shouldn't hurt your feet, or cause you to have a total freak-out on me."

She smiles indulgently but I see the concern behind it as she stands up, taking my upper arm to help me to my tender feet. I lean against her.

"Thank you Alex." Only three words but I stumble over them.

"I don't want your thanks, just buy me chocolate," she says with a quiet laugh that attempts to sweep the bad things away. "Now go and get dressed."

She pats me on the bottom, a gentle nudge in the direction of the bedroom before turning to pour herself another coffee.

I step into darkness, the blinds still drawn against the morning light, and snap the light on as I move towards the dressing table; still strewn with the confusion of cosmetics Alex painted me with a lifetime ago. I pull a tissue from a box and swipe half-heartedly at some spilled powder, a lipstick smear, before giving up and discarding the fragile cloth, it can wait. Lifting my favourite lipstick I go to slot its lid back on before frowning into the little silver tube. The colour is almost gone, the end jagged. I twist the tube to find barely a millimetre of it left. I hadn't taken it with me last night and it had been whole when I used it before. I meet my own frowning gaze in the mirror.

I lay the tube to one side and pull open the drawers beneath it, extracting underwear and a plain white vest. I fumble with the vest and drop it on the floor, turning my head as I bend to retrieve it to avoid banging it on the back of the dresser chair. The broken part of my lipstick is at the foot of the wardrobe, flattened and smeared, the shape of a foot that then dragged itself clean on the carpet.

"Alex?" I call and she is beside me immediately. "Did you do that before we went out?" I point at the floor and she looks at it with a shrug.

"Yep, it's a terrible habit of mine, smushing people's make-up into the carpet and not cleaning it up. The mums are making me go to counselling for it, all the neighbours have complained."

I look into her bland expression and sigh.

"So that's a no then!"

"Of course it's a no. I would have at least made an effort to clean it up, you doughnut."

"I don't remember doing it."

Her face grows less sardonic, more gentle.

"I think that last night is a bit of a blur anyway, Sarah, I think a bit of spilled make-up is irrelevant right now."

And I nod, because she is right, it must have been me.

Chapter Thirty-Eight

We sit opposite each other, her in the armchair, me tucked small and insignificant into the edge of the sofa. I'm sitting above the crack at the side of the cushion, the crack that hid the cufflink that became a snowball that sped away from us all and wreaked destruction below.

The room is in a misty kind of gloom, the curtains drawn, a little light spilling in through the tattered edge. My father once told me that a mouse got in one day and nibbled on the edge of the curtain, stealing it away in his big fat pouches. I imagined that somewhere behind the skirting boards there was a little mouse family – mother, father, brothers and sisters – and they had curtains just like ours but in perfect miniature; made by tiny little paws for a tiny little window. I imagined that the mother was kind and sweet and that the father was always there for his tiny little mouse children. I wish I was with them, that they were my family too.

She moves then and my eyes fly to her hands, waiting for something to happen, something to carve a path through the still, silent, oppressive room. She lights a fresh cigarette from the stub of the old one, breathes more fog into the air. I hear a car go past outside the window, somewhere down the road a lawn mower stutters into life. Beyond these walls normal life is unfolding for people, their days are full of routine, of events that slot neatly into the normality of their lives. They are not me. Down the hall the clock is ticking the seconds away, a fly is buzzing. I try to make my breath silent in my chest; try to fight the cough that rises in my lungs as her smoke fills them.

She is wearing a yellow sundress, it sits off her shoulders and the scant light from the window pools shadows by her collar bone, makes her beautiful face angled and harsh. Her hair is piled on top of her head in curls and waves; her neck looks too thin to hold the weight of it up. I am still wearing my pyjamas, they are pink and stained and they smell unclean. I can't remember the last time she washed anything. I can't remember the last time she ran a bath for me, rubbed shampoo into my hair, pulled a comb through it. She looks perfect and ready to face the world and I am sitting here, dirty and fading, behind the curtains where nobody can see me.

I should be in school today. I should be sitting in my sunshine classroom, pencil in my hand, learning maths or spellings or geography. I should be running around the playground playing hide and seek or skipping or just talking to my friends. I should be sitting in the school hall eating the lunch that they put in front of me with fresh fruit and yoghurt, a drink of juice. I should be putting something in my belly, something that chases away the painful empty feeling. I should be an altogether different little girl living an altogether different life.

But I am not. I am here in this space full of smoke, and my mother, who loved me once but seems to have forgotten, is staring at me from across the room. The time drags on and on forever and ever and I think I will sit here until I die. I will rot into the chair, seeping slowly into the fabric and my mother will still sit there, opposite me, in her yellow dress with her yellow lungs and her yellow fingers and she will stare and stare and stare at me as I slowly bleed away, turning into a skeleton and crumbling to dust.

Chapter Thirty-Nine

Alex is talking on the phone in the kitchen, her voice hushed, determined. I don't know why she doesn't want me to hear what she is saying. Perhaps she is afraid that if I overhear her recapping the events of the night before, I will spin out completely and sink slowly into lunacy. I pluck at loose threads on my jeans, rub the bruised and painful soles of my feet, wincing as I do so and scrape the flaking nail varnish from my fingernails with my thumb, all the while trying not to hear the occasional word that filters through to the silent space in which I sit. I wonder how many times in my life I have sat in a room while someone beyond a doorway speaks about me in a voice that implies I shouldn't overhear. I hear the beep of the phone as she hangs up chased by a sigh.

"They're going to send someone out, but they can't say for sure when it will be. They say it isn't their highest priority."

Her fingers curl into imaginary quotation marks, her tone mimicking the voice she has spoken to, her perplexed expression informs me that she cannot understand how this could be. How her friend potentially being drugged and abducted could be viewed with anything less than urgency.

I think of what could be before me on the list, picturing a car with the roof peeled back like an open can, a young woman in her skirt and bra expecting to go on a date but instead being told her family are dead, gone forever, apart from a weak and fragile heartbeat that blips softly across a screen. There are a million things worse for the police to face than a drunken night that ends in disaster.

"Do I have to wait in for them?" I ask.

"Judging by what they said and reading between the lines, as there is no obvious sign of... of an assault, I don't think they are in any rush to get here, they do suggest that going to the walk-in centre is a good idea though, if you have any concerns."

And I think how could I not have concerns? I try to think clearly, to work out what may have happened and when, but the more I try to think things through, to place them in some kind of linear order so that it all makes sense, the more confused I become. Nothing is making sense at the moment, everything is blurred and incomprehensible. I sigh and brush at the varnish flakes that have fallen onto the leg of my jeans, watching as they tumble slowly to the laminate flooring where I can sweep them up later. I think of lipstick pressed into the carpet and wonder what I can do to get that out.

"What do you think happened to me?" I ask and her look is sympathetic. "Do you think I was drugged?"

"I don't know, but something has definitely happened and hopefully the doctor will be able to shed some light on it. What about the man you were having a drink with, do you think he could have dropped something into your drink?"

I think back again to what I can remember of Cam. I see the tattoo, the delicacy of the black, soft lines of the angel wings. I see sadness in his face, the grief that he carries so plainly and unashamedly around with him.

"I just can't see that at all, he seemed so nice, so gentle and he had friends with him, he wasn't drinking so he could drive them all home. I doubt he would have drugged me and bundled me into a taxi before that."

"You're probably right. Is there anything else coming back to you, anything at all, even if it's little?"

"I can't remember anything else. Maybe something will come back." But even as I say it I think that nothing will, it is one more thing hidden away, lost.

I stand up and walk into the kitchen, taking a glass from the draining board and filling it with water to ease the dryness in my throat. One of the drawers is partially open and I move towards it, thinking that Alex must have left it so. As I reach out my hand to close it there is a flash of yellow and instead I pull the drawer outwards. Inside there is a doll dressed in a vet outfit, one of her shoes missing. I stare at it for what seems like an hour and then Alex is next to me, staring too. I think of lipstick on the floor, dolls where they shouldn't be.

"I think someone has been in here."

"What makes you think that?"

"This doll, I didn't put it here. I don't even remember packing it come to think of it. Leah said it was mine when I was a little girl but I haven't looked at it for a long time, I didn't think I had brought it with me."

"Perhaps Leah brought it over and popped it in here when she realised you'd left it behind."

I meet her eyes as she looks for the rational, the obvious, in a day which began with none.

"Leah has never been here," I say and Alex tries again, perhaps I overlooked it, perhaps I forgot I put it in here. But I know that I didn't, I would remember, I am too determined to keep everything in its rightful place. Eventually my confusion spreads through the air, meets Alex's rationale.

"Have you noticed if anything is missing?" she asks as we walk back into the lounge and I shake my head.

I don't have anything of value here; sentimental things perhaps, pictures of my dead family, my diaries. But other than the larger electrical goods, which are still in plain view, there is nothing.

I shake my head. "Not that I've noticed."

"Well that's something I suppose. Are you sure, Sarah, sure that it wasn't in the drawer?"

194

And I think that I am, perhaps. I think about how forgetful I can be, how unaware. What if this doll is another symptom of that, a physical reminder that I should make that appointment?

"I don't know, I can't remember putting it in there."

"What do you want to do?"

I know she asks because she herself does not know, that her suggestions are fading and she has nothing to fall back on.

"Have you called Leah to let her know what is going on?"

I stare at the floor, at the coloured broken flecks of nail varnish that stand out sharply against the pale flooring.

"She isn't there," I say. "I tried to call her earlier and she has gone away for the weekend."

I wonder if Alex hears the betrayal in my smaller voice, she has known me for long enough to know that Leah has always been there for me. Not now though, I tell her that the phone in her house had rung out, that Jane had been unable to pass on a message.

"What about her mobile?" she asks and I shake my head.

"I can't call her, I don't want to ruin their weekend."

Alex nods and beneath the concern she looks almost proud.

"Ah well, I'm here to hold your hand and chase the bad things away until she comes home." She pulls a light-hearted expression across her worried face.

"That will be more chocolate I owe you then," I reply and rest my head against her shoulder.

The NHS walk-in centre is busier than I imagined at this time on a Saturday morning. All of the seats in the waiting room are taken and some of the waiting children resort to sitting on the floor, reading books they find in a rack against the wall, near some giant building blocks and a spinning wall maze.

A thirty something mother sits pale and faint, leaning back against the pallid blue wall, three children arguing indifferently with each other at her feet. She appears not to have the strength to stop them and closes her eyes as their voices wash over her. An old man with a bald, age-spotted scalp faces an equally elderly tiny woman in the far corner of the room, he is holding her hands in his and looking deeply into her eyes, she smiles at him in a way that excludes everyone else in the room but there is concern on his face and every so often he looks around, his smile fading, as if willing someone to be there with them so he can make everything right.

A wild-eyed man with a matted beard and filthy clothes wanders back and forth near the door, muttering to himself and once in a while swearing loudly, his words chased by muted laughter from the older children. The ill-looking mother glances uneasily at him before looking back at her children.

The majority of the others are in their late teens or early twenties, many with the hooded, painful look of the morning after. They sit in isolation in this crowded room, looking a little embarrassed, obviously wishing they were anywhere but here. I remember that this centre also holds a sexual health clinic and wonder how many of those waiting are here for emergency contraception or sexual advice of some kind.

Alex and I sit in silence, holding each other's hand. There is nothing to say that I want overheard by strangers and Alex's stillness tells the same story. By the time we are called in to see the doctor, the waiting room has almost emptied and filled up again. My throat is dry and I lament the fact that I have no change on me to buy a drink from the lone vending machine. Alex walks with me up the stairs and to the doctor's room but chooses to wait outside and I am grateful for my solitude as I step over the threshold.

The blonde-haired woman at the over-large desk introduces herself as Doctor Ferguson as I take a seat and begin telling her what I think may have happened, realising as I speak, the fragility of my words, of my knowledge. Not for the first time I curse the vacant spaces that have taken up residence in my head.

"So as far as you are aware there are no signs of sexual

assault, no soreness, bruising, bite marks, anything like that?"

I shake my head. "Well it doesn't feel like anything has been done to me, I don't feel uncomfortable or sore at all and I'm not bleeding there either. I would be bleeding wouldn't I, if anyone had done anything to me?" My voice climbs an octave and I lower the volume to compensate.

The sympathy on the doctor's face as she looks at my red face, my trembling mouth, brings tears to my eyes.

"The likelihood is that there would be some discomfort if you had been raped or sexually assaulted, yes. But if you want to be certain I can carry out an examination for you."

I consider it for mere seconds before I shake my head, too embarrassed to agree. It is not just ignorance that spurs my refusal. Despite the harrowing hours during which I walked through the night, the unknown moments that lead up to it, I believe that I was physically untouched. Surely I would know on some level if something had been done to me.

I tell her so and she looks at me with compassion and understanding, she has heard excuses like this before and no doubt knows that sometimes, even in situations such as these, ignorance can be bliss. Can be necessary.

"So," she says after typing some information into the computer on her desk, "where would you like us to go from here?"

I look out of the second-floor window, over grey rooftops covered in seagull feathers and droppings. I don't meet her eyes as I speak.

"I want to find out for sure if I have been drugged or not. I've been having some confusion lately, I've been a bit forgetful, I was brain damaged as a child and I've been getting quite a few headaches recently. This felt different somehow and I'm concerned that I may have been given something that might make me ill or have some really awful side effects."

She writes something else down before meeting my eyes. "I'm afraid there isn't anything I can do for you in that respect. I know that on television and in films there are often these

197

incredible toxicology screens that tell people what is going on with their blood etcetera but sadly, the reality is that those tests are expensive and pointless. I could take your blood and send it off, but many of the date rape drugs pass out of one's system within just a few hours. By the time the test results came back in three or four weeks, even if the results were positive any symptoms would be long gone and so the test results would be unnecessary. All I can really do is treat any symptoms you are displaying at the moment and as you don't appear to have any then the chances are that, if you were given anything untoward, it has already left your system."

I must look crestfallen, I certainly feel it.

She leans forwards and peers up through long eyelashes. "I can understand that you want to know for sure what happened to you and I'm truly sorry that I can't give you a definitive answer. I can tell you that in my experience of working in this centre the most common drug routinely used to incapacitate people is actually alcohol. Rohypnol and others such as Gamma-Hydroxybutyrate are much less common. It is possible that your drinks were spiked to make them stronger, but we have no way of testing for that."

My hands lay clasped in my lap and I stare at them as she talks, wishing I hadn't chipped some of the polish off and made them look rough and cheap; wishing, too, that I hadn't come here, hadn't sat for hours in the waiting room wondering about the others there, wondering if they would be okay. I wish I had stayed at home and idled the time away. Alex has wasted her day beside me, too, as I seek answers that don't exist.

"Well, thank you for seeing me, Doctor," I mutter, feeling stupidly formal, underprepared for the ending of this conversation, the lack of answers. She nods and smiles around her mouth, her eyes still grave and concerned.

"If all you really want is a definitive answer, regardless of what that would mean, if it is simply a case of wanting to know so that you can try and make sense of what has happened to you, then you could go and see a private doctor. They would almost certainly do a test for you. You would have to wait a few weeks for the results and there are no guarantees anyway as any drug may have left your system by the time the tests are conducted. I'm not sure I would recommend that route purely because you could end up paying money and being no closer to the truth, but that option is there if you want to take that chance." She gives me a genuine smile. "One further thing, it's probably better to be on the safe side and make sure there is someone with you for the next twenty-four hours if that is possible. Just to monitor your behaviour in case there is some kind of drug in your system. It's just precautionary you understand."

I nod, stand up and thank her, closing the door behind me. I go to ask Alex if she minds the thought of babysitting me until tomorrow.

Chapter Forty

When I woke up, the house was in darkness. A vague glow came from behind the thin curtains. If I opened them I knew I would see the dark branches of the oak tree waving in silhouette in front of the house, the flickering glow of the streetlamp behind the limbs playing hide and seek. The path would look cold and two-dimensional, the road darker still. Parked cars would reflect the light from their roofs while their windows remained blank, insides hidden. All would be still and calm as the world slept. I had watched it before, looking out with wide nervous eyes into an alien world of muted colour. I had been afraid of the stillness, of the lack of vitality and life amid the flat and bleak reality outside my window.

I winced when I moved, whimpered quietly beneath my breath. I could not let her hear me. I must not wake her up. She would come running, her voice shrill and piercing; there would be punishment written across the palm of her hands. I was more afraid of her than ever before and I realised that my father's presence had held her within the realms of normality; while he was near she had been forced to hide her cruel self from him. She had been compelled to pretend in the days when she could look at the clock and see the hour hands point to an opening door, a cheery hello. Since he had gone, since the door had failed to open at the end of the working day, the clock was no longer her monitor, she had forgotten it altogether and it sat dusty and grim on the mantle, dusty and grim like her.

There was no more routine, no more school, no more mealtimes. There was just us, her and me, dancing around each other carefully like fighting birds and my fear of her grew daily. Her eyes blazed in my direction, her cruelty thoughtless, casual almost. If I looked at her or spoke to her, if I moved in the wrong direction, stepped too loudly, flushed the chain at the wrong moment, sighed too forcefully, it would bring the sword of Damocles down upon my fragile, frightened head. I was careful to never meet her stare, her eyes and the vacancy in them burned deeply into my nightmares. I wondered when I had stopped thinking in terms of making her happy and focussed instead on ways to avoid making her angry.

My empty stomach was quietened with dry crackers, green-flecked bread, cheese that had gone shiny and cracked at the edges; whatever I could find in the cupboards to stop the churning, protesting ache in the hours before she woke. One morning I watched the milkman deliver to the neighbours; not to us, he never stopped at our house. I looked at the milk bottles, blue-white and glistening against the red-painted front door and I couldn't resist. I let myself out into the cold morning light and cautiously crossed the street, my feet bare and numb against the freezing cold road. I snatched up the bottle and tucked behind the smelly bins as I drank it greedily. It sat sickly and foul in my stomach for the rest of the morning. Later I watched through my window as Mr Cambridge came out and looked at the bottles left behind, perhaps he thought it an error on the milkman's part and nothing was ever said. The guilt of it sat inside me, rancid and nauseating.

My school uniform was curled into the dusty, filthy bundle of clothes at the bottom of my wardrobe. When I looked at it I started to cry. I wondered what my friends were doing, what my teachers were thinking. Had they given my seat to someone else, someone who bothered to turn up? Had they forgotten all about me? I wondered if my class teacher, Mrs Jacobs, had had her baby, if the school trip to the zoo had taken place, if I was in trouble for simply ceasing to be. I wondered if anybody ever thought of me. I had no idea how long it had been since I walked through the double doors into my brightly coloured classroom. It was long enough for me to think that I was totally forgotten, totally invisible. But then something happened, something changed and I wasn't invisible anymore.

They came that morning, the visitors in their suits, sincerity on their faces, eager to help. But it seemed that she was their focus and that they only wanted to help her, not me. I was nothing to them it seemed. Afterwards, I realised that she knew they were coming, she had been expecting them. All the signs of their imminent arrival were there but I was confused by them, uncertain, at least until I heard the knock on the door.

She got up before me, an unusual occurrence after I became used to the dim mornings spent in isolation, moving like a ghost through the dust motes hovering in the light that poured through the gaps in the plastic kitchen blinds. She cast aside her dressing gown and I heard the increasingly unfamiliar sound of water flowing into the bath; the loud whoosh as it moved through geriatric pipes. By the time she emerged – steam billowing through the open door like some kind of ethereal mist – her skin was scrubbed and pink, she smelled like lilies.

Stepping into my room she took me by the arm and pulled me from beneath the covers without once opening her mouth to speak. Her movements were frantic, hurried and determined as she pulled me quickly after her into the bathroom, where I was unceremoniously stripped of my nightdress and plonked into her used water. I squirmed as the intense heat pushed sharp and tingling against my skin, I tried to hold myself away from the greying soap scum that lapped at the gritty tide line on the stained enamel. I tried not to cry out against the coarse treatment as she scoured the grime from my skin, rubbed me roughly with a harsh towel.

"Go and put something clean on."

Her voice was pinched and anxious. I hurried down the hall to stare forlornly at the contents of my wardrobe and wonder what clothes I could put on that wouldn't make her mad, wouldn't offend her. The only items that were clean belonged to last year's child, an altogether happier little girl, who still remembered what her father's aftershave smelt like when he kissed her goodbye in the mornings. I hesitated in front of my old clothes long enough for her to wonder where I had got to. She walked up the hall on silent feet and looked around the door, making me jump. Her eyes zoomed in on where I stood in my sagging grey underwear.

"Hurry up for fuck's sake."

I turned quickly, randomly snatched a dress from the back of the rail, an old blue corduroy pinafore that I hadn't worn for months, and slipped it over my head, surprised at its looseness, at how time was making me slowly fade away. She stepped into the room, sat on my bed pulling me in front of her and began brushing my hair. There was no gentleness, no careful teasing of the days and days' worth of knots, she put the bristles at my fringe and pulled back, her hand braced against me so I didn't fall onto her. My head snapped backwards and she smacked the back of it with the flat of the hairbrush.

"Keep your head up, please."

Her voice was light, cajoling, though her actions were harsh and I cried against the pulling at my scalp; she didn't seem to notice. I heard in her voice the mother she used to be, my fairy tale mummy who had somehow been replaced by an evil step-mother, a woman who looked the same, talked the same but had forgotten to love me, had forgotten to care.

By the time they knocked on the door – sounding official even in the way they rapped with their knuckles – I was primped and preened and clean for the first time in days. As she invited the two women in, showed them to the unusually tidy lounge, a space with open curtains and daylight penetrating corners that had been hidden for too long, I hovered near the doorway awkwardly and wondered who they were.

"Come here, darling," she said, her voice like meringue, crisp and soft.

She gestured with a smile and though her face was warm her hand movement was flustered, disjointed and I hurried to do as she commanded, to keep the smile on her face just a little while longer. She turned her face from me.

"She has been a godsend you know, with everything that is going on at the moment. I really don't know what I would have done without her."

Her voice was wounded, delicate; a little hitch in the middle that her words found difficult to climb over. I saw the understanding, the sympathy grow on the faces of her audience and I thought that I was lost, done for, that she had sucked them in with her lies.

She turned to me then and planted the gentlest of kisses on my cheek, a soft and perfumed reminder of what we had once been, of what I had lost. I touched where her lips had been with my fingertips, lightly, as though I were afraid I would knock the kiss to the floor where it would fester and become meaningless. I didn't yet know that it would be the last time she ever kissed me.

Her gaze met mine; briefly and without the usual scorn and she saw the tears that threatened at my lashes. I tried not to see the brief pinch of irritation that flashed in her eyes. She turned me deftly, lightly, until I faced the door.

"Would you mind going and playing in your room darling,

just while us grown-ups talk for a little while?"

She spoke as if her request were unusual, as if she never wanted me out of her sight. She spoke as if asking me to leave pained her and she would miss me even for such a short separation. I knew they would be charmed by her, when she was like this, most people were. I had been until the moment she no longer tried, until she put away her mask.

I left the room, pulling the door shut behind me and I listened for a little while as she lied and spun the web of a different life, where she was the victim and I was loved and cherished. Her voice was small and failed to push all the way through the wood of the door to where I stood, but I heard enough anyway. In a plaintive voice she told them that she knew it was wrong not sending me to school but she needed help, she wasn't well. Her doctor told her she needed someone to look after her and what choice did she have? After all, my father had abandoned us both and left her floundering, helpless.

I turned then and headed up the stairs as quietly as I could, so the three women in the front room wouldn't know I had stayed there and listened to words not meant for me. Even the whisper of my feet against the carpet sounded loud to my ears and I thought she would know anyway, she always seemed to sniff out any wrongdoing on my part, even when it was made up in her head, even if the only place it sat was among the voices that told her what a horrible person I was.

I sat on the edge of my bed amid the stale musty odour of neglect and waited for them to leave, fearful of the fallout from their visit, of where the blame would lie for it. By the time I heard the front door close and her feet treading heavily up the stairs what seemed like hours later, I hadn't moved from the place I sat down. I watched the door and tried to gauge by the weight of her walking the kind of mood she was in. Eventually it pushed inwards with

205

a whispered sigh and she leaned against the doorway, her face heavy, bleak with exhaustion.

There were deep grooves near the corners of her mouth, carved by unjust anger. She walked slowly across the carpet towards me. Leaning down she reached out her hand, and saw me flinch from it. She seemed unconcerned by my reaction as she stroked my hair gently and I fought the sudden urge to rest my head against her palm. After a moment had passed, her hand curled into a claw, tighter and tighter until my hair was gripped in an iron fist and she pulled me to my feet. When she started speaking, her voice almost a whisper, she punctuated her words with a sharp tug on my hair that pulled me one way then the other.

"Well, that was all good fun wasn't it? It's all your bastard father's fault you know? He walked out on me and left me with nothing. It's not like he's been to see you at all is it? But it's me that gets the blame for not coping. Typical bloody man, nothing more than a glorified sperm donor. Well fuck him, fuck him all to hell!"

She threw me then, backwards against the edge of my bed, the wood banging into my hip with such force it stole my breath away. She looked down at where I cried on the floor, her eyes full of indifference before she turned and walked out, slamming the door as she left. I stared wet-eyed at the dirty white surface, my stomach hollow and queasy.

Fuck him all to hell!

It was the last thing she ever said to me. When I woke up the following morning – my pinafore bunched up by my bruised and aching hips and twisted uncomfortably around my torso – she was gone. I could still feel her Judas kiss on my cheek.

Chapter Forty-One

The knock at the door comes as I look in the mirror and imagine the lipstick stain at my feet. I came back from the clinic with Alex and watched as she placed some tissue over the stain and ran a hot iron over it to soak the waxy cosmetic up. The next day after she had gone I did the same thing, but the carpet was still marked and looking at it made me feel edgy. Now, two weeks later, I stand over the fading mark and see in the mirror the lines that draw down the corners of my mouth and make me appear older, more worn. I feel shaded in when I stand here, black and white, and I don't quite know why. I am Lady Macbeth and the red stain plagues me.

No matter how much I try to convince myself that I somehow dropped the lipstick onto the floor and stepped on it, that I am responsible, I cannot help but imagine the ghost footprints across my floor, the subtle traces of some unknown intruder. They cannot be erased. They walk through my memory, leaving traces and doubt, whispering to me that I have to learn to live with them.

When Alex had gone, I phoned a locksmith and he came out as a priority that cost me over a hundred pounds, and changed the locks in the flat. I felt more secure once he had left and the new keys were securely tucked away in my handbag. There were three altogether, two of them for me and I asked for a spare to give to Leah so that she always had access to my home. I knew, perhaps more than most, how emergencies could arise and change the path of someone's life and I trusted her to keep it safe, to not let anyone else have it.

Leah had phoned me shortly after she got back and I ignored the call, too raw from the events of the weekend to feel able to speak normally. She would hear the strain in my voice, insist on being here and I couldn't bring myself to tell her yet what had happened. The phone rang out and she left no message, a sequence that repeated several times over the next couple of days. Eventually her small voice spoke into the answer phone; she is concerned about me, she hasn't heard from me, am I okay. I can't ignore the worry in her words and brace myself to call her back.

The conversation is stilted on both sides. My side of the talking tainted by the previous weekend's events, her ignorance of all that has happened acting like a dam, stopping words that I don't even know how to begin. My knowledge of her trip away and the shadow of her accusation, her lack of communication before she went, the growing gulf between us, act like interference on the line, an obstacle neither of us can feel our way around or over. Our sentences are too short, the pauses uncomfortably long. I don't ask her about her weekend and my silence adds further layers to the barriers between us.

"I wondered if you wanted to meet for lunch one day next week, Sarah, just the two of us."

Would she have clarified that before, that there would be no-one but us? When had it ever been different? I sense the reassurance in her voice, her desire to tell me that nothing has changed but the difference is there in her need to say the words and we both feel the rocky surface beneath our feet. How often have we talked on the phone before this? Apart from a quick call or text to say I would be late in for work there has never been any need before, we were always orbiting each other, like binary stars. Now I balance on the telephone line that links me to her, carefully stepping forwards, feeling my way blindly and hoping I won't fall.

"That would be nice. Where and when?"

"How about Gerald's on Thursday?"

Her words are spoken fast as if to prevent me changing my mind, chased by relief that I have agreed. Her choice of my favourite restaurant near the Cathedral speaks volumes about the foundations she is trying to lay for this particular bridge.

"Sounds perfect," I say and try to mean it. "About one o'clock?"

She murmurs her assent and we end the call simultaneously, saying goodbye in a way that merges together, the words losing volume and meaning as they collide.

How can I sit opposite her and tell her what happened? Would she blame herself for not being there? I am in two minds about what to do. If I don't tell her and she finds out then surely it will only add to the growing distance between us. But it isn't that easy. Through the hurt of being left out of an important part of her life and the confusion of feeling she wanted me out of her home there is also that part of me that remains glad for her that her life is no longer intrinsically linked to mine. I want to see her happy and beneath my childish jealousy I am pleased at the idea that for the first time in my memory she has someone else to turn to, someone to lean on. She has carried a lot on her slight shoulders for far too long now.

Deciding not to talk about it at all becomes easy in the end. For her sake I will stay quiet until things have settled in with her new man, until I know if he will be hanging around long enough to cope with my difficulties by proxy. I think about all of this as I look in the mirror, thoughts that are scattered when there is a knock at the door that makes me jump.

When Alex called around, when the locksmith turned up they both pushed the doorbell on the ground floor. I had spoken to them through the intercom system, identifying them before I pressed the button to release the doors and let them up. Someone knocking on the inner door is different. Whoever is the other side of the wooden barrier has gotten through the security of the outer door, up the stairs and to the door of my apartment.

I freeze where I stand as I think of the doll in the drawer, the blood-like stain on the bedroom carpet. The coffee churns like lava in my stomach and sickness rises to my throat. Surely this must be something sinister, the secret person who knows the way into the building, who knows the code, who until recently may have had a key for the very door they are knocking on. Who else can it be? Who else would come in through the lobby without buzzing up to me first to announce their arrival? My fear renders me speechless and still until I can do nothing but sit here and not respond.

When the knock comes again it is louder, more insistent and followed by a deep voice that sounds impatient and gruff.

"Miss Phillips, are you in there? This is the police."

I snap out of my horror and hurry to the door immediately, a Pavlovian reaction, an altogether different type of adrenalin coursing through me as I wonder what has happened before pausing and remembering what Alex said days before, that they would come round, that they hadn't treated this visit as urgent. I look through the fisheye in the door, the distorted shapes of two uniformed officers filling the elongated lens, before releasing the chain and swinging it open.

The two men who stand there look young and fresh-faced; they don't appear to be much older than me. One is shorter, rounder, the other pale and blue-eyed.

"Miss Phillips?" the shorter one asks and I nod, wondering at the weight of their uniforms, at the many items attached to them.

"May we come in please?"

I begin to nod then stop myself, hesitating. "Can I see your ID?" I ask, seeing the nervous energy leap from my mouth towards their ears like a blown kiss.

"Of course," he replies and they both remove their information from one of their many pockets and hand it over. "There's a number on there that you can call to verify who we are," he says helpfully, his voice holding only a hint of resignation at the delay.

Instantly I feel silly and over the top, a swooning Victorian woman. I stand aside and wave them in to the lounge, inviting them to sit and offering tea or coffee before realising the tea is nonexistent. I am relieved when they decline and sit opposite the space where they perch awkwardly on the edge of the sofa as if reluctant to get too comfortable.

"I take it you are here about the night out," I say. "I've been to the walk-in centre and the doctor there said there is no way of knowing if I was drugged or not."

My voice runs ahead of me like a steam train until I catch the sidelong glance between the two men and careen to a halt. "What is it?" I ask, looking from one of them to the other and back again.

"We aren't here about that, Miss Phillips," he says and his voice is serious.

My heart skips a beat as both men look at me with raised eyebrows. "Then what is it, what's happened?"

"We have received a complaint about someone at this address from an individual, Miss Phillips. That is why we are here, to investigate it further."

I cannot hide my surprise, it opens my mouth, pushes my eyebrows up. "What complaint? What individual?"

"Do you know a man called Robert Jay, Miss Phillips, from Reading?"

My mind scrambles instantly across years and experiences, fleeting tastes of old kisses fill my open mouth as I step into a past that I still own, a time that stays in my memory and has not been stolen away by amnesia.

"Well yes, I mean no… " I try again. "Yes I knew Robert Jay but last I heard he was living in Scotland, not Reading.

Though that was years ago," I reply as if this makes all the difference to the randomness of their questioning.

Again there is the look between them and I wondered if they could speak at all without having this silent communication first. I wonder if they are trained to do this to enhance tension, to prompt questions from the person who looks at them and queries why they are visiting, what else they may have to say.

The taller of the two speaks next, his voice higher-pitched than I expected as if he has been stretched upwards and it pulled his vocal chords tighter and thinner.

"The police service in Reading received a complaint from Mr Jay regarding malicious phone calls that he has been receiving over the last few weeks. These have been fairly significant in number."

I wonder how it is that the police can come out for malicious phone calls but they have yet to put in an appearance regarding a night out that ended in fear and confusion. I am about to ask them that very thing but they meet my eyes with such gravity that I keep my words behind tightly sealed lips.

"Is there anything you would like to tell us, Miss Phillips?" The shorter of the two speaks again, as if they are a tag team, little boys taking it in turns.

"I don't understand what you mean. What could I tell you? I don't even know why you are here talking to me about this. I haven't seen Rob Jay for more than five years."

I hear the rising of my voice, the indignation fed by puzzlement.

"We began investigating these calls a few weeks ago, Miss Phillips, and originally they were coming from a different source but as we were preparing to pay a visit to the caller, the location the calls were made from changed. We are here, Miss Phillips, because the calls are being made from your landline number."

Chapter Forty-Two

The house was still, an occasional creak or popping sound carving a path through the silence as the heat of the day faded and the walls and joists tried to catch up. In the pit of my stomach was that feeling I hated, the feeling I got when I watched a scary film or when my eyes fell onto an animal torn and distorted by a car's tyres. It was the feeling I had when I heard my mother's footsteps and waited for the door to open. But this was like nothing else I had felt before, everything was different now.

Those footsteps I had been terrified of, the sound of her breathing, the resonance of her raging anger; I would have welcomed any one of them, perhaps even the sound of her hard palm slapping against my skin. Even that would be better than the utter solitude of the house I now moved through. I was a ghost now, nobody knew I was here, nobody could see me.

It had been four days and a handful of hours since I woke up alone in a house that seemed to hold its breath in anticipation of what would happen next. The calendar hung in the kitchen, ragged-edged and curling; the pictures were of green spaces, beautiful landscapes, dramatic mountains and multicoloured heathers, places in Britain I had never seen before, places that seemed a million miles away from here. I looked at the calendar that morning after turning on the television to watch the early programmes, leaving the news on to find out the date. I made a little mark on slightly greasy paper with the edge of my blunt purple crayon. I knew I would be punished for that when she came back.

The following morning I did the same, and the one after that. Now there were four purple marks and the afternoon sun pushed through the grimy window and dripped light onto the photo of the dramatic hills and mountains of the Cumbrian fells. I felt as though I had been alone forever. I wondered if I would ever be found.

On that first morning I had woken up, my hip smarting and painful, knowing that I couldn't put off the moment I must leave the relative safety of my bedroom, knowing that I would have to move, to go downstairs and wait for her to get up. Each bleak step was slow and light as I tried not to wake her, my injured hip adding difficulty to every movement. I held onto the banisters, trod carefully at the outer edges of each stair and breathed a sigh of relief when no sound came from above me.

The kitchen cupboards yielded little food but there was still some dry cereal and I poured it as slowly as I could into the bowl I placed oh so carefully onto the kitchen table. I wondered if today would be the day my dad came home, if today would be the day I got my real mother back. I tried to hold his image lit and beautiful in my heart, but every day brought a dimming of that hope, a fading of possibilities. In my head he was taking on almost mythical proportions and he stood side by side with Father Christmas and the tooth fairy as a visitor I looked forward to arriving.

I crunched on my dry cereal, it was slightly stale, soft and dusty. I ate with my fingers and drank water to take the dryness from my throat. When I finished there was still no sound from upstairs, so I wiped out my bowl and put it back in the cupboard, knowing that if I didn't I would be punished for making a mess of a house that already had dirt crusted into its seams and corners.

In the front room I fought the urge to switch the television on, to stare mindlessly at the morning cartoons and remember a world of vibrancy and colour. The television would make a noise as I switched it on, the noise would wake her, the fear would grow. In silence, as still as a rock, I waited for her appearance, for the burden of her anger and unpredictability to descend. I waited and there was nothing. No sound from upstairs, no creaking of the bed as she moved. I listened to the world come alive outside the curtained window and still there was silence inside our walls.

An image popped unbidden into my mind, the harshly lit horror image of blood on white enamel, of slimy red-stained towels festering in the corner. Indecision clawed at my ankles as I moved slowly from the kitchen and into the hallway. Standing at the bottom of the stairs I felt tiny and insignificant and far too afraid to take the steps one at a time. Closing my eyes I tried to feel her presence, imagining it settling around me, pushing at my skin. There was nothing but the enormous-looking stairs and the absolute silence from the rooms above me.

I held my breath and took the first stair in slow motion, pausing to listen when both feet were firmly on the tread. Silence hung over the stairwell and I paused and listened again. Each step that followed was tortuously slow as I moved one foot onto the stair and then the other, bringing them together slowly and silently before pausing and holding my breath. I tilted my head, leaning my ear towards the first floor and waited to hear if there would be any indication that she was stirring above me, that she wasn't lying across her bed with her wrists bleeding out onto the already stained carpet.

Step, step, pause. Step, step, pause. It seemed to take forever and when I eventually reached the top of the stairs, having heard no sounds from above me, I paused for much longer. Trying to hear above my own heartbeat, trying to work out if it was her breath or my own that whispered into my ears. I moved to the centre of the hall, my steps becoming smaller as I went, delaying my arrival at a door I didn't want to open.

Perhaps I should just stay this side of the wood. Perhaps if I lingered long enough then she would wake up, jerk the door open and scare my faltering heart into stillness. Perhaps I should just go back downstairs and wait it out, wait for her to put in an appearance. But I knew that I couldn't. What if she really was bleeding beyond that door, in her darkened room with its spilled cosmetics and piles of clothes too lovely for the floor? What if she lay there with her eyes fixed and staring at a world beyond this one, what if she were already dead, what if she was just trying to scare me, what if she had a man in there? Because of this last one I hesitated further, knowing that if this were the case and I disturbed them, then the punishment would be so much worse.

I don't know how long I stood there waiting, torn by indecision. Perhaps if I just very lightly pushed the door she might not hear it if she was only sleeping; she would never hear it at all if she were dead. I took a step forwards, placed the palm of my hand against the cold, painted surface. I could feel the pulse in my hand, felt it press against the door as if trying to knock lightly, as if trying to betray me.

The hall stretched out and I looked down towards the door to my room, thinking perhaps I could just go back to bed, hide beneath the covers, pretend this day had never been. If I went to sleep then sometime soon she might wake up. It would be like waiting for Christmas morning to come. The sooner I slept the sooner my mother would come and wake me, shouting at my laziness, but that would be okay because she would be there, she would be alive and the world would be normal again.

But I didn't go back to bed. Instead I reached for the cheap plastic door handle and pushed it down, releasing the latch so that my beating palm could push the door inwards. It swung slowly open, revealing a dark rectangle with vague lighter shapes beyond it. The room was bleak inside and smelt stale and rank. I listened intently and heard nothing, no movement, no breathing, no life. I knew I should turn the light on, I knew I should look to see what she had done yet still I faltered.

I thought of us playing I spy, the smell of her perfume. I thought of the way she had loved me once, of the way other people looked at her, coveting her loveliness, or gazing with envy at the way she drew people's eyes. I thought of the sheer life of her, of her fading effervescence and couldn't fathom it gone, couldn't imagine it simply ceasing to be, ending here among rumpled, greying covers.

Lifting my hand to the light switch, I could no longer distinguish between heartbeats. I felt my heart burst from my chest and fly away from me, beating so fast it felt like nothing more than a vibration as it went; a hummingbird. I bit down on my lip as I snapped the light on with an audible click. The light shone painful and bright on her empty bed. The covers dishevelled and thrown back.

I pushed the thoughts of her broken and bloody form from my head and tried to fathom an altogether different reality, one I hadn't even considered; a reality in which she was alive and well and simply not here. I moved into the room and looked under the bed, in the wardrobe; I even rooted through piles of discarded clothing, dirty underwear and stained blouses, before turning my attention to the rest of the house. I searched in every corner, behind furniture, under tables. I looked out of the windows into the front and back gardens and finally – when I was no longer afraid my voice would wake her wherever she lay sleeping – I called out for her, over and over again. Until the answering, impenetrable silence told me that she was truly gone.

Chapter Forty-Three

I sit in another waiting room, in another chair, waiting for another doctor, a doctor whose face is not already mapped out in my mind. I do not yet know where his smile begins, where his laughter lines plough their furrows, if they are bigger than his frown lines. I do not count these new tiles or hopscotch my way over them. I don't look at the artwork on the walls and berate the artist for sharing a bleak vision that fails to brighten up my day. I don't hear the familiar voice of my aunt buffeting against gruff and unfamiliar tones as they spill from the invisible room beyond an open doorway.

The appointment had come through the post, redirected from the tiny cottage that still felt like home despite all that had happened. I stared at the typed words, the calling forth and wondered why I ever agreed to it. The very thought of going filled me with dread and self-loathing. Yet the answer to my agreement, to my eventual arrival here, could be found along a road I followed while terrified and alone after I had been propelled from the taxi. It lay in the dark shadows and the rustling leaves with the fear that seemed great enough to kill me, the forgetting, the nothingness that had led up to that moment. It lay in phone calls I hadn't made from a phone in my apartment and in the hands of an old doll found in a drawer where it didn't belong.

I needed to find answers. I needed a solution, a get out of jail free card so that it couldn't happen again. I felt trapped, bound by the ignorance of what had happened to me. And so I booked the appointment and now sit alone and wishing I hadn't come. I am trying to project calm poise whilst inside I am in turmoil. Inside my heart races and tells me that I should be afraid, that I am somewhere new, that all is not well and I should run. The clamour of my heart makes my hands shake against thighs that feel weak and powerless.

The seat I sit in is a bucket style, covered in mock tapestry that looks worn and threadbare, perhaps purposefully so; it gives the impression of long use, tells whoever sits here that they aren't the first, that many have passed through before them, they are not alone in their malaise. I tuck my feet close to the fading print and look at the glass-fronted cabinet opposite, not at the contents but at the flicker of myself that appears in the reflective surface. I look insubstantial, wide eyes in a pale face. I wonder if I look like my mother and wish that she hadn't died, that I had known her, that she was here with me. I wish that she was not lost in the dark places of my memory so that at least in some way she would be here to hold my hand, even if I couldn't feel it.

I had asked Leah about her and been told that she was beautiful and kind but also that she was fragile and uncertain, that perhaps she was never meant to be anyone's mother as she could barely look after herself. My father was her rock and he adored her until the end. I wanted to ask if he had gone to the funeral, if he had cried over her grave the way we had cried over his, but I saw in Leah's face a painful look, the discomfort that she often got when she was rubbing at past wounds and finding them raw and painful.

I look around the waiting area and think that, if anything, it is warmer and more comfortable than the room I sat in waiting for Doctor Marsden. The fabrics here are less practical and clinical, more homely; there are cushions on the seats, magazines on a coffee table. The tiles are a terracotta colour, the walls cream with a faint border of autumn leaves. I wait for what seems like days to be called and again wish into that waiting space that I hadn't come at all.

"Miss Phillips?"

I look up at the door that opens silently and see close-cropped salt and pepper hair above eyes full of curiosity and welcome. I stand, brush my jeans down and follow him into a room that is smaller than Doctor Marsden's and more cluttered. The air smells of dust, potpourri and faintly of cigarettes, the latter coming from the man who looks at me with a slightly raised eyebrow. In a strange way I find it a comfort, that this man before me has a habit like smoking; as if it makes him lesser somehow, not quite so laudable because he should know better, he is a doctor after all.

"It's nice to meet you Miss Phillips, I'm Doctor Charles and, as you know, you were recommended to me by my friend and colleague, Doctor Marsden. Or is it the other way around? Was it I that was recommended to you? I can't quite remember."

He looks a little puzzled yet sounds smooth and well practiced. He reminds me of the policemen who came to my flat and asked about the phone calls to Rob Jay, but I am less wary of him, he has not yet given me bad news. I shrug my shoulders slightly and wonder what difference it makes, I am here regardless and uncomfortable to be so. He looks at me silently for a few moments until I begin to feel exposed, on show, before he looks down at the notes on his desk and reads something there, moving his lips silently as he does so.

"I know from Doctor Marsden that you have always been rather reluctant to come and see me, despite his assurance that you would be in good hands. I do understand why, of course, I know that there is a certain kind of stigma attached to seeing a psychiatrist. With that in mind, Miss Phillips, during this first session what I would like to do is explain to you some of the avenues open to us. I will tell you a little bit about how I work and then I will give you the opportunity to run like hell and never look back. How does that sound?"

The smile in his voice spreads across his face making him look friendly and more welcoming. I like that he doesn't take himself too seriously, that he appears to want to put me at my ease.

"Call me Sarah," I say and he smiles again and nods.

"I have been going through your files, Sarah, so I am familiar with the issues that have been plaguing you recently. I understand that you regularly re-experience the traumatic event, the crash you went through?"

"Most nights. I dream about it almost every night just before I wake up."

"When you have these dreams, how do you feel on waking?"

"Traumatised. My heart is thumping, my skin is sweating, I feel shaky and disorientated. It's horrible really. It makes me not want to go to sleep so I can avoid the dreams."

He nods again and I wonder at how difficult I find it to truly put into words the abject terror of reliving the moment that I became an orphan, the moment I was made solitary, different.

"From your notes I can also see that you no longer travel by car, that you are forgetful and introspective and that you have certain compulsive behaviours – such as not deviating from a given route, counting your steps etcetera – that affect your day to day choices. I also understand that you have no childhood memories whatsoever. Are all of those things still applicable?"

It is my turn to nod at his more articulate summation.

"Is there anything else you would like to add?"

I look away from him. How can I tell him that just lately I feel haunted, afraid, that my fears are no longer about the hidden things in my memory, but are grounded in a reality that is threatening and unseen? His eyes have not seen the doll in the drawer, the destruction of the grave, he has not witnessed the events in the nightclub. I wonder if I put my concerns into words will he add paranoia to my list of anxieties and not see the reality, the truth of them? And so I stay silent and he takes my lack of response as a negative answer.

"From everything that I have read in your notes and the conversations with Doctor Marsden, it seems highly probable that you are suffering from Post-Traumatic Stress Disorder. The re-experiencing of the event, the avoidance of new situations, the amnesia and periods of forgetfulness and vagueness, difficulty concentrating and the nightmares, these are all recognised symptoms of PTSD."

I look down at my hands and sense his eyes touching the top of my head as I pick at my nails and feel weak and pathetic. What would it be like to be normal, to have my childhood, my family? What would it be like to not be so different from everyone else? I sit in front of the doctor's kind eyes and gentle demeanour and regret having to meet him, having him know me as a clinical subject, as something to cure, as though I myself were the disease that dwelt in my own skin.

Soldiers from warzones often suffer from Post-Traumatic Stress; the hideous things they have seen, the trauma, the horror, over and over and over again. Surely they have more right than me with all that they have been through. How can I sit here and say that my life is anything like theirs? A life I can't even remember, a trauma that is nothing more than a fragment in my nightmares, a trauma that allowed me to paint a new scene over the blank wall of my past. I feel guilty, ridiculous and I tell him so.

"That is a surprisingly common reaction, believe me. But what you need to remember is that Post-Traumatic Stress Disorder isn't related to the size of the event that triggered it, nor is it only relevant to a specific type of person. Yes, soldiers who have been involved directly in warfare can get it but so too can car crash victims, rape or abuse victims, even bystanders who have witnessed a horrific incident such as a murder or brutal attack. PTSD can potentially occur in anyone and it is no reflection on you as a person. What we have to look at is a way that we can try and help you to overcome it."

How nice it would be to live without, to not have to count

my steps, to see different roads and pathways. How liberating would it be to get into a car and go somewhere new, somewhere off the beaten track? But even as I think this, even as I imagine being able to travel places, to the beach or to the moors, my heart races at the thought of pulling a seatbelt across my chest, of slamming a door that would trap me inside the metal can. I turn towards the window, not wanting the fear of this nothing, this thought, to show in my eyes.

"There are several ways that we can treat your symptoms, Sarah. The first thing that I would normally suggest is fairly obsolete in your case I think. Frequently, symptoms can change and improve over time and it is simply a matter of watching and waiting to see if this is the case. However, as you have been experiencing your symptoms for an extended period of time I think they are unlikely to improve of their own volition."

His pause grows into the silence of the room as I look at his desk and think of Julie, Doctor Marsden's receptionist who would have fetched some tea by now. I think of Newton and reflected windows. I wonder what Doctor Charles would do if I turned up to our next appointment with a Newton's cradle as a gift. I wonder if I will turn up for the next appointment.

He sees the faraway look in my eyes, the lack of motion in my face as I look at the world beyond him. "What are you thinking?" he asks and my eyes slide toward the kindness in his face.

"I am thinking that you are nicer than I thought you would be. I am wondering if I will hold on to the tiny bit of hope that you can hand me a normal life or if I should just stand up and walk out now and fulfil my own prophecy. And on top of that I am thinking that, right about now, I would really like a cup of tea but that I have seen no sign of a Julie to make one."

He looks puzzled for a moment and chews at the inside of his cheek, digesting what I said as if trying to put a flavour to the words I have served him. His smile returns slowly as he stands and moves to another desk I paid no attention to, one cluttered with books and papers and what looks like folded-up tablecloths. From beyond the mound of clutter the sound of a warming kettle chases the click of a switch, the rattle of cups.

"The tea I can provide. I have no Julie, though I do have a Marie who is, sadly, off sick today. I am glad that I am nicer than you thought and I hope that you will stay long enough for me to try and help you." He gives a very Gallic shrug, palms facing the ceiling, eyes fixed on my own. "I cannot give you any guarantees other than the one where I say I will do my best to make your life a better place and if at any point I feel I cannot help you, then I will be honest and tell you that. Do you think that sounds fair or shall we shake hands now and say our goodbyes?"

I look away again as I consider his words, looking deep into the cloud of rising steam emanating from the invisible kettle. I seek portents and clues in the swirling white while he waits patiently for my response.

"We'll see," I say finally and he smiles.

"That's better than goodbye."

His hands are busy beyond the pile of clutter making a cup of tea that he says is Earl Grey but I think tastes of hot dishwater. We settle down again, each holding a hot cup to hide behind. Mine is a shield, a distraction I can look at when too uncomfortable to meet his eyes. Long after it is empty I stare into the dregs and try to see my future there as his voice washes over me and tries to find the doorway in my head to let himself in.

"So if we can't adopt a wait and see attitude, what other options are there?" I ask as I stare deeply into tea dust that looks like a heart and a comma and wonder what they signify, what comes next.

"Psychological treatment for PTSD can take several forms. There is Cognitive Behavioural Therapy, Eye Movement Desensitisation and Reprocessing and there are various forms of medication that can be used to manage the symptoms and your responses. Regression can be used in cases of amnesia and Dissociative Amnesia to try and unlock the hidden parts of memory. In situations like yours, Sarah, I would use Cognitive Behavioural Therapy to focus on the trauma you have suffered, using mental imagery and experiences in such a way that it enables you to take control of your fears and your distress response to them."

"I thought the idea was for me to get away from these stress responses, not to create them."

I hear the scepticism that pours from my lips into the cup in front of me where it sits toxic and thick, trying to mask the terror I feel at the idea of such exposure.

"I understand what you're saying and yes it does seem strange at first to deliberately expose yourself to something that makes you so afraid. However, the idea is that the exposure is done in a gentle and controlled manner, gradually enhancing the contact to enable your stress responses to remain calm and stable. Eye Movement Desensitisation and Reprocessing is another type of therapy that can be used alongside CBT and which helps the brain to process the information from the trauma so that you can come to terms with the experience. It seems a little odd at first but it can be enormously effective."

I nod as if what he says makes sense to me when the reality is that I hate the idea of any of it, of exposing myself to the very thing I have spent years trying to get away from. The thought of attempting to live a normal life, of walking down new paths, of getting in a car and being something other than the pitiful creature I have become, is enough to grip my chest tightly and threaten to prevent the breath from entering. I am certain that I cannot do this, that my fear will push me away from here. When I speak, the words gush out in a flood that pours quickly over my teeth as if they are desperate to be heard before it is too late, before I change my mind and leave.

"And the medication, what about that?" I ask, thinking it can't possibly be that easy, surely. That it isn't simply a matter of popping a little pill and finding that all is suddenly all right with my world and that my fears are gone.

"Medication I would use as a last resort if none of the other treatments worked. PTSD responds well to medication known as Selective Serotonin Re-uptake Inhibitors or SSRI's and the tablets can help to minimise the symptoms greatly. Again they can be incredibly effective but personally I like to try most other therapies first to attempt to undo the pathways laid down in your brain by the trauma that you have been through."

He pauses and waits, looking at me while I process what he has said, knowing that he is giving me the choice of walking this path with him or leaving and never coming back. I meet his eyes, his sincerity and speak through the fear in my mouth.

"Okay, I'll go along with it for now but if it gets too much I can still walk away can't I?"

I hear my own fear, the hitch in my voice and the words sound alien to my own ears as he nods and looks at me like my decision matters, as if he really cares.

"The CBT and the EMDR usually take place over eight to twelve sessions. We can do the first couple and see how they go, that will give me a better idea of how many more sessions we will need, and give you the chance to decide if you want to continue."

I glance at my watch and put the empty cup on the desk between us.

"I'll send you an appointment as soon as Marie is back, hopefully tomorrow. Usually there is about two weeks between the initial consultation and the follow-up appointment, so you won't have to wait too long."

I hear his need of his personal assistant in his voice, his lack of coping with anything other than the patients that sit in front of him needing help. I stand up and hold my hand out to him, he takes it warmly in both of his own and gives an odd little squeeze rather than the traditional shake.

"Next time I'm bringing my own tea bags," I tell him and he smiles and says goodbye as I turn to leave.

Chapter Forty-Four

I am with her as she makes the journey back from the doctor's. She does not notice me there watching her every step, treading the same paths, sitting in the same busy train carriage. I wondered how she would cope with going to different offices, housed in a different building, seeing a different face. All things that previously would have sent adrenalin rushing through her body.

Leah has not made the journey with her this time; she was not waiting outside for her beloved niece to come out of the unfamiliar place. I wonder if she even knew about the appointment, if she stayed in Exeter biting her lower lip with her little teeth as she always did when she worried and pondered. For the first time ever, Sarah made this entire journey alone, leaving her apartment, getting to the station, boarding the train. Things she had never done before without someone there to hold her hand.

When I watch her now it seems that there are differences in the way she moves; subtle and indistinct but obvious to me, someone who has watched closely for so long. There seems to be a life about her now, a vibrant kind of tension that didn't exist before when she was just a shell. The apprehension bubbles around her, there is anxiety when she glances cautiously at the people nearby.

It seems to me that the fear coursing through her veins has set alight that dull, slowed heartbeat, making it leap and skip, creating faster and less certain steps. She is a deer standing downwind, nostrils flared, skin edgy and tense. And as I watch her skittish movements, her frequent glances over her shoulder, the way she keeps her head upright and alert instead of fixed on the pavement ahead, I think to myself 'I did that for you. I created you. I brought you back to life'. I think she should thank me for what I have done, for the steam train that I represent through her life.

I wonder if I will ever get the chance to tell her my own story, to explain that I knew what she was going through, that I too knew what it was to feel haunted and afraid. I wonder if I could tell her about my childhood, about abandonment and terror, and if telling her would bring an understanding, an acceptance even. Would she see my reasoning?

I want to shake her and say, 'this is how it was, this is my own fear. You are not the only one'. I want to tell her, to share with her my own image of a young girl walking through an empty home. A terrified little scrap who was running out of food and filling up instead on panic and dark imaginings. I want to tell her about being alone in a house that seemed more and more silent, more and more still until in the end I heard the very silence as sound and believed that there were ghosts that shared the space with me.

I want to give my childhood memories to her, because she has none and it is unfair that my burden should be so heavy against the weightlessness of her past. I long to show her that she should not mourn or grieve her lack of memories, that sometimes nothing at all could be a good thing, preferable even. Why could it not have been me that forgot? I envy the void of her memory. I covet her life, wanting it instead to be my own so that I can forget too.

When had my mind first started playing tricks on me, making me feel that I wasn't completely alone after my mother had gone? Somewhere among those first four days, when the hours had dripped past and I watched the light ebb and flow beyond the curtains. I turned on the television, watched children's programmes, brushed my teeth and discovered that sucking dry pasta for a while made it go soft. I looked out of my bedroom window at my neighbours going past, unaware of my gaze upon them. I listened to my own breath and wondered if it would stop before anyone else ever heard it again.

The first time I heard a sound I thought it was the front door opening, I thought my mother had come home. I felt joy and relief leap into my heart as I raced on bare feet to the hallway only to stare puzzled at the closed door. There was no breeze around my ankles to tell me it had been recently opened. As my heart slowed and settled back dismally into my enforced solitude I decided that it was my imagination, my desperate need for someone other than myself within these walls. As I made my way back to the front room I thought I heard the sound again.

This time my perspective was different. As I stood with my back to the front door the sound came from ahead of me, up the stairs. I paused and then ran, thinking she was home after all, that somehow she had snuck past me and gone into her room. I took the stairs two at a time on weak, hungry legs and ran into my mother's room.

It should have been in darkness, I remember thinking that. I was certain I had left the room after discovering her absence without touching anything other than the light switch. The bulb had gone dark and her curtains were still closed, I was sure of it... wasn't I? Had I imagined that I could still see the dark hole of her room beyond the doorway as I pulled the door closed behind me?

Now the door was open and so were the curtains. Sunlight tried to pour through the dirty glass. The same piles of clothes sat on the floor heaped into corners, the bed was still unmade. But those curtains were not the same, those curtains had been touched, changed. Slowly I peered behind the door and saw nothing but torn wallpaper over sickly green paint.

"Mum?" I called and heard the weakness, the uncertainty in the shaky question.

There was no reply and I backed out of the room, more scared than I had ever been. Fingers of terror crawled slowly up my spine, chased by the sensation of being watched and I pushed my back against the wall and slid slowly along it, wide eyes peering down the stairs as I passed, seeing nothing out of the ordinary there. I wished I had stayed in the front room watching the TV. I wished I had heard nothing.

Later, after darkness had fallen outside the window, after the television became an object of confusion and sinister images, I returned to the landing at the top of the stairs. For the second time that week I found myself outside my mother's door thinking I should open it, yet too afraid to raise my hands. What would I do if I opened the door and found the curtains closed again? What would I do if I looked behind the door and found something other than torn wallpaper and flaking paint?

I stood helpless and still, straining to hear something other than silence. Was that something, above the ticking of the clock, the creaking of the wood? Could I hear breathing other than mine? I tried to hold my breath, to wait and be still but the more I tried the less I could hear. My stomach gurgled, a dog outside barked as if spooked by something crawling in the darkness. The floorboard I stood on creaked slightly at the tiny, barely perceptible shift of my weight as I tilted my head.

I ran to my room and scrambled beneath the musty, damp duvet. Curling into a ball and hiding my head I began to pray that someone would come, someone would find me. I called out for my father, hoping it would be him that first walked through the door rather than the mother who had left me to care for myself. I prayed that I would fall asleep and not wake up to another day alone.

My sleep that night was bitter and fragmented, my fearful mind taking images from the last few days, images of my mother's descent into cruelty and pictures from the post-watershed television and blending them. One terrifying image after another shook me from my sleep and each time it was harder to wipe away the sweat onto already damp sheets.

By the time morning light stained the horizon I was half-delirious with tiredness and lack of food. My mouth felt dusty, sticky, my eyes seemed permanently half-shut. I crept silently towards the top of the stairs, dragging with me the fear that had become my permanent companion. I was relieved to see that the door to my mother's room was still closed. But as I reached the top of the stairs I heard a sound from my nightmares, it sounded to me like a door creaking open and in my half-asleep state I thought it was the door behind me.

I ran forwards and slipped as I reached the top of the stairway. There was a moment of total understanding and awareness. A moment where I knew what was coming and that it was going to hurt. In that tiny fragment of clarity there was a strange sense of relief. I wondered if I were about to die, I wondered if I minded. And then, as my knee made first contact with the stairs, I stopped thinking altogether.

I felt bursts of pain simultaneously, my knee, my shoulder, the side of my head. I heard something break and wasn't sure if the sound came from me or the banister. I fell forever and ever. If I close my eyes now I can still feel myself falling, the vertigo of it, the sense of it never ending. At the time I seemed to feel everything yet looking back the thing I remember most is the falling, the twisting. I remember that it didn't seem to stop for a long, long time and I remember the intense moment of utter stillness when it did and there was nothing in the brief moment before the pain started.

Agony exploded through every part of me, radiating out from my left thigh, washing over me and sweeping me away. Perhaps it is merciful that there my memory stalls and leaves me for a little while; there is peace in that space between memories, I am calm there. I don't know how long I lay at the foot of the stairs. I can't remember the rest of the day passing, or the night coming around again. I only really know what came next because I have been told.

The postman came and was surprised that when he lifted the letterbox a groaning cry poured out. He paused and waited and another whimper came. That was when he looked through the letterbox and saw me lying broken and twisted at the bottom of the stairs, one leg beneath me, blood on my face. I am told that my eyes were open and staring straight at him, that had it not been for the noise I was making he would have thought me dead. I am told that dead is exactly what I would have been had he not found me when he did.

It seems strange that someone who played such a pivotal role in my life, who stepped into it and prevented a premature ending, should have no name in my mind. He has a face that almost certainly my imagination has given him, a kind voice. I know this because it was he that called the ambulance and to do that his voice must surely have been soft and gentle and warm. Yet he still has no name and I don't know of any way to find out now after so much time has passed. I wish I could, I think that perhaps I would have liked to say thank you. I wonder if he ever thinks about me, wonders what came next in my life.

When I opened my eyes in the hospital, my leg in plaster and everything swimming at me through a fog of painkillers, my father was there. Shame filled his eyes, he looked sober and guilty and he struggled to form the words in his mouth. After a moment he stopped trying to speak and instead reached for my hand. I felt the warmth of his palm, the engulfing, folding of his large fingers around my tiny frail ones. I drifted back into sleep feeling safe and protected and, above everything else, relieved that it was him that was here and not the mother who had left me to die.

Chapter Forty-Five

The familiar smell of old books fills my nose as I move slowly through the shelves. This has always been a place I find peace, where I can reflect or escape into lives far more exciting than mine, bound neither by fear nor compulsion. Through their pages I find a freedom with which to view the world, to see the things I often hide from.

The librarian is the same woman who stood behind the counter and greeted me on my very first visit when I was a too-thin teenager with a head full of scarred confusion. Nothing about her has changed in that time, she watched through the same pair of old-fashioned glasses as I grew inside my bubble. We are on first name terms and she knows my tastes well enough to recommend books that I almost always enjoy, consuming them in a matter of hours.

The tips of my fingers pass gently over the exposed spines, absorbing titles as though they are Braille and all the while my eyes pull towards the clock on the wall, leaving me wondering why time is going so slowly, wondering why my sense of peace has deserted me here, in the one place I can usually rely on it. If I look back over the few short weeks since I moved away from Leah's I don't recognise them as belonging to me. The sense of calm understanding, of acceptance and normality seems to be falling away leaving me looking over a stormy landscape I don't recognise. The control over my life crumbles beneath my fingers and I feel scorched and lost. There is no sense to any of it, and I can see no way past this bewilderment.

When the policemen sat in my apartment explaining why they were there, listening to my denials, I saw disbelief in their faces, a sense of having heard it all before. I tried to tell them that they were mistaken but I could offer no plausible explanation other than the one they had mistakenly grasped at. There was nothing satisfying in the fumbled possibilities that I offered them in place of the coffee they had refused. Eventually they had cut impatiently across my stammering.

"Miss Phillips, Mr Jay has no desire to take this any further. He has asked for nothing more than that we give you a warning not to do it again. Should there be any further occurrences, then you will face possible arrest and prosecution. Do you understand what I am saying to you?"

I nodded helplessly, knowing that they had made up their minds, that as far as they were concerned I had obviously done what I was being accused of. The unfairness of it all washed over me as they stood as one and moved towards the door.

"Goodbye, Miss Phillips. Hopefully, we won't be seeing you again soon."

I closed the door behind them and rested against it, wondering what the hell was going on in my life.

Now their spectres, the gross injustice of them chased me here, to a place I normally embrace as a sanctuary, a haven. Tranquillity hides from me in the dark corners that I can't quite reach, along with the books that no-one wants, the fine film of dust that sits on their pages and makes hands feel dry. With a sigh I turn to leave, empty-handed except for my frustration and growing sense of dissatisfaction.

I walk slowly towards the town centre, surprised at how quiet the streets are. I am used to being barged, nudged, cursed at as I walk with my eyes on the floor and lack awareness of those around me. Now though, I walk freely without anyone coming close, which makes it all the more surprising when a pair of feet move in front of me, toes facing mine, forcing me to a stop. The shoes are black and clean but the slight wear on them says they are not new, simply cared for. I feel a hand on my arm and look up, surprised, into blue, smiling eyes.

"Sarah, I thought it was you."

He is smiling in a self-conscious way, he lifts his hand to smooth his hair and looks shy and uncertain, not knowing quite what to do now that he has got my attention. I catch a glimpse of the angel wing tattoo beneath the sleeve of his jumper and wonder if I should be afraid, if he is, after all, the person who slipped something into my drink.

His face is warm and open, looking genuinely pleased to have bumped into me and I think, surely not. I smile up at him, the movement slight, not quite complete.

"Cam, it's nice to see you again."

"You remember me, then. I'm relieved, I thought I might just be about to embarrass myself."

I think of him sitting opposite me, of the way my memories of him disappeared into nothing and I wonder at what came next, what happened afterwards. How could I ask him, what would he tell me in response? I try to find the words to begin but then he starts speaking again.

"I'm sorry I didn't get to spend more time with you that night. I mean, I know maybe the time wasn't right anyway because you looked a bit upset and everything but I was hoping to catch up with you and check you were okay. By the time I got away from my friends you were gone and I couldn't find you anywhere. I guess you left early."

He catches the frown on my face and stops talking. I wonder at his words, at this knowledge of me that he possesses, a knowledge that doesn't exist in my own mind. I don't want to talk about it out here in the street where other people might hear us and wonder blindly at my secrets.

"Do you maybe have time to grab a coffee and I'll explain a bit more?"

He glances at his watch and nods, looking pleased that I asked.

"I've got about half an hour before I have to be back at work, how's that?"

"Good enough."

We walk towards the nearest cafe I feel comfortable in, making small talk as we go. He doesn't ask me about the choice of venue, seemingly happy to go along with my unspoken choice. I ask him what his work is.

"I'm a photographer."

He is proud of this; I see it in his open face, the half-smile.

"Nothing seedy, just babies, families, weddings, that kind of thing. I know it sounds a bit boring but it pays the bills. In my spare time I do all the arty farty black and white stuff. One day maybe I'll have my own exhibition."

I file his dream away and think of the meaning that people place in photographs, of how important they can be in the right hands, at the right time. I think of a picture of me when I was a little girl, mop-haired and round-faced, an unguarded smile stretching my cheeks wide as I look at the lens with innocence and a lack of embarrassment. And next to me stands my sister, her smile and everything else smaller as she stands further back from me, slightly in the shadows. I do not remember this moment when we stood together and were frozen forever into this still image but I am glad of it, because it tells me that she did exist once, at the same time as me, breathing the same air as me. I look up at the man beside me and like him more because of the paper memories he hands to other people.

"How about you?" he asks. "What do you do?"

I think for a moment before answering. "You know, that one isn't quite such a straightforward answer. Can we leave it for another time?"

"Ooh curious. Are you a spy? A secret agent? If you tell me will you have to kill me?"

I laugh and say yes, that's exactly what I am.

"I've just had a thought. If we have to leave it for another time then that means you would like to see me again."

He sounds pleased but I hear the question in his voice as if he thinks I might follow his words with a denial.

"Well, we'll see," I say with a smile and he holds the door open for me.

We collect our drinks and move to sit down as I try to explain what happened that night. I don't tell him about my fear and why it exists, I don't tell him about my screaming ejection from a strange car in the middle of the night. I speak only of my suspicions about being drugged, of how the night disappeared into nothing. He is horrified, appalled.

"My God, that's awful! And the doctors can't test for that?"

"Well, they can but it's pointless as it takes too long and ultimately might not prove anything anyway, so they don't tend to bother, they just treat the symptoms. I was lucky really because nothing seems to have happened, I wasn't attacked or anything like that, at least, I don't think I was. I just can't remember at all and that's what scares me. You were the last clear memory I had of that night so I wondered if you'd seen anything."

He shakes his head and takes a sip of his coffee, it leaves a little bit of foam on his top lip which he licks away with the tip of his tongue, I find myself staring at his mouth as he talks.

"Not really. We sat and chatted and had a bit of a laugh about your friend on the dance floor, then you said you had to go to the ladies. Only you never came back. I thought I'd been ditched but then I saw you briefly after that, you looked upset."

"Was I on my own then?"

"You were. I didn't see anybody else hanging around. You looked a little bit worse for wear. You left before I had a chance to ask for your number." He smiles a little, but there is concern around his eyes, as though wishing he had followed me, made sure I was okay, seen me home safely.

In this moment I know for certain that he was not the person who slipped something into my drink. His face is filled with genuine concern and I fight the urge to tell him everything else that happened that night, the taxi ride, the long walk home. I wonder what he would make of my fragile mind, of my weird habits, of every counted step. It is a surprise that I want him to think well of me, that his opinion matters.

He glances at his watch, "I really have to go, I have a sitting in about ten minutes." When he looks at me there is a hint of hope in his eyes. "I'd really like to see you again."

"Me too," I say and reach into my bag for a pen and paper to write my number down.

There is no hesitation, no second thoughts. When I hand it to him, he takes the pen and paper from me and tears a strip from the bottom, writing down his own number before he rolls his eyes at me in false exasperation.

"And please don't do that thing where you think you have to wait for three days otherwise you appear too keen. Carpe diem, that's what I say. I won't think badly of you if you call too soon."

"Or I could just wait for you to call and then you decide for yourself how long the wait is," I reply with a smile.

"You could, and I promise you I won't be waiting for three days either, so don't think badly of me if you think I am being a little premature."

I pick up my bag from beneath the table and turn to face him. He says goodbye with a soft kiss on my cheek that I will still feel as I get ready for bed that night.

Chapter Forty-Six

I watch as his lovely, friendly face moves closer to hers, as he kisses her lightly on the cheek with a smile. Of course I remember him from that night, the man with the angel wing tattoo who had tied the tear in my top and made me wish I had met him under different circumstances. There was something special about him, a kindness in his eyes, a genuine sense of completeness as though he knew exactly who he was and never had to pretend otherwise. I liked that kind of honesty, that kind of openness.

Her interest in him is obvious, a bright rainbow against a bleak, dark sky. It is something that I haven't seen in her for years, that coming alive, that feeling of longing. With reluctance she talks about the past, I hear the hesitation in her voice, the slight catch, the too-long pause. Hidden amongst her abridged version of the night's events are secrets he can't begin to guess at. Secrets planted and watched with delight as they grow. I cannot blame her for keeping them to herself. Faced with the truth of her, the reality of her I think most people would run far away without ever bothering to look back.

There is something compelling in her responses to him, something in her body language that draws me towards her, intimate and close as if it were me she gazed at with her soft eyes and slightly parted mouth, as if her fingertips rested lightly upon my forearm and scalded my skin. I look on as he responds to it, leaning into it as though she is a strong wind on a clear day. A slow smile spreads across his face as he sees nothing but her.

I think of all the possibilities, of the things I can do to change the scenario playing out before me. I could find his number in her diary where she will write it later, no doubt in a colourful cloud. Would I dare, though, to phone him and pretend to be her? Perhaps I can follow him and see where he works, send him a gift from her that makes him turn and leave it and her far behind. Jealousy undulates beneath the surface, about how he could have been mine, how he could be leaning into me, his breath soft against my lips. Is it wrong of me to think that she doesn't deserve him, his kindness, his warmth?

Yet as I look on, envy and bitterness molten against my tongue, he reaches out his hand and lightly touches the back of hers. A brief touch that seeps life into her shy smile, that brings her eyes to life and suddenly I want desperately for her to reach out and grab his fingers between hers. I want her to stroke the rough skin on the back of his knuckles, to run her thumb lightly across the delicately painted grief on the inside of his wrist. I want to sense her emotion as I watch and imagine it is I that trace the veins beneath the surface.

Sometimes touch is everything, I know that only too well, touch can save people and pull them back from the edge of the abyss. Suddenly I feel sad and lost, in this moment I look at her and see my own reflection, as if we have briefly changed places and her strength unexpectedly becomes my weakness. And I think of then and of how it was, of how I had lived.

When I woke in the hospital, touch was the first thing I felt: the weight of the blankets, the softness of the pillow, a slight breeze. All of it felt gentle, more beautiful than anything I had touched upon for a long time. I was held in the present by it, in that moment when dread tried to pull me backwards into tumbling pain and solitude. And most of all it was the touch of my father's hand telling me that he was there and hadn't left again. The softness of the fleshy pad beneath his thumb, the depth of the creases on his palm, they all told a story that I was no longer alone. I felt that touch above the pain threading through bruises and snapped, splintered bones.

How many times did I hear the words 'I'm sorry'? How many times did I wake to feel his hand, to hear his tears before I opened my eyes and saw them wet and shiny running down his grizzled cheeks? It was how I knew I had come close to not making it through, I heard it in his guilt, in his remorse and saw it in the shadows that never again departed from his eyes.

He rarely left my side and amid the scant moments that took him away, I floundered, feeling bereft, my eyes constantly pulling towards the door of my room in terror that it would not be him that returned, that it would be her and she would take me away, somewhere I would never be found. Each movement beyond the doorway threaded adrenalin through every fibre of my body until a face that was not hers appeared and said that I was safe, that they were someone other, someone better than the thing she had become in my mind. I lost count of the moments of anxiety lining the corridors of each day.

When my father prepared to take me home, packed my meagre belongings and said goodbye to the ward staff, he saw the fear bloom across pale cheeks, his assuasive hands stroking calm into my shoulders, my face. His palm painted colour beneath it as he held me and told me everything would be okay, speaking in the same tone used for terrified animals, softly, slowly, feather-light. He had already known how I would feel in my returning, had already chosen a different path to walk, a turning away from the past.

242

By the time he carried me from the hospital – followed down the brightly lit corridors by the cheery smiles and waves of nurses who had become familiar – it was to somewhere else entirely, somewhere new. No skeletal branches that whispered to me from beyond my bedroom window, no sofa that held appalling secrets waiting to be discovered, no piles of clothing that smelt of mould and indifference. I could no longer look out of the hall window and see the woods where the spectre of Brian still played. I found instead that he ran through my memory anyway and that it was enough, it was better because I could think of him without the smell of her in my nostrils; I could remember him without seeing the door that slammed onto his tiny body. He was untainted and free and he ran ahead, urging me to run with him.

The house Dad took me to was further away, out of the city and along the motorway. It was smaller, brighter, with rooms that smelt of care and sunshine, with fresh flowers on the kitchen table and laundry hanging in the garden, flapping softly in the breeze. There was no dust to tickle my nose, no threadbare carpet or torn wallpaper. I wasn't haunted by the smell of my mother's perfume, the dark gaping hole of her bedroom. Everything in my room was new and clean as if created there with me in mind.

"When you're feeling up to it we'll go shopping and get you some new clothes," he said.

His voice asked me to love him, to forgive him. I heard the sorrow there and found it a lonely, tainted thing. I stood on the edges of him and watched his self-loathing, his continual questioning of actions that would always be regretted, that could not be undone.

His guilt underpinned everything he said, everything he did. I caught him looking at me often, his brow lined with worry and regret as he rushed to help me in the earliest days when my limping made me unsteady and clumsy, when the plaster on my foot clumped hard against the ground. I believed without question in his remorse, in his desire to make things right, to create a different future for me that I had dreamed of in my delirium at the bottom of the stairs. But despite my belief in him, my awareness of his will to remain my anchor, I still called out in the night to make certain that he was there. I still slept with the light on and needed him beside me.

Sleep was harder than ever to come by, every noise roughly propelling me from dreams as I imagined the front door latching behind my father, his image obscured in the smoky glass of the front door as he left me alone and vulnerable. I checked down the edges of the bright blue sofa, looking for the magic token that would undo us all. It became a habit, a compulsion. I could not rest until my hands had pushed into the space between the cushions, had felt around for something that should not be and come up empty and relieved.

As my impulses grew, his manifested vocally, his habits grew from mine, fed them, gave them autonomy. He developed the habit of singing if he was not in the same room as me, even for a moment. I could hear him when his voice poured through the walls and around the doorways and knew he was there, that he was not gone. Hearing his movements without his singing transported me back to a different house, a different presence. I needed that baritone, that vibration to keep me in the present. Without it I began to slide, slowly at first, into a hateful past.

As my bones healed and my weight climbed back to where it should have been I heard him talking on the phone, hushed conversations that spilled urgent secrets I wasn't meant to hear. But I was used to listening carefully from dark, hidden corners and I knew he talked to the police, that they tried to find her, that she was gone. No matter how many times he told me she could never find me I always thought she would, I always started at sudden noises and creaky floorboards.

By the time I looked normal again, all the bruises hidden, all the terror beneath the mask, preparations had already been made for me to return to school. Not the same one as before, I would never see my old friends again. I would make new ones, I would fit right in, I would be normal. Dad tried his best to make everything seem like an adventure but at the end of the first day in my tiny village school, the other mothers cast suspicious eyes over the man in their midst and spoke among themselves. As I walked out, relief at the sight of him standing there, I felt their eyes upon me, felt their questions and curiosity. I thought perhaps that I would always be different, that her actions had tattooed my skin and that everyone could see it but me.

Chapter Forty-Seven

The restaurant is almost full. Rustic wooden tables and mismatched chairs share space with pinstriped legs and briefcases, bags of shopping and exhausted faces. The noise hovers somewhere near the ceiling and I attempt to climb over it to find our table. She is already seated and I watch her from my place among the unknown crowd, see her hands flutter around the table, straightening things that don't need it, creating symmetry in which her concerns, her nervousness, sit more comfortably. I follow the trail of her fingertip as it meanders through the condensation on her large glass of white wine. She looks smaller than usual and her mouth is downturned beneath her casually pinned blonde hair. She looks sad, awkward.

Shifting in her seat, her eyes find me among the anonymous. Life blossoms across her expression, chasing the sadness away and it is my turn for sorrow as I take in her pleasure at seeing me. I watch as it lives for a few seconds, feeding from old habits, before being chased away by concern and distance. In this moment I want more than ever to take away the faceless thing that holds us in opposite corners, gum shields sliding into place. I miss her and that emotion meets hers in the seconds before I reach her and feel a warm familiar kiss given with unfamiliar reserve.

There is silence as we sit, I paste on a smile in the place of conversation and her hand reaches out to offer me a menu. I already know what I want as my eyes browse the columns, seeing nothing more than black type on white, meaningless in my disinterest. Her eyes graze, rough and conspicuous, across the top of my head. I feel them like the teeth of a comb, snagging at the occasional knot. I lift my own to meet hers, my mouth opening in the hope that I will find words inside, just as the waiter arrives and nods his familiarity.

"How are you both today?"

He is young and good-looking, his full mouth almost obscenely sensual, a kissing mouth curled lightly into a smile beneath dark eyes and raised cheekbones. I love the awareness of him, the fact that he is always here and that he fits into my thoughts and memories of this place perfectly. He started work here not long after we started eating here. He has become a perfectly integral piece of my obsessive compulsions, same restaurant, same decor, same waiter, same food.

Leah orders her steak medium rare, her salad without dressing and as I go to place my order, the waiter smiles and shakes his head, holding up a finger to say 'wait a minute'.

"Let me guess, tagliatelle alla carbonara?"

I nod and return a smile that reaches no further than the corners of my mouth. Still holding the menu I have hidden within, I feel embarrassed that I even pretended to look and a glance at Leah shows me sympathy and understanding. He reaches down and plucks the offending article from my fingers before assuring us that he will be right back with my drink. She reaches across the table and squeezes a hand that feels too cold. Concern fights for control of the face that looks at me with relief and love.

"How was your weekend away?" I ask her and she withdraws slowly, back behind the lines.

"It was nice, a little awkward, a little strange." She smiles slightly and shrugs. "I felt like an inexperienced fool really.

Last time I was in a situation like that was a good few years ago and I was shored up with alcohol and a twenty something's energy. Now," she gestures towards her upper torso with a sweep of her hand, "well, let's just say everything isn't as it once was and I faced it all sober."

"Is he nice?" I ask and she looks relieved that I asked, that I am the one to mention him, that there is an element of interest.

"He is. He's kind and gentle and patient. Probably the opposite of the sort of person I would have gone for when I was younger. Then I was all Billy Idol and motorbikes, now I'm all about comfort, slippers and hot chocolate. It must be an age thing. I don't think I could keep up with the wild ones anymore," she says with a smile.

It is a phrase I have heard her use before, one that had once meant boring and old before their time. She had described my father the same way, slippers and hot chocolate, as though it were a uniform one donned when stepping into a role of responsibility. Often when I think of him, when I try to conjure an image to hold on to, he has a steaming cup in his hand and slippers on the feet that I can't remember the size of.

"How's the new apartment?"

There is an interested smile pasted over her concern, the lumps and bubbles of worry showing through as I tell her what she wants to hear, that everything is fine and happy in my brand new independent world. I can see from her expression that she isn't entirely content with my response, her knowledge of me painting the lie into my tone. She looks thoughtful for a moment before biting her bottom lip and preparing to ask me what else, what am I hiding? I get there before she does, heading her off at the pass with a topic that will draw her in and force her response.

"I went to see that new doctor, the one that Doctor Marsden told me about."

Emotions roll across her face like billowing clouds. There is no hiding the fact that she is initially pleased. I see it in the rounded cheeks, the smile that shows her little teeth but it is tainted by the knowledge that she wasn't with me when I went, that she hadn't even known for certain that I was going, only that it was a possibility. I read in her eyes the realisation that we are two points on a map, separated by a widening gulf.

"I'm sorry I wasn't there with you."

Her voice is small and I wonder for the first time whether or not I would have had the courage to go if she were there holding my hand and making me feel less alone. If her support, her care, would have made it less necessary somehow for me to find a way through the shadows left behind by yet more missing memories. I wonder guiltily how much of my helplessness is down to someone else shouldering my burden, holding me up when things got tough. I tell her that it is okay, that I understand, that I coped, all the while wondering if she is apologising to me for not being there or if her remorse is that I hadn't felt I could ask her.

"How was it? Is he nice?"

"He seemed nice, a bit scatterbrained maybe. Not at all like Doctor Marsden. He thinks he may be able to help anyway."

"Well that's good. Who knows, maybe he'll be able to help you recover some of your memories. Did he say anything about that?"

"The impression I got was that he'll treat my symptoms as a whole, that they all boil down to the same thing anyway, which is this Post-Traumatic Stress thing and that he's going to try and deal with all of it."

It feels alien to be talking to her like this, to be filling in the blanks of my life with someone who has been there for everything up until now. My words are awkward, stilted, like I am talking to a stranger on a train. Our waiter places the food in front of us with a flourish, asks if we need anything else and Leah is quick to order another glass of wine as if needing the false courage given to her by the alcohol to even continue this conversation. We lapse into a strange uncomfortable silence as we eat, in which nothing is as it should be, as the foundations of our relationship alter and shift seismically beneath our feet.

After a while she lays her knife and fork down beside her plate, the meal half-eaten.

"Can we talk?" she asks.

"I thought that was what we were doing," I say and she shakes her head.

"We were making conversation, Sarah. Light-hearted conversation. I meant really talk, about what has been going on lately."

I think for a moment that she is referring to my disastrous night out with Alex, that perhaps she has phoned my friend's mothers and been told a variation of the night's traumatic events. I flounder in the void between sentences as I try to find the words to explain, before she starts to speak again with resignation, about me and her and things left unsaid.

"I'm sorry that I didn't tell you about Matt."

Her eyes move to the table, avoiding mine, waiting for my response. I follow her gaze to the woven placemat; take in the weave where the strands rise slightly as they cross one another before themselves disappearing out of sight.

"I understand why you didn't," I say and mean it.

She looks puzzled, as though this is the wrong response and I should have said something altogether different.

"I'll be honest and say that I was a bit upset at first that you hadn't told me, but I also know that I don't react to change very well and deep down I know that you were only trying to protect me." I hear the ghost of my conversation with Alex in my words.

"So you're not angry or upset because you found out that I was going on a date with someone?"

Her voice is genuinely confused as though she has planned this conversation out in its entirety, scripted the lines and organised her thoughts around it only to find that it has gone off at such a tangent that none of it makes sense any more.

250

"I was surprised at first, just because it had never happened before but the more I thought about it the more I realised it was about time really. You've been on your own ever since the accident, it's about time you had a bit of your own life back."

She has the beginning of tears in her eyes.

"But I thought you moved out because of it."

It is my turn to look surprised, to stumble.

"What made you think that?" In my head I see a brochure on a pillow, a decision made with haste. This conversation appears to be making no sense to either of us.

"I was speaking to Alex's mum and she told me that you'd asked Alex about me dating and then when you said you were leaving home you told me it was about time I had a life of my own. I thought I'd somehow managed to push you away, that you thought you had to leave. And then when Jane passed on the message that you'd called when I was away and that you hadn't seemed surprised that I had gone for the weekend I just put two and two together and assumed you were pissed off because of it."

I stare at her for long seconds as though she is speaking a foreign language, words fluttering onto the table between us, fragmented and torn, fitting nowhere into my sequence of events.

"What about the brochure you left on my bed?" I ask eventually.

I find that I can't meet her eyes now that I have brought it out into the open, that I don't want to look and see the guilt on her face as she answers my question, apologises for the blunt way she chose to do things.

"What brochure?" she says.

And my version of the world changes around me.

Chapter Forty-Eight

Between the river valley and the city centre the wind whips at my hair, rendering me blind to the distant hills, the rushing clouds that roll in dark and grave from the sea. I lift a heavy hand, tuck the strands back behind cold ears. The skyline is cut in two by a crane that moves slowly as if the breeze catches it too and is spinning it like a pin wheel.

I wonder if I jump now, will the void I feel as I fall match the emptiness inside as I stand and contemplate an ending? Would I fall forever into a darkness so total I would never come face to face with the mythical perfect light of whatever came next? How much closer to death than this thought, this moment, would I have to be to have a near-death experience? Would it be another step, a climb over the railings, halfway through the fall to the road far below? Never? Perhaps Death himself knows, far more than me, that I won't be joining him quite yet. Perhaps he isn't even looking in my direction.

I step up onto the crash barrier, the palms of my hands resting lightly on the rough stone wall that holds me safe, that prevents me from falling. I wonder what would happen if I took the next step, lifted my leg, perched my buttocks on top of the railing feeling the cold of the tarnished metal through the thin cotton of my dress. And if I jumped, if I lost my footing accidentally, deliberately, would anyone even know me? Would I be recognisable in any way? I wonder if I would be free then from the thoughts that plague me, from the trap I have built around myself, this self-made prison of memory and nightmare. There would be nobody to grieve, not anymore and I find somehow that in this moment I don't mind so much.

And if I went ahead, tasted that freedom, what would become of Sarah? Sweet, broken little Sarah, who is in my thoughts even now. Where before there had been spaces, a turning away in which I thought of other things, made other plans, she has become like the rhythm in my pulse, always there, ever present. She seems to live in every second of my thoughts. I am bound by her as surely as if I am her prisoner and I am, I am. Never making a single decision without thinking of how it may affect her, of what I could do to bring more change, more chaos to her every, ordinary day. She has become like a drug and the more I take, the more I need.

And so I think about her as I contemplate my small feet hanging over the edge, dangling in the air. I think of her as the wind blows at my face as though pushing me closer to the fall, the violent landing. I want to hold her, to cling on to her as I fall, to see the look in her eyes as we plummet towards release. I wish I could kiss her goodbye.

Even in the thought of such an ending there is dismay. She would never know I watched her, that I played such a part in the unfolding of her life, in the creation of the path she finds herself on. She would never know the subtleties at play, the plans I wrought that were unintentionally but wonderfully so effective. There would be no more opportunities to confront her, no pleased to meet you's, no grand unveiling.

I lean forwards, the railing on the top of the wall pressing against the lower part of my rib cage and acting as no kind of deterrent to anyone serious about ending it all. The ground seems so far away, so vague and uncertain and I watch as it swims away from me in a river of vertigo. I sway on weak legs as a car drives into the car park behind me and pulls me away from the edge, away from morbid temptation as if a spell has been broken and once again the ground beneath my feet is solid, substantial, welcome.

I breathe in deeply through a curtain of hair and pull it roughly back into a ponytail, sliding the band from around my wrist and doubling it over until it is tamed and my eyes are no longer blind. I hate the weight of it against my neck, as it pulls me further away from the drop in front of me. Eventually I turn my back on the wall and think that Death was right to look elsewhere, that I won't be joining him today.

I wonder what my mother would think if they were to find me five storeys below, clothes burst at the seams, blood running slowly into the gutter. Would she cry for me after all this time? Had she ever? Perhaps I should ask her, pick up the phone after all this time, introduce the grown-up me, the scarred and broken and angry me. I could go to her house, the house I grew up in, was abandoned in, the house she returned to when I was long gone and healed. I could knock on the door and demand answers, watch her expression change to one of fear when she realised I am not afraid of her, that I am more than a match for her. I smile as I think of the look on her face. Would it be the same look of terror that twisted mine as I tumbled down the stairs, the expression that was knocked senseless by the first solid hit against the edge, before the snapping and breaking of bones?

The beeping of a horn, urgent and long twists me from my mind, I have drifted while I was looking inside; stepping backwards away from the edge until I danced into the path of the vehicles leaving the car park. The huge silver Audi passes close enough to pull at my skirt and makes me stumble against the slowly moving side of it.

"Fucking moron!"

His mouth opens wide but the shout is dull and muted, a child in the front passenger seat has eyes wide with surprise. I cannot argue with him. He is right, I am. The name sits among the other labels, both given and self-created: moron, weirdo, stalker, crazy, victim. I am none of them yet perhaps all of them. I wonder which of them would be granted by Sarah if only she knew who to aim the words at and when to pull the trigger.

Chapter Forty-Nine

I think of lipstick trodden into the floor, of keys in doors and silent footsteps in a darkened room, of phone calls made to my past from an apartment that should have been safe and secure. I think of nightmares that wake me screaming, of nights that disappear into thin air. I think of misunderstandings and questions that should have been asked instead of assumptions being made amid stupid, secret anger. And I think of brochures placed on pillows that lead to somewhere altogether different, somewhere alien and strange.

Leah's face reflected genuine shock when I told her about the brochure. Her innocence obvious, the incomprehension as she looked across the table and failed to understand my words. I suddenly wondered at how long this had been going on, this subtle, furtive invasion? How long had some unseen tourist been watching my life, acting upon it? And then I remembered what the policeman had said and wondered how I had failed to notice, to realise at the time. That originally the phone calls to Rob Jay were coming from another number, another address, perhaps from the telephone in Leah's house. I should have asked but was so stunned by my past sitting uncomfortably on the policeman's lips that I didn't think to do so.

I feel haunted and afraid, seeking clues and vapour trails in the scant moments of my life that have been different, unusual. There are none that I can see. I have never caught someone's eyes lingering too long upon me, never become aware of footsteps timed perfectly to inconspicuously match my own as I walk with my head down and my shoulders bowed. I have never felt anything less than alone.

I let myself into the apartment looking behind me as I do so, wondering what I would do if someone were there watching, ready to jump. Locking the door after me and sliding the bolt firmly into place I breathe a sigh of relief and feel safer behind newly changed locks, Rapunzel in her tower with the subtle difference that I don't want to be rescued. I put the two remaining keys on the coffee table where I can see them, wrap them in my hands and feel their comforting solidity every time I leave the room to get food, to use the bathroom, to stretch my legs.

I gave the spare key to Leah and made her promise to keep it with her at all times as I fielded her concern and made light of it, just another of my obsessions ha ha. I saw her doubt and tried to pay it no attention, unwilling to give voice to the abject fear I could feel coiling through my belly, serpent-like and slow. Even so, the truth pushed against the inside surface of my teeth, clamouring to escape. And I almost told her of the shadow behind me, went so far as to open my mouth.

Her phone ringing pulled her attention away. There was a brief conversation, she said where she was, who she was with. She said goodbye with a warm smile, a vague flush to her cheeks and my own words remained unsaid, unwilling as I was to yet again steal that smile from her. I told her instead that the brochure was nothing to worry about, that I had taken the local newspaper upstairs and it was probably an insert that had fallen out. The lie coated my expression like greasepaint and she stared at its garishness before frowning slightly and saying nothing, as though afraid to question my version of events, to drive that wedge deeper.

And now the silence in my home is total, the television muted, all the windows closed against the sound of the city in the evening. Every movement made is sharply accentuated, exaggerated until my ears are full of the sound of myself and nothing else. I sit statue-still, breathing slowly, calming my heartbeat, wondering who may be outside my door at this moment. Who might be raising a hand to knock, to do me harm.

It is into that silence that the telephone rings sharp and jolting. Fumbling for it with shaking hands I mutter a choked hello through the lump lodged in my throat.

"I told you I wouldn't wait three days," he says and I hear the smile in his voice as my breath slows and pours more calmly into the mouthpiece.

"I'm glad you didn't," I tell him and mean it, feeling less alone with his voice against my ear.

"Me too. However, before you start feeling awkward because you are talking to a stranger, I'll get to the point quickly. I just called to find out if you wanted to meet up on Saturday? If the weather is nice maybe we could have a picnic. Maybe we could even if the weather is crap. We could take big umbrellas and afterwards feed the ducks. They don't mind a bit of rain."

My smile further chases the heavy silence to the edges of the room.

"I'd love to. Rain or shine. Would you mind if we went to Northernhay Gardens? I like it there."

I don't add that it is on my psychological map of places I can go, that I won't panic or lose count on the familiar paths and walkways of the city centre park, that I have been there many times before.

"Hmmm, bit of a shortage of ducks in Northernhay, but I guess we could feed the seagulls instead. I always feel sorry for them stuck in Exeter far from the open sea, feeling homesick and distinctly lacking in fish. So yes, Northernhay it is, I'll make salmon sandwiches for them, a little taste of home. Do you like salmon sandwiches?"

"Er, no actually I don't but that's okay, I'll bring something different."

"It's a date then," he says and I feel my stomach flip a little.

"Is it?"

"Well, yes if you want it to be. If you don't then no, no it isn't, it's just a nice wander in the park with Exeter's answer to David Bailey."

"It's a date then."

He announces that he has to go and photograph fat babies but is one o'clock on Saturday afternoon okay. I murmur my assent, arrange to meet at the entrance to the gardens and hang the phone up to find a silence less total than before.

The day begins to feel a little lighter, begins to evaporate into a mood not quite so bleak, a light not quite so dull. The mysterious appearance of the brochure still weighs heavy in my thoughts but now it shares space with something equal and opposite, something to look forward to. A distraction my thoughts choose to visit in place of fear and uncertainty. The hours roll together and disappear into vague traces and dreams.

By the time evening has drawn in close, I have planned over and over what I will wear, changing my mind one way and then back again, laying outfits on the bed, trying different hairstyles, all of which hide the faint white scar on my temple. The walk to Northernhay is meticulously planned out in my head, each paving slab, every kerb, every corner indelibly forged in the obscure and scant pathways of my brain. I can picture the route with clarity and ease, everything aside from where cars may be parked or a rubbish bag might have been placed.

I put on my pyjamas and dressing gown and lounge in front of the television with a mug of hot chocolate. The programmes are tedious and dull and I find my thoughts wandering elsewhere, outside the room, across the city to my old home. Wondering what Leah is doing, if she too is alone. What would she make of my plans for Saturday? She would be pleased that I am creating new paths, that I am following her lead, I'm sure of that much at least.

I check the front door, switch everything off in the kitchen and follow a routine I grow more and more accustomed to. There is solidity in the kitchen knife handle against my palm as I check under the bed, in the wardrobe, behind the sofa. Its weight is almost farcical in my hands when the bad dreams are being held at bay by possibilities and smiling blue eyes. I return it to the wooden block in the kitchen, smiling at my own folly when I know that the locks are changed and that I am safer now. I sing a little as I walk towards the bedroom, shedding my dressing gown as I go.

And it is into that lighter mood, that uninformed moment that the second phone call crashes in. Because of the previous call, I anticipate something far better, far lighter, something not quite so cataclysmic. I answer the call with a flourish, a breathy hello, a coquettish stance that speaks of expectation and the voice that replies is unknown, female, nervy.

"Hello, is this Sarah Phillips?"

"Er, yes it is." I deflate a little as the words leave me and take my expectant air with them.

"I'm sorry to call out of the blue like this but when I got your message I wanted to talk to you straight away."

I don't know of any message. I have no idea who this person is. And what she says next confirms these thoughts, that the name is right but the number is wrong because what she says, the words she speaks cannot be real, her words could never belong to me.

"Sarah, it's me. Your mother."

Chapter Fifty

The children at school called her The Little Orphan, I remember it well. She flinched from it, turned away as the words washed over her back and clung to the fibres of her school uniform like a cloak. But then they called her many things, orphan, survivor, loner. She had been so isolated, so different until meeting Alex, who was also set apart, was also different.

She never doubted that what she was told was true, never questioned the absence of her mother's grave. There were no memories to tell her otherwise, lost as they were deep in Pandora's Box. The idea came to me as I stood at the edge of the multi-storey car park contemplating an ending, a leaving behind.

It was the greatest lie between them, the tale of a death whispered into lost memories, filling a small corner of that vast empty space with the taint of deceit. Even in the depths of grief, Leah had used tragedy to sever that fetid tie; the weak and pitiable bond between the two of them, mother and daughter.

Little Orphan Sarah, a poor tragic little thing, lost and all alone with nobody left but her grieving aunt and the rancid remains of her family. And into that little scenario was poured the fiction of her wretched cancer-stricken mother, buried far away in her lonely unknown grave. It would all have been so terribly, horrifically sad, a tragedy of Dickensian proportion, except for one small detail: her mother was alive. Leah had lied about her death and I knew it, just as I knew why.

I knew the street where her mother lived, knew how close it was to the familiar paths Sarah stuck to with such rigidity. Had they walked past each other and not even realised? It made me wonder if perhaps she knew the truth somewhere deep down in her subconscious. Was there, somewhere inside of her, a klaxon that sounded if she veered from the familiar, recognisable paths? Did it exist just to keep her safe, to keep her away from an unseen truth? Had this bizarre compulsion of hers come about from self-preservation, from hidden awareness? I didn't really care. I just knew that it was about time the lie came tumbling around their feet.

Yet even though I thought it was a wonderful idea, that here was something, once again, that would jolt her out of her tired old patterns, I hesitated and tried to ignore the nagging second thoughts, the pushing away from something potentially ill-conceived. Struggling with myself to lift the phone, I heard the mosquito buzz from the earpiece, the tonal beeps as I pressed in the number I had memorised and all the while my thumb hovered over the disconnect button offering me a choice, I didn't have to speak, she would never know who had called.

An answer machine picked up and even the recording of her voice telling me to leave a message, the self-conscious tone, the overlong pause, the knowing that I would not have to speak to her in person, even those things did not calm my heart, transporting me, as they did, light-years away from the room I stood in. I waited for the beep telling me it was my turn to speak and I know I left it slightly too long, waiting for my adult voice to take the place of a frightened child's. Surely when she returned home and picked this message up she would think at first that the message was nothing more than white noise, a vague breathing sound. Perhaps she would hang up before I had even found my words.

My own voice, when I began to speak was too quick, spewed with latent venom and beneath the anger, infused into the gush of words, there was the fear of a life time ago. For a mere moment I felt a fraction of uncertainty at this particular choice, this course of action until I thought of Sarah and her pathetic piety, her lack of life, the absence of her past.

"Hi Mum it's me, Sarah. I know it's been a long time but I wanted to talk to you. I thought you were dead you see. Perhaps you could call me when you get this."

I left the number of Sarah's apartment and hung up, thinking that regardless of anything else, no matter the fear and indecision, it was done now and far too late to change it.

Maybe she wouldn't call. Maybe she would listen to the message and delete it without ever wanting to find out about the voice on the answer machine. There could be disbelief, guilt even that so long had passed and her daughter was a stranger to her. Would she be surprised at the voice of an adult coming from her child? Would she hesitate to be reminded of a time long gone? Perhaps she wouldn't care at all.

But what if she did call back? What would happen then? I could imagine all too easily the storm blowing through Sarah at the thought of it, the angst and the shock so tangible I could almost feel it. And what if they arranged to meet somewhere that wasn't in public, somewhere they couldn't be seen? What if they were alone together and nothing had changed? What if she became angry or violent towards the pathetically innocent Sarah? I knew it was possible, that violence was something she was entirely capable of. I had always known it, always feared it. I had witnessed it first-hand after all, she was my mother too.

Chapter Fifty-One

That word 'mother' is hard to describe. Its emotion, its connotation, they are descriptions that do not come easily. The word feels ashy and dry on my tongue, acrid almost. And its feeling is a hollowing of my stomach, the creation of a vacuum, a churning vacancy.

I doubt that voice, of course I do. I think it an error, a scam even. There is a rush of memories, or recent incidents, recent helplessness that push suspicion and anger into my words. I snap them through my teeth; force them through the tiny gaps and edges where there are imperfections, crookedness.

"You have the wrong number, my mother is dead."

And even after all this time there is still grief and loss there as I speak these words. I still hear the fragments of regret. There is a pause in which my breath catches and I think that now is the time to hang up, to end this call, carry on with what little remains of the day. But there is hesitation and something, something that I can't quite put my finger on, something that holds me still until she speaks again.

"No wait!"

The voice says, as if she senses my finger hovering over the button to end this.

"I know you thought that. I guess Tom told you that and I don't blame him at all. But it is me, your mother. At least I am if you are Sarah Phillips, daughter of Tom, sister of Annie."

This time there is no hesitation as I replace the receiver with boneless fingers.

Within seconds the phone rings again and I watch it feeling walls crumble around me, foundations tear apart. I count the tones, they reach twenty-one before falling into a silence in which I continue to stare at the curved lines, the small square buttons and will it to not ring again, to stay quiet, to hide unwanted voices deep inside. I want to doubt her. I want to dismiss her as a kook, a crazy. I want to roll away that stone and find dust and bones and decay.

But there is doubt, indecision and, beneath it all, beneath the stirring surface of catastrophe and disbelief there is something unexpected. Beyond everything else, through the emptiness carried behind my eyes there is a tiny stab of familiarity, something in her voice, the tone, the way she breathed through her sentences. Somewhere hidden away in the dark spaces where I am blind and floundering, there is a tiny inexplicable sliver of recognition. I feel it dragging at the edges of the black hole, a calling forth, a siren sound into hidden valleys.

I stand for a long time, staring beyond everything. Feeling nothing more than exhausted and overwhelmed, a blown circuit with nothing left but a blackened spot to show where there had once been something more, something live. Light moves, slow and pale into my peripheral vision and I turn towards it, coming face to face with the moon as it tells me I have stood for too long, that hours have been lost as my thoughts grew still and tired.

Reaching for the phone I dial one, four, seven, one and listen as a recorded voice gives me the last number that called. A stranger's number, a liar's number and yet perhaps not, perhaps a mistake, vast and unthinkable, has somehow been made. I run through the possibilities of how that could happen. What if there were two patients in the hospital with the same name, the same condition, what if the wrong one had died and, thinking it was the other, they informed the wrong family? What if it was a case of mistaken identity, that Leah had been fed the wrong information? Information that she then passed on to me as she held my hand and told me she was sorry, that she was now all I have.

As I write down the number it occurs to me that perhaps the caller is in fact the person who has been following me, the person who is responsible for the immense, arduous changes in my life. The call could be a ruse created by someone who knows my history, my orphan status and wants to play on my insecurities, arrange a meeting, get me alone. And what would I do then, if I went along with it, put myself in danger?

I think again of Leah, of the brochure, the taxi, the phone calls. It is all too much of a coincidence. Despite the growing lateness, I dial her number into the handset and wait for her to answer. Three rings later I hear the beep as we are connected.

"Hi Leah, sorry it's a bit late but this is just a quick call, I just need to ask you something." She sounds surprised that I have called so soon after meeting. She tells me to go ahead and ask my question, her voice is sleepy.

"Did my mother have any other family, perhaps more distant relatives that we don't know about?" There is a pause, at once brief and immense.

"Why do you ask?"

Her response is stilted, uncertain and I wonder at its hesitance as I begin to speak again.

"I don't know, I was thinking about things, that maybe there were other people from my past that I can't remember. I had a phone call this evening, and the caller knew a few things about me and it got me wondering who could know me that well."

There is another pause, deeper and millpond-still and when she speaks again her voice is more awake yet quieter, an air of urgency clinging to every fragment of her speech. Her words are separate drops in a black ocean.

"What did the caller say?"

I take a deep breath before replying.

"She said she is my mother."

The silence from the end of the phone is total, complete. I wait for a response, for something to meander its way into my ear piece and make light of everything, her tinkling laugh perhaps or safe words to dismiss this strange new turn of my world on its axis. I wait but nothing comes. The silence grows longer and more profound and I begin to feel afraid as something of the truth, or some variant of it, blooms within this space. I begin to hear the shocking legitimacy of a stranger's words as I wait for denial from the one person who has always been on my side.

"Sarah," she says and nothing else is needed, her voice shaken and knowing and bleak.

I do not know what to say as my words rust solid and I hear the silent confession in her tone.

"You lied to me?" I say and I don't want to believe it, I brace myself against the hideous tide of betrayal that pours through me like a tsunami.

"Sarah, please."

Her tone is pleading, guilty and I know then without doubt, without reservation, that I am right and that for some unfathomable reason, Leah has allowed me to grow up believing I have no-one but her, that I am utterly alone.

In a burst of disbelief and rage I throw the phone across the room, watching as it clatters through the kitchen doorway, skidding along the tiles and breaking out of sight against the wall.

I pace the room, my disbelief giving momentum to a body that had been winding down for sleep. Penned in and claustrophobic I gather my bag and coat and leave the apartment, slamming the door behind me. I have no idea where I am going to go but I have to get out before Leah turns up, as I know she will, and pleads forgiveness, tries to make me understand something that to me, in this moment, is beyond comprehension.

Chapter Fifty-Two

I hear the door slam as she storms out of her apartment and strides away from it. Purpose and anger resound in each determined, heavy-footed step. Her head is up, chin jutted out as if leading the way somewhere important, somewhere urgent. There is real fury in the set of her shoulders, the length of her stride. Down the pedestrian shopping centre, past the little statue of the blue boy that once stood in the courtyard of St John's Hospital School but that she has never looked at long enough to understand the meaning of, who he was, why he was there. Past the chrome and glass frontages of the restaurants and cafe's that spill their tables onto the pavement.

She turns right at the end of the street, past the designer clothes shops and the glass sculptures that shine out in different colours when the night draws in. Instead of continuing as she always does, towards the familiarity of the High Street, the place where the walkways are known and safe, where everything is solid, memorised, she turns left, as if she has done it many times, walked this night-time path towards Cathedral Green, without fear, without anxiety.

Her step doesn't lessen as it normally does as she nears unfamiliar routes, her chin does not drop to her chest, her eyes do not follow its feeble journey to point towards the floor. She is a scandalised puppet and her anger the hands in charge, pulling her upright, forcing her steps onwards, sharp and undeviating.

Somewhere near the grounds of the Cathedral, near the grass that is sparse in places from the many visitors that sit to take in the air of peace, the fight slips from her feet into the flat, cool ground. Her steps slow as if caught in mud or quicksand and her shoulders move slightly, inexorably downwards. And still she doesn't look around her with the eyes of fear; still she doesn't gasp her sudden panic out in front of her shocked face. Instead she steps slowly towards the low wall that circles the Green. Her hand reaches out towards the rough surface and she follows it, sitting down delicately as if in pain. Turning in on herself she hunches over as if weariness pulls her inwards, forces her eyelids closed. Her head shakes a little and the long curtain of hair slips to hide her face from prying eyes.

I think of her here, in this place that is strange to her and wonder if she will ever see the victory in this moment. Does she even know, in her anger and shock, where she is? Does she see the newness of her experience in the old grey stones, the gargoyles that watch over her? Does she even notice her own vulnerability as she sits, a young woman alone in the night, the occasional drunk passing by and looking at her curiously?

Lost in my own thoughts I fail to notice her moving away until she is vague and distant and I am alone. I make no move to follow, becoming instead what she was, a young woman drawing the attention of passing drunks. The difference being that I am aware, I know they are there, I am not held captive by the depths of my own thoughts.

Retracing my steps back to the apartment building I key in the code, wondering why it has never occurred to Sarah that whoever it is that follows her, lives in the same place. It seems obvious to me, like Occam's razor, that in this case the simplest explanation is most certainly the correct one.

But she has not got that far yet, her thoughts are not calm, they are not rational. Her controlled life, one in which there is no change, no variation, is crashing around her, leaving her caught, a rabbit in the headlights.

Perhaps I was wrong to make the phone call, perhaps it was a step too far, but everything I have done so far has brought her here, to somewhere new. Like a chick emerging from an egg there is a sense of freedom in her, a sense of choice and I find an almost obsessive delight in watching her unfolding, becoming.

I wonder how long it will be before Leah can speak to her of the truth, and of the reasons behind it. When will she be able to give an explanation for the lie that has lived with them, grown bigger than the pair of them? I knew the truth, the validity of her reasoning where Sarah was concerned. I knew of her mother's arrest, of her sentence and an eventual psychiatric evaluation that left her in and out of treatment, in and out of rationale. I guessed at Leah's wish for Sarah to have a normal life, a life free of that cruelty, that drama and uncertainty where there had already been far too much.

But I also saw Sarah's anger, the betrayal that wrapped around her, holding her still inside her rage. Angry enough that her eyes became blind, her ears became deaf and I knew that, for the present at least, Sarah would not hear anything Leah had to say.

I stand outside the door to Sarah's apartment, knowing she isn't there, that the rooms will be empty and dark. The door is solid, safe. I know of the bolts on the other side, the bolts designed to keep her safe, to keep me out. I smile to myself as I reach into my pocket and pull out the shiny new key. It feels cold and solid against my fingers as I slide it into the lock and open the door.

I don't bother turning on the lights, the vague glow from the streetlamps are enough that I can make out where I am going and I know this place well, I have been here often enough. I make my way to the kitchen and slide open the drawer, finding what I want there, before turning and seeing the shattered remains of the phone on the floor. I step over it and head back into the lounge. I think of sofas that hide secrets, of lives unravelling and I go and sit in the seat closest to the door, curling up into the arm of the sofa and reaching down to see if this one holds a secret for me.

Chapter Fifty-Three

Right at the very top, above the slope that begins gently then grows steep and jagged, there is a loose stone. It teeters a little, rocks from side to side and eventually it tumbles, turning end over end, picking up momentum and speed. Other rocks, stones, shale, knocked loose by its passing begin to slide too, joining in the race. They tumble end over end and more and more join until it becomes an avalanche tearing down the rocky face, bearing down to the bottom where I stand and fail to move. This is my life. This is where I stand and wait to be swept away, knowing that it will hurt, that it will tear at me and that I am helpless to prevent it. I cannot even run from it, my legs grown weak and useless.

I go over this morning's events, time and again but it makes no more sense with the repetition, there is no rational explanation. There were twelve steps to my sofa, twelve whole steps. At first there were twelve and a little bit and so I moved it, tried again, got it perfect. There were twelve steps to my sofa. Until this morning. This morning there were only ten. And I knew for certain then that this was not my imagination, that I had been right all along, someone had stood where I stood.

The man opposite me looks my way with curiosity. There are wrinkles around his eyes which are sharp beneath greying eyebrows, his hair is a uniform grey and buzz cut all over and his nose is long and pointed, making me think of a bald eagle. I am uncomfortable beneath his gaze, like prey waiting for the inevitable. I shift on my seat, glance around me and wait for him to speak into the uncomfortable silence.

"So, Miss Phillips, tell me again what happened."

And so I do, even though the words sound ridiculous to me, even though I can see in them the reason for the disbelief in the policeman's eyes.

"For a while now I've had the suspicion that someone is following me, there have been things in my apartment, things that I didn't put there. I noticed this morning that my sofa had been moved." I can feel my cheeks colouring beneath the wry look he sends my way. "I have certain... compulsions, I tend to count things and the steps to my sofa, they... they weren't right. And then when I was pushing it back to where it should be, I noticed that something had been pushed down the side of the cushion."

"What was it, Miss Phillips?" His tone is bored, disinterested.

"It was a cufflink."

I look away from him and see again the glint from the corner of my eye, something that had not been there before, something I had never seen. I reached for it and found a small golden cube, it sat in the palm of my hand. There was hardly any weight to it but I struggled to hold it. I ran to the kitchen then and dropped it into the bin, backing away as if it were a bomb that would explode if I turned my back.

And then I looked up and found her. The string tied around her neck, attached to the flex of the light. She swung slightly in the breeze made with the door, the plastic smile on her face clownish and hideous in the circumstances. I describe her to the man opposite me and his expression remains neutral, as if what I say is nothing new, is not capable of tearing at my foundations.

"The doll had been in a drawer, but I hadn't put it there

either, I had found it in the drawer in the kitchen, where it shouldn't have been, and then I found it hanging."

"Did anyone visit you last night, a friend, boyfriend maybe, that could have been playing a prank?"

"No, no, I wasn't home until very late. I... "

And I stop because I don't know how to say where I was, that it would open another floodgate that would confuse the moment, make it even less plausible. But he sees my hesitation and it is too late to stay silent.

"Tell me about last night."

"There isn't much to tell," I say instantly and he backhands the words from the air with a rapid gesture as I sigh.

"My aunt and I had a bit of an argument on the phone and I went out for a walk."

"What time did you get home?"

"I'm not sure," I admit. Accompanied by my anger and lost in the thoughts that spurred on my steps, I had again lost track of time.

"Had you been drinking, Miss Phillips?"

And I realise then, through his questions, that he sees what happened in an altogether different light. I feel threatened, terrified, and he sees overlaying my fears the mask of a forgetful drunk, an angry, foolish woman. He looks at me with cynical eyes as my own beg him for help, for protection.

"No," I say and hear my own weakness, my own insecurity and uncertainty.

"But you aren't sure?"

"I was distressed last night, something incredibly traumatic occurred and I was very angry and upset. I went out for a walk, it was late, I was tired. I am aware that I wasn't thinking too clearly but I didn't stop anywhere for a drink because that is not the sort of thing I would usually do." Annoyance taints my voice and I see him shut down against it.

"But, according to you, these weren't usual circumstances, so perhaps you behaved unusually."

He tells me and I do not know how to answer him because

his mind is made up and it is me that is at fault for being annoyed, for walking alone in the dark.

"What was this 'traumatic event' that you mentioned?"

"I'm not sure I want to go into that," I reply tightly, thinking some things should be left unsaid, hidden away where they can't be scrutinised, given credence.

"It would help me to understand more about your frame of mind and the sequence of events," he says and simply waits, leaning back on his chair, stretching out his legs a little as if this is a social visit and he has all the time in the world.

The clock ticks away the seconds and I grow edgy against its beat.

"I was brought up by my aunt and believed my mother to be dead. I found out yesterday that she might still be alive. That's all."

As if it is nothing and people come back to life all the time, as if I hadn't wasted years regretting the absence of my family both physically and in my memory. How small these words are, too small to describe the magnitude of emotion, the vast wasteland of the lie I have been told.

"I can imagine that would shake someone up quite a lot, something like that, maybe make them a bit irrational."

His eyes are on my hair as if he cannot meet the way I am looking back at him.

"I am not imagining this," I shout, knowing it to be futile.

He simply watches me quizzically, watches my hand shaking as I press it against my cheek, lower it back to the table.

The door opens and another younger policeman steps in and beckons the man opposite me; he gets to his feet with a groan of middle age and stretches as he walks towards the other. They step outside and shut the door leaving me in total silence.

Before I found its hidden secret I had moved the sofa back to its normal place and then checked and rechecked that I had it right. Twelve steps, just as it had always been. Was it

275

possible that I had got it wrong? But I knew the answer to that already, there was no way, no way at all. I was too meticulous about it, too compulsive to make a mistake like that. But even so there was a tiny element of doubt, until I went to sit down.

I saw a flash of light out of the corner of my eye and reached down to see what it was. The cufflink, something I had never owned, never seen before, had been put between the cushion and the arm of the sofa. And in that moment there was no doubt. I knew for certain that someone had been coming into my apartment, that despite the locks being changed, they had found their way in here somehow.

When I backed away from the hanging doll, pulling the door closed behind me so I could no longer see her, I could see the front door from where I stood, could see that the bolt was unfastened. Had I left it like that when I returned last night? It seemed unlikely that I would do such a thing when I was so edgy, obsessive about it. But the fog of my anger would not lift and my memories were still inside it. I couldn't recall an exact sequence of events, only footsteps on cobblestones ringing out in anger, a feeling of defeat and loss.

I went to get the phone, remembered that it lay in pieces on the kitchen floor and fetched the spare handset from the bedroom. I called the police and they told me to go to the station. Almost glad of an excuse to escape, I carefully locked the door behind me and ran all the way along familiar paths to Heavitree, where I had to pause to catch my breath before opening the heavy door into a quiet waiting area.

The policeman returns, pulling me away from my thoughts, he carries a file in his hands and a frown on his face as he reads it. I get the feeling that it is nothing more than posturing, something to hide behind and put words into his mouth.

"I see that we visited your apartment quite recently, Miss Phillips?" he says as though I am the one being questioned, as though I am under suspicion.

I nod anyway, "What does that have to do with anything?"

He glances up at my irritation as though looking at me

properly for the first time, finding me more interesting now he holds some history in his rough hands.

"It's all about context isn't it?" he tells me. "We come to visit you about malicious phone calls being made from your apartment and now this. Does it seem like a coincidence to you?"

"I think it was happening before I moved in, when I was still living at my aunt's house. There were a few odd things that happened then too. My family's grave was vandalised," I say and he looks back at his notes, looking for a record that won't be in there because my aunt's discovery had set her to war against her loyalty.

"Did you report that to the police?"

I lower my eyes and shake my head. "My aunt decided not to." My own voice is quiet in my ears, chased by the voice of the policeman as he asks me why not. I can't bring myself to say it, can't meet his eyes and so he asks again and again until I lift my chin and look at him.

"She thought that I might have done it because I was angry with her, we had argued."

"It seems that you and your aunt argue a lot, Miss Phillips, am I seeing a pattern developing here?"

"I don't know what you mean, of course not," I say and he glances down at the file again.

"You argued with your aunt and the grave got vandalised, then you argue with your aunt and someone breaks into your apartment. I wonder if you argued with your aunt every time a malicious phone call was made."

"I didn't do this," I repeat and the words evaporate like smoke.

"I'm not saying you did, Miss Phillips, I'm just trying to look at all the angles."

The surface of the table is worn and pitted. I look at the cup of tea that has been made for me, the drink that will remain untouched until it is tipped cold and unappealing down the sink.

"I take it that you aren't going to do anything about this," I say, helplessness stirring my words into a maelstrom, "that you expect me to just go home, and sit and wait for the next thing to happen. Maybe next time they won't come in while I'm out, maybe I'll be sitting right there when they decide to pay me another visit, let themselves in, hurt me, have you thought about that? Or just maybe, with these phone calls I'm being set up for something, but the easiest thing for you to do is to sit there and assume it is me because then you won't have to get off your doughnut-filled arse and do any real work."

My eyes stab into him from across the table and he lowers his to the file as he closes it.

"What I am going to do, Miss Phillips, is to have one of my colleague's escort you back to your apartment. He is going to check things out for you and see if there are any signs of a forced entry. I will also look into the possibility of getting a personal alarm set up for you. I would also suggest that you take a look at your stereotyping. Not all police personnel eat doughnuts, Miss Phillips, it's a myth fostered by too many fictional television shows. Personally I'm more partial to a bag of salted peanuts."

He stands up and moves towards the door, holding it open for me. A few minutes later I am standing outside persuading another policeman that I will meet him back at my apartment, that I want to walk home. He shuts the car door and drives away, after a few minutes I follow, looking around me continuously as I walk.

Chapter Fifty-Four

He unlocks the door for me after taking the key from shaking hands and steps through first; he seems sympathetic and I feel better for it, believed. He glances around slowly before moving out of the way to allow me in beside him. I appreciate the chivalry, knowing that it speaks of an element of doubt, of uncertainty. Two letters shine white on the dim hallway floor and I bend to retrieve them both. One looks official, a return address informing me that it is from Doctor Charles, no doubt an appointment. The other is a plain postcard, hand-delivered as there is no stamp, no postmark. It simply says: *Please, please call me. We need to talk. Leah.* I put both to one side on the hallway table and turn away from them.

"Would you like to wait here while I take a look around?" he asks.

He appears younger all of a sudden and I realise that even for him, someone who is trained, who knows what they are doing, there is uncertainty in these moments, of the unknown, of possibilities. I think that if it is okay for him to be afraid, then it is more than okay for me to be afraid too. I stand still as he moves away from me and begins a slow search of the rooms.

For several minutes there is utter silence punctuated by the movement of cloth against cloth, the slow scissoring of his legs. Then there is a tiny scraping sound and he returns to me holding the doll, the string trailing from her neck.

"Did you leave this on the side in the kitchen?"

I find that I can't remember. Had I untied her and laid her carefully on the side, or had I left her hanging there, slowly spinning? Has she been moved yet again when I was not here to see? I think of how vulnerable I am here, knowing that someone is getting in, that I cannot seem to stop them. A tremble begins near my feet, moving upwards swiftly until I have no choice but to sink to the floor, holding out a hand to find anything that might help to slow my descent.

He tells me that nothing seems out of place except for the phone that is smashed.

"I did that."

For a moment he looks at me differently and I sigh against this new judgement.

"I was angry," I say and it doesn't make it any better, but he holds out his hand to help me to my feet and acts as if it is normal that I have chosen to sit suddenly on the floor.

He moves away slightly and opens the front door, checking its edges, the lock. I think about offering him coffee but stay quiet as he stands and turns towards me.

"There are no signs of forced entry here, Miss Phillips, nothing untoward at all."

"Apart from the doll that was hanging in my kitchen, you mean?"

He nods, looking uncomfortable, "Yes, apart from that."

I turn from him, feeling helpless, covering my fear by walking to the table to retrieve the mail. I open the letter as he silently watches and I think that perhaps he really doesn't know what to say, to him this is a small thing, no obvious crime, no wounding.

I read the sheet of paper with blurry eyes, an appointment has been made for me to see Doctor Charles the following Tuesday. It seems like a lifetime since I saw him the first time. I wonder if I will keep it, if it will do me any good trying to find my past when my present is so turbulent. I think for a moment about not bothering to show up, yet even as I do so I know I will almost certainly attend. There is little left to lose that I am not losing already, perhaps there could be solace for me somewhere if I can uncover my past, find a way to be set free from the fear that blasts my landscape.

I consider calling Alex, asking if I can stay with her for the night, perhaps the next too. But in the end I don't, shying away from the questions that would follow, the conversations I am not ready to have. And if I went there, Leah would find out. Surely it would be her first port of call if she could get no answer from the apartment or my mobile phone. Perhaps she would turn up to talk and I cannot face her just now, unprepared as I am to hear her voice, her reasons. There can be no justification for her actions, such awful, awful deceit. There can be no excuses, no sensible reasoning. I do not see a way through the fog of her lies.

The policeman clears his throat loudly into the silence.

"I'll be on my way now, Miss Phillips. Someone will be in touch with you soon about installing a personal alarm that links directly to the police station."

I say thank you and he smiles and looks a little shy and uncertain – perhaps unused to being thanked in a job that often brings him face to face with violence. I silently wish him not to leave, to stay here to keep an eye on me, to watch me while I sleep so that I know that I am safe. But I open the door for him anyway, say goodbye and watch as he waits in the hallway beyond for the lift to arrive. I hear another of the apartment doors open and close my own quickly, not wanting my unknown neighbour to know that it was me the policeman was visiting, not wanting them to think badly of me as people often automatically do in situations such as these.

I lock and bolt the door behind him, wondering at the futility of it, wondering at the lack of forced entry, at my lack of understanding of what is happening in my life. I move towards the sofa, cautiously checking down the sides of it, even though I know the policeman did the same and found nothing, and then I spin the sofa round until it is facing the door. Sitting down I stare at the bolts, willing them to stay closed, praying that the handle will not move slowly with an external attempt to open the door.

And there I sit all day, ignoring the occasional ringing of the phone, or the vibrating of an arriving text message. I sit and stare, not moving, breathing slowly, as the day fades away and I grow tired and drift into a disturbed sleep in which the darkness becomes solid, becomes form and chases me through unfamiliar streets.

There is a pain across my shoulders when I wake, I have fallen asleep sitting up, my neck bent awkwardly, the muscles protesting. The light is still on and pushes against the daylight pouring through the window. Confusion blurs my thoughts as for a moment I forget everything and only see the strangeness of my waking. But then the doll with string around her neck marches into my thoughts and scatters the bemusement she finds there.

I look at the door and realise with horror that the bolts are undone. My heart races away from me, stealing the breath from my lungs and sealing my throat. I cannot look away from something that shouldn't be, that can't be. I locked the door and shot the bolts, I know it with such deep certainty. Ignoring the pain in my neck I raise my head from the back of the sofa and it feels lighter somehow, odd.

I reach up to rub my temple and stare incomprehensibly at my hand, at the wisps of hair that have come away and stuck to sleep-damp palms. The fear in my throat sounds like a dog whimpering as I push myself away from the sofa and stare in horror at the hair I leave behind, the dark curls that fall onto the seat I have vacated. Touching my head I feel blunt ends, jagged edges and as I look down at the clumps of hair on my shoulders, on my arms, I see the scissors on the floor, the vintage curve of them, the old dressmaking scissors Aunt Leah had given me because I found them lovely and unusual.

They are half-open, discarded, strands of hair still clinging to the blades.

I run then to the kitchen and grab two knives from the block, one for each hand, the tips juddering madly as I stand with my back to the corner of the room, staring wildly around me as though my attacker might still be there. I don't know how long I stand like that, terror paralysing my entire body. Eventually I force myself to move, checking rooms, under the bed, in the wardrobe, all the while holding the blades before me like a talisman to ward off evil.

There is no-one here but me, no dark shadow in the corner, no snake waiting to strike. Putting both knives in one hand I collect some things together – clothes, toiletries, my diary – and throw them into a bag. Standing at the door I draw in a shaky breath and wonder if I will come back here, to revisit this new beginning, to start over. I doubt I could ever stand here and feel safe again. I put the knives down on the hallway table and see my appointment letter as I do. I add that to the bag and turn to leave, locking the door behind me.

The hotel isn't too far away from the apartment and the streets are busy, if anyone follows me or chooses to watch from a distance, there is no way I will see them, pick them out among the crowds of shoppers. I try to leave my fears behind in the apartment, hoping they will stay inside the locked door with the tangled mess of my hair, but a thread of them snags on to my clothing and comes with me anyway.

Chapter Fifty-Five

Sorry to text you like this but something has come up and I'm not going to be able to make it on Saturday. Please don't take this as a brush-off. I still really want to meet up, just got family crises going on at the moment. Forgive me? X

I click Send before I change my mind and there is regret attached to the message as it leaves my phone. I don't unpack the few clothes I brought with me, I don't wander around the mediocre room I have booked, nor familiarise myself with its mass-produced wall art and cheap flat-pack furniture. I lean back against the pillows on the surprisingly comfortable bed, my diary closed on my bent-up legs, and stare into space wondering how I came to be here when my life has always been so easy, so straightforward.

My mobile rings loud in the vacuum I sit in. It is Cam and for a brief moment I consider not answering but then I remember the excitement in my belly, the soft kiss on my cheek and I realise I can do nothing else. He speaks before I finish saying hello.

"I am gutted! How can I possibly forgive you? Those poor seagulls. How can we ever make it up to them?"

My smile is small, real. "We'll have to make double for them next time."

"Are you okay? You sound sad."

And I wish he was here with me, even though he is new and unknown. I sigh. "Just family stuff, you know, getting on top of me a bit. I just need to get some stuff sorted. I meant it when I said I still want to meet. This isn't a brush-off, honestly."

"I'm glad, is there anything I can do to help?"

There isn't, there is no magic wand to change the past, to make lies into truth, to give back the years I feel I have lost.

"I don't think so, but thank you, I appreciate the offer." And I am smiling but my cheeks are wet and even though he is new and not yet precious, I hope that he is not another thing I will lose, another thing that I will one day have to grieve for.

"Let me know if there is anything I can do. I mean that too," he says, his sincerity unmistakable.

"I will do, I promise."

"You know," he says solemnly. "Promises mean nothing unless you pinky swear."

I laugh, I can't help it and somewhere on the line between us his laughter meets mine. "Okay, I pinky swear." I tell him and then he says goodbye and there is nothing more but the occasional noise from the corridor.

I stare at a patch of wall, seeing nothing but my own thoughts projected there; a jumble of confused imagery and change, of bitter deceit and sadness. 'I have a mother.' It goes around and around in my head, shouting louder than everything else, louder even than my aunt's betrayal. I lose my identity in that thought and struggle to remember who I am, the heavy cloak of an orphan slipping from my shoulders. The knowledge changes me, makes me less solitary as it hands me future possibilities – a grandmother for my children, someone to walk beside me down a make-believe aisle in one possible future.

And then another thought, black and weighty, pushes through the cacophony of change. Why hasn't she tried to find me? Was I told that I was dead too? That I had faded away in the wreck of the car along with her other child, her husband? Had she too wondered at the location of an unknown grave and pitied those who lay beneath for having no-one to tend them, no-one to care?

Into the silent, calamitous thoughts the ringing phone intrudes. I look at the screen, at Alex's name and I press the reject button. Seeing, as real as any projection on the wall opposite, a sequence of events I know would prove true: my aunt arriving at the apartment to try to explain, to ask for forgiveness, finding my home empty and dark. It is only logic that would drive her literally or metaphorically to Alex, to question my whereabouts. Had she explained why I was gone? Was the truth altered, abridged to make it sound less extreme, to make sure that the first person that hears the explanation for the lie is the person it affected the most? Did she try to justify what she had done?

Whatever has been said is enough to spur Alex to try to call several times within the next hour. I put the phone on silent and know it is ringing only because of a slight vibration travelling across the bed covers, little more than a whisper against my thigh. When I pick up the phone again I have missed twelve calls altogether, eight from Alex and four from Leah. Alex has also texted saying she is concerned for me, asking me to call, please call and let her know I am okay. Yet how can I when it would be a lie to tell her that I am? How can I tell her I am okay when my world has shifted on its axis?

There is no desire, no urge in me to respond. No way that I can contemplate saying hello, explaining, saying where I am. No-one can reach me here, no-one knows where I am, no-one can lie or betray or question me. No police could turn up with their accusations, their disbelief as I try to share my truth with them. No whirlwind can blow through and leave me terrified and changed and gasping. No hand can wield scissors while I sleep. There is only me and suddenly, through the cloud of days spent in fear, I feel safer than I have for a while. Safe and hidden away where no-one can see me.

The bland carpet is harsh and brushes against my feet as I stretch my legs. I carry my bag to the bathroom, pull out my toiletries and as I do so the letter from Doctor Charles tumbles out, skidding across the shiny tiled floor that looks worn but is otherwise clean. I bend down to retrieve it and read it through again.

For this there is a compulsion, sudden and surprising, a desire to keep the appointment, to set that change in motion, to fix things that I thought permanently broken, to find memories hidden in dark places. Is it because I have learned the truth about my mother and I want to discover everything about her, to make sure we meet as equals, known quantities?

Standing in an anonymous room with nothing familiar to bring me comfort, feeling miles removed from everything I know, I realise that my life simply can't remain as it is, and there is no-one else to turn to but this cluttered stranger with his terrible tea who offers sincerity and possibility; who offers to shed light on dark places even though it comes without a guarantee that anything can be fixed. In a reality that has become changed, he is the only one who offers me anything without a hidden agenda of his own. There are no secrets, no hidden past, no echoes from a life I no longer recognise as my own. Aside from him and the possibility that Cam holds, in this moment, what else do I have?

Chapter Fifty-Six

My footsteps seem different in the space she has left behind. I step softly, gently through her apartment. The sheets in the bedroom still smell of her, traces of toothpaste linger in the sink where it trickled into the plughole. In the corner there is dirty underwear, socks balled up and thrown onto the pile, a tomato-stained T-shirt. Her shorn curls tumble down the back of the sofa, across the seat, some have tumbled to the floor.

Yet despite all of these things, in spite of the signs of life, of recent movement, the rooms feel discarded and cold, as though no-one has lived here for a long time and the decay is already beginning to permeate into the walls, the fibres, the soul of the place. There are dirty dishes in the sink. A tea cup with a hardened stain, liquid becoming solid, toast crumbs, congealed grease, a frying pan.

I fill the sink and squirt in detergent, watching it foam and bubble, light reflecting off the tiny orbs as I take my time over the task, scrubbing at the stains and the filth that she left behind.

I am safe here. I can do this, step into her life like this, without fear of disturbance, knowing that she will not be returning anytime soon. I do not have to fear her responses. I no longer have to consider the impact my actions will have on her. Is this a small way in which I am trying to make things better? Changing things so that she will not have to return to find them filthy and gross in a sink that smells of mould and decay?

In some bizarre way I think I am beginning to find my maternal streak. It began in that moment when I looked at her and felt her devastation. Too late I began to see things through her wet and fearful eyes. She had lifted her face, open and afraid, to mine and I hid behind it, finally beginning to see the world as she did, a world of sensation and fear and blank empty spaces that no-one could fill. I wanted to smooth her skin beneath my palm, brush her ragged hair and tell her it would be okay, that she wasn't alone, that I was here and I would never leave her, I would always be here for her.

I dry my hands on a tea towel I find in the drawer and fold it up beside the draining board before drifting slowly back into the living room. The carnation sits on the coffee table. I found it on the way here, alone on the pavement beneath the over-full hanging baskets that swayed gently above my head. It seemed wrong to leave it there where no-one could see its beauty, where it would be crushed beneath the careless feet of people who never bothered to look down, to see what was passing beneath them.

I reach out and lift the bloom to my nose, a vague sense of a scent that is almost nothing, little more than a shadow. But the petals themselves are perfect: red and soft. I caress them with gentle fingers before walking to the bedroom once more and placing the flower on her pillow as if I were laying a wreath. Flowers for the dead, because she has gone and I find myself grieving her absence. There are tears on my cheeks as I turn to leave.

Chapter Fifty-Seven

The phone rings and I grope blindly for it. It doesn't take long for the room to become familiar even with my eyes closed and foggy with sleep. The display on the phone says the number is unknown and I am instantly awake, aware. I do not answer the call. Moments later there is a beep from the handset that tells me I have a message and I brace myself to hear it, to hear unwelcome words from unwelcome people.

I hold the phone at some distance from my ear so I can snatch it away quickly, not hear words that I do not invite into my life. I recognise the voice immediately. The policeman I spoke to – I insulted – at the station says hello to my answer phone service and asks me to call on a number he rattles off without hesitation. I move to the window and look out on the morning's slow-moving traffic and grey skies before calling the direct number.

"Ah, Miss Phillips, thank you for getting back to me." His voice is polite, bland, speaking of routine calls, nothing interesting.

"It's fine," I say, though it isn't, it is awkward, unpleasant.

He clears his throat. "Okay then. I just wanted to phone to arrange a date to come and see you to fit the personal alarm in your apartment. This would be a direct link with your local police station so that officers could respond immediately if you sounded the alarm."

I tell him that I'm not at home and that for the moment all is quiet, there has been nothing further to tell him. I will call him on my return and arrange a date then. When he says goodbye I hear the relief in his voice, the delight at being able to end his association with me. What I said to him is true, there has been nothing out of the ordinary. I do not feel watched even when I venture out as I have already done, a visit to the hairdresser to reshape my butchered hair, to buy supplies, to count the steps to Gandy Street and watch the shop, wishing I had the courage to go in, to confront her. I have felt no eyes upon my back as I walk to my hotel, caught no threatening movements out of the corner of my eye.

Over the previous weekend the phone calls to my mobile petered out. Time passing could have been recorded by the falling away, the frustration in the ring tone, the lack of success. The calls had gone from several times an hour during waking hours, to one or two to none at all. In one instance a call had come in at two in the morning, I was still awake, pretending to read but thinking of my sister. The screen had flashed up Leah's name and I turned from it, trying not to feel her worry, her desperation in the early hours of a rainy morning.

Eventually she sent a text: *I understand you are not ready to talk to me but please, please let me know that you are all right. I don't know where you are and I am worried about you. I'm sorry.*

I considered not replying, the way I hurt inside pushing away any consideration of her feelings. But then I imagined her, too easily, lying in a dark bedroom, curled up beneath her pink candlewick bedspread, feeling alone as I did, wondering what had happened to the last unravelling thread of her family.

Before I could change my mind I texted back: *I'm fine.*

I didn't add a kiss. Her reply was almost instant but I put the phone aside without reading her message. I had assuaged my guilt, but I couldn't see how it would ever be possible for her to do the same. And that was days ago but I lose myself in thoughts of her as another day passes slowly and I feel the tension in the band of stress that knots across my brow, dragging pain behind it. Laying down I am gripped by the morbid fantasies that often seem to exist only in the early hours of the morning, when there is no-one else around to bear witness. But now it is daylight and the fear, the irrational weight of them, is the same.

I think that I could die here, that no-one would know, until eventually the hotel staff realised I hadn't been seen for a few days. I had placed the Do Not Disturb sign on the door. How long would it be until they ignored it, looked beyond it? How long would it be before I faded away into the background and left a vacant space in the world, too tiny to be noticed? I lean over and reach into my bag for the painkillers that will chase the crushing pain back into the darkness.

Chapter Fifty-Eight

And this is how it ends.

With a day that starts somnambulant and slow. The sort of day that should be full of sunshine, heady with the scent of roses. There are thick grey clouds in the sky, the smell of rain and damp grass. It ends with me waiting for her to look my way, with a falling away, a removal of the masks that we wear. It ends when she looks at me, sees me properly for the first time and realises who I am. It ends with her legs losing strength, with her falling back, her eyes rolling into her head.

Or maybe I should say that this is how it begins.

Sometimes I wonder if life is a dream. If all the daydreams or the real dreams, the sleeping moments and the lost in thought moments, if they are, in fact, the real us. If the day to day grind of walking the treadmill is the dream and we are so much more than that, so much beyond the reality. I search through myself and find a slightly bitter taste, an element of disgust at what I have wrought. Barely finding my motivation, any justification, within the barren scene of guilt and regret.

She leaves the hotel early before the shops have opened, walking behind a street cleaner who looks half-asleep as he goes about his job, perhaps he too is dreaming of a world more real to him than this moment. There is a strange kind of stillness, a calm as if snow has fallen, invisible and muffling. She looks brighter, more aware of the world around her and I feel that old familiar sense of envy creeping up inside me. Until I think about the dark circles that meet her eyes in the mirror, the way her mouth turns down at the corners when she thinks that no-one is looking her way.

She has not set foot in her apartment since I left the doll for her to find, since I took scissors to the hair she grew to hide the white scar at her temple. She is still holed up in the anonymous hotel that seems to suit her better – with its lack of personality – than her own home. As though having people around, strangers, makes her feel more secure, less alone. There is no threat in them, nothing to fear; their eyes hold their own secrets that don't intrude upon hers and they sit alone at breakfast looking only into themselves, not seeing the vague shadow that sits in the corner and eats quietly, keeping herself to herself.

She hasn't seen her family and friends for days and their absence weighs heavily on her. I think that she sometimes pretends, to herself and no-one else, not to care and I wonder if she dreams about walking with them, breathing the same air, perhaps there are thoughts of forgiveness, of letting go. I wonder if her anger has begun to change, alter into acceptance. If her jagged, sharp sense of betrayal now has worn-down edges and a sanded, smoothed surface.

She checks her bag as she walks, hands moving through pockets guided by the sensation of touch rather than sight. She finds gum and pops one in her mouth, chewing slowly. Her steps seem light where they should be held firm against the floor. She appears to be an altogether different person than the one she once was. I carved, with a flick of my wrist and some sleight of hand, a new face over the old; a face upon which living seems to sit a little easier even when it hurts.

I have a choice now, just as I have always had a choice. To continue the path I have begun, perhaps more gently, a path that must surely lead to further change, perhaps ultimately to confrontation. Or I can fall silent, back away, pretend I have never been walking two steps behind her, watching every move that she makes.

She crosses the road heading towards the train station, the edge of the white envelope bearing the doctor's name protruding slightly from the handbag carelessly left open, ready for a pickpocket's hand. I think, perhaps, that I should give this up now, let her live her life, let her go her own way without any more interference from me.

But then, there is this new doctor she has finally agreed to see, the doctor who has the potential to unlock the mystery of her blank, hidden past, who could lift a signpost high above his head that says 'this way, get all your answers here'. And I want to know them too, I want to know where he will lead her, what he will say, what will happen if she ever learns the truth. I want to know if anywhere, in the darkness of her memory, I am waiting.

I look at the envelope again, catching a tiny glimpse of the jagged edge where it has been ripped open. I make up my mind in that moment to follow where it leads, bread crumbs in the forest. I follow behind as she heads to the station. Holding the newly bought ticket in my hand I climb into the carriage and as the train pulls away I look out of the window, pretending not to notice the girl whose life I have turned upside down.

Chapter Fifty-Nine

The once-absent Marie greets me by name as I enter. She doesn't ask if she can help me, she doesn't look down to check who I may be. She has the sort of smile that takes over her whole face, an artfully arranged messy top knot of caramel blonde curls, a gentle voice. Her welcome is warm enough to chase away some of the fear at the thought that today my therapy will begin, today I face the possibility of exposure to things I thought locked away forever, those things that have kept me prisoner, that I never wanted to face.

"Would you like a cup of tea or coffee?" she asks me. Ordinary, calm.

"Is it Earl Grey?" A feigned shudder at the thought of it, bland and insipid, against my tongue.

"Well, we do have Earl Grey, but we also have Yorkshire Tea or chamomile."

"Yorkshire Tea would be lovely," I say gratefully, and she nods and eases out from behind the reception desk telling me she will be right back. The phone rings immediately as the door shuts behind her, she doesn't return to pick it up.

I wait and hope it won't be long before Doctor Charles calls me through. I keep company with my thoughts and find in them too much to fear, too much to try and escape. The longer I sit with nothing but the churning mass of them, the more likely I am to turn away from this moment, to fade rapidly into the background before a stray bullet can find its way to me as I hastily desert. Fingertips drum against denim-clad legs, sounding hollow and too loud as my mouth grows dry; any desire to talk evaporating into the air above my head.

In a flow of synchronicity, Doctor Charles opens his door as Marie returns with my tea, backing into the room with a small tray perfectly balanced. She smoothly detours into his room, bidding me to follow her. There is no departure of a previous patient and I wonder if I walk into the room will I discover one cowering beneath the desk, terrified from too much exposure, too much confrontation of their own fears?

I know that it takes me a little too long to get to my feet, that my legs are weak and unstable as I walk. By the time I step into the room, Doctor Charles is once again sat behind his desk and looks up at my entrance, sympathy rippling across his face as he takes in my pale skin and tense shoulders, the way I hold my bag close to my stomach as if defending myself from an expected body blow. He glances briefly at my hair but makes no comment on how short it is now.

Less chaotic than I remember it, the room smells fresher, more welcoming; where the kettle previously played hide and seek amongst piles of detritus there is a clear expanse of wood and a jar with flowers and a handful of leafy branches. I cannot meet the eyes of the man opposite me and he glances down at his large hands clasped on the edge of the hefty pitted desk.

The tea is placed in front of me and I reach my hand for it, noticing the obvious tremble I cannot control, a rapid snatching back before it is seen. I risk a glance at the doctor and find his eyes on me, speculative and sympathetic. He rubs at his chin before biting a nail; a cartoon character playing at pondering a subject. I follow his exaggerated movements and wait for the axe to fall.

Abruptly he nods as though reaching a conclusion as yet unconsidered. Elbows on the table and fingers tented in front of his chin; I begin to feel uncomfortable beneath his gaze.

"How are you feeling about being here today?"

I clear my throat loudly into the vacant space beyond his question, twice, the sound filling the void clumsily.

"Terrified," I say and I do not exaggerate. "The thought of being exposed, even a little, to any of the things I'm scared of makes me want to leave and not come back. If I'm honest, it's amazing that I made it this far. I kept on wanting to turn away, go home. I still do."

"But you haven't, which is very positive indeed. It means that at least part of you is ready and willing to face up to your fears."

I say nothing and wonder which part it could be, the tiny crescent moon at the base of a fingernail, the hair follicles on my forearms perhaps. And where is this part of me hiding now when I need to find even a faint residue of courage to get me through this painful exchange?

"How would you feel if we postponed the first session of Cognitive Behavioural Therapy and try something else first?" He asks, contemplation still in his voice, a spur of the moment decision that changes the direction we are facing.

My initial response is a vast wave of relief that encourages me to agree to anything as long as he sticks to what he says and changes the proximity of the starting line. The thought of not having to face the beginnings of exposure, of testing the water and finding it too hot or bitterly cold, sweeps out of me and through the room on a rush of gratitude.

"That sounds preferable."

He smiles at what is obviously an understatement, at the relief that turns knuckles from white to skin-coloured.

"I thought that perhaps it would." He raises an eyebrow and smiles, looking too young to be him for a moment, as though he wears a disguise most of the time and the reality of him is far less serious than his title, this room.

"The way I see it is that your issues are multi-level issues, though of course all stemming from the same source. I'm wondering if the key to unravelling your PTSD lies with

unravelling your amnesia, or perhaps the other way around."
He stands and walks to the window that looks out on bricks
and pathways and falling leaves that blow in the wind.

"I'm sensing that you have some degree of anxiety at the
thought of the Cognitive Behavioural Therapy which is, of
course, totally normal. Few people welcome the thought of
facing and addressing those things which have lead to such
enormous and fundamental difficulties. Am I right?"

I nod and keep my eyes fixed at a point on the carpet
between us; the colours fade one into the other, fibres mashed
by hundreds of feet until they blend like paint.

"So my suggestion would be to perhaps begin with some
form of hypnotherapy, a gentle probing if you like into the
wall of hidden memories. Perhaps if we can locate them, find
out where they have gone and why, then we stand more of
a chance of unravelling your past and getting to the root of
your PTSD."

I sense that he wants me to see this as a gift, this changing
of his mind. Did he plan this before? Was this whole ploy
designed to make me feel discomfort at the initial idea of
exposure only to be handed relief at the kindness that
followed? Yet it leads to a different kind of discomfort,
slower, more hesitant.

"I'm not sure that option is any better." The thought of being
hypnotised, out of control, vulnerable makes me shudder.

"Believe me, it isn't all showy like these stage hypnotists
you may have seen on television. I won't make you pretend
to be a cowgirl or a ballerina. The whole thing is much more
gentle than that. The chances are that you will remember
everything that is said and, in case you don't, the whole
scenario will be recorded using the webcam attached to my
laptop. A timer will be visible on the screen to show the passing
of linear time so that you know nothing is being hidden from
you and, on top of all that, Marie will sit in with us for your
own peace of mind." He smiles a little wryly. "I've heard
everyone's concerns so many times regarding hypnotherapy

that I have tried to cover all bases when suggesting it."

"Will I be able to watch the recording back?"

"Of course you may. Knowing that should enable you to feel more confident in the process. This first session would be a simple straightforward one, just a little look, a bit like a mini exploration to see how far beneath the surface these memories are and even if we can find them at all. Sometimes they can be rather well hidden and have to be unpicked gradually over time."

"Can I stop at any time?"

"If you wish to then yes. All you need do is indicate to me that you want the process to end and it will. You should remain in control of yourself at all times. The hypnosis will take the form of suggestions and a kind of guided searching rather than myself taking charge and forcing you to seek your memories out. How does that sound?"

I sip at my tea and sigh a little before nodding, hiding behind my eyelids as I reply.

"Okay, we'll try it," I tell him, because it is marginally preferable, because I will maintain a level of control and it is better than slowly immersing myself in a dark pond full of trepidation.

The tea in my hand is still warm as once again I sit in the waiting room while the room is arranged, readied, and the cup is empty by the time Marie's smiling face calls me back through. The light is changed, more subtle, the curtains now partially drawn making the room seem smaller and more intimate. Cushions have been placed on the sofa to lean back against and an upright chair is positioned nearby but not so close as to block the small round ball of the webcam from seeing into the moment.

I lean back, get comfortable, put my feet up on the couch, worried about outside dirt on the bottom of my shoes and all the time there is an uncomfortable awareness of something out of the ordinary, something different. My hands feel cold, my fingertips numb. I lean my head back and try to relax but my heart thumps like a racehorse pawing at the gate and I close my eyes against the room until it only exists in the delicate scent of the flowers that leave a darker residual trace on the inside of my eyelids.

Into that deliberate breath, that conscious slowing of responses, the doctor's voice speaks low and steady. His tone sleepy and shrouded in peace as it washes over me. I hear his words and feel no different. I don't feel entranced as I expected to, I don't feel sleepy. He tells me that he will count backwards from five and I almost smile at the cliché before he begins. And then I find only silence, nothing, and so I open my eyes into the stillness of the silent room.

"I must be one of those people that can't be hypnotised," I say apologetically into his professional mask and he smiles a little.

"That is a statement I've heard before," he says as Marie busies herself with the laptop, adjusting the screen a little.

I still feel chilled as I see the image of myself paused on the screen, eyes closed, appearing asleep.

"I'm going to show you the tape of this session before we move on to discuss further appointments and treatment."

There is something present in his voice then that hasn't been there before. A rigidity, a lack of emotion as though he is reading from a textbook, Psychiatry 1, 2, 3; everything by the book, no deviation. A linear process whereby every step must be exact, carefully followed. I look at Marie, smiling Marie and find her eyes are facing away from mine as she busies herself with the task in front of her before she turns to leave without glancing my way.

"If you would like to sit up and make yourself comfortable I will play the recording for you and then we'll talk about your next appointment."

I nod, my voice growing small and disappearing into my throat so I cannot find a loud enough response.

He moves the mouse pointer over the play button and clicks it down, the sound sharp into the relative calm and peace. I feel a little embarrassed as I watch myself, almost completely still and silent on the screen, a fingertip moving slightly, tongue flicking out nervously over my lower lip.

His voice echoes out from the speakers and I wonder how it is that listening to a recording does not have the same effect. What would happen if we both sat here and fell under the spell of that calm, peaceful monotone? Who would save us then? I hear him count backwards again and watch more closely, expecting to see my eyes open, my rueful smile but the time in between grows longer and I glance at the doctor puzzled.

"Keep watching," he tells me and so I do, his voice pouring out of the speakers.

"I am going to begin by asking you a series of simple test questions to help relax you further and so that we can build up slowly to the questions connected with your treatment. Do you understand?"

I listen intently as I hear myself reply in the affirmative, thinking this can't be real, that if it was I would surely remember. But I don't remember, I heard a countdown then opened my eyes and in between there was nothing, a fragment, a second, nothing more. Confused, I see myself on the screen, existing impossibly in a place and time that is null, invisible.

"Okay then," the image of the doctor says, "we'll start with the basics. What is your name?" There is a pause before the answer, as though I had been caught out by the simplicity of the question and then I watch as the me on the screen, the me that I have no memory of, smiles beatifically. And the voice that pushes through that smile is no longer mine somehow, is lighter, more accented.

"My name is Ellie Wilson."

Chapter Sixty

There can be no continuing from this point. No ignorance of me when the blindfold is lifted and there are others that have borne witness. I feel it in her confusion, her immediate denial, her conviction that this is a ruse, a game for some reason that she cannot fathom. I feel her as she chases her disbelief, tries to hold onto it even though it is slippery and keeps escaping her grasp.

The doctor is gentle with her, and kind, but it is not enough, in this moment it can never be enough. I am the fault and she the glass I dwell in and she fractures and breaks around me as everything comes to the surface. Is there anywhere inside her that this makes a strange kind of sense? Is it possible that she feels a kind of recognition, of everything suddenly coming to the surface, a moment of relief that finally, finally, she has the answers to the puzzle? I cannot tell, I do not have access to her thoughts and have never been able to tell what she is hiding there.

She is worryingly silent. First Doctor Charles and then Marie speak to her and she does not respond. But she is there, I know that she is there because in this space in time I am not the one behind her eyes, I am in the background, an observer and she stands in front of me. But I can sense her stillness as her body turns to stone. I feel the rigidity in her limbs.

I do not know how she feels in these moments when she has looked at me, seen someone other than herself, someone who looks like her, someone she doesn't know. Does she feel anything? I sit with her as she fails to respond to gentle questions, hands on shoulders, worried glances. I do not fade out as I often do when the boredom of the days become too much, I do not lose myself in thoughts and vacancy. I stay with her as phone calls are made.

Is it selfish of me to say that I expected something more? That I wanted something far more explosive, far more intense than a silence I have had to bear for too long? I wanted her to rage, to fight me, to steal my breath away with her reaction but beneath my desires, my wishful thinking, I already knew that this was how it would unfold. In these moments of unmasking, of exposure, it is impossible for her to be anything other than what she has always been, the one who hides, the one who needed me.

We wait for Leah to come, though I'm not sure Sarah knows she is waiting for anything other than the return of normality, a backward step into yesterday where I was unknown. Leah will come and take her home and I wonder if everything will look different now. Whichever home she goes back to, the apartment, the little terraced cottage, even the hotel, surely it will not look the same now that she knows I am there.

In her silent mind, in her stillness, does she even realise the irony of Leah's status as next of kin on the forms that Marie seeks out? Does she remember the revelation that her mother lives? That *our* mother lives? Does she think anything at all?

I sit with her and feel the chill of her skin, the silence in her bones. I can only guess at the shock coursing through her veins like a toxin, washing through her and leaving this empty shell behind. Marie's face is no longer smiling. Concern etches into the corners of her eyes, the edges of her mouth. She fetches a blanket and places it around Sarah's shoulders. I feel the warmth from it and know that, in this moment, Sarah doesn't. She has drifted away, switched places with me as she often does when things get too uncomfortable.

I step in to push back the monsters, just as I always have, to keep her safe, to lock the bad things away. I look at Marie and smile my thanks, watching the relief cross her face as she finally gets a response of some kind, any kind. I pull the blanket closer around shoulders that feel cold as marble to touch. There is nothing I can do to help her, to make this easier and so I do the only thing that I can, the same thing I have often done. I keep her company, watch over her, respond to the people around us as if I am her. I try not to draw attention to the two of us, and inside, where nobody can see me, I imagine I am holding her hand.

Chapter Sixty-One

I don't remember getting to Leah's house. I look into my memory and see myself on a screen and my legs go weak, there is the sense of fading away. Nothing in me speaks of this return, or hastily made beds, a settling down, tucked up warm with a duvet and worried arms around my shoulders. If I could find a way to ask the one who looks like me but isn't, would this be a different story, would she remember this moment that for me is elusive, gone? Was this her moment, her personality, her life, so separate from mine?

I cannot equate this day with my life, my existence. I am surely not the person Doctor Charles talked about as once again another medical professional looked at me with curiosity and intrigue, labelled me as some exotic bird, some freak of nature. How many more years would have to pass before I felt I stood on even ground with the man who sat opposite me and made no promises that he could help, that he could fix this?

The roots of my shock forced through my feet, pushing into the ground, holding me captive and still, so still that I had to think to draw breath. It took all my focus, every ounce of energy to fill my lungs, push them empty. What if she were there in the shadows, what if she held my breath when I didn't want her to? Could I die like that, with a stranger at the helm, a doppelganger who took charge? If she decided not to breathe for me, would I die that way? Could she stop my heart if she chose to?

When I wake it is to be greeted with pure darkness and recognisable odours. I am home, safe, in this space where I know how to place my feet, where I know the path that leads safely to the door even in the dark. The light snaps on beneath probing fingers and the illusion of familiarity fades slowly away into plain walls and bare furniture. I am not here in this place anymore. My own things, the traces of my personality, which once lingered in familiar fabrics and clutter-filled drawers, are gone. This room is plain and bare, meant only for the guest that I have become and nothing more. Yet I still know the stairs to avoid as I descend, I still remember the way light pools softly on the floor in the downstairs hallway.

The front door is locked, the chain slid into its holder and for a moment the urge to step out into the night, to fade away amongst strangers, is stronger than anything else. But then I think of who I am, what I may become, the helplessness of ending up somewhere I don't know, a taxi ride into darkness, and instead I step into the kitchen slowly closing the door behind me.

And that is where she finds me, a woollen shawl around my shoulders, a cup of cooling tea in my hand. She glances at the clock as she enters and I follow her eyes. It is three in the morning and she looks as though the path to sleep has not yet been discovered. She busies around, boils the kettle, fills the pot and puts on the tea cosy before carrying it all to the table and placing it in front of me. The remains of my own mug are poured down the sink to make way for a fresher brew. And all the while neither of us speaks, our eyes don't meet.

The clock ticks away the seconds into this waiting place in which the words fail to appear. The night is still, close and we sit like strangers on opposite sides of the white painted table. We gravitated automatically to the spaces we have always occupied, ever the creatures of habit and yet nothing else about this scene feels familiar, safe. Neither of us are the people we once knew. But am I less or am I more? I feel diminished, weakened and yet there is this other, a whole new entity, a different version of the face I see in the mirror. How can I not be twice the person I was, how can I feel so much smaller?

Leah pours us both tea, adds milk, replaces the cosy. A familiar ritual we have repeated many times. And then she sighs, the sound of it filling the kitchen, hovering above us in condemnation.

"Your mother didn't die of cancer."

Is this for her, for us both, an easier topic of conversation? How strange that it seems to be so when only a short time before these words would have stayed mute, the elephant in the room. Did the things we must avoid swap places and change as circumstances changed? Was this betrayal, this lie she told, easier to face than the knowledge that I am someone other, someone hidden? In spite of it all, my surprise that this is where she would begin, I respond. My identity slides away from me by the day as I lose sight of who I am but perhaps in this moment is a truth I can carry the weight of, a reality more acceptable than the one presented to me in a meaningless office at the end of a train line.

"I know," I tell her. "She left a message on my answer phone."

Leah nods slightly in acknowledgement and pauses as if wondering how to begin or how to end.

"Your mother was so beautiful, so delicate. She was the kind of woman that other women tend to turn their backs on, yet men seem to want to take care of."

"You've told me that before."

She nods again in response and smiles wryly in my direction. "I know, I'm just trying to lay the foundations I guess. She was very weak, highly strung. And so very jealous of anyone your father came into contact with. Her behaviour was often erratic, never quite normal. Everything in the house revolved around her moods. Tom was run ragged trying to juggle work and your mother and you girls."

Her lips purse and her jaw tightens over her mug of tea as I try not to move, in case she should have a sudden realisation of who she is talking to and remember that this is not right, this is the great unspoken and should remain in the darkness.

"Annie had always been closer to your mother, but you, you were a real Daddy's girl and that was like a thorn in her side. She thought that Tom should only have eyes for her, that you were no more than an extension of her, not a person in your own right. As her behaviour grew more extreme, more erratic, you became more withdrawn.

"And poor Tom, if he wore aftershave or made an effort to look nice she never saw it as being for her, it was always for someone else. She called him all hours of the day when he was at work, even phoning his boss once to check he was where he said he would be. She stifled him completely, sought out the company of other men, made your home a battleground and eventually her behaviour became too much for Tom and he left. It was always his intention to set up a home and then come and collect you girls but by the time he did it was too late. Your mother abandoned you, left you in the house alone." She shakes her head slowly from side to side as she tells the tale of a life I do not recall, as if it belongs to someone else, someone altogether different, more interesting.

"Why did she leave us? Where did she go?" I ask and she looks down at clasped hands.

"Why did she leave you? It's a question I've asked myself quite often. It was even harder to fathom because she took Annie with her, it was only you that she left."

Her sympathy is such that I can hardly bear the weight of it as it settles around me and digs in, uncomfortable and harsh.

"It was as if by leaving you, Daddy's little girl, she was getting back at Tom for daring to leave her. You were alone for a few days and during that time there was an accident and you were injured, you fell down the stairs. I can't even imagine what went through your mind. You were so young, so vulnerable. The postman found you, heard you crying through the letterbox and raised the alarm. Tom took you away then and when the police found your mother, Annie was handed into Tom's care too. Eventually the case went to court and your mother was charged with child neglect, she was found guilty and sentenced to six months in prison. It wasn't enough."

"Why have you never told me any of this before?"

She sits opposite me and pours out the story of my forgotten life as though it is yesterday's news. But it isn't, not to me, it is another new thing, another confusion.

"I don't know. I always meant to, but when I realised the extent of your memory loss, when I watched you floundering every day with your physiotherapy, your day to day agony, I couldn't bring myself to hand you one more story of insecurity, one more reason for you to doubt your worth. After the accident, your doctors told me that you needed a stable environment to continue your recovery, that everything needed to be calm and tranquil and she wasn't, Sarah, she was anything but those things. I couldn't bear the thought of her stepping back into your life and turning it upside down once more with her erratic behaviour. I was terrified that she would get you back and I wouldn't be able to keep you safe. I owed it to Tom to keep you safe."

She gets to her feet, refills the kettle, goes to the cupboard and removes a pack of biscuits before placing them between us on the table without taking one for herself; the action little more than something to fill the space as she waits for my response. I sense her agitation, her guilt that she did the wrong thing, a weight she has carried for far longer than this moment.

"You should have told me," I say and she nods.

"I know, just as I know that saying sorry isn't enough. But all I can say in my defence is that I did the wrong thing with the best of intentions. I lied because I didn't want her to hurt you anymore."

"You said I was injured, in what way?"

It is strange not to know, as though I am sharing stories about someone else, tragic tales told for no other reason than the drama of it all.

"You fell down the stairs and broke your leg quite badly."

I think of a little girl, all alone, lying at the bottom of a staircase, crying and in pain. And suddenly I am glad that I cannot remember this, I am relieved that the memory is hidden from me and I don't have to recall it and know the fear and agony I must have felt at the time.

She watches me intently across the horizon of the mug I hold near to my lips, close enough to touch, to taste, yet I hold it still, redundant. She waits for me to respond to her story, to pull the trapdoor from beneath her feet and let her hang or to offer respite, absolution.

But I say nothing, no words of censure or any of forgiveness. I am mute and helpless while she waits for me to decide her fate, our future. I know that if I speak into this moment, no matter what words I use, whether they placate or condemn, they will be little more than a lie, a mistruth. Because in this moment as we sit, awkward and stilted in the circle of the overhead light, all words are meaningless. I feel nothing about the little girl who was once me before she disappeared behind a wall of forgetting; my emotions lay waste and barren and burned. I am insignificant, empty as I step through the wreckage and leave this past echo behind me.

"What if they cannot cure me?" I ask and watch as she raises the fingertips of both hands to her mouth, holding in fears, sorrow, consoling kisses.

"We'll find a way somehow. It will all be okay."

And she reaches a hand across the table towards me, palm upwards, waiting for alms. For several seconds I look at the lines on her skin, the grooves and troughs of a palm reader's fortune and slowly I reach out my own hand in return, feeling the smooth wood of the table against my palm until the warmth of her skin grasps onto mine. And as I feel the comfort pour from her into the circuit made by our hands I cry, silent and deep, and she does nothing to stop me, for which I am grateful.

Chapter Sixty-Two

It would be a mistake to say that I am she and she is me. If only it were that simple. Perhaps once that would have been the truth, that we were the same, that her experience was mine and vice versa. It is not so anymore, rather we are like a river, the two of us; where once we followed the same path, twisted and churned our way through the same landscape, we somehow became separate, took alternate pathways. Though we had the same source, the same beginning, now we are as different as if we had never been joined. All rivers look the same when you glance too closely only at the water that flows in them. You need to look with better eyes than that, at the flora and fauna that line the banks, at the subtle twists and curves, at the rocks and stones that lay beneath the surface.

Perhaps it began with the cruelty of my mother. Did I become me in the moments when Sarah tried to hide inside herself, among happier memories, better moments? Was I the one who stood up only to take the fall, to bear this burden? Or perhaps it was later, in the tearing wreckage of a car, in the moment that she looked upon the dead bodies of her father and sister. Did I hold her even then, place my hand over her eyes and bury her traumatised head into my shoulder until we became distinct, separate?

Perhaps the main difference between us is that I know of her, her neuroses, her fears, her blinkered sight, I have witnessed her daily life, the steps that she takes, the conversations she has. I see her face reflecting back in the mirror as I peer out from behind her eyes, whereas she has no awareness or knowledge of me at all. Only that sometimes she is forgetful, sometimes she has blank moments, sometimes time just evaporates. She did not know that it is in those spaces that I live, where I am, where I wait.

I have walked the same constantly dull pathways of her life, the tedium of her days, while remaining helpless to deviate from them. Never stepping forwards for long enough to choose somewhere else, never willing to change the route that she might take, hoping instead that one day it would change and she would begin to live more, enjoy more, so that I too could experience these things, so that I too could live within any given moment and find it new and exciting.

From the time I became truly aware of her, of me, I watched her from the darkness inside and, in the time that followed, grew restless, angry at the wasteland that her life became. A life I would give anything for. I felt slighted, affronted that she seemed to have the best parts of us and yet she squandered them with her refusal to live, her refusal to alter her course for any reason.

It was hard enough that I was the one who carried the memories of a bleak and tormented childhood while her memory stayed mercifully blank. I would have given anything to forget, to be free of the uncertainty of my mother's cruelty, of her eventual abandonment. I had more reason than Sarah to dwell in dark places, to find peace in misery and wallowing, but it was not my choice to do so, I was stronger than that and perhaps that is why I had moved away from her, become solitary within our shared physical self. Was it because I could cope, I was strong enough? Had she subconsciously poured over me those things she needed to isolate, those things she could no longer endure?

Was my intervention in her life her fault too, another subliminal plea to my thoughts, my consciousness to interfere with the futility of her life? Did she grasp the edges of her red flag and wave it where I would catch its movement in the wind, simply because I wanted to live, to experience, to be happy? Because it was her reluctance to do any of those things that had forced my hand, made me step up and place obstacles in her boring, familiar path.

I changed the map she walked upon, blocked routes, opened others upon which she stepped gingerly. Did I imagine her steps becoming stronger, more certain as the setting changed dramatically around her? Did the choices I gave her present challenges to overcome, or more to fear, to hide from? I like to think that from the moment I started to peck gently at the shell around her, she began to experience a sense of freedom, of choice. She tasted the air outside and found it sweet in spite of its unknown tang, its vague scent of danger, of difference.

And now that I am present, now that she knows of me, what does the future hold? I too grow helpless in this moment, this exposure harsh and raw against my skin, yearning to be known, to be acknowledged when I have only ever been invisible, when I have only ever been her. I see the question in Leah's eyes as she turns towards us and wonders who it is that sits before her, if I am truly in here. What do I say to her? Where do I go from here?

Chapter Sixty-Three

"I don't know who I am anymore."

He looks at me with sympathy and nods a little. "That is, of course, entirely understandable. But let me tell you. You are Sarah Phillips, you are the person you have always been. That much hasn't changed."

"Of course it's changed. This thing is inside of me. How would you feel? It's like a parasite, a possession. I can't get away from it." I sigh a little, look away, feel the warm squeeze of my right hand as Leah tells me silently that she is there and the touch of her skin against mine, her hand within my own reminds me of something.

I cannot help but think that she will one day take over. That she will insinuate herself slowly until I am nothing more than a square inch of feelings that slowly disappear. I cannot get away from my own skin. I am trapped with her.

I look over at the sofa I chose not to sit on, opting instead for a chair in front of the desk. That sofa belongs to her now, it can never be mine. I could never sit on it and not feel her shadow there, joining me with her unwelcome, uninvited company.

"I cannot pretend to know how you are feeling in this moment, Sarah. From a professional viewpoint, I have never worked with someone with this condition, so I have no prior experience of what it is like for the patient. It is unusual but you are by no means alone and I can reassure you that many people with this type of dissociative disorder live independent, healthy lives."

Doctor Charles is apologetic in his ignorance, I don't feel any better for it. I want him to wave a magic wand, make it go away.

I have another diagnosis, another condition that may not be fixed. The Dissociative Amnesia, brought about by a traumatic childhood and the horrific car crash that left me with no past and a deep scar, is in fact symptomatic of Dissociative Identity Disorder, once known as multiple personality disorder. It isn't simply that I cannot remember my childhood. In the fog of trauma and recovery my damaged brain separated out those horrific memories too awful to cope with and, instead of placing them in a box where I could no longer see them, handed them over to a personality stronger than mine, someone more able to stand still and solid beneath the weight of them.

She is inside me, part of me. I sense her now crawling beneath my skin and feel nauseous, terrified. She is stealing little pieces of me, taking me over, wearing my face, my body. She is the one who stole my childhood from me, who knew my father, who knows to grieve for him; the one who left me with a blank space and only photographs to fill it. When I feel myself grow vague and distant, there is a sense now of urgency, of panic. Almost like a dream in which I am falling because I know that she is there in that silence, she is waiting for me to fade away.

"The treatment for your condition is similar in many ways to the treatments recommended for Post-Traumatic Stress Disorder; that is Cognitive Behaviour Therapy, hypnotherapy work regarding your amnesia, attempting to unlock your hidden memories, which we now understand belong, in part at least, to an alternative personality. We will need to meet more frequently than previously planned, at least once, perhaps twice a week and... " for a moment he looks awkward, sheepish perhaps; he knows where he led me before, how we fell down the rabbit hole into an altogether different reality. "… the treatment I can offer will partially need to be conducted under hypnosis. In order to treat you effectively, it will be necessary to treat both you and the alternate personality."

"But why? Surely treating me will stop this, will make that disappear."

And then my words dry up, because I don't know how I can ever do that again, hear him count back from five and find that silent moment where she lives.

"The important thing to remember here Sarah is that, although she is separate from you in that she has different memories etcetera, essentially she is you. She is most likely a part of you that became distinct when you were experiencing significant challenge or trauma. In order to effect any kind of cure it is, in part, that trauma that we will need to try and heal. And it is the alternative personality that may hold that trauma, which you yourself have no memory of. We need to access those memories and treat them individually with the same treatments I have mentioned before, Cognitive Behaviour Therapy and so on."

"And what then? If you succeed in unblocking the memories, finding them somewhere and treating them, will she simply cease to be?"

I hold my breath and wait for his reply before he shakes his head and makes me feel even more hopeless.

"It may be possible that the separate personalities can be ultimately integrated, but realistically, it is more a case of trying to achieve a position whereby the alter, or alternative personality, can live harmoniously with the host." He points at me with a vague smile as if I have won a prize at a fairground and he is the stall holder, "That's you."

"Why is it, what makes me the host personality?"

"Because yours is the birth personality, put simply, you were there first."

"How do I know that though? It could have been her. I don't remember my childhood, what if I am the interloper? What if I get all this treatment and I am the one that disappears, that fades away?"

"You were the one that was christened Sarah Phillips. The host personality is the original one, therefore Ellie came later. However, I believe it unlikely that either of you will fade away, so to speak. Normally it is, as I said before, a case of learning to co-exist."

"Normally? There is nothing normal about this though, is there?"

Hearing her name makes her seem more real somehow, more distinct and I realise how trapped I am, how helpless. Without treatment I am infected by this other, this alter, who controls my body, who guides my hands but with it... what would happen to me, could happen to me? What if I were the one to lose out, to be cast aside. What if it were me that ceased to be? And if the trauma she took from me is too vast, too unbearable, what will happen if it is given back, what will happen if I cannot bear the weight of it and I fracture further apart?

By the time we leave Doctor Charles' office I am no less helpless, no less afraid.

319

Chapter Sixty-Four

There is no straightforward cure. We learn this together, sitting in the doctor's office with Leah, and I don't know how to feel. I hear Sarah's disappointment in the tears that fall for a short time before she pulls them stoically inwards and braces herself against any further information. I know completely how she feels about this truth, this announcement, but my own emotions are a mystery.

What if there was a cure? What if an answer could be found inside a pill capsule to be swallowed down with water and hope? Like her, I wonder would there be a gradual fading away, blank moments where my existence was ceasing to be? I wonder if it would be preferable that way, to slowly disappear, to become ethereal? I wonder if that would be better than to live like this, trapped within a body that does not belong to me, unable to truly live, to truly be.

I have hated her often for the way she has squandered the preciousness of her days. For the way she has chosen the quiet, nondescript path and walked it always the same way. I seethed at her refusal to live her life to the full, at the knowledge that given the chance I could have done so much more with such a precious gift. But my rage was not born of malice. Rather it was the frustration of a caged animal that could see the distant hills bathed in sunshine yet had them forever beyond their reach.

I listen as Doctor Charles explains that there can be no easy severing of Sarah's alternate personality, of me, that I am Sarah's coping mechanism, the seeds of which were almost certainly laid down long before the car accident as I thought they were, planted somewhere amongst the cruelty and loneliness of life with an abusive mother. And there the separation began, this slow dissociation that ended with complete disunity, with an alternate personality whose metaphorical shoulders were big enough, strong enough to carry the burdensome weight of such horrific childhood experience; experiences that then ceased to exist in Sarah because they came to rest, unfairly, in me.

Doctor Charles thinks that there is a possibility, with time, that there could be a drawing together of these separated aspects, that with treatment and support there is a possibility of some kind of unity, some kind of harmony. I hear in his tone that he himself thinks it unlikely that the dual aspects of Sarah's personality, that the two of us, can ever be truly united in one mind, in one character. Rather, he says, it would be a case of simply learning to co-exist, of finding a way to live harmoniously. It is possible, he says, it has happened before.

Perhaps the most unusual part of us, and the saddest, is that neither of us has any memories of Annie. She is not there and perhaps it is possible that she has a little dissociative space of her own in Sarah's broken memory, watched over by someone else, another personality that I do not know, that is utterly separate. She does not exist in my version of our childhood, through all of the memories I have, through all of the difficulties, I stand alone. She was not there to hold my hand, she is not a voice heard in the distance, a shadow moving in my peripheral vision, she is simply absent and I know that Sarah grieves for her just as I do.

Perhaps her absence is a reflection of how Sarah felt,

of her increasing sense of isolation, a sense that was ultimately to become mine. And for Sarah, too, with her missing memories, her lost childhood, Annie has never been there. I feel sad about it, that this is the truth of her, of this little girl that died too soon and faded away inside damaged memories.

Perhaps I should have known that coming face to face with Sarah would simply be a beginning, a difference. I think I saw it previously as the pinnacle of our individual experiences, it was the summit I strove to reach and once there everything would be better. Yet the truth is that my reality does not change. I am still little more than a shadow in the background, the hider under the bed. I know that Sarah is afraid of me, that she finds it hard to act normally in moments when she thinks too long about the other person she carries with her; when she tries to come to terms with the strangeness of it all, the truth of it.

Leah watches her like a hawk and I know what she is doing, she is looking for signs of the switch, trying to identify that moment when I step in and Sarah ceases to be. Her eyes weigh heavily on me and I find that when I come forwards I cannot meet her stare, I look at the floor and move awkwardly to the door, ignoring her calling after me as I leave the room. And once, just once, as I turned from her and stepped through the door, I heard her call Sarah's name before quietly, and with obvious hesitation she said, "Ellie?"

I carried on walking and did not answer, shocked by this tiny word appearing in the mouth of one I have known for so long, where she has not known me.

It is in one of those changeover moments, those switches, that I make a decision, that somehow I will have to introduce myself to Sarah, that in some way she will have to get to know me so that she is no longer afraid, so that I am no longer seen as a threat, a monster. Perhaps it is something I should have done before but would she have accepted it before she knew the truth of me? Would it have been to her little more than the threatening activity of the stalker who was finding their way into her home and wreaking havoc?

I make my way up the stairs on the tide of Leah's voice calling only Sarah's name and find a pen and paper in the bedside drawer. I sit down on the bed and begin to write.

Chapter Sixty-Five

The weeks following the revelation that I am not alone, that I possibly never really have been since the piecing back together of my fractured life, are an anticlimax of sorts, a nothing. Did I expect more, something more dramatic? Yet what could be more dramatic than the realisation that this other is living inside me, wearing my face, living my life?

I notice now when time becomes vague, where before I would dismiss it with a shrug – just one of those things, just me being forgetful – now I know it to be something other, something sinister. It is a violation that I have no awareness of, no control over. I see her echo, her shadow in these lost moments and I know that I cannot outrun her; she will always run quicker than me. I cannot escape her. I am trapped inside myself, haunted by the face I see in the mirror. I search it for hints of her and find no shadows, no trace in my skin, behind my eyes.

And then she begins to leave me notes. It is strange, alien to find these sheets of paper next to the bed or on the dining room table and know that it is my own hand, controlled by another, that writes them. There isn't the same fear that accompanied the hanging doll, the moving of the sofa. I no longer have to look to find the face at the window, the stranger at my door.

It is through her words that I learn she has always been aware of me, that though she lives only in my blank moments, my vague absences, she has always had that knowing, she could always see me. There is an unusual quality to this knowledge. I do not know how to feel about having an observer, how to react to the awareness that I have always had this company, though she also tells me that sometimes she sleeps, or fades, or goes elsewhere. She writes that she cannot see me one hundred percent of the time.

The notes are sometimes short, sometimes overlong yet strangely her handwriting is different to mine, less tidy, though her spelling is slightly better. She tells me of her childhood, the childhood that is also mine. There are tales of fear, of hunger and of falling. I am reading someone else's story, so distinct from mine, and when I read between her lines I see that she asks for understanding, that she is trying to excuse her existence in my life.

I cannot equate her story to myself, though somehow it is more personal, more tragic hearing it from Ellie than from my aunt, who wasn't there and didn't know first-hand the horror of it. I read my absent childhood in her words and I can see it in my head for the first time, though the images are her memories and not my own.

She tells me of what it has been like for her, to be a part of me, to will me to grasp life, not just for my sake but for hers, so that she too can experience new things, limited as she is to the brief moments when she takes over. And through the words that appear over days, weeks, I come to a strange and unexpected understanding of the frustration of her existence, the way I have held her prisoner through my reluctance to take a chance on any kind of a life.

I read her name out loud and find the sound strange yet also familiar somehow against my tongue. The sound of her name seems loud in the room and yet it belongs, as though it is recognisable in the subconscious part of me where she lives.

Between Leah and Ellie, these patchwork tales come together, forming a quilt I surround myself with as I try to make sense of its patterns and squares. Sometimes the pieces fit, tessellating together perfectly, yet others seem a million miles apart, seem to have no place in the same lifetime, the same universe. I try to think that she is me and I am her but it doesn't fit somehow. We are not the same, we are each of us unique and separate. And though I know I too lived this awful childhood, it is her that I grow to pity for the weight that she has to carry. She appears stronger than me, more determined and I find in some strange way that I envy her for it, even as I learn about her, about us and how we are pieced together, where the seams are.

In my vague moments, the blank spaces that I can never recall, Ellie is there, looking through my eyes, speaking through my mouth, wearing my clothes. She is the Dilly Daydream my aunt referred to, the one who left the brochure, who left the doll, who moved the sofa. She is the one who climbed into the taxi, thinking to have me home before I took over again. In one of her notes she tells me that she is sorry, that she just wanted to go for a drive. I was never drugged, though she drank more alcohol than I normally would have. There was no threatening man with ill intent, though she did have a run-in with a man she didn't like.

It was Ellie who made the phone calls to Rob Jay, initially from Leah's house and then from the apartment. Of course there were never any signs of a break-in, she was there all along and difficult though it is, strange though it is, I find this truth to be less threatening than the idea that someone wished me harm, that a stranger walked into my home.

When she writes me the letter of apology, she tries to explain why she has done what she has done, that she wanted to shake me awake, force me to live. She assures me that there was no intended harm to me, though sometimes these things were done with anger and frustration. She deliberately chose things from my past and my present that she believed would affect me the most. With the phone calls to Rob Jay there was a part of her that hoped he would pick up the phone and call me back, even in anger, because his voice may have been a reminder of what it is to look at someone else and feel that longing, that desire to be less alone.

Her words make a strange kind of sense. If I think of her as someone other than myself, as a different person altogether then there is forgiveness in me, a sense of understanding because in some ways I am the one who turned my back on the life she wanted. I forgot what it was to live and in doing so denied her the right to discover it for herself. Ellie is trapped in her cage just as I am trapped in mine and when I think of her as separate I cannot help but carry the responsibility, feel the guilt for that.

Eventually I discover that I cannot think of her as part of myself, I have to believe she is distinct, I have to think of her as other, because if I imagine her as someone hidden, someone who watches, I find that I cannot sleep with the light off, that I feel constantly as if someone is behind me. I cannot think of her beneath my skin, inside my brain, guiding my hands.

And so I see her in my head as the helpless child I once was, the vulnerable child I no longer am. She becomes distinct, separate in my mind. I see her as the one who fell, the one who was alone, who was abandoned; and when I see her as a terrified, powerless child, I can feel sad for her, I forgive her, and then I can carry some of the responsibility, some of the weight that she has held for me. I whisper an apology for the burden she has carried – for the fear she has borne for both of us – quietly into the room and hope that, in this moment at least, she is listening.

Epilogue

I was surprised when Sarah told Leah, three months after the discovery of me, that she wanted to move back into the apartment. She explained that she no longer felt unsafe there, that she no longer felt threatened now that she knew of me, of who her mysterious intruder was. Leah made her promise to stay in touch, to keep the weekly appointments with Doctor Charles, to call if she needed her.

As the days passed I wondered if perhaps she saw me in the same terms she viewed Annie; as a sister, someone separate. Maybe it helps her to see me as distinct, different, instead of the messed-up part of her, the part of her that needs treatment. We are not the same, she and I, and we are both learning that.

When Sarah spends time with Cam, which is something that is happening with increasing frequency since she got in touch with him after everything had calmed down a little, I try to absent myself as much as possible. I lose myself in thoughts. I am trying to learn to be more contemplative, meditative in some way, in the hope that I can remove myself from these moments and not encroach on something private, something just for her.

If it happens that we switch during her time with Cam then I will walk away from him and not intrude. She has told him that the injury to her brain gives her powerful migraines, that they come on suddenly and the only thing she can do in that situation is to go home, to lie down in a dark room until it goes. I am the one that walks away. It is a lie, but for now it is the best she can do, the truth would be too hard to explain.

Sarah intends to meet up with our mother sometime soon, a thought that makes me so deeply afraid, even though it was me that phoned her and led Sarah to the truth behind the lie. I cannot yet come face to face with these fears, the awful memories, this helplessness. I cannot imagine sitting across a table from her and it feeling safe, right. Perhaps I worry needlessly and it will not happen any time soon, if at all, as mother has not phoned back again.

I go to the graveyard to visit the family that are also mine and I take seeds and a cloth with me, hoping in some way to repair the damage that my anger caused. I polish the faint scratches on the stone and plant the wildflowers that will appear in a bloom of colour during the spring and summer. And while resting on my knees I apologise for what I did, knowing that there can be no excuses, hoping that I am in some way making it right.

As I kneel there I feel that strange shift, a momentary vagueness, a turning away until Sarah is there with me. She does not seem surprised to find herself here in this place, looking at the curling marble names of her family. I have written in a note that I will not take her anywhere unfamiliar; while she needs me to, I will only follow her counted pathways. I step backwards and make space for her as we both look down at the place where our family sleep, the father only I remember and the sister who remains a tragic stranger to us both, and in that silence we stand and grieve together.

Acknowledgements

As always there are many things that go into the research and writing of a book. Behind every writer there is a support network of people that humour, cajole, nag, read, edit, sort, inform, hold and nurture. Without all of those things, *To the Edge of Shadows* would have remained simply an idea.

Thanks go to the wonderful team at Legend Press for their hard work and dedication. In particular to my editor, Lauren Parsons, who has to deal with my frequent punctuation errors.

Much gratitude also goes to Ariella Feiner for working with me on the original idea for the story.

Significant thanks go to Dr Christopher Gardner-Thorpe, whose neurological expertise and understanding of traumatic brain injury proved invaluable during the writing of Sarah's character.

Thanks also to the staff of the Accident and Emergency department at Royal Devon and Exeter Hospital for answering my many questions about the impact of date rape drugs and to Heavitree Police Station for answering my questions about police procedures.

On a personal note, I want to express my eternal gratitude to my wonderful family who are possibly too many to mention, but I shall try… Mumfies, Pete Wilson (aka Daddykins), my siblings Cathy, Peter, Kevin, David and

Becky, my lovely children Kiera and Sam, Aunty Stella, my nieces and nephews (who are all magnificent but there are a lot of you so you must be thanked as a collective) and many more. If I've forgotten you it's because I don't like you and you smell funny!

I would not have gotten through the last year without the help of some extraordinary friends and must thank Chen and Worge for their ongoing and continuous support, Sam Whitehead and Sacha Feehan for being magnificent, Dan and Dee, for all the personal support, Eve Jones for the book club intro's and fashion promises and John Earthfire Reeves who delivers reminders at the perfect time. I love you guys.

Enormous gratitude also goes to Kate West for my spangly new office and to Deborah Reeves for bravely seeking out the mistakes.

And lastly (but not leastly) my love and thanks go to Mark Webber - I'm still looking up.

*Lacey Carmichael leads a solitary life. To her neighbours
she is the mad old woman who lives at the end of the lane,
crazy but harmless.
Until she is arrested on suspicion of murder.
When Rachel Moore arrives in the village, escaping
her own demons, the two women form an unlikely bond.
Unravelling in each other tales of loss and heartache,
they become friends.
Rachel sees beyond the rumours, believing in her
innocence, but as details of Lacey's life are revealed, Rachel
is left questioning where the truth really lies.*

ISBN (Print): 9781909395671
ISBN (Ebook): 9781909395688
Available online and in all good bookstores

Come and visit us at
www.legendpress.co.uk

Follow us
@legendpress